I0609689

The Site:

ONLY THE DEAD KEEP SECRETS

JULIE HARRIS

The Site: Only The Dead Keep Secrets Copyright © 2011, 2013 Julie Harris
First published as *The Site* © J. Radford Keir by Pan Macmillan, Sydney, 1996.

All rights reserved. *The Site: Only The Dead Keep Secrets* is a work of fiction and any resemblance to any person, living or dead, or to any actual events, is purely coincidental. No part of this book may be reproduced or transmitted in any form or by any means, electronic or mechanical, including photocopying, recording or by any information storage and retrieval system, without prior permission in writing from the publisher.

ISBN-13: 978-0-9873456-3-9

ISBN-10: 0-9873456-3-X

CHAPTER 1

South West Queensland, Australia, 1992

Kerry had three ladies, two of whom were so regular he wondered if they were born of a Swiss timepiece.

The first was a younger woman who seemed intangibly familiar to him. For a few weeks he never knew her name. Her appearance was so consistent that Wednesday became a day of anticipation.

She rode into town on a Yamaha farm bike each Wednesday morning at eleven thirty. First stop was the Mallen grocery, then Mallen's newsagent and, finally, Mallen's bakery.

And Kerry would watch without watching from his window—it was habit, perhaps an unjustified one these days. She'd come in, ask for three loaves of sliced multigrain and she'd depart. If he tried to talk, she'd say she was too busy, had to run... And he'd watch her walk out of the bakery, place her goodies in the red plastic basket on the back of the bike, and he wouldn't see her again for another week.

She was the only person in Mallen, population 982, who never stopped to talk. Then he discovered that her name was Lacey and she worked at the pub sometimes. Ella, who ran the post office, had come in one morning as Lacey was on her way out. After giving each other a wide berth, Ella said, 'Strange one, that Lacey,' and unlike everyone else in town offered no further information.

The second on his list of regulars was Mrs Mallaby. 'Call me Dora, young man,' she'd said after the introductions. She came in each day at six minutes to ten, spent twenty-two seconds scanning the display of French pastries and she'd say, 'One high top, young man,' without looking any further afield than the top button of Kerry's shirt. And when her mouth opened to say, 'high-top', Kerry always saw a smear of brilliant red lipstick across her front teeth. Dora would totter out, catching her high heel on the carpet tile that hid the sensor.

Emile Rollet, who ran the only decent pub in town, eventually informed Kerry that no one had seen Dora Mallaby wear make-up for twelve years. She took to it with a vengeance the day after Kerry Staines moved to town.

For Kerry, it was a move not unlike any other. Relocating personal possessions and furniture had become a habit. He hoped his latest move to Mallen would be his final one. He'd had two options: the bait shop at Hutters Bay or the bakery at Mallen. A toss of the coin later, Mallen won. Heads I win, tails you lose.

Mallen, far south-west Queensland, consisted of two pubs, and although there was no segregation as such, the Indigenous population congregated at The Metro whilst the Non–Indigenous met at The Australian Arms. There was a post office, one general store thinly disguised as a supermarket, one electrical, one hardware, two banks, two garages, one Catholic school plus a state primary and a state high, two churches, Catholic and Church of England. A small group of Seventh Day Adventists met in the town hall library. The McCoskers had converted a derelict secondhand store next to the electrical shop into a movie rental outlet. That was Kerry's religion—watching movies.

Mallen boasted one doctor and most folks thought the vet a better choice in an emergency. Or they'd travel two hours to nearest major town. Henry Martinelli was too old to be practicing and hadn't bothered to update his practice or knowledge since 1957, or so the story went.

But small communities like this one were full of stories and Kerry's arrival added one more. Mallen hadn't had a baker since Eric Bateman died. Kerry didn't know who Eric Bateman was until the afternoon pulled his Toyota Rav into the drive of 11 Margaret Street and found Eadie waiting.

She was number three on his list of regulars.

He'd been driving seven and a half hours to get to the edge of the desert, the furniture van was supposed to be there at midday. He was hungry and for the past few hours he'd dreamed of six frosting cans of ale only half as much as his cat dreamed of waking from his nightmare. He didn't appreciate pet-paks much. Maybe it was Dire Straits on repeat because Kerry couldn't eject the CD from the car system that had both man and cat with that fifty-yard stare too often associated with combat fatigue.

She was sitting on the fence, waiting. Black curly hair foaming its way down her back, long legs sliding out from tiny denim shorts, toenails painted glorious red. She was picking at them when she said, 'Gidday,' the moment he alighted from his car outside of number 11, his new and hopefully permanent home.

From a distance she looked twenty-five. Closer add ten years. Maybe she thought she was still eighteen. 'Afternoon,' Kerry replied, stretching, aware he was under serious scrutiny and not caring. All he wanted was a beer and the beers were in the cooler somewhere in the back of the Toyota.

'Did you have a good trip?' she asked, although it sounded like 'didjavagoodtrip?' If he was to live here, he'd need to round out his vowels more to fit in with the native population's speech patterns.

'Fine, thanks,' he lied.

'The name's Eadie,' she said as she inspected her little toe.

'Kerry Staines. Pleased to meet you.' Another lie. It was out before he realized it.

'Yeah, I know who you are. Everyone does. We been expecting you for a week. Elspeth told me you was coming.'

'Elspeth?' Do I know an Elspeth? he wondered.

She answered his unvoiced question. 'She knows you. She's been waiting for you.' Eadie went back to picking her toenails, all the while watching Kerry take the pet-pak off the front passenger seat.

'She's back, you know.'

'Excuse me?'

'Elspeth. She's back. Always comes back this time of year.'

He'd seen that gleam before. No, it wasn't a gleam, it was more of the fixed, wide stare of a serial confessor. I don't need this right now, he thought.

'Just thought you'd better know.'

'Aha'

'She killed Eric, you see.'

His brain stopped on the word "killed". 'Who's Eric?'

'Eric Bateman. He used to live in this house you bought. He's still there you know.'

'You said she killed him.'

'Yeah? So? He's still there. So's Elspeth.'

Ghosts? Kerry thought. Ghosts? Jesus, why me? Why is it that every nut case for fifty miles always zeros in on me? 'Look, Eadie, is that your name?' She nodded, her face came alive. Maybe he shouldn't have used her name. 'If he used to live in my house and he's dead, he can't still be there. It's not *possible*.' But she smiled. Kerry wished she hadn't. 'She killed him in the kitchen, you know. Had a bit of fun first. She was like that with fellers. Liked a bit of fun... Both barrels. Bang. If it wasn't for the finger, Doc Martinelli wouldn't have been able to identify him.'

'Finger?'

'Yeah. This one.' She held up her right index finger. 'Eric got it cut off once. Back in the days when the roo works was here. Back in the days when everyone had a job.'

'Oh, right.' The good old days have reared already. Please, no, he thought. Not now, not ever. I just want a beer. A beer and some privacy.

'It wasn't suicide.' She got off the fence and walked towards him. 'Elspeth got him. Just like she got Mitchell and Brady on Starks Road that night. Police say they hit a roo, then the tree. Bullshit. Elspeth jumped out, not some roo.'

Kerry decided if he didn't respond, she might go away.

'You don't talk much, hey?' she noticed. 'No worries. I like quiet fellers, what don't wear cowboy hats.' She stood terribly close, so close that his eyes almost watered from the fumes of the cheap perfume she'd bathed in.

I must get a Stetson, Kerry thought and smiled, then turned and put another cardboard box on the grass. Soon she'd have to get the message and leave.

'Did you see this dump before you bought it?' she asked.

Kerry looked up at the house he had seen only in real estate photographs. The old, run-down, "renovator's dream" came nearly free with the bakery. Eighteen stairs up. Eighteen stairs for Kerry would be like climbing Ayers Rock with a broken leg. He took four boxes from the car before he discovered the esky cooler and decided, impolite or not, he had to get inside and quickly lock himself away and relax with a beer.

'Bad limp you got there,' she called as he took the stairs. By the time he'd reached the top she was behind him, cardboard box in arms. She was going to help him move in. Kerry noticed it was a box of books, and Moby Dick was on top.

'Just here'll be fine, Eadie. Thanks.'

She dropped it on the verandah and he stopped Moby Dick from falling off with his foot.

'Em says you used to be a cop.'

'Detective Senior Sergeant.'

'Em says you got shot. That right?'

'Uh-huh.' Had he offered an invitation to pry? Who the hell was *Em*?

'I got shot once, too. Sort of. I was helping a mate re-load bullets. See?' She pointed to her foot. Kerry saw the scar and the wince was automatic, not empathic. 'Kept getting infected, damned thing.'

'Bullet wounds can do that.'

'Comes back every year. Just like Elspeth.'

'Who is Elspeth?' Kerry asked. They were still standing on the verandah and he was as yet unwilling to open the front door because once he did he'd never get rid of her.

'You'll find out soon enough,' she said. 'Like I said, she told me you was coming. She's been dead for seventeen years this December. Was me best mate.'

He couldn't avoid it much longer. He had to look into her eyes. 'Eadie, I don't believe in ghosts or life after death.'

'That's what they all say.'

'Look, I don't want to be rude,' he lied, 'but the van'll be here any old—'

'You did murders when you was a cop?'

'I'm not a cop any more.' He took the stairs down.

Eadie followed. 'I guess you'll know a few of the bad guys then?'

'Excuse me?'

'You know, when they build the super, you beaut, new fangled, hi tech prison here. We don't mind. Might save the town from dying.'

More words flowed but he wasn't listening. Mallen had been second on the shortlist of possible locations for the new prison. 'When did you hear this?'

'Some feller came out and talked at the town meeting last week. I thought you knew about the prison.'

Kerry said nothing.

'Think you'll know any of the bad guys, Kerry?'

'Maybe,' was all he dared say. The odds were very favorable that he'd definitely know a few bad guys. Twenty minutes in Mallen and the past had already surfaced. What else did these people believe they knew?

You was a cop.

Until a forced retirement which left him with a permanent limp, even less faith in humanity and a reversion to his first trade: a baker. Kerry had left home at seventeen, headed for med school, by nineteen he was both a qualified baker and topping his classes. At nineteen and a half he returned home to hold his mother's hand while she died; he ditched study and became a paramedic instead, specializing in air sea rescues until the police service called. Now he was thirty-eight years old and had to begin over again. Some days his willpower was as temperamental as his old Honda bike had been.

A prison. He only ever knew the darker side of humankind and when some light shone, habit had him searching for the shadows. And now there was a correctional facility for 400 maximum security prisoners about to begin construction four miles from town. It was one of those multi-million dollar joints with a staff of ten and run by computers. Just what Kerry needed.

Most folks probably thought that the new arrival had bought the old established bakery and residence in the hope of making a small fortune through contracts with the Correctional Services Department. Kerry decided to let them think what they liked. Any opposition simply loosened the gossip elastic. After all, there wasn't much else to do in Mallen except talk and drink yourself blind and talk some more.

He was forced to let Eadie into his house—he couldn't stand on his own verandah forever.

'When's the rest of your stuff coming?' she asked.

You tell me and we'll both know, Kerry thought. 'Two hours ago?' he replied.

She smiled at his pathetic joke. However, she must have seen his face the moment he opened the front door because she said, 'I better go. Might see you tomorrow, hey?'

And around the corner, the furniture van rattled.

The house was jokingly called 'an historic Queenslander'. If not for the golden words, "renovator's dream", he'd have had just cause to sue for false advertising. After one beer, Kerry helped the removalists lug the furniture upstairs, but it was Kerry who fell through the rotting verandah floorboards. Looking up from the darkness he saw sunlight shining through the ragged hole, and a face with a rollie cigarette glued to the bottom lip asked, 'You right there, matey?', unconcerned, as if people fell through rotting verandah floorboards every day.

The front doors didn't even close, let alone lock. The ancient carpet runner down the dim hall spewed dust with each step. It had been nailed down, covering, Kerry discovered, another carpet runner. The walls were original pine and unpainted, giving the impression that they may disintegrate if touched by the brightness of day. Painting throughout was imperative. He did not want to become accustomed to such dismal darkness. It could only lead to dark thoughts or suicidal tendencies and he'd come to Mallen to live again, not die further. Even undercoat, he knew, would be a vast improvement.

On his first night he discovered what the ancient Aboriginal stone axe-head was for—it fitted neatly under the door and defied the dry westerly's attempt at bursting through. Maybe houses in this town never had the need for keys.

There was a fireplace which hadn't held a fire for years and perhaps the chimney hadn't been swept since the last brick was placed but he had seven months until winter so that could wait. The TV fitted perfectly against the lounge room's southern wall. Then he discovered there was no reception apart from the ABC.

The house had four bedrooms; each opened via French doors to the wraparound verandah. Cupboards in the kitchen yielded the skeletons of three rats, the chopped wood beside the wood stove was riddled with redback spiders. All the plates on the electric range worked, although the range hood did not.

Kerry had thrown the cat into the bathroom and hadn't seen what lay in there, waiting, until he opened the door three hours later when the van left. The cat shot out, using Kerry's bare feet as traction. 'Suss the perimeter but be back in ten, pal,' Kerry said to himself. The cat was long gone. Kerry then inspected the bathroom. It contained one cast iron tub with turned lion's paw feet and a wash basin with stains only Stephen King could successfully describe.

The laundry was downstairs and a half-finished alcove near the bathroom displayed someone's attempt at installing a toilet. Whoever it was hadn't got around to the cistern yet. Kerry leant against the wall and stared at that pan for a long time, only beginning to contemplate the motive behind the previous owner's suicide.

Eventually he picked up his wallet and decided to walk to the pub. He always did his best thinking with a beer in his right hand. Yang was busy scratching in the only spot of loose dirt in the acre of overgrown yard. He saw Kerry and let forth his yowl which Kerry had, over the past six years, learned to translate as meaning, "wait for me!".

So the new baker and his cat made their way to The Australian Arms on High Street. It was here he first met Emile Rollet, the 'Em' Eadie had mentioned. Kerry had never heard his name pronounced with a French twang before as Emile introduced him to a handful of regulars.

Frank Purvis was the plumber who made more money fixing septic systems than running cattle. Johnny Logan was a painter and Kerry soon realized that a quick hello to either of them could last up to two hours.

Purvis was a giant of a man, ex-SAS commando with eyes Kerry could not read to satisfaction. Logan, always smiling, had come to the Mallen district when his family bought Laguna Station ten years before. When asked what it was he did for a living, he'd replied he was a painter. He neglected to mention his Impressionist pieces, the abstracts and the occasional charcoal portrait, and from then on, his income was derived from painting houses. Had he said artist, he'd still be in the family partnership working sheep and Mallen would be full of unpainted homes. The story had been told so often that everyone in the bar moaned, 'Jesus, Johnny, give us a break.'

The people here were so ordinary that Kerry found listening to them a gentle yet refreshing bore. He had no underlying cause to search for deeper meanings behind a simple hello. A few icy cold beers later he'd almost readjusted. It seemed that the people he most needed to meet were all waiting patiently for his arrival. The painter and the plumber could start work immediately. Kerry figured they'd been at the pub all day waiting for him to show. Tradesmen were scarce this far west.

Everyone knew the state of the Bateman house. Everyone assumed that the new owner was a city boy who needed his little luxuries like painted walls and a toilet that flushed.

The bakery, however, was in good working condition. It had been leased after Eric's demise and the lessees had lived in a Winnebago on site. They'd probably taken one look at the house and bolted.

In the space of one hour, Kerry was told the recent history of Mallen. But no more information was forthcoming after his simple question, 'What's the story with Eadie and who the hell's Elspeth?'

Everyone in the bar turned face to their glasses—suddenly he was a stranger in town. But that was when he saw Lacey for the first time. She was sitting on the carpet next to the pool table, chalking in the meal menus. One glance was enough. She had to be the prettiest female he had seen in a very long time. She wore an Indian-type black skirt with tiny bells on the hem, and a faded pink blouse with straining buttons. Her hair was caught in a ponytail and she looked away the moment he smiled at her.

Undaunted, Kerry took his beer, stood behind her and watched her work. After a little while she turned and, as on each future Wednesday, her face hid its smile whilst its color deepened.

'Is it worth the risk?' Kerry asked.

'Pardon?'

'The food. Is it worth the risk?'

'I hope so. I'm the cook,' she said quietly as she returned to the chalk board and the decorative artwork no one ever noticed. All they saw was a meal description and the price. 'Order at the bar after six,' she said quietly, killing his question before it rose.

'Do I know you?' Kerry asked, trying to pin his sudden bout of intangible familiarity to one set location or situation.

'I don't think so,' she lied, packed up her chalks and damn near ran into the kitchen. Kerry sighed. Well, he thought, that was over before it began.

He didn't eat at the pub that night because he knew she was expecting him to. He put her out of his mind and bought a frozen roast dinner and a can of cat food at the grocery just on closing. He and the cat walked home in the twilight.

It was anyone's guess which box contained the microwave, so Kerry put his dinner into the electric oven and he sat and waited. It was too quiet. So quiet, even his heartbeat was loud, and the cat washing himself after his feed was too noisy. It wasn't a situation like those ads on TV a few years back where the solitary person ate his frozen dinner whilst assuring the caller he was looking after himself. Because anyone who may have cared in the past stayed there. In the past.

Kerry scanned the mountain of boxes, wondering again at unpacking time why a body needed to collect so much crap over a lifetime. Such wonderings only arise during a relocation. He looked down at the nearest box. Framed photos. The Shiva masks and bronze Indian ornaments, the gold-plated Buddha Annie had given him as a pre-wedding present. He put them all in the places where they had been in Brisbane, the photos on the mantelpiece, the ornaments stayed in the box for now.

He went back to the photos. He couldn't see them up there. He should hang them on the walls. He should do a lot of things. Annie, Kerry, Michael and Julia. Now only a memory of the happiest and most meaningful time of his life. Annie had had the photos taken a month before the bus crash. His wife and children were on their way to Sydney to see Annie's folks and never made it past Grafton. He'd begged her to fly but no way could she do that alone with two little kids, one of whom, at the time, had a middle ear infection. Kerry touched the paper faces under glass. His son could have been a clone of his father. His daughter had taken her first steps two days before she died in Grafton hospital.

By the time his dinner was ready, his appetite had departed. He slept on his sofa—he hadn't the energy to make his bed. It had been a long day and as he dropped into sleep, he thought of two things, how tomorrow he'd find Eadie and pay her to help him unpack. And he wondered why the name Elspeth was always surfacing in his mind. He could not push it aside.

During these seedy, hypnogogic mists, he saw a middle-aged man sitting on the floor of the kitchen, a double-barrelled 12 gauge cuddled as tight as a teddy bear.

Kerry opened his eyes, blinked a few times. The man was still there.

Who the hell was that? How'd he get inside? He wanted to move but he was frozen, paralyzed. He saw a girl walk by, stand in the doorway. She had long blonde hair, muddied and dreadlocked to her shoulders. The man on the floor looked up at her, shook his head a couple of times, pure terror lighting his eyes. *No. No.* She took no notice. She pulled her top over her head, stepped out of her shorts and stood there, stark naked over him. Then she sank down, straddled him. Kerry wanted to look away, but couldn't. *Do it, you gutless bastard! Do it!*

And the man on the floor complied. After the shot came peals of laughter. The scream of denial was stifled by a choke. And then the kitchen was just that, a kitchen, with boxes all over the benches and floors. Finally able to move, he did, shakily. There was no one on the floor, no brains up the wall, just a half-eaten frozen dinner lying in the sink and Yang helping himself to it.

Kerry got another beer from his fridge. His hands were shaking again. Not a good sign.

He didn't sleep at all that night.

Welcome to Mallen, he thought. Your new life is about to begin.

CHAPTER 2

After three weeks, Johnny Logan was still at work, burning off the chipped paint from the exterior of the house. The interior was finished in a pale, soothing blue throughout and although it wasn't the color Kerry had chosen initially, he liked it.

For three weeks, Kerry had wanted to ask if anything strange had ever happened whilst Johnny was working inside the house. The guy always stank of garlic, always wore a crucifix around his neck. Unfortunately it wasn't to ward off vampires—his wife was Italian. Johnny Logan was thirty-three, and he kept his long red hair in a ponytail. He wore Reebok sweatbands on his wrists and forehead, and for a painter he never seemed to attract many spots. Or spooks. If the girl with dreadlocks hadn't reappeared... maybe it was a case of residual memory of a traumatic experience forever imprinted on the atmosphere? Something like that. Annie explained most hauntings that way. Unfortunately Kerry never took much notice of her theories. She'd looked everywhere but under her nose for the secrets of life and happiness. Most folks did.

So many times the question formed, but never rose to the surface. Kerry would look at Johnny Logan's grin and immediately drown the enquiry. I'm going mad, he thought. It only happened once. I was hallucinating.

On the Tuesday at 4.00 p.m. when Kerry got home from work, he was met by Johnny Logan who said, 'Eadie came by today. She left you some stuff. Said it'd help keep Elspeth away.'

'Who's Elspeth?' he asked, casually.

'People don't talk much about that one,' he said and went back to his mini flame-thrower. 'Oh, and whatsername rang, too. I said you were at the shop. She said she'd see you tomorrow, usual time.'

'Whatsername?'

'You know, Dolly.'

'Dolly?'

'Works at the pub. Big tits. The sheila with the market garden outa town. Starks Road. You know...'

No, Kerry didn't know.

'She rides the Yamaha,' Johnny said slowly, still struggling for a name.

'Lacey?' Kerry tried.

'Is *that* her name?'

Kerry sighed. Another one who saw only the form. Is that all Lacey was? The sheila from the pub, the one with big tits who rode a bike and had a market garden?

He took the eighteen stairs, walked inside and immediately saw and smelled what Eadie had left behind. There was a large vase of flowers—daisies, roses, two other kinds Kerry recognized but could not name. The perfume filled the house, too, till he realized that his stale cigarette smoke was smothered by an incense burner reeking of sandalwood. He carried it out to the verandah, then he opened all possible windows and doors but there was no breeze and the smell was thick and lingering. 'What's all this crap in aid of, Johnny?'

'Keeps Elspeth away. I told you.'

'Who the fuck is Elspeth?'

'Ask Eadie. Ah, no, don't. She's cracked. Ask... whatsername again?'

'Lacey.'

'Yeah, her. She'll tell you. It happened long before my time, man. Hey, Kerry!' he called just as Kerry was turning away. 'I tried the Strat, man. Little *beauty*. Too bad about the valve amp, though.'

Kerry's mind went blank. 'You what?' Suddenly he was on the verandah rail, leaning over, peering up under scaffolding.

'Didn't think you'd mind, man.'

He couldn't believe it. Logan had taken the Fender Stratocaster from its dusty case, and used the Fender valve amp which was working perfectly last time he'd used it eight, nine, maybe twelve months ago?

'It's okay. I got some spare valves at home. I'll fix her for you. She's worth a bit these days, mate. If I was you I'd keep it under heavy guard. You never know...'

Kerry was more surprised than angry. He never let anyone, *anyone*, touch that guitar.

'Blew the arse outa the house, too. But I fixed the fuses. These old places—you know I've got a mate who's an electrician. You could do with a safety switch.'

What's next? The house needs rewiring?

Johnny climbed down from his scaffolding. 'You any good?' he asked as he lit a smoke.

'At what?'

'What'd you play? Lead or rhythm?'

'Both. And bass. Keyboards sometimes.'

'Yeah?'

'A long time ago, yes.'

'Wanna make an extra—'

'No.'

Johnny didn't want to press too hard. He knew the look of the retired rocker. But there was one small question remaining. 'Vocals?'

'I said no. Well, not right now at least.'

Logan recognized the weakening. 'Give us a bell if you change your mind. Band's called *Deceptions*. Straight covers. Classic rock, a bit of C & W. You name it, we play it. Anything from the 60s to late 80s... Fridays and Saturdays at the Arms, weddings, parties, piss ups, we do the bush dance circuit and play in Wilton sometimes.'

For a while there was silence. *Deceptions*. His old band had been called *Misled*. Kerry wondered how long he'd be able to resist the temptation.

'Where's Eadie live?' Kerry asked, changing the subject.

'Let's see, 13 George, I think.' Johnny studied the house, the work for today. 'Should be right for the prepcoat tomorrow unless we get some rain.' He scanned the cloudless late afternoon sky as if secretly praying for a miracle. Then he cleaned up, left his gear under Kerry's house and headed home.

Kerry looked down at the incense burner. George Street was a block away. This time the cat did not follow as Kerry walked across the narrow pot-holed and weed-filled streets, taking a left along Race and a right into George.

Number 13 had the only garden in the street. Bottlebrushes, banksias, cotton palms, bohenias, roses and the unknown flowers amongst a thousand agapanthus. The house was low set original Federation. A beaten-up Mazda van sat rusting in the carport. Kerry sighed. The tires were bald, the vehicle looked as if it'd been rolled once or twice. The number plate was obscured by dust and black smoke. And it hadn't been registered for two years. This would have a worse effect on the ozone layer than fifty farting cows, he thought and was immediately reminded of Annie, hanging out of the car window and abusing any driver of an unroadworthy vehicle that spewed black smoke or worse.

Kerry put Annie away for a while and knocked on the front door. He heard the sound of music from within, so he knocked louder. The way he used to: police style, the authoritative syllable knock.

Open the door, I know you're home.

It never failed. Well, almost never. He knocked again. No answer. The folks next door were on the front verandah, watching. So was Dora, across the street. Kerry found his way to the back of the house and found more garden. Plants everywhere. He concussed himself on something trailing green from the pergola roof and stifled the inevitable curse.

The music was louder from the opposite end of the old house. For a moment he considered putting the burner down on the outdoor table but the urge to go inside rose strongly and couldn't be ignored.

He knocked again, louder this time. Nothing. 'Eadie?' he called. No answer. Kerry tried the door. The knob free-turned but the door was caught on something. 'Eadie?' he called and pushed. It gave a few centimeters, enough to squeeze inside and see what was barricading the door.

Eadie.

She was semi-conscious, whimpering. His first thought was rape. For a moment, he wasn't game to touch her.

'Who did this?'

At the sound of the voice, she tried to crawl away.

'No. No, I'm not going to hurt you. Who did this?'

Eadie covered her face as if expecting another onslaught. Her dress was torn. She was lacerated, bruised. Muddy. Muddy? It hadn't been raining.

Kerry, on his knees, gently eased the shield of arms from her face. 'Eadie, it's me. Kerry.'

Kerry? She recognized something in his eyes and for a second, the animal terror disappeared. The shaking did not. 'Kerry?' She caught him by the neck in a death grip, a grip which eased when he put his arms around her, held her.

'Eadie, who did this?'

'The boys,' she whimpered. 'Ain't done yet. They—' And she was pulled from his arms, letting forth a scream that almost decalcified his spinal column.

And Kerry saw no one. Nothing. He lunged for her bare foot. A frantic tug of war with an unseen force was soon lost. Kerry was kicked by an invisible boot—a boot which left black mud on his shirt. All he could do was watch while Eadie was dragged across the length of the kitchen floor and under the table, until the sink cupboard barred any further movement. She no longer screamed, she was crying softly, almost as if she were resigned.

For Kerry, an innocent witness, logic had no meaning. Each time he attempted to get closer, to help—something, anything—that boot caught him again. And again.

'Go,' she screamed. 'Away. Get away!'

Who, though, was she screaming at?

Silence fell, eventually. She rolled to her side, tried to crawl back to Kerry. He couldn't move, again, only able to watch. Eadie was kicked to her back, and looked up at a myriad of invisible faces as if she were surrounded. She was, but by what Kerry didn't know. He couldn't think. Kerry saw the imprint of another muddy boot flatten her chest. Then there was nothing more, except perhaps faint whispers, but from where, from whom?

Eadie lay on the floor of her kitchen. She was covered in black mud now, although the area was currently in a drought and any dirt for miles was bright, bull dust red. The stench of decay filling the room was nauseating.

'Eadie?' he tried, voice no more than a hoarse croak.

She rolled to her side again and tried to pull her dress together but she had neither the strength nor the will. Only then was the spell broken completely; only then was he able to move.

Kerry dived for the phone. Then he realized he didn't remember the doctor's name, nor was there a hospital within an hour's drive. He couldn't remember his own name for a cloudy moment. His fingers wouldn't find the right page in the phone book.

Someone brushed his arm, almost sent him into the ceiling. It was Eadie, on her staggering way up the hall. She said two words. 'I'm okay.'

Then the name came to him. Martinelli. He found the number, dialed and an old man answered with a tired 'hello'.

'Dr Martinelli? Kerry Staines.'

'The baker?'

'Yeah. I'm at Eadie.. Eadie...' Shit, he thought, what's her surname? He heard the doctor's voice.

'She'll be fine, son. Happens each year near Christmas. Give her ten minutes, throw her in the bath and she'll be right as rain till tomorrow night.'

Kerry couldn't believe he was hearing this. 'Look, you don't understand.'

'Oh, I understand. You saw it happen, didn't you, son.' It wasn't a question.

'Well, yes, but...'

'Go have a whiskey, boy. That's what you need.'

'But she's, she's…'

'Trust me.' The old man hung up. Kerry stared at the wall for a few seconds. His brain was completely blank. What the hell had he walked into this time? As if in reply, the portable stereo on the kitchen bench lifted, flew past his nose and bounced off the fridge. It was enough to get him out of the room. Quickly. He leaned against the closed door, heart pounding. From up the hall, he heard water falling. Kerry followed the sounds.

Eadie, sweating, shaking and teeth chattering, was perched on the edge of the tub, staring glassy-eyed at the tiles on the floor while the hot water sprayed the shower recess walls. She was grey, motionless. Shock, he thought.

'Eadie?'

She heard the voice but didn't acknowledge it. Kerry leapt aside as she dived for the toilet and hung over it, limp, heaving, crying in turn.

He dared ask nothing. He dared think even less. He tested the water hurtling from the shower head. Too hot. He adjusted it and waited for the woman to stop throwing up before he put her into the shower. Her knees refused to lock. Kerry held her upright with one arm while he pulled the torn dress off and washed the mud away. She was lacerated, bruised, and welts were appearing all over her body, even on her feet. But the blood which oozed was black. Putrid.

'Eadie, what's happening here?'

She looked up as if only then realizing he was there, that she wasn't alone. And she gave in, turned her face into his shoulder and howled. Kerry didn't realize until later that he was wet, too. He turned the water off and, still holding her upright, reached for a towel. He wrapped her tightly. She was still shaking. She couldn't walk. He carried her into the nearest bedroom, sat her on the edge of the bed.

'Talk to me, please.'

'Leave me be. Why can't you just leave me be?'

Kerry found a nightie across a papasan chair, pulled it over her head and rolled her into the covers. As he watched, trying to make some logical sense of this, her right eye swelled, closed. Her lower lip split. Oozed blackness. For a while he thought he was experiencing some kind of delusion, a waking nightmare. For a while he convinced himself that any moment he'd wake up. Soon the alarm would go off, it'd be time to head off to work.

There were footsteps coming up the hall and a face he'd never seen before peered in. The doctor. He gave Kerry a cursory look as he stepped in and asked, 'You're the one who rang?'

'Yeah.'

Kerry put his hands behind his back, clasped tight to ease the shaking. The old man noticed, expertly pretended he didn't and looked down at Eadie. 'I was on the way past. Go and get a strong drink, son. I'll talk to you about this in a minute.' Kerry stayed where he was—he had no intention of leaving Eadie alone. Not that she would have known. The old man touched Eadie's face, patted her cheek, said something Kerry didn't catch. But a half smile appeared on Eadie's face. What was it, reassurance? The old doctor checked the welts, the abrasions on her arms, her throat. And he turned to Kerry. 'Will you be here tomorrow, son?'

'Why?'

'Tomorrow will be worse.'

'Excuse me?'

'She relives what she thinks happened to her friend. Every year, like I said. Lasts three days all up. She'll sleep for a bit, she'll be fine later on. Till tomorrow. How much did you see?'

Kerry tried to explain what he'd witnessed and as a reward was patted on the shoulder. Friendly or condescending, he didn't know. 'You'll get used to it. I've seen this every year for seventeen years now.'

The old man left as quietly as he'd arrived. Fifteen minutes had elapsed from the time he first knocked on her door. It felt like forever. Kerry sat on the edge of the bed, studied his hands for a while before he took Eadie's pulse—something the doctor hadn't bothered with. Normal. Her color was returning. Her breathing was normal. 'Jesus, Eadie,' he mumbled, still too aware of the size ten boot imprints on his ribcage.

The eyes opened, focused on Kerry's face. 'What are you doing here?' she asked.

A thousand questions welled, none surfaced.

'You shouldn't be here. Neighbors will talk.'

Kerry squeezed her hand and watched her drift into a peaceful sleep.

Martinelli's words returned. *She relives what she believes happened to her friend.* Elspeth. And he wondered exactly *what* had happened to Elspeth.

'What you here for?' came the slurred words.

It was a good question, to which he didn't know the immediate answer. Then memory returned. The incense burner. What had he done with it? He didn't want to go back into the kitchen—not alone at least. But the house was quiet now. Too quiet. Kerry pulled the covers higher, swept wet hair from her face and said, 'I think I came to say thanks for those flowers you brought to my house today.'

'Keeps Elspeth away ...'

Elspeth. 'What just happened to you?'

'Happened to her. Not me.' Her eyes closed again and this time he let her sleep.

Kerry looked around at Eadie's room, the walls covered in fantasy posters and unframed prints. Unearthly views of purple worlds with reversed moons, of white-winged horses flying to Merlins, of Egyptian goddesses holding crystal balls.

Crystal chimes hung over the window. A locked window.

He looked at his hands. Yes, they were still shaking and he hadn't had a heavy drink in weeks, but he sure as hell needed one now.

When Eadie woke at 7.00 p.m., Kerry Staines was sitting in her papasan chair, watching her intently. He tried to smile at the confusion on her face. Apparently she didn't remember what had happened, but he'd never forget what he'd witnessed. 'Can I get you anything?' he asked.

Eadie touched her face, looked at her bruised arms and up into Kerry's dark eyes.

'How long you been here?'

'Two and a half hours.' He looked at his watch. 'And fifty-five seconds. Are you in pain?'

'No.' Eadie threw the covers back and struggled from the bed.

'Where are you going?'

'May as well make you a cup of tea. Did you come in the front door or the back door?'

'Back. Why?'

'Anyone see you?'

'No,' he lied.

'Bullshit,' she said quietly and padded down the hall. None of the bruises or abrasions had disappeared and she was limping. Kerry couldn't believe she wasn't in pain.

'I wasn't expecting you to come visit.' She opened the kitchen door, saw the mp3 in two pieces on the floor. Eadie sighed. 'Happens every year. Guess what I get myself for Christmas?' she asked, turning to him, trying to smile.

'Eadie, why'd you bring me those flowers?'

'Didn't Johnny Logan tell you?'

'No, he didn't,' Kerry lied.

And she looked at him as if she knew he was lying. And he knew that she knew. 'I don't want her hurting you. Hurting you or worse.'

'Who could hurt me or worse?'

'Are you stupid or are you making me feel stupid? Elspeth. Who else would I be talking about?'

'That's your dead friend, right? And flowers keep her away?'

'Flowers make her sneeze.'

Kerry sighed. She's dead. Dead people do not sneeze. 'Sit down, I'll make the tea. Then you can tell me what's happening.'

He made her tea, sat opposite and studied her face for some time. As she picked up her cup, Kerry saw her fingers were bruised, swollen. And Eadie kept her gaze averted. She was so different to the extrovert sitting on the fence the day he'd arrived. It felt as if forever had turned full circle since then. 'You won't believe me.' She fixed her stare to the table top and took a deep, shuddering breath.

'Why do you think I won't believe you?'

'What I think is that you better go, Kerry. You better go right now. You should never have come here. Man like you. Was a mistake. A bad mistake. And next time you want to visit, you ring me first. Okay?'

'If I don't know your name, how can I know your number to call?'

She looked up into his face, at the dark brown eyes, so dark you could get lost in there forever. He was wearing a sleeveless T-shirt, his arms and shoulders were brown. He used to work out a lot, traces of it remained. Either that or that's the way God made him. No wonder Elspeth wanted him bad, she thought. Real bad. She'd always dreamed of a guy like this one. Perhaps a little old, but age never worried Elspeth. Alive or dead.

'My name's Eadie Ross.' Then she felt the warmth of the hand on hers, felt the question in his eyes. 'No, I ain't hurt. Just looks it. Scares me a bit, that's all. What they did to Elspeth ... it shows up on me every year. Lasts a few days, goes away. Tomorrow'll be worse. Come Friday...'

'Friday?'

'The day she died. December third. I told you.'

'And how did she die?'

'I dunno. I don't wanna know.' It came too fast. The lie wasn't convincing, even to herself.

'Eadie, do you remember the first time we met?'

'What of it.'

'You were waiting for me. You were going to tell me about Elspeth then, weren't you.'

She said nothing.

'And you could have,' he lied, 'but I only got half the story. You can't keep it all locked inside. Seventeen years is a long time, Eadie. I'm here now, I'm ready to listen to whatever you want to tell me.'

Maybe it was the way he looked at her. As if he was interested. As if he truly wanted to know. As if he could help. As if *wanted* to help. Still she asked, 'Why?'

'Because whatever it was that was attacking you got me as well. I wasn't going to tell anyone, but I think I saw your friend my first night here. And if what I saw was real, then you were right about Eric Bateman. He didn't suicide.'

'What do you want to know?' she asked so quietly it was almost a whisper.

'Whatever you feel I need to know.' He had both her hands in his now, gentle squeezes of reassurance that had never failed him before.

'She was my best mate, the only friend I ever had. I reckon we shoulda been sisters, you know. Twins. What they did to her, they did to me, too. But I ain't dead.'

'They?'

'The boys. She used to get hurt or get sick, I'd feel it. They reckon it happens sometimes. You ever heard of it?'

'Empathic reaction? Yes, I've heard of it.'

'You think I'm crazy? You think I'd wish this on myself? Hell, why not, everyone else does.'

'I'm not everyone else.'

'Around here, they call me the Christmas Spectacular and they think I don't know.' Eadie sighed. 'We was both eighteen when Ells went missin'. 17 years ago when the army came playing war games she went out to the camp for a bit of fun and nobody ever saw her again. But I know what happened.' Tears in her eyes again. She wiped them away before the flood began. 'Cops said she'd run away. They didn't give a shit. Whispers were the town was a better place without the likes of her in it. But it took her three days to die, Kerry. Three fucking days.'

'I assume her body was never found?'

For a while there was complete silence.

'What did Elspeth look like?' Kerry asked.

Eadie brightened a little and fetched a photo album from a kitchen drawer. She put it on the table in front of Kerry, opened it and leafed through. 'Here. That's Elspeth.'

He looked down at two young women, dressed to kill. She used to be very beautiful, the dark, sultry Eadie. Elspeth, the blue-eyed blonde who belonged within the pages of a women's magazine, smiled up at him. She had the long legs of a model, a perfect hourglass figure. For a few seconds he was magnetized to the smile. The eyes. She looked so much like Annie. Too much. And the girl in the photograph barely resembled the ghost he'd seen on his kitchen floor.

'This was taken at our high school formal. We looked good, huh. Sure as hell didn't look seventeen. We had lots of good times, more good than bad.' Then the army came through town. And Eadie's story began.

If every small town had one, then Mallen had two. Eadie and Elspeth had served the men in town well, or so it seemed. When Eadie was young, Mallen's population boomed due to the opening of the roo works, but when the works closed four years later, the population dwindled back to one thousand. Elspeth's father decided to stay in Mallen—he had nowhere else to go anyway, except prison.

For Elspeth there wasn't much to look forward to except the daily grind as check-out operator at the Mallen grocery store. After work on any given evening there were two options, either go home and watch the ABC on TV, or go to The Australian Arms until closing, play the jukebox until all songs were exhausted or play eight ball in the public bar. Most nights, she'd offer her services for fifteen dollars and fifteen minutes of her time near the stack of empty kegs behind the beer garden.

Once a month there was a picture show at the drive-in—although it couldn't be called a drive-in as such, just an open space next to the rodeo grounds. Those who came to watch the feature movie—which was usually fifteen years old—sat on the bonnets of their cars, or in fold up chairs, and heard the soundtrack through one crackling loudspeaker.

It was Elspeth's influence on Eadie, of course. Not that the roo shooters or meat workers minded, there was always a queue for the best skirts this side of the Nulla siding. Mallen townsfolk feigned indifference to this scourge of morality—there would always come a time when the town's secrets were safe.

When Elspeth Mackenzie disappeared Eadie Ross was never the same again. The summer of that year was horrendous. The drought showed no sign of breaking. Farmers walked off their properties. The population again dwindled, the school closed. It was so quiet that one could hear the blowflies buzzing in the town dump. Mallen was dying.

Then the army moved in, just for a little while. Town spirit revived, for a little while. It was war games time and the occupation of black-banded enemy forces was to be taken seriously. Elspeth and Eadie couldn't believe their luck—a serious man-drought broken by a monsoon rain of young soldiers. Suddenly the town was alive with camouflage uniforms, army trucks and helicopters, and a tent city popped up, too, four miles from town on the edges of The Swamp.

On the first day, the rail siding was taken by the black bands. There was one train a week and it had been and gone two days before, so the two privates guarding the siding became extremely bored but somewhat heightened in job satisfaction when Eadie slunk into enemy territory and decided to stay the night.

Not for Elspeth two mere privates on the floor of the rail siding. Using binoculars whilst perched atop the Anglican church, she discerned in the distance the glow of the enemy camp. Tent City. They were obviously plotting a way to take the entire town before the good guys arrived.

The tents were inviting and Eadie was two hours late. She couldn't wait for ever. At 8.30 that night Elspeth strolled into the public bar of The Australian Arms and she stayed until closing. Then she walked off alone in the dark and no one ever saw the girl again. And no one except Eadie missed her over that lengthy weekend. No one missed her until the army left town. And what was worse, no one cared. Not even her own family.

'If you reported her missing, wasn't there any kind of investigation?' Kerry asked, breaking the glassy stare in Eadie's reddened eyes.

To his question, she laughed. At least, he thought it was a laugh. 'I know what they did to her and I know where she is. When they come to build the prison and drain the swamp next week, they'll prove me right. They'll find her bones, I know they will. Maybe when they find her and she gets buried proper, maybe then she'll give us all a rest.'

'Would you show me where you believe the body is?'

'I won't go there and you can't make me.'

'Would you draw me a map?'

'No.'

'Don't you want her body to be found? Don't you want this resolved?'

'No! It's bad land out there, Kerry. It was cursed by the Aborigines a long time ago. It's one of them places no man's supposed to go. No white man, no black man, no one in between. It's not for *people* out there.'

'But you think her body's out there.'

'I know it is.'

'How do you know?'

'She told me.'

Kerry tried to ignore that. 'If you believe Elspeth is haunting you, why would she want to haunt me, too?'

'Look, if I'd gone with her that night like I said I would, I'd be dead, too. Maybe she's mad 'cos I'm *not* dead? Or maybe you look like the guy she always talked of marrying?' Eadie looked into his dark eyes, reached out and touched his dark hair. And he didn't flinch away when she touched, either. He wasn't scared of her. Maybe he *didn't* think she was crazy. 'She likes you. You're exactly what she always wanted.'

He tried to smile.

'What Elspeth wants, Elspeth gets.'

'It would take more than a ghost to scare me, Eadie Ross.' Except perhaps invisible hands, invisible kicks. Invisible forces dragging a woman across a kitchen floor, but we won't mention that. Let's try to forget that.

'I think you better go home now.'

'I can stay a while longer if you want.'

'No. I'm used to being on my own. I like it.'

'I want you to call me if you need anything.'

Eadie led him to the front door. 'There is something you can do,' she said quietly as she opened the door. 'When you walk out, go out smiling like you had a real good time. Give the neighbors something to talk about. Thanks for what you did. For staying, making sure I was all right. You're okay, you know?'

Eadie didn't say goodbye and after the front door closed, Kerry heard four locks click into place—four locks when everyone else in town had trouble finding their house keys.

That night he ate his frozen dinner and tried to watch TV. Too much snow. No music interested him. He couldn't even think of anyone he could call, except maybe Belinda. But that was a futile consideration: Belinda would probably never talk to him again. He'd read every book he owned at least twice. Kerry simply could not settle.

The alarm was set for one thirty. Living and working in Mallen had given him his longest days yet but he wasn't tired. He'd begun a routine of bed by seven thirty, up at half one for opening at seven, every morning except Sunday.

It was now nine and he knew that placing his head on a pillow would immediately force his eyes into a wide stare, engage brain to full alert. Something gnawed at his gut. He hadn't felt that for a long time—the knowing that something was wrong, screaming to be righted. It could have been the effect of the silence, broken only by Yang as he curled on the end of the bed and purred himself into oblivion. It could have been thoughts of Eadie, of what she'd said, how she'd said it. The marks, welts and bruises were some kind of stigmatic-empathic reflex that occurred once a year. Like people who bled at Easter. Anything, he knew now, was possible.

And again, that name would not leave him alone.

Elspeth.

It took her three days to die. How could one young woman disappear from a small town and no one raise one eyebrow of concern?

Kerry reached for the phone and he hesitated at first. What would Demetri say? He dialed the very familiar number and looked at his watch. 9.05. Demetri would be at the Chinese, getting takeaway. Providing he was on a 3-11 shift, of course.

No one answered for a time, which meant they were either in a swarm in the kitchenette or all out. It was odd, because Tuesday nights were normally quiet. Kerry almost hung up, then a familiar voice answered: 'Detective Sergeant Barlow, CIB.'

'Hey, Belinda.'

The pause was infinite, thick. Twelve hundred kilometers of crackling, uncomfortable static. 'How have you been, Kerry?'

'Fine.'

'And the job?'

'Working out so far. You?'

'Still in therapy. What can I do for you?' she asked, cutting him short in the only way she knew.

'Is Migraine there?'

'Somewhere... Hold. You take care.'

Before he could reply, she'd held. Then another voice he knew too well picked up: 'Hey, buddy. How's the ulcer?'

'Resting uncomfortably, no thanks to you.'

'What do you want?'

'A favor.'

Another pause which needed no explanation. 'Kerry, it's not worth my job—'

'Can you look up a missing persons—'

'No.'

'You owe me one, Demetri.'

'I owe you *fuck all.*'

Dial tone. Kerry hung up and stood staring into inner space.

Well, at least Belinda was back at work. Her voice wasn't the same though. He hadn't expected miracles after that bust at Maleny. For a little while, he wanted to cry. Flood the past from his mind, for wherever he looked, it reared to attack again, always when he was unarmed and unprepared.

Kerry went to the fridge, but didn't extract a beer. He took Johnny Logan's business card instead and dialed the number. He told Johnny he'd changed his mind, he'd give the band a try.

Johnny was waiting for the call. 'See you tomorrow unless we get some rain,' he said.

Rain? No chance of rain, Kerry thought.

He went to bed, momentarily forgetting about Eadie and Elspeth's body in the swamp four miles from town; forgetting about badlands and curses; black man, white man, brown man, no man. For a while after he turned out the light there was nothing, except the cat lying stretched out on the bed, purring, while the fan groaned, squeaked and wobbled precariously from the high ceiling. For a moment he could have sworn that Annie was beside him again, curling into his back like she always did. And the arm went over him and hugged tight. Then she played little. Lifted the covers high and slid down into the bed. And as always, he closed his eyes to the touch, the relaxing ecstasy of her mouth, her hands, until he realized that Annie never had long fingernails. With a sudden jolt he was awake.

Kerry reached to turn the light on and with illumination came emptiness. There was no one in the bed. He turned the light out, told himself that his imagination was out of control. The cat moved, stretched out as he always did when he was being stroked. And he purred louder.

But Kerry wasn't touching him.

Someone was standing at the bottom of the bed, leaning over, stroking the cat. Then she turned her face towards Kerry and smiled.

Elspeth.

With a yelp of fright, Kerry dived out of bed, crashed into the wall, then the kitchen door which he hadn't remembered closing. She was right behind him. Kerry grabbed the vase of flowers and held it high. Elspeth smiled at him.

Kerry took one step backwards. 'Get away from me!'

She put her head to the side, an inquisitive puppy.

'What the fuck do you want?'

Elspeth smiled, pointed to the corner of the kitchen. Kerry dared look towards the corner: a garbage bag with his raincoat on top? It wasn't there before. He was sure it wasn't. 'What do you want from me?'

The dead girl looked at him curiously, semi-amused, then she turned away and walked through the kitchen wall and out of sight.

Kerry put the vase down. So much for flowers keeping Elspeth away.

Kerry didn't remember crawling back into bed until he woke from a dreamless sleep at midnight. There was a loud crack, and for a while he thought he'd been shot again. Thunder? Rain, *heavy* rain, roared down onto the galvanized iron roof. Something cold hit his cheek. His nose. His forehead. Water? The roof was leaking and his raincoat was hanging from the wardrobe door.

CHAPTER 3

Lacey put the phone down and stared out into the thundering darkness. The swamp in the near distance lit for a heartbeat with each lightning strike.

Storms and darkness were the only times she felt alone, slightly afraid. She didn't like her sleep interrupted by phone calls, by nightmares of what could have been as opposed to what now was. And the nightmares only came with thunderstorms. Both were nearly over, now. It was just a matter of time.

All day she'd been haunted by that phone call she'd made. And she knew it had been a mistake a few seconds after she called Eric Bateman's old number. If she was lucky, Johnny Logan would have forgotten, but Lacey knew the new man in town would remember eventually. Some people were haunted by the past all their lives. She was one of them.

At work, Lacey remembered overhearing gossip about the new baker. Most of it was prematurely cruel, but the town was full of bored and mainly empty minds which refused to listen to hearts. God knew what had been said when she arrived in town, permanently, five years before— she often asked and received no reply. She learnt quickly to keep away. Keep away yet be civil, be as kind as possible and not fuel imaginative fires. At times it was indescribably hard.

More than once when delivering the counter meals she'd want to upend a plate over an unsuspecting head but as long as the regulars wore the carpet down a little more each day she was assured of work, of regular income. Most of the men who frequented The Australian Arms talked to her breasts anyway, and talked some more about what they'd like to do to the rest of her when she returned to the kitchen. If they were aware of thin walls separating the public bar from the kitchen of The Australian Arms, they never cared.

Just when she thought she understood human nature, she moved to Mallen. The divorce settlement was more than enough to buy the farm; there weren't a lot of people in the town and she was under the mistaken impression that in Mallen, she'd be left alone. She'd thought the stories of lone divorced females were nothing but fiction. Within a year, old belief systems had flown out the proverbial window.

The new baker was different to the average hard-working, beer-swilling Ocker. He was quiet. Intelligent. He had a presence which could weaken knees in a woman of any age and the effect was reinforced by his ignorance of that fact. The bakery was doing well. The main attraction wasn't the quality of the product—Kerry Staines was his own living advertisement.

Lacey tried very hard not to meet that dark gaze whenever she had to go into town to do the weekly shop. The most he'd ever said to her was that quip at the hotel on his very first night in Mallen. He hadn't been into the pub since, that she knew of. Not frequenting the pub was questionable behavior. Mallen had a new, handsome male under forty years old who didn't go to the pub every day and this came as a shock to everyone. What did he do with his spare time? was the main question. A question Lacey knew the answer to. He wants to be left alone. One hermit always recognized another immediately.

After that afternoon in The Arms, he'd tried vainly to make conversation when she visited his shop. Yet when it came to the point of no return, of introducing herself, she always sought and found an escape route. She'd lower her gaze, smile, and hope her face and voice were not familiar to him.

He had a kind face, till she looked into his eyes. Eyes she couldn't look into long enough to read, or ever hope to. And he had nice hands, too. Healing hands. If one day she was ever able to glimpse or, in her dreams, study those hands, she'd know more about him than a lifelong friend.

He was different. Magnetic. What would he want with me? she repeatedly wondered when her daydreams spilled into reality.

The storm was intensifying.

With a will of its own, her mind incessantly rehearsed, Kerry and Lacey. Lacey and Kerry. No, it didn't fit. Too many y's. What am I doing? she thought. Fantasizing about this poor guy again. I've been on my own too long. Far too long. It may not even *be* him. How many police officers had faces like that? Hands like that? A voice like that? No, it was him. Had to be. She never believed in coincidence. It happened to others, not her.

To the north there was a ground strike, so close the entire house shook. She bit back a yelp. What good was fear? She was no better than the old black Labrador whimpering under the table. Yes, they needed the rain but why, oh why, were prayers always answered with violence? The swamp lit and stayed lit for a succession of spectacular ground strikes.

And through the rain and howling wind she thought she saw people out there. One, two, five people. They wouldn't be campers—people tended to avoid that area. All was plunged into darkness again. Lacey waited for the next strike. When it came, nobody was out there. Just the rain. Hard, incessant. Hard enough to flatten her tomatoes but enough to heart the lettuce. Flower the potatoes. If, of course, the pigs left any.

That was the reason for the phone call. Pigs. Or so she told herself.

She climbed back into bed, yet sleep was elusive. There was nothing to do at three in the morning. Nothing except to listen to the radio, the insomniac shift on relay from the coast for all the lonely people... She answered Paul McCartney's eternal question: Where do they all come from?

They come from Mallen but they don't belong here.

In the bakery, Kerry flicked the radio on as he walked by. 'Eleanor Rigby'. The electrical storm interfered with the AM band and the constant static annoyed him. No chance of decent FM this far west. And as he worked on, he wondered how many prospective suicides Carl the DJ would have this morning. What was in the atmosphere at this time of year? Sudden storms, a couple of weeks until Christmas, stifling heat, plenty of despair. A few lost souls reaching out for the gun or the rope or the pills... Kerry filled the mixer and suddenly remembered where he'd seen Lacey. The light finally shone in the dark tunnel and for a moment he hoped it wasn't an approaching train.

He was still in uniform back then, the eleven till seven graveyard shift. It was winter. Cold, wet and foggy. It was an early morning call to a flat on the western side of town, a few streets from his favorite watering hole. An attempted suicide. An hysterical old lady had called in. There'd been a hell of a fight between a father and daughter; father drunk and abusive had left thirty minutes before and the little old lady had tried to get in. It was unlike the teenager to lock herself away and not answer the door. Please, do something. She's so unhappy I think she might try to kill herself, I really do.

Kerry remembered it well; it was one of his first attempted suicides. He had to break in—something he'd been good at when he was fifteen. He'd entered through a bedroom window, found her in a full bath of very hot water. She'd taken half a bottle of Serepax. Then the cops came. She saw his face and used the razor anyway, her right arm slashed from wrist to elbow. She didn't say a word. She didn't have to. The look in her eyes and the bruises on her body told him all he needed to know.

Thinking back, he was almost certain the sixteen-year-old attempted suicide and Lacey were the same person. And if he hadn't broken in, she wouldn't be cooking at The Australian Arms today.

Now it made sense why she couldn't meet his gaze. The incessant nagging dissipated now that he knew the reason for the vague familiarity.

He looked at the time. Quarter to four. The vicious storm had passed and left in its wake soothing rain. Normal people would be sleeping through this, unawares.

Kerry fired the ovens to The Supremes, 'Stop, in the Name of Love.'

He immediately thought of Belinda Barlow, who had the chance of turning professional and so had he to a lesser degree. Kerry tried to persuade her to take the opportunity and run. As a professional singer, Belinda's life would have taken a new highway, straight to the top. But she stayed in the force. These days she could barely talk.

Tonight Carl the DJ was taking calls from every lonely heart in the south of the state. Voices over the airwaves were soon lost in the scream of mixers, the work, the new job. Everything was lost.

I need to employ someone, Kerry thought for the sixteenth time. Some kid I can train and trust. Again he wondered at the logic of this proposition. Had it been wishful thinking that a new town and a new job equaled a new life? He had an innate aversion to routine; not for him the safe parameters of a self-imposed, barbed-wire, nine to five grind. Most of all, he needed something, someone.

It may have been fulfilling enough for Dora Mallaby to be chatted to every morning at six to ten. It sure wasn't enough for those three twelve-year-old girls who lingered by the drinks fridge each morning at eight-thirty.

Kerry supplied the primary school with pies, rolls—one errant thought occurred that he should incorporate a takeaway, too. But Mallen already had a cafe. Plus, he couldn't afford to employ anyone yet.

Around eight-thirty the girls strolled in, stood by the fridge, stole the normal shy, giggling glances. They shared a can of coke and an iced donut for breakfast every day. When Kerry spoke, they normally split with laughter, but that Wednesday, the freckle-faced girl with dark auburn hair asked, 'Are you really joining Deceptions?'

Kerry shrugged and again wondered about Mallen's information retrieval system. A turbo-charged bush telegraph.

'Please say you will,' she said, her face as red as her hair.

'What stuff d'ya play?' another asked.

'Anything and everything,' Kerry said with a grin, and thereby gave the three primary seniors something to tell their friends. After they left he sat for the first time in three hours.

Damn the storm. Damn Eadie Ross's delusions. Two hours sleep wasn't enough. There was a time, a few years back, when he could stay awake and remain lucid for 72-hour stretches. And make love four times in one night. Now he was closer to forty than thirty-five, his hip hated the cold, too many cigarettes had depleted his fitness and left him a superb candidate for a heart attack. He'd noticed grey in his hair and on his face if he didn't shave for a few days. Grey implied age but grey he could live with. If the youth disappeared from his eyes, then and only then would he worry.

He'd never had trouble advancing towards a female target. In his youth and early career days he was known as The Bandicoot—eats roots and leaves. For ten years he was proud of it, too. Fortunately emptiness welled and he found Annie. He was working undercover at the time. Her car had broken down on Ipswich Road. She'd seen the leather-clad bikie stop, get off his bike. One look was enough for Annie—she locked herself in her car.

Feigning boredom to neutralize her fears, Kerry discovered that the fuel filter on her Nissan hatch was blocked. He cleared it. By the time the Nissan started, he was on his bike and waiting for her to pull out. She walked to him instead, tapped on his visor. Kerry lifted it.

'Thank you!' she yelled.

'No worries,' he replied and smiled.

One month later she admitted her knees had become jelly because of that grin. She'd dreamed of a Prince Charming on a white stallion. She got Kerry Staines on a Honda instead. For three months he avoided the issue of employment. She didn't run away the night he said, 'Police'. It came in the afterglow, the endorphin rush a moment before sleep. It was always his most vulnerable time but she was still in his bed the next morning. Maybe it was her bed. He couldn't remember. He'd married her within six months and he'd had her for nearly three years. But she was only on loan. Like Michael and Julia. On loan.

'Oh, Annie,' he whispered quietly. 'You'd hate it out here.'

How long had she been in his thoughts? Was he thinking of her last night, wishing so hard that imagination overrode sense? That for a moment he actually believed she was in his bed? Doing what she did so well? Did he really believe that Annie had metamorphosed into that missing Mallen girl? Illusion. Delusion. That's all life was.

Kerry looked at the time again. Each second was lasting for sixty. It was nearly nine o'clock. It felt like two. It's going to be one of those days, he thought. He knew it. He felt it. People had filtered in and out, two took advantage of the corkboard. A 175 cc Yamaha dirt bike for sale. Too much. If it'd been a Honda 900 Kerry may have been interested. The other notice was a house for rent. At least he thought that's what it said— the printing was illegible.

He watched the passing traffic, though traffic as a word was an overstatement when applied to the occasional farm pickup, old sedan or double-decker sheep-transporting eighteen-wheeler. No one used the Stop sign. No one knew what a Give Way sign meant.

Then Lacey parked her bike outside the bakery. She was two hours early. He hadn't seen her for a week, he hadn't eaten at the pub yet either, although he always meant to. She'd traveled a fair distance, her bike was covered in mud. Unlike everyone else, she scraped her boots before entering. And she didn't linger idly chatting. She was about as subtle as an Exocet missile launch.

'Emile said that you could probably help me. I don't have time to ride to Wilton. I went once but everyone was out.'

What the hell is she talking about? he wondered.

'What do I have to do to get a gun?' she asked.

Jesus, he thought.

'I already have a couple of old rifles that,' she lowered her voice and looked to the door, 'no one knows about. Do I have to get a licence to keep them even if they're already licensed but to someone who died?' She looked up into his eyes.

A hint of the despairing sixteen-year-old still lived there. 'You want a handgun?' Kerry asked.

'Not want. It's need.'

'Can I ask why?'

'I'm having trouble with pigs.'

'Pigs?'

'Look, if I can't get a gun legally, I'll get one anyway.'

Any way was how most people got one.

'Would you like me to make further enquiries?'

'Would you?'

'Can I have a contact number?'

'Oh, sure.' She put her plastic bag down, scrounged through her wallet for a card. It said Marguerite. It was a Brisbane number. 'Can I have a biro?'

Kerry handed her a pen and she held it a while then stole a glance before the old number was obliterated by a single stroke and she wrote Lacey Kilder, 253112. She returned the pen and gave him the card. Fingers touched momentarily.

And now he knew her name. 'Pigs?' he asked again.

'I have a market garden on Starks Road. I've tried trapping. I've tried fencing—'

'What kind of rifles have you got that no one knows about?'

'If I knew anything about them, would I be here? Besides, Emile said you did two years in Tactical Response.'

Oh, did he? And where's Emile get his information? 'I tell you what,' Kerry said. 'I finish here about three. I'll take a look.'

'You'd do that? You'd look at Dad's old rifles and teach me to shoot?'

Had he said that? Was she a mind reader? This Lacey Kilder, aka Marguerite, was more than the normal three steps ahead. She was breaking the finish tape. 'I'll see if they're safe to use first.'

'Do you know Starks Road?' she asked.

'Off Weir Road?'

'Go right at the five ways. It's sealed for two kilometers, then it's very, very rough gravel for three. Just before the road sweeps to the right, there's a turnoff on the left. You can't miss it. I'm opposite the swamp.'

Kerry kept his thoughts to himself. How far was her place from the proposed prison site? Were wild pigs really her main problem?

No, his brain had been foreseeing the shots again. Closing at 3.00 p.m. would leave several hours of daylight at this time of year. He'd started two hours early anyway and late afternoon was always his slowest time.

'You don't mind?' she asked at the door.

'No problem,' he said.

He watched her get on that muddy bike and ride off. His heart lifted. Now he had an excuse. And she was getting prettier each time he saw her.

Getting away proved a large problem. He attempted to reverse the open sign three times and people who rarely stopped to chat seemed compelled to break old habits. It was 4.15 by the time he showered, shaved, fed the cat and noticed that Johnny Logan hadn't shown for work. Kerry collected his mail and reached for his Beretta 92 in its designer nest in the bookcase. God help anyone reaching for Moby Dick.

The gun wasn't there.

Any anticipation died a quick, painless death. He spent another twenty minutes in futile search, trying to remember where the hell he may have put it. It wasn't a replica, no way would he have put it with the others. He was certain it came in the car with him and the cat.

He decided to tear the house to shreds tomorrow. He was already two hours late for a meeting with the first woman he'd been attracted to in years. She spoke quietly without the rounded bush accent. Shyness was not enough mask the interest in her eyes. For three weeks each had pleaded indifference to the sparks trying hard to ignite.

By the time he was out of town with Dire Straits still doing the endless circuit, he'd forgotten about the missing weapon. He'd forgotten almost everything.

When she'd said the road was rough she wasn't joking. Just before the road swept to the right he noticed the mail box—a forty-four gallon drum painted in rainbow colors.

Tracks in the settled road of one bike, knobbly tires. Over the first grid and to the right, noticed about ten acres devoted to a market garden— tomatoes a week from picking flattened because of last night's storm.

Then he saw the farmhouse. High set, oleanders in bloom. One fence was covered in flowering bougainvillea. Kerry stopped near the side gate to the house yard. His attention was taken by sheep in the fifty acres to the rear of the woolshed a hundred meters ahead. Market garden, sheep—here lives one busy woman. Kerry got out of his car and was met by an ancient black Labrador. She sniffed his boots and waddled off. Great security system, he thought and unlatched the gate. He followed the path. The lawn was green kikuyu, short, well kept. Clothing hung from the hoist and music blasted from the house. It was futile knocking, like catching a whisper whilst standing in a 500-watt Marshall amplifier.

A white cockatoo in a cage by the steps lifted its crest in surprise and said, 'What you doing?'

Kerry looked at it.

'What you doing? Give us a smoke. I need a smoke.'

A woman, living alone, a long way from town with one ancient dog and a psycho parrot for company.

'Turn it down!' the bird screamed.

Kerry watched as the parrot opened the door of its cage, climbed out, and waddled across the lawn. It walked like a duck but repeated, 'Turn it down! Turn it down!' and disappeared around the corner of the house. A moment later it reappeared in a faster Charlie Chaplin waddle.

'Charlie! Get back in your cage, right now.' Lacey, digging fork in hand, appeared and saw Kerry standing by the back stairs. 'Oh, hello. I didn't think you were coming.'

'Nor did I for a while,' was all he said.

Lacey picked the bird up, put him away. 'Did he swear at you?'

'Abusive little bastard, isn't he?'

'Oh, God. I'm so sorry. I didn't teach him to swear. I inherited him. He lets me know if someone's here. Doesn't matter where I am, he lets himself out and manages to find me. Shouldn't call him a he—he laid an egg the day I was born. Come on up.'

Lacey ran upstairs. By the time Kerry made it to the top and through the screen door, there was silence. Cool, clean. 'Come in. Sit down. I'll get the rifles... Oh, that didn't sound very good, did it? Sorry.'

Kerry walked into the huge kitchen and from afar heard, 'The rain was terrific. I won't have to irrigate for four days.'

'You work this place alone?' he called.

'Just the patch. The rest is all agisted. It helps ends meet. They never embrace, but occasionally they touch.' She appeared with a .243 plus infrared scope in one hand and an M16 in the other. 'This place is the only one with natural springs and pasture most of the year round but I still have to irrigate. You saw the swamp?' she asked.

'Yeah,' he lied.

'It's an aberration. Shouldn't be there.'

She put the weapons on the kitchen table and walked out again. The house felt good, bright. Something was different. He didn't notice at first, till he sat and saw the color of the ceiling. Bright canary yellow. Gloss. The walls were off-white. He wondered what color her bedroom was.

Lacey came out again, this time with a 12-gauge shotgun and a bolt action .22. Kerry expected her to vacate once more. What would be next? A .32 carbine? Maybe a .30 cal? Uzi? She went to the fridge instead and took a large jug and two large glasses from the freezer. 'Wild lime juice,' she said softly as she poured and handed him a glass.

'Thanks.'

'Well? What do you think?' she said, sitting on the edge of the table, sipping her drink, swinging her leg idly.

Kerry inspected the firing mechanism of the .22 first. No wasp nests in the barrel. Whoever had owned it had cared for it. It was the same with the .243; the shotgun. 'Your father's?'

She nodded.

'What did he do?'

'A truckie. I only lived with him two years. Well, what do you think?'

'I think you should put them away and forget they exist.'

'Why?'

'Too easy for someone to turn it back on you, Lacey.'

'I doubt a pig would do that.'

'A woman alone, isolated, what if—'

'I've been here five years. Nothing has happened and nothing will. People are not a problem. I days ago, I was shifting the irrigator and I swear the pig I saw coming for me was the size of a bloody Shetland pony. Have you seen what a wild boar can do to a person?'

'You seen what a 12 gauge can do?'

'If I hadn't been able to get to my bike, it would have killed me.'

'Supposition.'

'You said you'd help me.'

'I said I'd look at the rifles.'

'Thanks for nothing.'

Kerry pretended he didn't see the fire in her eyes. 'Have you ever used a weapon before?'

'Not really.'

'Is there any ammo for the .22?'

She disappeared again, her absence this time a lengthy one. Kerry sipped the drink. One sip became the full glass and he reached for a refill as returned with an assortment of ammunition boxes.

'Would the .22 stop a feral pig?' she asked.

'Depends where you hit it and what you mean by stop.'

'I don't like killing, Kerry, but it's him or me. It's war now.'

"Got some old tins?' he asked.

He took the .22, ejected the magazine, loaded fifteen rounds and walked downstairs. Lacey followed with two dog food cans from the garbage. Kerry placed both tins on the strainer post in the backyard and said, 'There's a hell of a difference between a tin and something that's breathing. I hope you never have to experience it.'

'But you have?'

He didn't answer. He had selective hearing. He showed her how to hold the rifle, outlined safety procedures, how to trigger it. He shot first. The tin lifted, the cockatoo swore and the shell was ejected to the grass. Kerry gave the rifle to Lacey and she clasped it as if it were a life preserver. A few moments later she sighted. The first bullet lodged in the fence. She hit the tin with the fifth.

'The pig population's safe,' Kerry mused.

'We'll see.'

He liked the gentle defiance lurking in her eyes, that half smile on her face.

Getting him out here was as much an excuse for her but neither would admit it.

'Think you're capable of killing a living creature?' Kerry asked.

'I don't know.'

'When are the pigs at their worst?'

'Before sunrise, about sunset.'

Kerry checked the time—5.30. 'Show me.'

Lacey took him walking and with the walk, conversation came a little easier. The afternoon was mellow, golden. He wished he knew her better, he wanted to hold her hand.

'Why do you limp?' she asked.

'I got shot once. Actually I got shot twice. I'd show you the scars but I don't know you well enough. I'm kind of shy, you see.'

'Pig's bum,' she said.

'It's true. I am very shy. This, the me here now, cool, calm, it's all an act.'

She walked on, quietly. 'The first time I saw you I could feel your pain.'

'The doctors said I'd never walk again. I always wanted to prove them wrong and I did.'

'Is that why you left the police?'

'What's the story you heard?'

'I've heard four so far. One, you were busted for selling drugs at the folk festival at Maleny. Two, you were drunk and shot a colleague. Three, you stole money from a dealer. And four, you were involved in a child prostitution ring.'

'Shit, really? I've been busier than I thought.'

'Yes, that's what I thought.'

'If it's multiple choice, what's the highest score? A, B, C or D?'

'E for none of the above. You were set up and took a fall for someone else. A good friend perhaps. Someone you used to trust.'

'What are you, psychic?'

To that she turned, grinned at him and walked backwards for a while. 'Could be. But my ex-brother-in-law was a cop and gossip amid cops is worse than it is here in Mallen. Here, look. Proof.'

Kerry crouched, saw a cloven hoof print in settled mud near remnants of the fence which bordered her market garden. The hoof print was as big as his fist. She hadn't been exaggerating. A pig this size would only blink and wonder what the sting was when a .22 bullet bounced off its skull. He decided to teach her how to use the .243 instead. The Beretta, had he found it, would have been better, especially at close range.

'I'm trying to supply the town with fresh local and organic produce.

Summer is lettuce, beetroot, tomatoes, celery. There's asparagus over there but I have to wait another two years before I can harvest it. Potatoes over there, but the crop's not ready for harvest yet, of course.'

Kerry was watching her, not her vegetables, as she walked him through this huge expanse she called *the patch*.

'I can lose it all in one night, Kerry. It's happened before. That's why I had to get the job at The Arms. I prefer working my own way, in my own time, doing my own thing. But I have to eat, too. It's called compromise. Something I thought I'd never have to do.'

'Were you approached to sell your land?'

'Oh, yes, but what the government offered wasn't enough to relocate without begging at a bank.'

'Land value won't increase with the prison so close.'

'Maybe they won't build it.'

'Of course they will. Hell, I bought the bakery a week before the decision was made public.'

'You're a fatalist.'

'No, I'm me. No room for "should haves" or "if onlys" any more.' He had enough maybes tucked away in his garbage bag of pain. Sometimes he forgot it was there, mostly though it was too heavy to drag around. More often than not he just carried it, his own private set of weights. For a few moments he heard the silence. It was thick and sweet. Alien. And he breathed it all in. Savored it.

Kerry watched the darkening eastern sky. The swamp in the distance. 'Where exactly is this prison site?' he asked.

She pointed to the swamp. 'A mile or so beyond the swamp. The surveyors were there on Monday. I watched them for a while. It's going to be huge. I suppose there's some sense building a prison so far west. If there was any escape, they couldn't get too far.'

'You believe that, don't you?'

'I don't really have a choice. It looks like I'm here to stay. No use grumbling about decisions that can't be reversed, is there?'

He looked into her eyes and tried hard not to laugh. They had more in common than he had first thought.

'Ever considered poison for your pig problem?'

'Hell, no. It's too much of a threat to the wildlife. I couldn't be responsible for anything dying that way. Slow. Agonizingly slow.'

'Everything has a right to life?'

'Oh, yes. Definitely.'

'Except feral pigs.' Kerry didn't say what else was on his mind. If he had he knew it would be the last time he'd ever drive away from Rainbow Farm. He'd been watching. He'd seen the scar on her arm. Yes, she'd attempted suicide twenty-odd years ago and, yes, people's lives change. Some, he knew, changed for the better.

'I'll give you a situation,' he said.

'I don't like hypotheticals. They tend to take on a reality of their own.'

'It's two years into the future. It's nine at night. Moonlight. A storm twice as severe as last night's has just passed over. The road's impassable. The phones are out. The substation at the prison site's been hit by a ground strike and the electronics have died.'

'Six-inch-thick steel doors lock everyone in.'

'There's a malfunction.'

'With three back-up systems?'

'Funding cutbacks. They could only afford one back-up and there is human error responsible for its failure.'

'That's not possible.'

'Obviously you've never been a public servant. There's total malfunction. We have an assortment of maximum security prisoners suddenly let off the leash. I am one of them. Never to be released. If you knew me, you'd know why. I'm out. I look around. I see no other farmhouse for miles. The prison is in a direct line to your property. Flat, virtually treeless. It's direct and that's where I will go.'

'It won't happen.'

'Ah, yes,' Kerry said and took a packet of cigarettes from his shirt pocket. 'It won't happen to me. Fatal last words most folks utter. It *can't* happen to me. But it does. It does every damned day. It's not too late to change your mind.'

'I have nowhere else to go.' She watched him light his smoke. 'Kerry, there won't be a prison. They might try to build it but it won't eventuate. If it does, believe me, there will be one disaster after another which will continue until the place is forced to close. Do you know what that piece of land really is? Sacred ground. Ancient, sacred ground that was cursed ten thousand years ago. That's what the government is intending to build a prison on. Cursed land.'

'You believe in this kind of crap?'

'Nothing lives there. Birds avoid it. Even crows avoid it. The water in the swamp is black and putrid. It's dead. There's no grass, no trees, not even saltbush will grow on that site. The only vegetation that does grow is groundsel after rain and even it dies within a week.' She walked off and Kerry followed.

'Whatever reason you give I can find a perfectly acceptable explanation for the opposite.'

'It was cursed 10 000 years ago.'

'The water table's risen, turned a few acres into a salt wasteland.'

'One localized area exactly four kilometers square?'

'A geologist would—'

'No, Kerry. No one can explain why that piece of land is as it is.'

'I still don't believe in curses and Dreamtime fairytales.'

'What do you believe in?'

'Fate.'

She looked away from the smile—she had to. For a long time there was silence. God knew what he was thinking of. At any moment now, she expected his question. I know you from somewhere, don't I? 'I love this time of day. It's quiet, like a preparation for the darkness to come.'

'You're poetic,' he said.

'In more fits than starts, I'm afraid. Out here, sometimes—not very often—the sky gives off an eerie yellow glow. It's as if the color spectrum's confused for half an hour. Or God's wondering if anyone down here will stop long enough to notice the difference.'

'You know, your kitchen ceiling did that to me.'

'You noticed?'

'Nearly reached for the hat and sunscreen.'

'Yellow stimulates the thought processes. I do my best work in that room.'

'And what's that, exactly?'

'I write.'

'Yeah? What?'

'Metaphysics. The lounge is blue because that's where I meditate. My bedroom is fuchsia, the bathroom is purple and the loo, well, it's green. Each color affects me differently.'

Yeah, Kerry thought. A green dunny would be wonderful for a drunken Technicolor barf at 3.00 a.m. He looked at the time, threw his cigarette butt down and ground it out.

'Do you have to go so soon?' she asked.

'Not especially.'

'Would you like to stay for dinner? Nothing fancy.'

'That'd be nice. Thanks.'

They walked back to the house in silence. Kerry unlatched the gate and Lacey didn't bitch about going through first. She wouldn't bitch about a car door being opened either. At least he hoped she wouldn't. It was twilight by the time they entered the house and again it welcomed him. Like his mother's house used to. The place had a heart, a warmth that had nothing to do with outside temperatures. And he knew as he watched her prepare dinner just where that warmth originated. It all came from Lacey.

I could fall in love with this woman, he thought. As if sensing the gaze, she turned and smiled. Kerry scratched his head. He wasn't used to feeling vulnerable.

'Grilled chicken breast be okay?'

'Fine,' he lied. He didn't want to admit that he hated chook after once having been poisoned by an Indian curry. Death at the time seemed very inviting, but she'd obviously hoped he'd stay to eat and she'd gone to some trouble and effort for this, so he said nothing more except, 'I'll have to return the gesture one day.'

'It's not necessary. You taught me to shoot the .22, I fed you. It's not right that people go through life always feeling they owe something when they don't. Besides, it's nice having someone to talk to. Someone who looks me in the eye for a change.'

'What do you mean?'

'If my breasts could speak I'd have a captive audience hanging on every word.'

'I'm a leg man myself,' he said quietly, lying again.

She didn't believe it. 'There's a beer in the fridge if you'd like one.' She held up her hands, covered in flour and egg and herbs. Kerry extracted a beer. 'Want one?'

'Oh, no. I can't drink alcohol. I have an intolerance to it. I was born drunk, you see, and I dare not start again. I've been dry all my life but having half my mother's chromosomes, the temptation strikes me at times. Plus the two years I lived with my father were hell. He was an alcoholic—' Her voice faded. She wanted to tell him more but dared not. 'I'm harping again. I'm sorry. I either don't talk at all or I talk too much and I don't know which is worse.'

'Don't apologize.'

'Is the beer cold enough?'

'It's fine.'

'I *am* talking too much.'

'No, no. It makes a pleasant change to what I get day in, day out.'

'Farmers whining about the drought?'

'And when it rains they bitch about the wet. I've been here, what, three, nearly four weeks, and I think I have a mental copy of everyone's pedigree from 1939 onwards. Who does what to whom, where, when and how.'

'What do they say about me?' Lacey asked.

'Nothing. Look, I don't listen, Lacey. If I do it's selective. I just utter the appropriate noises on cue and everyone's happy. Keeps the customers satisfied, I suppose.'

'Do you think you'll like it here?'

'It makes no difference. I'm just filling in time.'

'Till when?'

'Till I die, I guess.'

She turned to him, and the bright blue gaze impaled every cell of his body.

'No, I'm not suicidal. Bored with life, maybe.'

'Already?' she asked, smiling. The smile lifted his heart, so much so that adrenalin-induced butterflies rose till they swarmed in his chest. He hadn't felt that for years. Seven years to be exact.

'How long were you married?' he asked.

'Four years,' she said. 'You?'

'How'd you know I was married?'

'Eadie told me about the photograph she saw in your house. I'm not prying. I know you don't let anyone through your gate.'

'I tend to shoot trespassers. I'm like you. Mind if I look around? I get nervous watching women with knives.'

'Just remember there's nothing worth stealing.'

'I have enough crap of my own, what would I want with yours?'

Kerry picked up his beer and walked into the lounge room. 'Kind of grows on you,' he said aloud as he looked up at the bright, glossy, pastel blue ceiling. 'So do warts,' he added softly. Kerry looked at the books which lined an entire wall of the room. Few fiction titles. Anthropology, history and metaphysical-New Age books dominated the display and, he noticed, three titles bore the name Kilder.

There were also alternate farming, permaculture and lifestyle books. A Complete Shakespeare. Oscar Wilde. T.S. Eliot. Darwin's Theory of Evolution. Freud. Jung. Plato's Republic. His gaze fell on a white cover inscribed with red: Science Against Crime. He took it out, leafed through. It was dated. Forensic science had advanced rapidly since this book was published. DNA was coming into its own. Lengthy and expensive, though.

'What did you do in CIB?' she asked from the doorway. The sudden voice frightened him, he turned quickly. 'What divisions? What squads?'

'Depended where I was. I've done Fraud, Vice, Juvenile Aid, Homicide, Rape, Drug Squad. Six months in Tactical Response, not two years. It's all past,' he said, turning pages in the forensics book. 'I thought you said you weren't going to pry.'

'I lied.'

Kerry turned to her again. She was leaning against the doorway, arms folded across that plentiful chest.

'Which gave you the most job satisfaction?' she asked.

'Oh, that's a tough one. Let's see. Booking Ford drivers when I was twenty-one and a petrol-head highway patroller, I guess. My partner victimized Holden drivers. Anything Japanese was fine with us...'

Disbelief crossed her eyes.

'Don't believe me? Okay, then. How about the time I averted the attempted suicide of a teenage girl?' It wasn't a question. Lacey looked at her bare feet. 'Lucky for her I'd been a paramedic.' He slid the book back in its place. 'It's not often you find someone so young who knew exactly what she was doing. She took the blade up her arm, not across the wrist. She was even lying in hot water for a better bleed.'

Still Lacey said nothing. She didn't have to.

'*Just let me die!* she kept wailing. She looked a lot like you. But I guess we've all got our double somewhere.' Kerry brushed her arm as he walked by and Lacey didn't move for a little while.

Oh, he was good, this one, she thought.

'As for job satisfaction, now and then someone would say thanks for playing God and intervening in another's life. That girl I was telling you about, she sent me a card when she was released from the psyche ward. It was a little white card with a red rose on it. She signed it, With love and thanks, Marguerite. Marguerite Lebsanft. I often wonder what became of her. For all I know she might have tried to top herself again. Went for a full bottle of pills, not half. Or maybe she aimed a car at a tree ten years ago. I guess I'll never know, will I?'

Lacey met his gaze. 'A lot can happen to a sixteen-year-old. Perhaps she had what she believed were good reasons for what she tried to do.'

'Did I say she was sixteen?'

'Isn't it the worst year of anyone's life?' she asked, question for question.

'Maybe,' Kerry said. He was standing a little too close so she moved away. 'Maybe there's a larger hand at work that sometimes sends the troops in when someone wants to get off the merry-go-round too soon. Know what I see when I look at you?'

'I'm not you.'

'I see one extremely attractive woman that most guys would queue just to be near. You're bright, intelligent. Kind. Patient. Cool. You talk like you've done some kind of public speaking and I bet you'd sing well, too. I'd hazard a guess that every guy in town's tried to get into your pants at least once, and I can't blame them for trying. Yet you live alone, miles from anywhere. It seems a waste.'

'I have the farm, I have my work. I don't see it as a waste.'

Kerry put his empty bottle into the kitchen tidy by her feet and he looked out of the kitchen window. Directly in his line of sight, the swamp.

'You know that teenage girl was me.'

'I never forget a face.' He turned, reached for her wrist and turned her arm, lightly tracing the wide jagged white scar from the bottom of her hand to her elbow. 'Wasn't worth it, was it?' He turned her face towards his and kissed her lightly. Tentatively. 'I won't mention it again,' he said quietly. 'But I will have another beer. Christ, that smells good.'

It had been a long time since he'd been in a woman's kitchen, sipping on a beer, watching her cook.

'You've been published three times,' Kerry said. 'Is it all spooky stuff?'

'It's psychic research. Different aspects from ageless wisdom to the UFO phenomenon.'

'Do you know much about hauntings?' he asked.

'Enough. Why?'

'Is it possible for a large object to be physically moved from one location to another?'

'But you didn't see it occurring?' she asked.

He shook his head.

'There have been verified reports of teleportation. What's the object you're talking about?'

'A heavy garbage bag. I'm thinking maybe a handgun, too. My Beretta's missing.'

'When did it happen?'

'The bag? Last night. A lot of weird things have been happening lately.'

'Did it start soon after you met Eadie Ross?'

Kerry told her the basics of what had happened, without emotion, as if he were writing a report. All this while they ate. He told her how he believed he saw Elspeth, but he did not say what he believed she had done to him.

'And what did Elspeth look like when you saw her?'

'She was covered in mud.'

'Like Eadie had been?'

Kerry remembered both images and said, 'Yeah, I guess so. I didn't get a good, close look at the blonde. She scared the shit out of me if you want the truth. Here's this ... *girl* pointing at my raincoat as if she wanted me to wear it.'

'And it rained a couple of hours later, didn't it?'

'This is going to sound weird, but it seemed as if she knew I walked to work and she didn't want me to get wet.'

Lacey said nothing to that.

'Eadie keeps saying Elspeth likes me, that she'll have me.'

'In what way?'

'I really don't want to know,' Kerry said quietly.

'I'm writing about Elspeth. Trying to. Personally, I believe she was murdered and can't rest, can't go on until her body's found.'

'What do you mean, go on?'

'To where she ought to be. She's earthbound, and her hate, her anger, is keeping her here. I think her body was dumped in the swamp.'

'That's what Eadie says. What the hell am I going to do? I don't particularly want to go home if she's going to visit me every night.'

'Kerry, she cannot harm you physically unless you allow it to happen.'

'I've seen what happens to Eadie. I tried to stop it, I got kicked out of the way.'

'The mind is a powerful thing.'

'It's more than that, Lacey. Much more. Eadie brought me flowers and stuff, said it'd keep Elspeth away. I feel like I'm being watched all the time.'

'Fear will intensify the phenomena.'

'So you advise me to, what, ignore it?'

'No, Kerry. I advise you to accept it. Everyone else has. Except perhaps every man in town who ever took advantage of that poor girl. She comes back periodically and makes them pay for what they did.'

'Eadie believes she was murdered by soldiers when the army came through town.'

'Soldiers? Maybe.'

'You're not convinced.'

'I just wish she could be at peace. So does everyone in Mallen.'

'Can you tell me something?'

'I can but try.'

'Why'd she pick on me?'

For a little while, Lacey was silent. Then she looked into Kerry's eyes and said, 'Well, maybe she's like every other woman in Mallen. A little fresh blood makes all the difference.'

CHAPTER 4

On the Thursday night, Kerry finally ate at The Australian Arms. He tried to pretend that all eyes were not following Lacey as she put his plate down and quietly returned to the kitchen.

What he'd hoped would happen on that wonderful Wednesday night didn't, of course. The most she did was put her hands behind her back and say goodbye as he got into his car. One of those awkward moments better left alone. But he'd departed feeling good, a rarity.

The pub was busy that Thursday night and he didn't want to disrupt any routine. Or start gossip. The most he said to her was a quiet thank you with a smile in his eyes. One day he'd get her alone again, that much he knew.

He remained quiet, non-reactive to the beer-induced talk close by. These people were pissing him off today. It seemed that not a great lot ever changed. People had pissed him off his entire life.

'What you think, mate? Like a piece of that or what?'

'Or what,' Kerry said bored, not bothering to look at whoever had spoken.

'I had it you know. I sure did. A while back.'

'Had what?'

'Her. Whatsername.'

Rory, a seventeen-year-old jackaroo who came to town once every three months, wore an Akubra cowboy hat so tight his brain was too compressed for normal operation. No doubt he'd picked a fight with everyone present at some time or another, even his reflection. But the days of fighting were long gone for Kerry. Best be quiet, no use throwing kerosene on embers. Even though he was half-inclined to rearrange this peacock's face with one well-placed jab, Kerry simply continued eating. The food he'd had at Lacey's house the other night was a lot better—a more personal touch added to the flavor.

Rory drawled on, an imaginative fantasy story about Lacey on a mattress in the back of his Toyota pickup. Kerry's hand, with a will of its own, began fisting. Picking up his plate and his beer, Kerry headed for the lounge. He wanted some peace. If he stayed much longer he'd probably kill that boy who would no doubt run like hell if Lacey so much as said hello. Which she didn't. Most of these men were open books. She was right. Mallen had more dickheads per head of population than anywhere else Kerry had ever lived.

A very pretty part-Aboriginal child kept grinning at him. She was about a year old, the same age as Julia was when Kerry was summoned to Grafton to identify the bodies of his wife and son. He had stayed in the hospital for two full days and nights, rarely leaving his baby's side. His life-supported daughter. Nurses offered him food, coffee, sympathy and advice. Get some sleep. There's nothing you can do.

That's all he remembered of it. A little like Maleny. He couldn't recall much about that either. Just lying in long green grass, feeling his life drain away. Eyes open enough to see Belinda. Not being able to warn her. Or help her.

The little girl smiled brightly at him. Most kids did. She didn't know about racial differences yet. She didn't understand true innocence—she displayed it. It hurt Kerry too much to keep smiling so he took his attention elsewhere.

A band's four way PA and equipment was set on the cabaret stage. *Deceptions*. Nine-piece Pearl drums, Fender bass. A Rickenbacker lead and Peavey amps. A Roland keyboard on a stand. For a while Kerry considered waiting for Johnny Logan to show. Hear what the band was like. But he was so damned tired. Later, he thought. Another night. Maybe Saturday.

No one visited him that night, nor were there any dreams.

Friday began as all days did. Tired of the emotional, introspective and dark poetry on the insomniac station, tired of listening to people begging to be heard, Kerry used his own music. Sang most of the morning away.

When the phone rang at 7.30 he knew who it was long before he answered: had Lacey finally shot the pig after an all-night stakeout? No. 'Have you heard from Eadie?' she asked.

'No, why?'

'Kerry, she hasn't spoken to me since Tuesday night. After you left her.'

'You sound worried.'

'With reason. It's the seventeenth anniversary of Elspeth's death today.'

'Look, Eadie's survived sixteen other anniversaries.'

'It's different this time. I feel it. Please trust my intuition?'

'I tell you what, if I get a chance this morning, I'll call in. Leave it with me.'

The tone in her voice could not be ignored. He tried to call Eadie's number, no answer. He waited until Dora arrived for her morning chat and asked if she'd help him out for a little while. She didn't refuse and the kiss on her cheek for good measure added more than a little sparkle to her day. Kerry discarded his apron and left the shop.

The Mazda was in the carport as it had been on Tuesday night, but today no neighbors were out watching. He knocked on the back door, heard the empty echo. 'Eadie? It's Kerry Staines.' No answer. No movement from within. The door was unlocked.

In hindsight, he wished he'd used a hanky around his hand. In hindsight he wished a lot of things could have been different. He was only human but he should have known better. The kitchen was exactly how he'd left it on Tuesday night. Her cup of tea, with a ring of scum floating on top, sat where she'd left it, next to the open photograph album.

'Eadie!'

He knew she was dead long before he skidded into her darkened bedroom. The stench was gripping the air. The nightgown he'd dressed her in was draped over the papasan again and the form covered by stinking, darkened bedcovers was immobile. Kerry pulled the sheet back and immediately turned his face away. In a corner of the room lay a pillow. It was holed and powder burnt in three places by a large calibre weapon—he guessed a 9 mm.

Eadie Ross had been shot, her body was drained of any color, of all blood. He saw three bullet wounds in the center of her chest, and all were point blank.

Kerry looked at his watch, closed his eyes and reached for the phone by her bed.

Finally he heard the magic words, 'Wilton police. Sergeant Gilmeister.'

'Detec—sorry, Kerry Staines. Mallen. I'm reporting an unlawful death. Edith Ross, white female, age mid-thirties. Three gunshot wounds to the chest. It appears that death occurred two or three days ago.' Kerry needed a hatchet to break the silence. 'Are you there?'

'Detective Senior Sergeant Kerry Staines?'

'Was.'

'And who's dead again?'

'Eadie Ross.'

'Eadie? Oh fuck.' Gilmeister cursed for awhile about needing to get the bloody CIB in.

'Look, Sergeant, if you don't mind, I have a business to run and I cannot wait here indefinitely.' Kerry gave the address and said he'd wait no more than an hour.

Later, he realized it had been a mistake calling. He could have just walked out and waited for someone else to find her At the time, calling seemed the right move to make. Then he had to wonder just how long it would take a crime scene squad to get to Mallen. Half an hour if they flew in. Two hours if they drove. For a change he was on the outside looking in.

Kerry drew the sheet back fully. Eadie's right leg was twisted under her as if she'd been pushed backwards as she tried to get out of bed. Probably awakened by an intruder. Or a regular. The pillow had been used to smother the discharges. Her mottled skin still bore those empathic marks—investigators would deduce a violent struggle had occurred. Hell, if he knew no better, he would have. Kerry turned the light on and studied Eadie's nails. Bitten to the quick.

Kerry turned the body over slightly—the bed-clothes stuck. The bullets would be discovered in the innerspring mattress if not the floorboards, because all three wounds had exits. Definitely 9 mm.

'Shit, Eadie, you sure as hell scared somebody.'

Without touching anything else, and trying to recall what it was he had touched on Tuesday night, Kerry went outside to wait. He sat on Eadie's front steps, reached for a smoke and inhaled deeply. He coughed, then he threw up into her nameless flowers. Nothing could ease the shaking except perhaps a half bottle of bourbon.

After a few minutes, he heard the familiar ring of a Yamaha farm bike coming down the street. 'Oh, Jesus, no. No.'

Lacey, in jeans and denim jacket over a black tee shirt, saw Kerry sitting on Eadie's porch with his head between his knees. 'Kerry? Is something wrong?'

'Go home, honey. Get on your bike and keep riding until you get home.'

She, like any damned woman, took four steps closer. In her hand a plastic bag full of green tomatoes.

'Go. Please, do as I say.'

'What's wrong?' she asked slowly, face paling. 'Is it Eadie? Is she okay?'

'She's dead, Lacey.'

'Eadie? How?'

'Go home, please.'

'You tell me Eadie's dead and then you tell me I should just go home?'

'I do not want you involved in this! Are you fucking deaf?'

'Don't you swear at me!'

Both were stunned into silence for a while.

'I know, you're playing some kind of silly game.' Lacey tried to walk past, Kerry held her back.

All was quiet. Too quiet. Kerry looked up into her face. He'd never seen anyone cry without uttering a sound before. Tears coursed down her face, tears she didn't attempt to wipe away.

'How?' she asked, voice shaking.

'Shot.'

'Who'd do that to Eadie?'

'You tell me.'

'But she talked to me on Tuesday night. She was talking about you. She said how easy it'd be to—'

'To what?'

'Fall in love with you.'

Silence again until Kerry said, 'She hardly knew me, Lacey.'

Lacey put down the plastic bag. 'I brought some, some...'

Kerry stood. 'I know. I have eyes.'

'She fries them. Loves them fried. Ever since we saw that stupid movie about about...'

He held her face tight to his shoulder. He'd seen *Fried Green Tomatoes*, too.

'I was going to come in yesterday but I had the fence to fix and I had to work and—'

'Good thing you never came.' He drew her away. 'She's been dead a couple of days. There's nothing you can do, or could have done. Trust me, Lacey. Go home.'

Lacey pulled away. 'When do you think it happened?'

'Tuesday night or Wednesday morning maybe.'

'Who would have done this?'

'I don't know.'

'Why?'

'I don't know that either.' But he had the feeling it was because of his presence in the town. His presence and a leaking deadly secret. About a murdered girl's body in the swamp.

'She never hurt anybody.'

'Lacey, I need to ask you something.'

She wiped her face on her sleeve and tried to look at his face. He seemed cold, indifferent now. As if a curtain had fallen somewhere behind his eyes. 'How many people here knew what I used to do?'

'Oh, everyone,' she finally offered.

'I think Eadie knew who murdered Elspeth and she's been silenced. Someone in this town is scared, scared enough to kill to keep the truth buried. And I'm the last person he or she needs living here.'

'How are you going to prove it? No one will help you.'

He said nothing.

'Kerry, you should never have come here.'

Fear, the same fear that lit Eadie's eyes was alive in Lacey's. Eadie had said those same words to him on Tuesday evening. You should never have come here, man like you...

'You okay to get yourself home in one piece?' he asked.

'I don't know. I think so.'

'Go now, please. I'll come by later. Go. I don't want you here when the police come. Trust me on this.'

Lacey walked to her bike and kicked it over. She looked back at Kerry before she rode away. He was sitting on the porch again. And at the corner she saw the patrol car with Gilmeister driving. Gilmeister had been born and raised in Mallen. And Gilmeister was one of the many who had used both Elspeth and Eadie at some stage. Used and abused. Now both of them were dead. Lacey didn't like the feelings which swelled and for a while she was tempted to go back to Eadie's, but she respected Kerry's wishes and went home instead.

Kerry believed that the first question would be, 'What time did you make the discovery?' Instead, the well-rounded bush sergeant took one look and barked, 'You keep the fuck out of this, you hear me?'

Wonderful, Kerry thought. 'I'm free to go, then?'

'Where'll you be?'

'At work.'

Two hours passed back at the bakery and with each successive customer, the word had spread. Enlarged. Did he know that Eadie Ross had been shot? Strangled? Stabbed and raped? Wasn't it awful? No one was safe anywhere any more... People would start locking their doors now. What was the world coming to?

What Kerry knew would happen did. At five to four, two suited strangers walked into the shop and said the magic words to Kerry, words he himself had said five hundred times to some poor, confused individual.

'Kerry Staines? We believe you could help us with our enquiries. Would you accompany us, please.'

'At least let me lock up.'

One of the two took a Coke from the drinks fridge. Popped it. Kerry saw the *I Gotta Charge Someone* look in the face and the expression was aimed solely at him.

As he was pushed into the back seat of the unmarked car, he knew that sixty pairs of eyes were watching. But his only thought was *would someone remember to feed my cat?* He didn't know how long he'd be away.

Kerry was silent for most of the journey to Wilton. He didn't need to risk an innocent word or phrase appearing later, twisted, in a Record of Interview.

He never thought this would happen to him. What was it? Karma?

'I hear you topped your class at the academy.'

Kerry studied the view and remained silent.

'That you were the youngest D.S. on the force.'

He was handcuffed to the door. Why? he wanted to ask. He hadn't resisted. He was not being charged, he was assisting.

Bullshit he was assisting.

Saltbush flew by and from the blurred vision came something much clearer.

A six by ten grey walled room with one small window and from the window he could see a bare, barren, desert landscape. And in the distance, he could clearly see a farmhouse. It was in a direct line from his cell. He was on the inside looking out. Unless he did something, quickly, as a last resort.

Lacey tried to call but no one answered at Kerry's house or at the shop. She should have taken notice of her feelings and not gone home. She should have been there whether he wanted her present or not.

When she appeared at workplace, Emile told her that Kerry was in Wilton, being questioned about Eadie Ross's murder. Lenny Gilmeister had intimated that charges would soon be laid. It was only a matter of time before he broke.

Broke? Broke? What the hell were they doing to him?

'Charges? What charges?'

'Murder. And rape, too, I think.'

'Kerry?'

'Lacey, you do not know this one. He was too quiet, too secretive, too.'

'*Was?* You're talking as if he's dead, too! Jesus, Emile! You of all people? Bugger this, I'm going to Wilton.'

'No, no, it is cabaret tonight.'

'I *have* to go!'

'If you do leave me now there will be no returning, cherie.'

'Really?' she asked.

One word coupled with a forceful, icy stare was all Emile received. He relented, quickly. 'Non, non, you cannot leave me.'

But she did and she did not look back.

Kerry had been in Wilton three hours, with great cause to wonder what Leon Prior, the young constable, was typing on the Record of Interview because he hadn't said a word yet apart from his name and address.

'I want this on video and audio tape.'

'Shut the fuck up.'

Sean Merrin had a wonderful vocabulary.

'I also want access to a telephone and legal representation if charges are going to be laid.'

'Lenny! Get your boys out to Mallen and search this fucker's house!'

'You get a fucking warrant first!' Kerry spat.

'Don't need one,' Gilmeister said. 'We're looking for *drugs*.'

'Oh, for Christ's sake, what is happening here?'

The backhander came so quickly Kerry wasn't sure of its origins. A hint of surprise lit Prior's eyes, so it hadn't been his doing. Kerry's hands fisted, he was ready for whatever fireworks they might be planning. And whatever they did, he would have to sit there and not retaliate. Maybe they knew that, too, but hoped he would.

'Let the record show that the time is 1825 hours, Friday, 4 December 1992.'

Kerry's application for bail was filed verbally. Most of the initial questions were affirmatives. No next of kin.

Contact?

'Lacey Kilder, Starks Road, Mallen.'

What relationship is this person to you?

'She's a friend.' He didn't say she was the only one he had. Whether after this fiasco she still would be remained anyone's guess. Least of all his.

No wife?

'Deceased.'

Mind if I ask how?

'Grafton bus crash. My son and daughter died as well.'

I see. How long have you lived in Mallen?

'Four weeks.'
And what was your relationship with Edith Ann Ross?
'Acquaintance.'
She was how old?
'I don't know. I never asked.'
When did you first meet Edith Ann Ross?
'The day I moved here.'
From where?
'Windsor, Brisbane.'
What was your previous employment?
'Police Service.'
Give me a brief history of your service, Mr Staines?
'Find my service record.'
Why are you unwilling to cooperate?
'Because I had nothing whatsoever to do with Eadie's death and you damn well know it.'

At this point of time, Mr Staines, you are assisting with our enquiries; is this clear?
'Yes.'
So you first met Miss Ross the day you relocated.
'Yes.'
How was she towards you?
'Friendly. Helpful. Curious. Where's this leading?'
One could say she took a shine to you?
'You'd have to ask her. I never knew what she was thinking.'
A detective senior sergeant of many years' active service and you never knew what she was thinking?
Did you have an intimate relationship with Edith Ross?
'No, I'm not an opportunist.'
After six years working undercover in the drug squad, and three in vice, Mr Staines, you expect me to believe you when you say you're not an opportunist?

Kerry sighed and stretched. This was going to take forever. 'Yes.'
And what caused your discharge from the police service?
'I was deemed medically unfit for active duty.'
So you liked Edith Ann Ross as a person, is this correct?
'I felt sorry for her.'
Why?
'I just did. She'd go to great lengths to get my attention.'
Such as?

'She said my house was haunted. She brought me things, things I felt best be returned. Flowers, incense oils, stuff like that. She was under some kind of delusional fantasy that a friend of hers was murdered. Elspeth Mackenzie. She disappeared in 1985. Each year around this time, Eadie'd show stigmatic-type injuries which she believed coincided with her friend's wounds.'

Sean Merrin said nothing. He'd heard about Mallen's Christmas Spectacular.

'Tuesday, I returned an oil burner she left in my house. I saw the phenomena occurring. I was not under the influence of alcohol or mind-altering drugs at the time either. To me it looked like she was being pack-raped. I walked in on it. I didn't understand what was happening so I called Dr Martinelli. He'd seen it too, seventeen times. He was not concerned in the least. I am telling you what I saw, what I know. She had injuries which she said coincided with her friend's—the girl she believed was murdered. But no body was ever found. She was being assaulted but there was no one there.'

You were there.

'Oh, for Christ's sake'

What were the injuries you 'saw'?

'Bruises, abrasions. Lacerations on her arms, shoulders, breasts, stomach, legs. Dr Martinelli will verify what I've told you. Anyone in town will. I put her to bed. Stayed with her a couple of hours and when she woke, she was fine. I got home around nine or so, called a mate at Headquarters, asked if he'd find a Missing Person's report for me. I wanted to know if one had been filed.'

You had an alcohol problem for a number of years, is this correct?

Kerry felt sick again. What was left now, diminished responsibility? 'I was not drunk when I saw what was happening to Eadie Ross. Now, am I being charged or not?'

You're assisting with our enquiries.

'How much longer is this going to take?'

That's up to you.

'I cannot tell you what you want to hear.'

What might that be?

There was silence for a while. No way would Kerry admit a thing. A phrase, a sentence misconstrued could have him on the inside looking out, mandatory life.

You called Sergeant Gilmeister at approximately 10.30 this morning, is this correct?

'Yes.'

Tell us what occurred this morning.

'Lacey Kilder called me around 7.30, worried. She hadn't heard from Eadie since Tuesday night. I told her I'd call in when I got a chance. I tried phoning, no answer...' He went on with what had occurred, but God knew what Leon was typing. Kerry wouldn't know till he was asked to sign the Record of Interview.

Tell me about Tuesday night.

Kerry obliged and, in the course of the interview, obliged seven times in all.

Do you have in your possession any unlicensed firearms?

'No, I don't think so.' It wasn't quite a lie, the Beretta was missing anyway. The Beretta 92. The 9 mm.

Nausea rose again but there was nothing left in his stomach to expel. Kerry knew, as he sat in the office at Wilton, that as he spoke, there were a handful of uniforms systematically wrecking his house in Mallen. If the Beretta was there, they'd find it.

You don't think so?

Best declare it, Kerry thought. 'I was given a Beretta 92 by a visiting LA officer back in 1986. A present of sorts. I think it's registered with the others, I'm not sure. You'll have to check.'

You're not sure if you do have in your possession an unlicensed firearm?

'I mislaid it in the relocation.'

You mislaid a Beretta?

'I never kept it with the others. It has its own special case. I remember telling Lacey I couldn't find it. Wednesday afternoon. She wanted my help. She was having trouble with feral pigs on her property. I went out there, she—'

Someone tapped on the door, it was answered, quiet whispers passed from one plain-clothed to the other.

They found the Beretta, Kerry thought. Jesus. Next will be a ballistics test.

The detective, Sean Merrin, paused the interview and left Kerry alone with the observer, Leon, who asked if he wanted a coffee. Kerry said yes, but he never received one.

Sean Merrin entered the other room and sat down. The big-breasted blonde asked, 'Where's Kerry Staines?'

'Being questioned.'

'About what? He didn't do anything. He did not kill Eadie. I know him.'

'You're Lacey Kilder?'

'Yes.'

'How well do you know him?'

'Are you charging him or not?'

'That depends what we find in the search of his house.'

The man swung in his chair and never took his eyes from her face. Nor she his.

'And have you seen Kerry today, Miss Kilder?'

'Yes, I saw him. I also talked to him on the phone, why?'

'Tell me about it.'

'I called this morning because I was worried about Eadie. I hadn't heard from her. It was odd.'

'Why.'

'Because I'm writing a book about her experiences and we speak...we *spoke* almost every day.'

'You write books?'

'Metaphysical. Psychic research. I've had three published in the past two years.'

'Really?'

'Kerry said he'd try to call in on Eadie if I was that worried. I didn't hear from him so I thought all was fine. I got to Eadie's about 11.00 a.m. and he was sitting on the steps. He was upset, quiet. He told me she was dead. She'd been shot. I didn't believe him, I thought he was pulling my leg.'

'You said he was quiet. Upset.'

'He didn't want me there. Didn't want me involved. He tried to chase me away.'

'Do you see him a lot?'

'Would it matter if I did? He came out and taught me to shoot on Wednesday afternoon'

'Why would he teach you to shoot?'

'He didn't want to till I showed him the hoof print of the boar that nearly attacked me last week. Bloody pigs are wrecking my market garden.'

'And did he?'

'Did he what?'

'Teach you to shoot.'

'He showed me how to use my father's .243 after tea. He'd seen the size of the hoof print, said the .22 wouldn't be much good. He told me he was having some weird things happening in Eric Bateman's old house and he knew what type of work I published, so he asked me some questions. Things were going missing, relocating in his house. He mentioned something about a gun of his going missing, a garbage bag that moved by itself, his raincoat hanging itself up just before it rained...'

'Did he say what type of gun was missing?' She had to think back.

'It started with a B.'

'Browning?'

'No. Beretta? Is that it?'

'Did he say when he noticed it missing?'

'That day. Wednesday. Two days ago.'

'Do you have an intimate relationship with Kerry Staines?'

'No, and who I sleep with is my business.'

'How long have you known him?'

'Long enough to recognize a decent human being when I see one. They're rare out here, aren't they? Now if you want me to make a statement, I will. Either you charge him soon or you let him go. He did not kill Eadie. So why don't you start by asking her old boyfriends? Do something constructive. Find a motive. Don't arrest the person who found her body, because it could very well have been me. Investigate. That's what we pay you to do. I am the public. You are the servant. So get off your fat lazy arse and find who murdered Eadie Ross or I damned well will.'

With that she walked to the door and then turned back.

'Did you get all that on tape? I hope so. Tell Kerry I'll be waiting to take him home and I'll wait all night if I have to. If he asks for legal representation tell him my ex-husband is a barrister who has taken on the Justice Commission four or five times. And he won. Good night.'

She slammed the door, too. 'That'd be fucking right,' Sean Merrin mumbled.

Lacey was waiting when Kerry finally walked out of the interview room at five to midnight. He was the color of the walls, exhaustion was almost complete. Then he saw her waiting. 'What are you doing here? Shit, Lacey, your job—'

'What job?' she asked.

Kerry rubbed his face and reached for her hand. It wasn't enough. He held her tight, took a deep breath. The perfume of her hair sustained him, lifted him. For a while there, he thought he'd never see her again.

'What happened to your face?' she asked.

'I fell over.'

'You want me to believe that?'

He tried to smile at her and holding her hand, they walked out.

He found his car parked outside the police station. 'Didn't think you'd mind. My bike wouldn't have made it with both of us.'

'I don't mind.'

'Want me to drive?'

Kerry nodded and was terribly quiet as he sat in the passenger seat. He had never been a passenger in his own car before, that he remembered, at least. 'Why you?' she asked.

'The people next door saw me going in on Tuesday afternoon. Saw me leave a couple of hours later. No one else came or went that anyone saw. If I'd been Merrin I wouldn't have let me walk.'

'Don't say that. They have no proof.'

'There's enough circumstantial to hold me. At least a DNA test should clear me of rape.'

'Kerry, you didn't do it.'

'I know, you know. But if they find that Beretta, I'm cactus, honey. I'm on the inside looking out. Probably at your farmhouse.'

'I told Sean Merrin what you'd told me last Wednesday. About the gun being missing.'

He looked at her as she drove and he reached out, touched her hair, her face. 'Why are you doing this?' he asked. 'It's my problem, not yours. Don't get involved.'

'I'm already involved. Voluntarily.' Lacey squeezed his hand and for a moment, no further words were needed.

'He asked if I was sleeping with you.'

I should be so lucky, Kerry thought. 'If I was him I would have, too.' Kerry stared out at the darkness. It was safer than looking at her.

'I don't lie that well so I had to say no.'

For a long time there was complete silence.

'I have to be at work in three hours.'

'Let it go for a day.'

'It doesn't work that way and you know it.'

'Kerry, you need to sleep.'

He closed his eyes to oblivion and was woken by a shake. He came up fighting, realized where he was. Lacey had parked in the driveway of his house.

'Come on. You're home.' She followed him up the stairs.

The front door was wide open. The entire house had been ransacked. The sight was sickening. But Kerry had been expecting it. He stepped over the shambles. Every room, every thing. He leant against the lounge room wall and covered his face. Lacey touched his arm, an attempt at reassurance but all he wanted to do was punch someone.

'No, no. Leave me alone, please,' he begged her.

'Come home with me. I can help you clean this up tomorrow. Don't stay here tonight.'

'But the shop—'

'Mallen will survive one or two days without you. Just till this blows over, please, stay with me. Please.'

Kerry lit a smoke with shaking hands. 'You see that?' he said and pointed to the floor where all his books lay in an untidy heap. 'I kept the Beretta there. In the bookcase. In a copy of Moby Dick. And if it's found, if it is the weapon that killed Eadie, I'll be on the inside looking out.'

'You didn't do it!'

'Jesus, girl, innocence or guilt doesn't count. What does is enough circumstantial for a quick clean-up. If a case like this isn't solved in forty-eight hours chances are it never will be.'

'Craig is a QC.'

'Craig?'

'My ex-husband.'

'An army of QC's is not going to help me, girl. I'm being set up again. I don't believe it, but it's happening. All over again.'

'You're coming with me and you're not arguing.'

By the time she'd turned off Starks Road, Kerry was dozing again. It didn't seem possible that this was happening. But it was. And the intensity of the effect on him was hard to adjust to. She didn't know what was circling in his mind. But she had an idea what it would be like if he was charged and convicted. Right now he needed a friend. Someone to be there, to share his thoughts with. If ever he would.

Kerry stroked the old dog on the way past, the cocky asked for a smoke and Kerry felt welcome. Very welcome.

'If you shower, you'll sleep better.'

Kerry headed straight for her purple bathroom, stripped and ran the shower. Lacey found one of her large tee shirts for him to wear and she pulled back the covers of her bed in readiness for the body to drop and lapse into unconsciousness. She prepared the couch for herself and was putting the pillow down when Kerry appeared. The shirt which reached her knees barely covered his thighs. She couldn't look at him very long. Lacey pointed to her bedroom and he walked in, and came out immediately.

'Jesus, I hate pink,' was all he said.

He walked to her and held her tight. She didn't try to get away. Kerry lifted her face. 'Thanks.' He kissed her, her mouth opened to the touch. Then he pulled away, quickly. 'I can't. I'm sorry. I just can't.'

Lacey turned off the light and he followed her into her room. Each climbed into her wide bed, and each stared at the ceiling for a long time. Then he snaked his arm under her head and she rolled into his side. He didn't say a word. His hand was stroking her back absently.

'I've been on my own five years now.'

Still he said nothing.

'Till I saw you that night in the hotel, I thought my body was dead.'

'Not now, Lacey. I can't.'

'I know, I know. I'm not asking for anything. I just wanted you to hear that.'

His heart was very loud in her ear. Thundering. Again, she wondered what was going through his mind, why he wasn't talking.

'Jesus, I can't take any more of this.'

She looked up. His voice was shaking, his heartbeat quickening.

'Try and be positive.'

'It won't help.'

She held him all night long whilst he slept in fits and starts, talked in his sleep. She kept repeating softly that everything would be all right and he clung in his sleep like a little lost child.

The cops came at six in the morning. And Kerry, as he had foreseen, was charged with the murder of Edith Ann Ross.

He couldn't even go home for a clean set of clothes.

CHAPTER 5

Kerry hoped the sight would last for ever—Lacey, standing in her nightdress, fingers in mouth, tears in her eyes, and the dog sitting by her feet. It was all obliterated by a dust cloud. At least he'd have something good to remember, even if he never experienced it again. Sometimes a photographic memory was an asset.

Kerry stayed quiet while the plainclothes talked about her—no better, no worse than pub regulars at any given time. But, as they were only after a reaction, any better than none at all, Kerry said and did nothing. He knew from experience that no reaction was very aggravating.

He watched the saltbush blur once more, the clear blue sky above, the flat, unending landscape further than the beyond, and he tried not to listen, not to think. Thinking was always his downfall. He felt like a doctor who'd just suffered a heart attack and didn't like the hospital he'd been taken to. The doctor though had a chance of recovery.

Kerry was looking at life. He was printed, formally charged and dragged from the tiny watch-house cell at 10.00 a.m. for round two with Sean Merrin. Not a solicitor in sight. Wilton's legal eagle who specialized in conveyancing and the occasional family law case was overseas for three weeks. Kerry was on his own and too aware of it. Too much information was withheld and what was not said aided in Kerry's silent compilation of the police-prosecution scenario.

Before long, Merrin's patience was wearing thin. 'You returned to Ross's house between 9.00 p.m. Tuesday night and 2.00 a.m. Wednesday morning.'

So they have a time of death, Kerry thought. Give or take three hours either side of midnight.

'At 9.05 I called Headquarters, spoke to Belinda Barlow and Demetri Aspromorgous. As I've said previously, I wanted some information on the Mackenzie disappearance. Soon after I called Johnny Logan and told him I'd changed my mind, I'd join his rock band. After that, I slept. I was woken by the storm at 1.15 a.m. Wednesday morning. The roof was leaking. So I moved the bed and decided to hell with it. I went to work earlier than usual.'

'Did anyone see you?'

'I don't know. It was pissing down rain. A hell of a storm.'

'And you walked two blocks to the bakery in this storm?'

'My car was bogged in the driveway. As for anyone seeing me at the time, talk to Ella Fitzpatrick. She was closing windows in the post office quarters. Maybe she saw me go by. It's worth a shot.' If nothing else, he thought.

He was surprised when Merrin noted it. A small, feeble light began to shine momentarily, until Merrin said, 'You had plenty of time to return to Ross's house. You found the back door unlocked, you walked in'

'No. I found the back door unlocked on Friday morning. Plus she slipped four deadlocks into place when I left Tuesday night. By the front door.'

'What time was that.'

'Quarter to nine.'

'Why would she have four deadlocks when no one's locked their house for twenty years?'

'I asked myself that. Maybe if she'd known me better, trusted me a little more—'

'Lost your touch with the ladies, Staines?'

'No.' And he meant it, too. What's this little shit heard about me now? Kerry wondered half-heartedly. 'A couple more days she'd have told me the whole story. Someone made sure I didn't get that time. Can I please have a cigarette?'

Silence.

His request was ignored. Nor did Merrin follow on the 'whole story'. How thick is this bastard? Kerry asked himself.

'What occurred when you returned to Ross's house on Friday morning?'

Kerry told him. Again.

'I say you returned between 9.00 p.m. Tuesday night and 2.00 a.m. Wednesday morning. She let you in the back door, you followed her to the bedroom, pushed her on to the bed.'

'No, I did not.'

'Your fingerprints are all over the house.'

'If my prints are anywhere, they'll be on a cup in the kitchen. On a teaspoon. On the cold water tap. On the kettle. On the teapot and sugar bowl. On her photo album, maybe the shower recess and possibly her papasan chair. But that is all.'

'Your prints are on the Beretta, too,' Merrin said, watching for a reaction.

'Well, fancy that. My prints are on my gun. I haven't touched it for a year. And it was pretty damned humid in the city when I left.' Merrin wouldn't meet Kerry's gaze. 'Exactly where was it located 'cos I'm damned if I could find it.'

'You tell me what the hell happened on Tuesday night.'

'I have no idea. I did not kill Eadie Ross.' Kerry was willing to sit there until the year 2000 and Sean Merrin knew it. If they wanted to take it to committal on an unsigned confession and hope the plea was guilty then it wasn't their day. Maybe Merrin knew that, too.

'I tell you what, Sean, knock off the typing, Leon. How long you been in this job?'

'Three years.'

'There was no sign of forced entry or struggle therefore Eadie knew her killer. More than a possibility.'

'She knew you.'

'Not enough. My guess is the perpetrator obviously does not want the truth about Elspeth Mackenzie to come to light.'

'How do you know that?'

'My gut tells me. Yours telling you anything?'

Merrin remained quiet.

Strike one, Kerry thought. 'Eadie Ross wanted to tell me who killed her friend Mackenzie but she never did. Whoever shot her figured it wasn't worth the risk. If you're after a motive you won't find one with me. I suggest you reopen the Mackenzie case and find the reason why there was never a full investigation of that girl's disappearance. That's what I'd do first if I were you.'

'You're not me, Staines. And what we have on you is enough.'

'What you have on me is circumstantial. When the Beretta went missing I had tradesmen in my house. One of them helped himself to my electric guitar, to the booze in the fridge, and Christ only knows what else.'

'His name?'

'Johnny Logan did the painting, Frank Purvis was the plumber. They had the place to themselves while I was at work.'

'Why the hell didn't you mention this before?'

'I don't make a habit of accusing tradesmen of theft. Do you?'

'What hours do you work?'

'2.30 a.m. to 5.00 p.m., depending on how busy it is.'

Merrin looked through his notes. 'You started at 2.00 a.m. on

Wednesday morning, and you closed an hour early.'

'So? I was going out to see Lacey Kilder. I wanted to get to know her better and I finally had an excuse. I taught her to shoot a bolt action .22 and then the .243. She was having trouble with feral pigs. I discovered the Beretta gone because I'd toyed with the idea of taking it out there. Something else. Eadie was in my house that Tuesday as well. She left flowers, an electric oil burner. So three people I know of had access to my house while I was absent. You know and I know that I should not be sitting here.'

'Why would Eadie Ross want to steal a Beretta?'

'Why did she have four deadlocks? You tell me, we'll both know.'

Sean Merrin studied Kerry for a long time. Kerry took no notice of the open thoughtful stare, he was accustomed to such things. He used to do exactly the same thing himself.

'Is there anything else you wish to add?'

'I did not kill Eadie Ross.'

For a while, Kerry thought an apology was nigh. That Merrin realized it wasn't as clear cut as he'd first hoped. That there was still more investigation to do.

'You'll be held in Wilton watch-house pending committal in the circuit court on 22 December.'

'That's three weeks.'

'It'll give you time to think about what you've said. Leon, get us a coffee and take your time.'

After Leon departed, Sean Merrin took a packet of cigarettes from his pocket and handed them to Kerry. The gesture took him by surprise. Kerry lit one immediately, offered the packet back. Merrin shook his head.

'Ella Fitzpatrick's already made a statement that she saw you arrive for work at the bakery around 1.45 a.m. I've also spoken to your friend at Headquarters. As for the Mackenzie girl—' Sean Merrin stuffed a photocopied wad of paper into Kerry's breast pocket. 'Bear with me another twelve hours,' was all he said.

A little while later, Leon Prior returned with two coffees and Kerry was taken back to the holding cell. A plate of sandwiches and a plastic bottle of orange juice awaited him. Finally on his own, Kerry took out the papers Merrin had slipped him. It was one of the shortest reports on a missing person he'd ever seen. The report was made by Edith Ann Ross in December 1985. There was an attached handwritten statement signed by Frank Purvis which said he had passed Elspeth as she hitchhiked towards

Wilton. The case was closed and no further action was taken.

The report was filed by Lenny Gilmeister who was then a senior constable. Apparently Mallen once had a policeman stationed there.

Kerry read it through again and he reached for a sandwich and lay back on the mattress. The concrete floor was cold. Three weeks of this would do his hip no favors. All he could do was hope for two miracles—that he'd soon be released, and that Lacey would bring him a toothbrush and change of clothes. He needed to see her face, badly.

He had spent time in the cells before, always knowing he'd walk—drug busts where the under-cover was arrested as well and usually wired. After a few hours, maybe a day, two at the most, he'd be home or back on the street. Unfortunately he was beginning to think he'd never see home again, leaking roof included. He wanted to know why. He wondered what Demetri had said to Merrin.

Kerry slept for a while. He had no idea of the time when the watch-house was finally unlocked and he heard two sets of footsteps. The outer door opened and a young lad in blue unlocked the cell.

'Visitor,' he said. 'You've got five minutes. No touching.'

Kerry forced himself to his feet. He wore yesterday's clothes—jeans, shirt, denim jacket. No belt, no socks. No shoes. He should have been pleased to see Lacey but she was as out of place in the watch-house as a camel on the Sydney Harbour Bridge. The lad in blue took the overnight bag from her hand and searched through it vaguely, handed it back.

'If the sarge hears about this, I'm dead. Five minutes.'

'Thanks, Pete. You're sweet.' Lacey gave him that 'I got what I wanted' smile and the young cop walked away, left them almost alone. Lacey put the overnight bag on the floor of the cell. 'Toothbrush, toothpaste, soap, deodorant, clothes. I rummaged through the dropsite for an hour to find all this,'

What is she, he wondered. The answer to a prayer?

'Kerry, have you seen a solicitor yet?'

'No. There's none available.'

'I called Craig but he's not free till January. Plus he'd want $300 an hour and that's a cut rate, as far as his favors will stretch. What else are bastards for? I suppose. So I managed to find someone. He's defended one murder so far. Unsuccessfully. But he's better than nothing, unless you think you can handle your own defense. He'll be here on Monday afternoon to talk to you, go over the Record of Interview.'

'I may be out by then. You said to be positive.'

'You weren't in a holding cell then, Kerry.' Tears welled whenever she looked at him.

'Don't cry. Jesus, I'm only tough till a lady cries, you know.'

He wanted to touch but the young constable was in line of sight, definitely in the line of hearing.

Tears filled her eyes again and Pete pretended he was blind for half a minute. Kerry wondered if smells had memories of their own as he held her tight. Then Pete Jameson appeared, agitated.

'The sarge is coming,' he warned them.

Lacey looked up into Kerry's eyes. He nodded, then she was gone. And half a heartbeat after Pete Jameson thrust her out the back door, Lenny Gilmeister walked in. He leant against the cell bars, casually. A stark, almost amused grey gaze held Kerry's but Gilmeister was the first to look away.

'Your first mistake was buying that bakery.'

Half a smile crossed Kerry's eyes. He waited for more, but there was no more. The young constable reappeared.

'You're wanted in the office, sarge.'

When the outer door clanged shut, Kerry said, 'Thanks for letting her in.'

'I wasn't doing it for you. This way to the shower.'

In his overnight bag, Kerry found the walkman he thought he'd lost two years ago. A wad of writing paper and a pen that actually worked. And an envelope. Sealed. Kerry slipped it into his pillowcase, gave the bag to Pete and was led away for a shower.

Half an hour later, clean, almost new, he settled on the mattress, took the envelope from the pillow case, faced the wall and read.

Kerry,

A note in case we can't talk. After they took you away I went to your house, found what I could.

I'm writing this at your place. Not that it matters.

If there's anything I've forgotten to pack, call me.

I should have told you this morning or last night. Why do important things always slip past?

Lenny Gilmeister lived in Mallen until the station was closed in 1981. According to Eadie, he and Elspeth had been good 'friends' since 1973. I have so much information in my notes, and on tape. Did I tell you I was writing a book about Elspeth? Anyway, in Eadie's words she knocked about with Lenny G. and Frankie Purvis long after Frankie married. The night Elspeth disappeared she'd been drinking with them both at the Arms, although proving it is another matter. No one says boo and the ranks are still closed tight. Will this help at all?

Lacey

No, not really, Kerry thought.

There was a post script on the other page. The writing was hurried, scrawled. The paper holed. She'd probably written it against the bike seat and in a hell of a hurry—it was almost illegible.

Dora's just asked me why the police had taken you away because she saw Frank Purvis going into Eadie's house just after the storm began. Kerry, she lives opposite Eadie Ross's and no one has questioned her yet!

I'm going to correlate all my notes into a semblance of order and confront Sean Merrin with it. God help him if he gives me that hysterical female look again or I may be sharing the cell next to you.

Yep, Kerry thought. There is a God after all. 'Pete?'

'Hey?'

'Where's Merrin?'

'On his way to Mallen. Why?'

'I want to talk to him. It's important.'

Pete appeared and leant against the cell bars. 'How important?' he asked.

'Call him. Tell him he missed a witness. Dora Mallaby. Lives opposite the Ross house. It wasn't me going into Eadie's house at 1.30 in the morning. It was Frank Purvis.'

Frank Purvis was fitting poly downpipe at the back of the Metro when the blue Ford pulled up. Merrin said to Leon, indicating the squawking two-way, 'Get that bloody thing, I'm not here,' as he alighted.

Frank didn't blink as he screwed in the length of pipe. 'Gidday,' he said. 'Rain's gone.'

'Frank Purvis?'

'That's me. The one and holy.'

'Sean Merrin, Detective Sergeant.'

'Yeah, I know. What can I do you for?'

'I'm hoping you can assist with a few enquiries.'

'Yeah? Hope all you like, mate. I know squat.'

'Would you mind coming down? Now?'

'Keep your shirt on.'

Merrin watched the plumber climb down. A man about forty-five, balding. A faded, raggy T-shirt hanging out of King Gee shorts that did not disguise a hairy arse, football socks and work boots.

'I've already told Lenny what I know about the bread man,' he said.

'Yes, I'm aware of that. You worked for Staines, is this right?'

'Did a couple of days. New crapper, put a basin in the bathroom. Shouldn't bitch too loud, at least the poor bastard paid me.'

Any drier, he'd crumble, Merrin thought. 'Do you remember a girl called Elspeth Mackenzie?'

'Who?'

'Elspeth Mackenzie.' Sean showed the photograph taken from the old missing persons file. 'She went missing some years ago.'

'Jesus, that's Ells all right. Forgotten all about her. Didn't she marry some AJ?'

'AJ?'

'Yeah. She did a bunk with half a platoon of grunts playing war games a few years back.'

'How well did you know this young woman?'

'Ells? About as much as any other bloke in town. Everyone else said no, she said yes. Get the drift?'

'Did she charge for her services?'

'If she did I never fucking paid. Why?'

'How well did you know Edith Ross?'

'Eadie? Fruitcake that one. What's to say? She was born here, she died here, what else is there? She was nuts. Gave good head but ... you know.'

'You visited her regularly at her home?'

'Now and then. Whenever I got the urge. No more than anyone else.'

'I understand you're a vet, is this correct?'

'So what if I am?'

'Special Air Service?'

'So?'

'Not many make selection, I'm told.'

'What the fuck do you want?'

There was a loud whistle and Merrin turned back to the car. Leon was beckoning. 'Thanks for your time, Mr Purvis.'

Frank watched the Ford drive away. He climbed his ladder again and from the hotel rooftop, saw the car disappear into George Street and stop outside Mallaby's.

He'd seen the old bitch talking to Lacey Kilder that morning at Staines's place when he'd driven by.

Silly little girl, he thought. Always meddling.

Asking about Elspeth was bad enough. As if she didn't know. So what if she thought she talked to a spook and wrote books no one could read— she could prove nothing. And hell, he could have fixed her pig problem in one hit but no, no, she, like every other female in town, had their sights set on the new baker. The ex-cop. Cursing to himself, Frank threw his gear into the back of his Toyota and he drove off in the direction of Starks Road.

'Give her fucking meddle,' he mumbled.

'Are you sure?' Sean asked. 'It was storming.'

'Yes. That's why I saw him. The storm had just begun, you see, and I was up to close all my windows. I was here,' Dora said, and relived the moment to the police as she stood in her living room. From the window she had a direct line to Eadie's front yard. 'Closing my window. There was a lightning strike and for a second it seemed as bright as day. Frankie's truck was on my footpath and I saw him jump Eadie's fence.'

'How do you know it was Frank Purvis?'

'Young man, I taught him from grade one to grade seven and he still cannot keep his pants up.' Leon Prior studied the ceiling, bit-back his mirth.

'Mrs Mallaby, you should have come forward with this information.'

'I thought you would come to me and when you did not, I took it upon myself to phone Lenny Gilmeister. I also taught him and he told me to forget about it. It was not important, they had found the person responsible. But it wasn't until I spoke with Lacey this morning that I knew who had been arrested. And I was outraged.'

'You know Sergeant Gilmeister well?'

'Oh, yes. They were all friends. My son Jackie, Lenny, Frank, Emile Rollet, Eric Bateman, Johnny Mitchell and James Brady. Only Lenny, Frank and Emile are left though. All the others have died. Or are missing.'

'May I ask what happened to your son?'

'He disappeared.'

'When was this?'

'10 March, 1986.'

The two men exchanged glances as Dora reached for a framed photograph of her missing son.

'Did your son know Elspeth Mackenzie?'

She was thoughtfully quiet for a little while. 'They tried to tell me that Jackie had run off to be with Elspeth. He was a good boy. He knew how I worried. He was in with the wrong crowd, realized his mistake... but I don't wish to talk about her and my son. The town's a far better place with the likes of her gone.'

So much pain in the old lady's eyes.

'You said, they tried to tell you your son had run off somewhere. Can I ask who you mean by they?'

'Lenny, Frank, Emile. The other boys before they died. Johnny Mitchell and James Brady died in a one-vehicle car accident on Starks Road. I don't remember when, though.'

'Mrs Mallaby, you'll be required to make a statement and possibly give evidence in court about what you saw.'

'If you promise me, young man, that this foolishness will soon be over and Mallen can return to normal.'

With a prison going up four miles from town, I doubt that, honey, Sean thought. 'I think I could manage that, Mrs Mallaby.' He turned to Leon and said, 'Stay with her till I locate Purvis.'

Lacey sat at her kitchen table and questioned the logic of it. Three years of asking endless questions, of note taking, and nine C90 tapes in a small box was all she had. Elspeth's story. The one with four false starts over the past year. She wrote longhand first, more of a habit. She'd settle to begin and her pencils would disappear. She'd attempt an introduction and the phone would ring. But no one would be on the other end of the line. A few books would fly from the bookcase, diverting her attention momentarily to the other room. She'd return. Whatever she had written was in the kitchen sink. Wet. Once she'd written three paragraphs, then the fluorescent light exploded overhead.

So she decided she'd write straight on to the Xerox computer. The A drive scrambled. The C drive disappeared, could not be found.

Thirty-five retries later, she rebooted but all she had now was the blue screen of death.

She dissolved into tears, only to feel that familiar and warm, small hand on her head, her shoulder. Elspeth's reassurance. She obviously did not want her story told.

Next day Lacey took the computer to the local tech genius. It booted for Benny Gray. He smiled at her, the same smile Sean Merrin had given her—you poor delusional creature. Benny could find nothing wrong. It was futile defending herself.

She arrived home, reorganised her notes, this time knowing exactly where to begin. It didn't boot.

Error reading drive C.

And Elspeth was laughing. She always had a lousy sense of humor.

Three years of questions, of hypothetical problems and solutions, of reference quotes to similar hauntings, similar cases. Nine C90 tapes for a book which would never be because a ghost did not want it to be.

There was an envelope containing photographs of Eadie Ross. Three days of each December for the past two years. This year she'd let it ride. Lacey could not take the photos out. Not yet. It was too soon. Sean Merrin would not believe this proof of Eadie's empathic reaction anyway. Unexplained phenomena rarely had a niche in a world of comfortable logic.

She had interviewed several people about their knowledge of Elspeth, their sightings of her. The only people who cared to remember were those who remembered Ells as a willing body recalled with ankles tickling ears in the backseat of someone's car. No one could remember the night she went missing. It was the only time the army had used Mallen for war games. The town was full of soldiers, but no one remembered what they were doing that night.

Paddy Martin remembered the snow in August 1943 and he declared he'd never go into a church again if that's what happened. But even old Paddy knew what had become of Miss Mackenzie. Basically, no one cared, and nearly everyone she spoke to had lied. Had told her to leave it be, how no good could come of digging up the past. Just let it go.

She had nothing here to offer Sean Merrin, except photographs of a woman considered the town fruitcake.

She'd promised Kerry she'd correlate her notes and confront Merrin with it all. She wondered why. She questioned the logic of it.

'Some help I've been,' she thought aloud. Kerry's cat looked at her then returned to his doze. He'd taken a fancy to the end of her pine table. He wasn't silly for there he caught a breeze from the window. And many face rubs, too. She reached out and touched. He opened his eyes, stretched out and purred. So she stroked him from head to tail and said, 'He'll be home soon. I *hope* he'll be home soon.' How she wished she were a pampered pet—fed when hungry, living the moment. No past, no future, just the present. Oh, what a life.

Purvis was not at the Metro. Sean drove down the main street, checked the parking area of the Arms. He drove the entire town, could not locate Purvis' Toyota anywhere. He stopped at a council road-maintenance crew of two who were filling in pot holes along Weir Road.

Sean asked if they'd seen Frankie and was told they'd seen him, in one hell of a hurry, low flying across the weir, coming so fast that one of them had to leap aside. He was heading for Starks Road and it was about time they got paid danger money.

Sean got back in his car, pondered the possibility of collecting Leon from Mallaby's and decided time was imperative. He'd bring the plumber in for questioning alone if he ever found him. He couldn't have got too far along Starks Road in fifteen minutes. Leon was useless anyway. Probably having cup cakes and tea with the old school teacher. Just his type.

Lacey put the envelope of photographs aside. The information that she wanted Sean Merrin to hear was on the fourth tape. It was labeled E. Ross, 25 December, 1991. Lacey remembered that Christmas day.

Christmas was always a bad time to be alone. There was no midnight mass within an hour's ride, so she went to the Anglican service instead. As she always did on the rare times she showed her face in a holy place, she stayed a while after, mainly to breathe in the still, the quiet. Eadie was there, too, doing the same thing, she supposed. So she slid in beside her.

'Most people have good things to remember at Christmas, not me,' Eadie said softly, tears stinging her eyes. 'Me dad died ten years ago,' she said. 'Arse over head during Christmas dinner.'

I wish mine had, Lacey thought to herself.

'Jesus, I miss him,' Eadie said, voice shaking.

With a sigh, Lacey put her arm around Eadie. 'Let's have Christmas together. You and me.'

'Jesus,' Eadie had said. 'You and me? Now we'll be gay. You wait.'

Lacey laughed, but Eadie, who'd lived in the town all her life, had been right. Again.

She found the tape, put the photographs and cassette into a larger envelope and was about to uncap her fountain pen when she heard a vehicle approaching. Kerry's cat lifted his head, stared at her and Lacey almost read its mind. The old dog barked a succession of triple warnings which, of course, alarmed the bird and he screamed his usual: Turn it down!

Lacey, followed by the cat, made it to the verandah in time to see Frank Purvis's truck take the second grid way too fast. It was airborne for a while.

Skidding into the lounge room, Lacey pulled the Indian rug from under the coffee table and lifted the floorboards. An assortment of pistols lay in the metal army ammunition box. No time to choose, so she took the top one, ejected the clip and inspected it. A full load.

The old dog was frantic now Another minute or two and Frank Purvis would be leaping up the back stairs. She kicked the rug back in place, slid the table to its usual position. She knew what he was like and that only intensified her fear. Each time their gazes met, by her accident or his design, the alarm bells screamed out the silent warning which was flooding her at that moment. Something wasn't right with Frank Purvis. She'd always sensed it long before she recognized it as real.

Lacey heard the driver's door slam. He had no reason to be here. He'd never had a reason.

Making sure the safety was on, Lacey slipped the handgun down the back of her jeans and grabbed her overshirt, put it on. Frank was leaping the house yard fence when she appeared at the back door and made no attempt to quiet the dog or the parrot.

'What do you want, Frank?'

'Call this dog off!'

'What do you want, Frank!'

'I need to talk to you. Call the fucking dog off!'

Calling the dog off would be giving him an invitation inside. 'So talk.'

'I saw you this morning with Dora. What the fuck were you saying to her?'

'It's none of your business, Frank. Go away.'

He took a step in the wrong direction and Kara, who had never bitten anyone in her life, took direct aim and sank her aged teeth into his left calf. And she hung on. But it had little effect. Frank kicked her off and didn't hear Lacey's enraged screams as the old dog rolled across the path and lay on the grass, whimpering. Hurt. 'You bastard!'

'I told you to call the old mongrel off!' He walked towards her. He wasn't limping but he should have been.

Lacey opened the screen door and took one step down. Frank looked up and saw an ancient handgun pointed at his face. An ancient handgun held in both hands by a frightened woman. Who couldn't shoot to save herself. He took another step.

'You get off my property, now!'

'Jesus, put it down before you hurt yourself.'

'Think I won't? Think I can't? Don't come any closer!'

Frank stopped and looked down at his bleeding leg, then up at Lacey. A dozen stairs lay between them. The more he stalled, the more indecisive she'd become. The easier it would be to disarm her. And have a little fun doing so. He reached for his tobacco ever so casually, rolled one, lit it and looked up again.

'I only want to know why Dora was talking to you at the bread man's house this morning, that's all.'

'Since when have I had to answer to you?'

'Come on, Lacey. We all know you're upset about Eadie. Who isn't? And we all know you're screwing the baker and we know you're trying hard to prove he didn't do Eadie. But he did. Okay? He did. What were you doing with Dora? Trying to convince the old bitch to say she seen me at Eadie's? Huh?'

'You were at Eadie's! Get off my property!' she screamed. Everything she knew about this man was rising in her mind. How he could kill quickly, without a sound, without a weapon. And how he enjoyed it.

'Where'd you get the gun? What is it? An old 92?'

'None of your business.'

'Cops are looking for a gun like that one. I bet it's the gun that did Eadie.'

'Don't you come any closer!'

'Looks to me like they arrested the wrong person.' One step closer. The gun was shaking in her hands. 'Why'd you do Eadie?' he asked. 'Were you fighting over the baker?' Two steps. She was almost within reach.

She fired but not to hit.

He felt the bullet fizz past his left ear. 'Okay, okay. I get the message. I'm going.' He retreated one slow step at a time, hands out at his sides in a gesture of defeat. 'I just wanted to talk some sense but if you want to go shoot at an innocent man, I'll just have to go to the cops myself. Tell 'em what's happened here.'

He retreated further, and considered momentarily the .30 cal with infra-red telescopic at five hundred yards. All he need do was watch for a while, take her in the open while she was in her market garden maybe. Or get the rifle right now. It was in the truck. 'I'm going,' he said. And he walked away. Kara was waiting by the gate so Frank vaulted over it, turned back to the old dog, tormented her a little through the chain-loop wire. The dog was almost rabid with hate, and Lacey was making no attempt to call it off.

Frank was reaching behind the bench seat of the Hilux when he heard another vehicle approaching. He looked. The same police car that had pulled up at The Metro half an hour ago. He had his hand on the rifle and hesitated momentarily.

The Ford had one occupant.

Frank decided to leave. Within seconds, he was in the Toyota and lost amid a cloud of red dust, tires straining for traction. He side-swiped the power pole and kept going. He had several options—the dam on the right, the market garden on the left, or the blue unmarked Ford dead ahead and skidding across the private road in a block.

Frank chose the market garden. Lacey had turned the irrigator off barely an hour before. The truck skidded sideways again and through the fence, and there it stayed, back tires churning, a waterfall of fertilized mud pouring out.

Lacey heard the engine stop and she heard Sean Merrin's voice:

'Out of the vehicle, now!'

She saw it all. Heard it all. The shots, the shatter of glass as the Ford's windscreen was hit. It wasn't like a stand-off in the movies or on TV. It was over so quickly she wondered when it had begun. One moment Frank Purvis was behind the wheel of his bogged truck and the next he was dead. Silence ruled except for the cockatoo's screaming obscenities.

Sean Merrin, alone, and still with his small gun in his hand, approached the patch very cautiously. Then he looked into the driver's window and all caution dissolved. The man who'd taken Kerry away that morning, who was standing in mud, looked at his feet for a moment, then he turned and kicked the back tire of Frank's truck. And he saw Lacey hugging her gatepost as if it would stop her falling over.

'Did you see this?' he called.

In reply, Lacey Kilder fainted.

She was vaguely aware of someone sitting her up, pushing her head between her knees Buzzing darkness slowly turned to daylight. All was quiet except for Sean Merrin's breathing and Kara trying vainly to lick Lacey's face.

'You right?' Sean Merrin asked, although he looked as if he were next to pass out. He tried to light a cigarette, his hands shook too much.

'Is he dead?' she asked, shakily.

'You saw it, didn't you?'

She nodded.

'Good,' he whispered. 'He shot first, right?'

'Yes. Yes, it was a rifle. He got it from behind the seat just before you came and—'

You little doll, Sean thought. 'I have to use your phone.' He helped her to her feet, guided her inside.

Kara didn't bother about this man's presence, nor did Lacey. Till she saw the Beretta on the bench near the back door. She leant against the bench top, pale, shaking, and pointed the way to the phone. Then she dropped the gun into the cardboard box by the door and covered it with the box of lettuce seedlings she'd bought.

She tried not to eavesdrop on the conversation. Everything was a blur except for: Purvis is dead.

'It'll take about an hour,' Merrin said quietly as he sat at Lacey's table. His face was white, his hands shaking a little.

'Are you sure he's dead'

'I'm sure.' Merrin rested both elbows on the table and let out a shaky sigh. Lacey opened the pantry cupboard and searched deep for a bottle of brandy someone gave her as a present ten years ago. It had never been opened. She put it on the table with a small glass but he looked up and shook his head. 'No. Thanks, but no.' He didn't need to have been drinking before or after. Something about her gesture, though, was reassuring.

'I was always under the impression cops never came when they were needed. Thanks.' Lacey put the kettle on. Here she was making a cup of tea and a dead man was sitting in his vehicle, outside. Two bullets in the head. It seemed ridiculous. Frank's dead. It could have been me. And I'm making a cup of tea.

'What was he here for?' Merrin asked, trying to contain rising nausea.

'I don't know exactly. He saw Dora Mallaby talking to me this morning. Talking about him at Eadie's the night she—'

'Yes, I know. I got the message. Why didn't you tell me first?'

'I don't trust any of you people. I have my reasons.'

He said nothing to that, it wasn't the first time he'd heard it, and it certainly wouldn't be the last. 'You're in trouble now, aren't you?'

Merrin didn't have to speak—his glance replied instead.

'But you didn't have a choice. He shot at you first.' She made him a huge mug of tea but one sip later she was pointing the way to the loo, trying not to hear him throwing up. She seemed to understand—she was nauseated, too. But all she'd done was watch. Before today, he was just a man doing a job. Perhaps wrongly but it was just a job. He came back looking paler but a little better and he resumed his seat and for a while, couldn't look at her. He was probably rehearsing what to say to his wife and kids. Worrying about the transfer, the promotion. Lacey knew his immediate future at a glance. 'You'll be okay,' was all she said.

He looked up, wondering how she knew what he was thinking. 'How long have you lived here?' he asked.

'Five years.'

'No one knows very much about you.'

'I keep to myself. It's safest that way.'

'I asked around. No one knew you wrote books.'

Lacey walked off and returned with her three books—Beyond Reality, Veils and Phenomenon. She put them down with, 'People out here read pictures, Mr Merrin. It's one of the reasons I came here. I wanted to be left alone.'

Mister Merrin? 'You can call me Sean.'

She said nothing. She looked at the clock. Fifteen minutes had passed. This would be the longest hour of her life.

'You said yesterday you were writing about Elspeth Mackenzie. What exactly do you know about her?'

'Her or the disappearance?'

'Whatever.'

'All I know is what I've seen. But only a minor percentage of the population sees what I see. I know she's dead. I know she was murdered somewhere near the swamp in December 1985. That there were five people involved. That Eadie Ross had an empathic reaction every year and the reaction lasted three days—as long as it took for Elspeth to die. Or so I believe. No body has ever been found but I know where it is. It's in the swamp.'

'Why haven't you said anything before this?'

'Well, put it this way. Len Gilmeister has his own touching way of keeping silences. Like Frank had.'

Sean remained quiet.

'Here. I was addressing this to you when Frank arrived. It's for you if you want it. But I need it returned. It's my research file. Such as it is.' She slid the envelope across the table to him and he looked at her questioningly. 'Look, I used to work with police a few years ago. Mainly on missing persons and only when I was asked. I never volunteered. The public never knew but it's all on record at Headquarters if you need to check. Inspector Cummins, if he's still there, will tell you all you need to know.'

Sean Merrin didn't know what to think now.

'I had a 95 per cent accuracy rate as a psychic. I also used the name Marguerite. I didn't want anyone here to know what I used to do. Can you understand that?'

His expression told her he didn't. His expression told her just how wary he was of all this psycho-stuff. For curiosity's sake alone, he asked, 'How'd you do it?'

'I'd be given an article of clothing. It's called psychometry. Inspector Cummins will—'

'He retired four years ago.'

'I didn't know that.'

Ninety-five per cent accuracy, huh?'

'I don't do it any more. This is my life now. Here.'

'Does Staines know this?'

'I don't think so, but with Kerry it's hard to tell.' The pause was indefinite. 'So many deep, dark secrets were finally safe when Elspeth died. No one took any notice of Eadie Ross. She was the resident nutter. Then Kerry Staines arrived in town, Eadie fell in love. Kerry has that effect on us.'

'Us?'

'Women. Of all ages, I suppose. I guess I'm the lucky one. He chose me. God knows why.'

Sean knew exactly why Staines had chosen her. Half a chance, he'd try as well.

After a sigh, she continued, 'The people who wanted the secret to remain buried—'

'Secret?'

'Elspeth's disappearance. Well, they couldn't afford any risks. Anyone who knew and threatened to tell met with an accident or they left town and were never seen or heard from again. Have you spoken to Dora Mallaby yet?'

'Yep. It's one of the reasons I'm here.'

'That's why Frank came out. He said he saw Dora and me talking at Kerry's place this morning. Said he knew what I was telling Dora to say to the police. That she'd seen him that night at Eadie's. Kerry didn't kill Eadie. He had no reason, no motive. If only you'd seen his face after he'd found the body... He was as frightened as you are now. Maybe because he knew what would come, too.'

Sean was quiet for a while. 'Do you know Len Gilmeister?' he asked, finally.

'I know he's frightened of me. I know I would not like to be alone with him. He's tried a couple of times but failed.'

'Like that, huh?'

'Like that. Yes.'

Sean rose and with a sigh, he leant on the kitchen bench under the window and looked out at the huge expanse of land. The swamp. 'You don't seem concerned about the prison being so close.'

'Should I be?'

'Construction begins next week, doesn't it?'

'Monday, I think. A few professional protesters will come out, paint themselves black and cry *sacred ground*. Trouble is, if it was needed by the local Aboriginals why aren't they protesting? No one wants that land. For a reason.'

Sean tried not to smile. 'Yeah, I've heard. It's cursed. Thanks for the tea. I'd better go outside and wait.'

'Sean?'

He looked back.

'Kerry Staines is a good man. Maybe he had some problems in the past, but—'

'I'll tell you something, Lacey. I haven't known a decent nark yet who didn't have a substance abuse problem.'

'He's not a murderer.'

'I know that,' was all he said and squeezed her arm as he went by to wait outside in the fresh air.

When he was gone, Lacey took the gun from the box near the door and put it back under the floorboards.

Two hours later, she was in Wilton police station, telling three police officers, one the district inspector, what had happened to her, what she had seen. Mainly that as far as she could tell, Frank had fired a rifle at the police car first. She read through her statement, signed it and was taken outside to wait for whatever else was to come.

Peter Jameson, the one who had allowed her to see Kerry, the one who was a regular visitor to The Arms on a Saturday night, brought her a cup of tea, sat beside her on the uncomfortable wooden bench and sighed as he stretched out. 'How you doing?' he asked, looking straight into her eyes. She liked it when men did that, saw her eyes first.

Apart from a forced smile there was little else forthcoming. 'How's Karen?'

'Good.'

She'd known him for a couple of years, but there was nothing else to say.

'You'll be right,' he whispered, patted her knee and walked off.

Kerry was finally led into the interview room for what he thought was round three, and he glimpsed Lacey waiting. She didn't see him, she was too busy studying the depths of a tea cup.

The first face he saw was Alf Graham's. Graham had been head of CIB when Kerry was on highway patrol, what seemed like an eternity ago. Now he was the District Inspector. 'Kerry.'

'Alf.'

'I made a few calls, verified a few points. The charges have been dropped. You're free to go.'

'And if you bastards had made a few calls a little earlier, none of this would have happened.' Kerry waited for something else, an apology perhaps.

'Sorry this had to happen, but we should have been informed of *all* relevant details.' More of a grunt than an apology.

'Yeah, sure.' Gazes met. Both were agitated, although Graham was embarrassed as well. Stew, Kerry thought.

'A car will take you, Miss Kilder and Mrs Mallaby back to Mallen. That's all.'

That's all, folks.

Kerry walked out and did not look back. He signed for his possessions, put his belt and shoes on and found Lacey. She looked up, surprise turning to relief.

'G'day,' he whispered.

She didn't reply. Tears welled in her eyes, so he sat beside her, put his arm around her and hugged her close.

CHAPTER 6

Lacey lay asleep against Kerry's shoulder on the late afternoon journey home. Peter Jameson was driving. Kerry knew he wasn't alone in wanting a beer and a bit of respite from Dora's incessant prattle.

Lacey had witnessed the Frank Purvis incident, had verified Sean Merrin's report and that was all Kerry knew. She'd apparently refused an offer of counseling from the government psychologist. Unfortunately Sean had no choice. Gilmeister was suspended pending further investigation.

Before Kerry was taken to Alf Graham, Merrin had spent a few minutes with him in the holding cell. Sean stood there, looking like he needed a week's sleep and he'd said, 'You were offered full reinstatement. Why'd you tell them to shove it?'

Kerry told him why but the answer was not pleasing to either of them. 'I couldn't take the hypocrisy, the politics. And pricks like you.'

It had been an incredibly long day, one Kerry would rather forget ever existed. Lacey hadn't let go of his hand in three hours. Even asleep she held tight.

When the patrol car finally stopped at Dora Mallaby's, Lacey didn't wake. Kerry moved her slightly—his hip had locked again. She mumbled and collapsed on his lap, stretched herself out across the back seat and finally let go of his hand.

'Won't be long,' Peter said and Kerry watched as the young uniformed constable walked Dora to her front door. Kerry looked across the street. Crime scene cordons were still intact across the length of Eadie's yard. And home was two streets away.

Five weeks ago nothing ever happened in this tiny place, he thought, not a damned thing. Then I arrive in town.

Kerry fumbled for a smoke and lit it. Under the streetlight on the corner of Race and George Streets stood a young woman. Waiting for someone. She looked directly at Kerry and waved. He didn't feel like it, but he waved back—a gesture only. He knew instantly it had been a mistake. She came across the street toward him.

She was a very pretty girl, barely eighteen. Her perfume was strong as she rested her elbows on the car window and said, 'Give us a drag, gorgeous.'

Kerry offered the packet Merrin had given him.

'No, just a drag of yours'll do.'

Kerry lit himself another so he wouldn't have to take the original back. God knew who she was or where she'd been, one glance gave him more than a fair idea. Something about her was familiar.

'Nah, it's not the same any more.'

Kerry said nothing as she dropped the cigarette on to the overgrown footpath.

'You wouldn't be going anywhere near Starks Road, would you?'

'No, sorry,' he lied.

'I've seen you around,' the girl said.

'I have one of those faces,' Kerry replied quietly. 'Bit of Abo, in you, hey?'

'Excuse me?'

'Who leapt the fence? Mum or Dad?'

'Excuse me?'

She leaned on the window again, stuck her behind out, wagged her tail a little. A very nice tail it was, too. She squeezed her arms together in an effort to enhance her already-enhanced cleavage. Kerry noticed the heart tattooed on the heart—hard to miss the way she was displaying her goods.

'Like me tat?' she asked. 'Hurt like hell.'

Kerry looked purposely into blue eyes he'd seen before somewhere. She vaguely resembled the girl asleep on his lap. The same eyes, at least. Same colored hair.

'I'm thinking of getting a job modeling bikinis at the Gold Coast. What do you reckon?' She didn't give him time to reply. 'Lenny says I'd make a great centerfold. You're shy, aren't you.'

'Me? No, far from it.'

'Bullshit,' she said. 'You live in Eric's old dump, don't you?'

'Ah, yes.'

'What you scared of? I don't bite. Unless you want me to.' She grinned and Kerry felt his face heat. Burn. Come on, Jameson, where the hell are you? Now's not the time for a cup of tea and more idle chatter.

'What happened to your leg?'

'Excuse me?'

'I see you out walking. You limp bad.'

'I got shot a couple of years ago.'

'Yeah?'

'Yeah.'

'Me mate got shot in the foot once. Jesus, I laughed.'

Kerry looked at the girl again, felt his blood turning to ice. Her right arm held bracelets to the elbow. Long fingernails painted red, a man's skull and cross bone ring adorned her middle finger. The hair was short and bleached, she wore a Celtic cross around her neck and was as alive as Lacey, deeply asleep across his lap. This is not happening, he thought. I'm on overload. This is some kind of psychotic delusion. She is not here. But her voice continued on. A nice voice. Girlishly deep, melodic. 'Don't get me wrong. I wasn't laughing 'cos she got shot. Hell, it was just so funny. What's your name?'

'Kerry.'

'Girl's name. Jesus, you sure got the wrong end of the stick. What'd you do in your last life that was so wrong?'

He tried hard to smile. He liked that. If we can't blame lifelong crap on some present issue, blame the past which can't be proved.

'I'm waiting for Rossi. That's what I call her. Rossi. You know, Cinzano? She likes getting pissed on it, says it never gives her a hangover. I like Scotch myself. Or rum and Coke. Who you waiting for?'

'Someone I know.'

'Yeah. Me, too. She's bloody late again. You want to come to the pictures in Wilton with us? There's a pile of us going.'

'What's on?' he asked, knowing full well that the Wilton cinema had closed nearly twenty years ago. He'd driven past it more than once.

'Mad Max,' she said. 'I love that Gibson guy.'

'Mad Max 1, 2 or 3 ?' Kerry asked.

'Get out of it,' she laughed and he felt the playful tug on his hair. 'There's only one! Oops, there's me lift,' she said. 'Rossi's late. Oh well, stiff. She misses out again. See you around, Kerry?' she asked.

Again, he tried to smile. Kerry watched her run across the street and get into a Kingswood ute. He didn't see who was driving, but saw the logo which read *S Bend*. The vehicle traveled about fifty meters down George Street before it disappeared, as if it had never existed. And he knew he'd just spoken to Elspeth, aged about seventeen, the year before she died.

He looked at his time. Either his watch had stopped or time hit a pothole because he turned towards Dora's house and Peter was still walking her up to the front door. She opened it, went in. Then he was on his way back. It wasn't night-time, either. It was only sunset. The streetlight hadn't sensed enough darkness to spring to life yet.

Kerry opened the car door and looked at the ground. It wasn't overgrown grass, it was a foot-path garden and no half-smoked butts lay in the petunias. Nor were there any footprints where the girl had stood. But her perfume was rank. What had he done? Slipped back twenty years to the time when Elspeth was alive? When overgrown footpaths encroached on the thinning bitumen? When the streets were not curbed and channeled? He put his hand on Lacey's shoulder. At least she was real. Warm. Soft.

Pete got back in the car and instantly said, 'Pooh. What's that stink?' Then he sneezed. Four times. His eyes watered.

'What stink?'

'Avon. Bird of Paradise. My mother used to wear that crap. Thank Christ they don't make it any more.'

Barely a minute later, Pete had stopped at Kerry's house and two shakes after that, Lacey was upright, disorientated.

'Peter will take you home,' Kerry said.

'No, no. I have to go to work.'

'Emile can do without you for one night.'

'No, it's Saturday. Cabaret.' She let herself out of the car and walked off towards town.

'Go have a beer, mate,' Kerry said. 'I'll take care of Miss Kilder.'

Jameson needed little persuasion. He drove off.

Kerry dropped his overnight bag over his fence and had to run to catch Lacey. 'Would you listen to reason?'

'No.'

'What time do you start?'

'Half an hour ago.'

'Okay, be an hour late. Come on.' He took her arm and led her back across the street and into his house yard.

'You're making me angry.'

'Yeah, yeah.'

'You haven't seen me angry.'

'I'm scared already. Go inside and shower at least. Please. Look at you. You can't go to work like that.'

She looked down. She hadn't realized she was still in her working clothes, an old T-shirt that had seen far better days. Barefoot. Shorts covered in patches. 'I went to Wilton dressed like this?'

Kerry nodded.

'Oh, my God. Would you take me home so I can change? Please?'

'I would if I had a car but someone used it and never returned it.'

Lacey realized both her bike *and* his car were parked by her house gate.

'Looks like we're marooned,' Kerry said.

'I'm sorry. I wasn't thinking. When the police came I had to go with them and... now what are we going to do?'

Peter Jameson was halfway through his first beer when the phone in the public bar of the Arms rang and the receiver was held out to him.

The patrol car's lights illuminated what was left of Lacey's patch. Even Kerry, this time in the front seat, whispered one word. Shit.

'It's futile,' she whispered.

The Toyota had been pulled out by a tractor and four months of back-breaking work was totally annihilated. Moving and impounding Purvis's truck had caused more damage than Frank had. It could only look worse in daylight.

Peter Jameson stopped by the gate to the house yard and finally drove off, hoping by some slim chance that he wouldn't be called back to Mallen for another week.

If Lacey looked tired an hour ago, she was exhausted now. Kerry followed her in. 'You're not seriously considering going to work are you?' he asked.

'I don't have a choice.'

'I'll call Emile, tell him you're sick.'

'No! Your keys are hanging on a hook hear the sink. Just go away and leave me alone.'

Kerry studied her for a long time. He was not about to pick up his keys, get in his car and go home. He saw the files and papers spread across the kitchen table, the bottle of brandy open.

'Something I said? Something I've done?'

'Kerry, please, go home. I'm happy that the charges were dropped but I have too much to do to stand here being nice when I don't bloody feel like being nice! And take your cat. I didn't know what else to do with him so I brought him home to stay here with me.'

Kerry took his car keys from the hook and left without a word. But as he took the stairs and the old dog met him, limping as bad as he was limping, he could hear her crying upstairs. He came to a stop, looked at the cockatoo in the cage. He had his head under a wing but was watching. And though Kerry wanted to go back up those stairs, he decided it best to just leave her alone.

Maybe she'd call him one day. Maybe he'd come out tomorrow, help her rebuild the fence. Maybe he'd just get in his car and keep driving. To hell with everything.

Yang was waiting on the fencepost. Kerry picked him up on the way past, threw him into the back seat and drove away. As he took the second grid too fast Kerry was hit by a much better idea. He'd get blind instead. So much for newfound freedom.

He returned to his rambling old house in Margaret Street, parked the car by the house and went inside to shower and change.

The place no longer resembled the drop site of Friday night. Lacey had spent God knew how long cleaning and tidying, and considering she'd never even been in the house since he took possession she'd somehow known each item's place.

Kerry opened the fridge first. In a microwave dish in front of his beers a casserole lay waiting. He took it out. There was a note taped to the plastic wrap.

Welcome home. Ella.

Kerry stared at it for some time, staring so hard that tears stung behind his eyes. Until now he hadn't realized just how hungry he was. Kerry put the casserole into the microwave, ran the shower over the Stephen King tub and washed the watch house mattress odor from his skin and hair.

Black Levis, a dusty red shirt. Aramis. A small plate of Ella's food and one beer later, Kerry had found new hope. There was a light in his eyes he hadn't seen for years—a light that only shone sincerely when he was playing or surrounded by friends and family. Maybe the light shining when he was alone was a good sign? Of what he wasn't sure. And he thought, as he walked to The Arms, that perhaps he had a few friends in Mallen he hadn't recognized before.

It was five to nine when he walked into the public bar of The Arms, scanned the crowd for a face he knew, a place to sit. At that stage all he wanted was to get quietly drunk. He could have done so at home, alone, but after spending a day in a watch house cell and contemplating a bleak future, he felt it wiser to be surrounded by people. The drunker the better. Drunks rarely judged.

Maybe no one was drunk enough yet. The place fell quiet the moment he entered, a scene from a bad western where a tall dark stranger steals women's hearts and saves the town from its plague of evil.

Kerry, feigning ignorance, walked to the bar where only one stool was vacant. It was probably Frank Purvis's seat, kept vacant in memory of a regular. People were funny like that. Mallen people funnier than most.

Emile Rollet put a beer down and didn't accept payment. 'We have heard already that these charges are dropped, that the case is now all closed. Welcome, Kerry. Welcome back.'

Kerry tried to read the hazel eyes because the voice grated with strained sincerity.

'We will all miss Frank,' Emile said.

No one commented.

'We will, too, all miss Eadie.'

'You're not fucking wrong,' a faceless voice called from the eight-ball table.

Noise returned and Kerry was thankful. People who had barely spoken a word when entering his shop were now crowding around, quietly quizzing, curious as to what had happened in Wilton. It seemed to Kerry that the last two days had been just a bad dream from which he was beginning to wake. He had to reassure so many that no, he wasn't about to leave town, he was here to stay. The shop would open again for business as usual on Monday at 7.00 a.m.

Emile's daughter, Chantelle, was working the bar with her father. Kerry caught the glances, smiled, and to his smile she replied with a face the color of a Stop sign. Which did his heart some good. Not a lot had changed. Kerry decided the beer would go down easier with a rum chaser. He felt the effects quickly and did not ease off until he was slapped on the back and he turned, feathers ruffling. Johnny Logan's grin was a beamer and instantly disarming.

He was pissed already. 'Jerry's got some bug and can't be more'n three steps from a dunny. How about it?'

Who the hell's Jerry? Kerry wondered. 'How about what?'

'Ever played a Rickenbacker before?'

The eyes smiled. Then Kerry touched his fingertips. No callouses these days but it wouldn't be the first time he played till his fingers bled. Welcome to the past. Do we pick up where we left off? Are the Gods being kind?

'Come on. Give us a hand.' Johnny pushed a typed sheet of paper into Kerry's hands and handed him a pen. It was a line-up. 'Tick what you know, write down what we don't and we'll meet somewhere in the middle. It's John Lennon night, okay? Gimme ten, I gotta find these other bastards yet.' Johnny waddled off.

There was a little of everything imaginable on Deceptions line-up sheet. Garth Brooks. Lee Kernaghan. Rolling Stones. A list of Beatles songs Kerry had been weaned on. ELO. Elton John. The Doors. Bob

Seger. Elvis Presley. The list went on and on. Most were numbers his old band had covered back in the good old days. So what if he was rusty? It was going on for 10.00 p.m. and by 11.00 more than half of the audience would be as paralytic as the band.

Kerry took his beer, the line-up sheet, and weaved his way to the lounge. The place was packed by people of all ages and varying degrees of color. This place was the only nightlife Mallen had ever had, or was ever likely to have. The Australian Arms on Friday and Saturday nights. High on the wall behind the band's set was a large video screen showing a silent copy of 'A Hard Day's Night'. On the wall, a mural of Sergeant Pepper. John Lennon in an army camouflage helmet.

Alive for the first time in two years, Kerry stepped on the stage feeling like Cinderella before the pumpkin episode. He turned the four-way PA on. Peavey amps boomed to life and someone killed the juke box. He didn't know many names to associate with the faces that watched him with bored expectation. Maybe he'd slipped back too fast because he turned to Belinda but she wasn't there. Just him. He studied the Roland, sat, and a few seconds later, 'Imagine' began.

The voice hit four pairs of ears simultaneously. Johnny Logan, Owen Richter, Ray Macquarie and Lacey Kilder.

'Who the fuck's that?' Owen asked, choking on a microwaved party pie—the only food he'd had since breakfast. He'd spent all day scarifying one hundred acres of his old man's land and was ready for a pink elephant to leap from the walls at any moment.

'The bastard's started without us,' Johnny said without much emotion.

Owen stuffed his mouth full of party pies as he departed, quickly.

But Ray stayed, as unperturbed as always. 'Sounds good,' he said, a hint of surprise in his voice.

'Should be,' Johnny said calmly. 'Ten years back he had the chance of going pro.'

'Who are you talking about?' Lacey asked. It was normal practice for the band to come into the kitchen and eat what was available before they played.

'Kerry Staines.'

'That's *Kerry* singing?' she asked, voice a squeak of disbelief.

'Sure as hell ain't Jerry.'

Lacey watched from the kitchen door—the man, the voice, the music, all combined to weaken more than her knees. At least Johnny, Ray and Owen let him finish his introductory solo before they swamped the stage and stole a little of the newcomer's limelight. But only a little. Every female of every age was magnetized to him.

Kerry had never told her he was a musician. Why not? But he never volunteered anything. He only ever half answered questions. Before you knew it, you'd forgotten what you'd asked, so adept he was at changing subjects to suit himself.

'Light My Fire'. Deceptions always began the night with that song. Johnny never sang that well, none of the band members could, but he soon took a back seat because Kerry Staines sounded too good. He wasn't off-key, either. And the guitar in his grip was almost talking.

Lacey leant against the back wall of the lounge bar room, her ears blasted by screaming guitars and booming amplifiers. She noticed Kerry seemed happy, alive, up there. She could no sooner do that than orbit the sun. For a moment she envied him, and then he saw her standing against the back wall, swaying a little in time to the music. And he grinned at her. She returned it, almost shyly, and then went back to the kitchen to resume filling the dishwasher.

Not a lot had changed. Johnny Logan had lost a friend that day and Lacey had seen it happen. He didn't seem too concerned; if he was he hid it well. There were many others all too ready to take Frank's place at the bar in The Arms.

For most of the evening, talk in the bar was of Frank. What he'd been like before he joined the army, then the war and what he was like when he returned. Some people's memories were long enough to recall with exaggerated clarity Frank's good points—however few there were.

It's almost over now, Lacey thought. Apart from Emile and Gilmeister, almost everyone else who knew what happened to Elspeth was dead. Emile never mentioned her; at the time of the incident he was a newlywed and although he may not have physically been there that weekend, he knew. How he knew. His position in the town hierarchy was cemented for life when he married the shire chairman's daughter. Now he was a widower and the town's mayor. With a few secrets of his own.

Lacey didn't have the chance to speak to Kerry that night. He was too busy being the center of every female's attention. So much had changed in a couple of days.

4.30 a.m. Saturday. Lacey had woken to find Kerry standing on the verandah, staring out at the breaking darkness. He had known what was to come. She'd watched for a little while, indecisive as to whether she should leave him alone or not. It seemed then, that he'd spent most of his life alone in one way or another. She'd walked to him, touched his hand. The rest was, as they say, history. Possibly a mistake, and what could be learnt from one mistake? She realized she could feel again? That he could dissolve a cleverly built barrier with a simple look, a word, a touch? Would he ever want her again?

Lacey had ridden home at midnight after giving two extra hours of her time helping Chantelle in the lounge bar. The band was playing on until 2.30 a.m. She hadn't the energy or inclination to stay any longer than necessary. Feelings of jealousy were overwhelming.

She decided tomorrow she'd rise at dawn and pull the fence down, salvage what remained or plough it all in. Tomorrow she'd think about whether she would begin again or not. Tomorrow.

But tomorrow took too many hours to arrive. Lacey could still smell him on the pillows beside her. She hadn't the time to change the sheets, nor make the bed. For hours she thrashed about, her mind in overdrive. When she finally dropped off to sleep, Elspeth came in a dream, a bad dream. Lacey woke clasping the spare pillow, her screaming choked, replaced by the scream of the alarm. 'Leave me alone, Elspeth. Why can't you just leave me alone!'

Her plea was answered by humor. Too much of it.

CHAPTER 7

Lacey looked up and groaned. Her heart should have lifted at the sight of the Rav, but unfortunately she was calf-deep in muddy ruts of squashed tomatoes and mangled lettuce, pulling up broken and buried barbed wire which seemed to have rusted overnight. And the pigs had been back. The ones with four legs this time. The last person she needed was Kerry. Or so she thought.

He wore a black tee shirt, faded jeans and old sneakers. He leant against his open car door, attempted to lift his sunglasses. Sunshine seemed his main enemy. He'd been right. It was far worse by daylight. Thirty per cent worse. His judgment was off due to the alcohol residue in his bloodstream. And feeling this way had once been normal?

'Gidday,' he called. Lacey mumbled to herself. 'Did you enquire about compensation?'

'I can't wait till I'm sixty-five for the government to put me on a shortlist.'

'Did you enquire?' Kerry asked again, only now able to take a few steps closer, lifting the glasses fully. Squinting.

'No. Did you? You were falsely arrested.'

'I wasn't convicted.'

'But you were charged.'

'It's not worth the trouble.'

'Don't preach at me, then,' she spat.

What's up now, Kerry thought, wondering again what it was he'd done or said. With women that was all he seemed to do—wonder. Time for your happy pill, honey, he thought as he watched her dragging tangled lumps of wire from congealed mud. He knew better than to offer assistance. If he did he'd have his sinuses cleared by a length of barbed wire. If he didn't, the same.

'I woke this morning and thought, good day for a picnic.'

'Rot.' Lacey threw a tangle of barbed wire on the stockpile. 'You woke this morning wishing you'd died during the night. I have no sympathy for you.'

'And then I thought, who can I picnic with?' He took a basket from the back seat and a cooler. He looked about as if he'd never seen the property before, then he headed for the dam, the grassy banks and a lonely, ancient red gum's welcome shade.

'Kerry,' she whined. 'I have to get this done. If I stop now, I'll never start again.'

'Sunday's the only day I can picnic with a pretty lady. Looks like you're it. It's lunchtime, so stop whinnying and making excuses. Get your arse over here before you collapse from dehydration and/or exhaustion. My first aid's lousy, you should know that.' He kept walking towards the dam, hiked over the kikuyu covered bank and disappeared from view.

Lacey looked at the time. Quarter to twelve. His timing was impeccable. He took it for granted that she'd been out since dawn, was tired, hot and hungry, and on the verge of walking away from everything. She followed, but not because he had ordered it.

He was lying on a travel rug, squashing the occasional green ant and sipping on a frosting Coke when she finally appeared.

Taking a place on the edge of the bank near the irrigation pump, she took off her boots. Socks. She walked into the muddy water and gave her hands a cursory wash, then her face. She stood in the water for awhile, bent over, hands on hips. Then she dived in, disappeared for five seconds and resurfaced in the middle of the dam.

'How is it?' Kerry called.

'Come in and find out.'

She didn't expect that he would. She certainly didn't expect to see him strip to his underwear, either. He grabbed the rope hanging on the red gum branch and tarzaned it into the middle of the dam.

The water was ten below freezing, or so it felt. For the first time in ages, she laughed. He tried to delete the expletive. He tried, hard.

'There's a sub-artesian river flowing under your feet. That's why it's so cold.'

'You could have warned me.'

'Me? Why? No one warned me the first time.' Lacey paddled to him. 'I heard you last night. You never told me you were a singer.'

'You never asked. Logan wants me to become a permanent fixture.'

'And?'

'There's nothing else to fill my spare time with. Or is there?'

She looked away from the teasing eyes.

'Looks like you have a few days' slog ahead. If I was you I'd go for compensation.'

'You're not me. It's not worth it. After consideration, I decided Frank could have aimed for the dam and taken out the pumping station instead of the vege patch.'

'Lesser of two evils?'

Lacey floated for a while—her shirt ballooned, and not with air. Kerry's initial thought was, honey, you will never drown with inbuilt floaties like that.

'I've been asking what I did to deserve this. I guess you've asked the same.'

'Nah. I know what I did.'

'And what was that?'

'Far worse to many people. I was just given a return taste, that's all. Life does that, always when you least expect it. Get around believing you exist in some invisible bubble of authority and superiority and sure as shit, someone or something will burst the balloon. Did I thank you for what you did?'

'It's not necessary.'

'I never expected the kind of support I got, from you, the townspeople...'

'Oh, come on. Think of it our way. No one wants to lose another baker, least of all me.' She never admitted very much, however when she did it was well worth hearing. 'That excuse for bread we used to get from Wilton never lasted more than one day and it was full of preservatives and God only knows what else... Who taught you to bake?'

'A cranky old Italian,' he said and smiled.

'I wanted to call you this morning, but I couldn't find a decent reason.'

'You don't need a reason,' Kerry said. She was so beautiful. He reached out and pulled her closer. 'You should take this off,' he said, playing with the shirt. 'Get waterlogged and drown, then I'll have to resuscitate.'

'I would if I could, but there's leeches in the water,' she said, matter of fact, 'which is why I wear clothes. I've been caught before.'

'Leeches? Why didn't you tell me?'

'You never asked. You just dived on in.'

Kerry swam out, inspected as much of his body as he could and found only one leech, adhered and swelling nicely on the inside of his left arm. Probably the only drunk leech in history. At least he died happy, Kerry thought as his cigarette lighter ended that small parasitic life.

Lacey, dripping and refreshed, sat on the rug beside Kerry. 'You didn't have to do that,' she said.

'What?'

'Kill it.'

'What are you, a Buddhist?'

Lacey stretched out, stared at the sky for a little while. 'Eleven years ago I was in Malaysia with Craig. We were talking to a Buddhist monk and I swatted a mozzie. I got a twenty minute lecture I will never forget.'

Craig. Please, not the ex, not now. 'Where's the mutt?' Kerry asked, trying to divert conversation.

'In her basket. Recovering. Frank kicked her. She'd never bitten anyone before, either.'

'Are you going to tell me about it?'

'What's to say? The cops came just in time. It's over.' Lacey sat up, reached over and opened the cooler, scratching around in the ice for a soft drink she liked. She expected it to be half full of beer but perhaps he'd had enough for a week.

'He threatened you, didn't he.'

'Not really. I threatened him.'

'With what? The .243?'

If he was waiting for an explanation he knew he'd wait for ever. Lacey rattled about in the basket this time. Sandwiches, fruit, chocolate bars ... She chose and pushed the food closer to Kerry. He was still content with his Coke.

'Okay, I can shoot. I lied. I lied to get you out here. Initially. I am guilty, your honor.' She ignored the laughter in his eyes.

'There was no need to lie.'

'You would never have come without a good reason.'

'Ever think you were reason enough?'

All was quiet except for two young magpies watching, hoping for some leftovers.

'Kerry Staines, you worry me.'

'How's that?'

'Well, you're incredibly handsome.'

Kerry almost choked.

'You're talented, intelligent, humorous, and here you are sitting on a dam bank having a picnic with me. I feel like I won you in a lottery.'

'How much were the tickets?' he asked.

'Why do you always answer with a question?'

'Do I?' he asked, teasing again.

They both studied the sky.

'Do you write your own songs?' she asked.

'I used to.'

'Were they love songs for your wife?'

'I'll write one for you if you want,' he said, avoiding a direct reply.

'But you don't know me.'

'Which is probably why I'm sitting on a dam bank having a picnic. I've got an accurate imagination. And loners are good ballad material. I've never met anyone as secretive as you.'

'Oh, yes, you have.'

'Who?'

'Yourself.'

'Amend that to defensive then.'

'You.'

'I'm not defensive. You're picking on me 'cos I've got a hangover.'

'No, if I was picking on you, you'd know it. Why don't you talk about your wife?'

'Because she's dead and it's past.'

'But you want to know all about me. It works both ways, Kerry.'

He was thoughtful for a minute. 'Me? Well, there's not much to say. I was adopted at age three by David and Karalyn Staines. Dad was a music teacher, had the blues bad.'

'As in manic depressive?'

'Dad? Hell no. He wanted to be a blues/jazz musician but never made it. He died when I was ten. Traffic accident. The driver was DUI, but only got eighteen months suspension.' He was quiet for a moment, thinking.

'Is that why you wanted to be a policeman? To fight for justice?'

'Is there always a deeper meaning with you?'

'Curious.'

'Dangerous past time. No, I didn't always want to be a nark. I considered being a doctor. Used to play doctors and nurses with the girl next door. I was in third year med when my mother died of cancer. I dropped out, became a paramedic, then a police ossifer.'

Memory had dimmed the light in his eyes. 'Do you know about your biological parents?'

'No. My roots mean nothing. I'm not on the Great Search, never have been, never will be.'

'You would have been a good doctor.'

'Bullshit. I'm too selfish.'

Lacey moved closer and leant across to get a better view of the basket's contents again. She was incredibly hungry—she'd been working since dawn. But all her hunger died when she saw the scars on his lower stomach. Some were from a scalpel, most were not. She wanted to ask what sort of gun had done that but decided he'd tell her if he wanted her to know. He'd said he'd been shot but she hadn't realized the extent of damage. No wonder he walked with a permanent limp, pain registering in his eyes constantly. 'What did it feel like?' she asked, touching.

'I don't know. No, honestly, I do not know. I couldn't move. My attention was on Belinda.'

'Belinda?'

'A young nark I worked with for nearly five years.'

Lacey touched again and saw in her mind's eye, felt in her own body, the numbing paralysis and a hazy image, at ground level, of long grass, a red-haired woman only feet away. Bleeding. She lifted her hand quickly.

Kerry intercepted, held her hand tight and pulled her down beside him, cradling her head in his arm. And every muscle in her body tensed. Not a good sign. So he pretended otherwise and simply held her. He talked on, quietly.

'The Maleny Folk Festival. Belinda and I were playing there. It was the culmination of a six-month undercover investigation. Belinda was a dog when I first met her.'

'A what?'

'Dog. Straight from the academy. Never known a mind quite like hers. Basically, we discovered a few things we weren't supposed to, there was a tip off and it all went wrong. We were buying—well, in the short and sweet version, she was shot, and I was shot, and a major dealer who was also some relative of the police commissioner's wife got a bullet in the head.' He sighed. 'Shit flew in all directions for months. Unfortunately, I didn't die and I wouldn't be silenced. And here I am. The shit's still falling. End of story.'

Her tension gradually eased, he felt it in her breathing, the ice was melting. He took his time. A look wasn't enough with this one—she had too many demons of her own, so a little at a time was his best strategy. Volunteer some personal information, gain some trust and proceed slowly. And the fingers trailing her arm weren't yet shunned. He'd rounded the first curve of this obstacle course without failing. 'I'm pleased I met you, Lacey.'

Tension reared again and was eased by his voice, his touch. 'Mainly because you have no expectations. And it doesn't feel wrong telling you things. Or anything for that matter. Know why?'

She said nothing, so he took it as a sign to continue. Kerry moved a little, wincing as his hip protested with a shot of pain that sent his toes numb. He rose on his elbow and looked down at her. Into her eyes. 'I've never heard you say a bad word about anyone. That's special, you know.' He brushed a straggle of damp hair from her face and touched her nose. It brought a smile, a facial contortion. 'Ticklish?' he asked.

'No.'

'First mistake.' He trailed his fingers up and down her arm, inside her elbow. She reacted. Ticklish.

'No.'

'Here?' Behind the ear.

'Kerry—'

'Stop it' he mimicked.

Then she drew her right leg up, ready to roll away, escape. He tickled her leg from knee to thigh.

'Kerry—'

He kissed her to cease the objections. And when he did her entire body relaxed. Mouth opened. The fingers trailed a circle on her thigh, under the wet shirt, across the elastic of shorts to bare skin again. Soft belly. And up to the bra, into it. His touch was hot and gentle. Not rough. Never rough.

Her eyes closed to the tingling. Immediate fires sparked. Kerry unbuttoned the shirt and laid it aside, watching her face as he slid strap off shoulder and pulled the cup aside. Tongue tickled, tasted, tickled, bit. Lacey's breathing grew deeper, quicker. So he kissed her again and slid his hand into her shorts. Her legs opened slightly. It was obvious after a little while that she hadn't been touched like this for a long, long time.

About as long as he, but he was simply guessing.

Practised, intuitive touches brought her to a quick, violent peak and he left his hand there a moment until the pulsing subsided and she opened her eyes.

He was still watching, intently. Nothing else showed in his eyes— nothing she could read, at least. Lacey touched his face and silent messages passed. He kissed her again and pulled her toward him, unclasped the offending garment. Kerry threw it over his head and took a moment for himself. Witnessing what most other men in town had only imagined.

She had a tattoo of a heart, the size of a twenty-cent piece over her heart. He immediately thought of Elspeth Mackenzie. Even the eyes were the same color. He touched the tattoo and almost spoke. Almost. But Lacey slipped her shorts off and hesitantly touched him from knee to shoulder. All thoughts of Elspeth and any yesterday dissolved.

'Lay back, Kerry.'

The voice of an angel. And time was forgotten. Now and then he raised his head, only able to see her damp head between his legs. He wanted to slow her down. Didn't she know he was as rusty as she? Kerry had to put his hand on her head to stop her, and almost manic eyes looked up at him. His heart leapt a little. So he smiled as much as he could to cover the momentary fright. For a heartbeat, she'd been Elspeth. Then Annie.

Then sense returned.

Lacey crawled astride his hips. He didn't mind. Not at all. It was less agony on his hip this way; maybe she knew that, too.

Kerry reached out and touched, held the heavy breasts looming above. She moved slowly. Too slowly. Kerry, almost peaking too damned soon, rolled her over and forgot his disability, his permanent curse which seemed to have been put aside for the first time in two years. Because for two years, his mind was willing, but his body had not been obliging. He'd thought that he'd reached the end of an era. Till now.

Ten seconds after he was finally done, he remembered the rubbers in his wallet. In the Rav. He closed his eyes and withdrew, pulled out of her death grip.

And for half an eternity they lay on a travel rug, oblivious to the ants, the magpies steadily gaining ground towards the basket and half-eaten food. Oblivious to everything.

Then she sighed, long and loud.

He was watching again.

Lacey sat up and reached for her shorts, struggled to put them on without standing.

Kerry simply lay back, watching. 'How long have you had the tattoo?' he asked.

'Oh, years. It was a mistake, but Craig liked me wearing low cut clothing. It turned him on. I hate the damned thing, always have. Back in those days, I'd do anything within reason to keep someone happy.' Her voice faded. 'I don't know what would be worse, the tattoo as is, or the scarring if I had it removed.'

Kerry sat up and reached for his undies.

'Did you have this planned?' she asked.

'What?'

'A seduction.'

'No. If I'd planned it there'd be flowers and candlelit dinners and soft music.' And probably complete disaster.

What lay in his eyes now? A promise of better times ahead? After that little encounter, could it get better? she wondered.

'Kerry?'

'Hey—'

'Why did you come out here today?'

'To see you.'

'There's something you should know about me.'

'I know all I need.' He meant it, too. Best not to ruin what remained of the moment.

'Why won't you eat something?' she asked. 'You went to so much trouble.'

What trouble? he thought. Fifteen minutes at the cafe is trouble? 'Tomorrow I will eat. Today I will suffer quietly.'

'No sympathy.'

'I never expected any.' Kerry stared up at the clear blue sky, shielded his eyes with his arm. The world was spinning and the Vitamin B overdose hadn't helped much. Nor had Lacey. She finished dressing and rested her head on his belly, stared up at the sky, too.

After a while he asked, 'Why'd you come to Mallen? You don't seem the type to live here voluntarily.'

'Type?' she asked.

'The only people who stay were born here and know no difference. City's a dirty word. And city people are alien life forms.'

'I needed something new. Like you. Maybe our collective judgments short-circuited when the pen was in hand and the dotted line signed.'

'True.'

'Today I saw what was left of five year's work and I wanted to walk away from it all. I nearly did.'

'I don't blame you.'

'But I never begin anything I can't finish. So I started over. Thoughts changed and moods changed and you came along. Here I lie, wasting valuable time. With anyone else I'd be impatient. Tell them to shove off.'

'Say the word and I'm gone.'

Lacey looked up at the sky and said nothing. He knew she wouldn't tell him to go, now or ever.

'Who's Marguerite?' Kerry asked, at last.

'Why?'

'Curious. She was on that card you gave me.'

'I shoved her off years ago.'

'Tell me about it.'

'Marguerite once lived in an executive town-house apartment with two matching Volvos in the double garage. She had a husband who was a Queen's Counsel and one day she found he wasn't the monogamous, faithful creature she was led to believe. She surprised him for lunch one day. Unfortunately, he was already eating. His secretary at the time took a little more than shorthand. So Marguerite walked out and never looked back. It wasn't worth it, you see. One could say she got tired of being nice to bastards and she's still not very good at it.'

'That's Marguerite's story? Beginning, middle and end?'

'Not quite. She used to be a psychic. Was consulted by police on one or twenty-three different cases. Maybe you heard of her.'

Kerry said nothing. He dared not.

'The time for proving herself to skeptics ended when she came too close to being charged with the murder of a six-year-old girl. So she knows how it feels to be on the wrong end of the stick. She knew far too much about the location of the body, the identity of the person responsible, the way the child died... After being subjected to police laziness, what she called the *you'll do* syndrome, she turned her back on her old life and went bush. Literally.'

'Why refer to yourself as she?'

'Marguerite died five years ago. She's dead in every sense of the word.'

'Why didn't you tell me?' Kerry asked.

'I tried to a couple of times. Maybe I didn't want you to know too soon. And it's not, relevant to the present. I write now, you see. I write, I try to supply the town with fresh organic produce and I put in some hours at the hotel. I'm back where I started, but this time I feel I'm doing something worthwhile. Money and possessions are just tools to help me achieve certain goals. I've lived with money, and I've lived without it. And nothing good comes from exhuming old graves unless one learns never to let past mistakes happen again.'

She was quiet for awhile.

'I had this insane notion that I could go it alone, that I needed no one. I figured we were born alone, we die alone, so it was a natural enough assumption to believe that I could live the rest of my time here alone. There are no problems that way. No one else to blame. No karma to generate. No one to tear your heart out and stomp on it eighty times and hand it back mangled. The first three years were fine, then it slowly dawned that I was wrong. Basing a probable future on past experience just brings more of the same old patterns, old ways. There was no one out here I liked enough to consider even trying again. Until you came along I was beginning to think I should have bought that takeaway at Hutters

Bay.'

The foot Kerry was jiggling ceased all movement. 'Say again?'

'I was going to buy the takeaway at Hutters Bay.'

'I was going to buy the bait shop at Hutters Bay.'

She sat up, quickly. 'You're pulling my leg.'

'Why would I lie?'

'Why didn't you buy the bait shop?'

'I tossed a coin. Mallen won.'

'Really?' she asked, eyes huge.

'Yeah, really,' Kerry said, surprised himself over this coincidental revelation.

'Seems to me the universe has thrown us together for a reason.'

Oh, God, he thought. The universe? What have I got here? Another Annie of the Magnificent New Age? He almost laughed. 'What reason?'

'Hell, I don't know, do you?'

'Maybe we're both good at solving mysteries.'

'Which is the reason you came out here today.'

'I came to see you. Talk. Ask—'

'A few questions. I thought you'd retired.'

'Know what happened to thought, don't you,' he said lightly. 'I got a call from Sean Merrin this morning. He wants my help. Off the record, of course.'

'And you agreed? After what he did to you?'

'He was only doing his job. Plus, I have my own curiosity to satisfy here. Sean's like me. If something feels wrong he won't let go till it's righted to satisfaction. Looking at him is like looking in a mirror.'

'Kerry, are you sure you know what you're doing? I wouldn't trust him.'

'When you talked to him yesterday you said you knew where Elspeth's body was. Is that right?'

'Kerry, you are not a detective any more.'

'Yes, I know. Eadie told me where the body was, too. So Sean and I are going to take a stroll through the swamp. Just him and me. He'll be here about two-thirty. But I did want to see you as well and I need you to believe that.'

'Keep away from that swamp.'

'I knew you'd say that, but I can't.'

'Why not?' Lacey asked.

'Because Elspeth Mackenzie talked to me yesterday outside Dora's place. She walked up to the police car, leant on the window and chatted me up. Now I'm either going crazy or what I saw was real and I don't feel crazy.'

'Are you sure it was Elspeth?'

'As sure as I can be. Her hair was short, she was dressed for... well, need I explain? She wore a bikie's ring on her right hand and she had the same tattoo as you. In the same place. When I think of it, she has the same colored eyes as you.'

'Kerry, she's dead. What you saw wasn't—'

'Real? Bullshit. I know what I saw. I also saw Frank Purvis pick her up in a 76 Kingswood ute. When he was working for me he drove a near-new Toyota. I went back in time, Lacey. I don't know how, or why, but it happened.'

She was very quiet for some time. 'Can I ask you something? Have you been having odd experiences all your life?'

'Odd?'

'Psychic.'

'Who, me?' he asked, and then expertly changed the subject. 'Eadie kept saying Elspeth liked me. If it's true and I think it is, then I hope she'll lead me to the location where her body was dumped. I don't expect you to come but I wouldn't say no if you agreed to. You know more about this stuff than me.'

'Sean told you what I used to do, didn't he?'

'He did some checking on what you'd said, yes. But I wanted to hear it from you.'

'I'm not going near that swamp and I don't want you to, either. Let Sean go. Not you. Trust me, Kerry. Even if Elspeth's remains are found, she won't move on. She died before her life had begun. She can't let go, she doesn't want to. She was a powerful and hypnotic girl alive and she's intensified those qualities in death and believe me, finding a few bones will make no difference. It'll probably make it worse.'

'I don't think so.'

'There's things about that place you don't know. Talk to the older Aboriginals. There's a tribal elder in town. His name's Murrumbingal. He'll tell you all about that swamp. What it does. Why it does.'

'Legend, Dreamtime bullshit? There's a logical explanation.'

'That place is evil, Kerry. It goes against the natural law, the natural order of things. I thought I told you this before. Please talk to Murrumbingal. It was cursed thousands of years ago. Cursed for a reason.'

'Superstitious crap, Lacey.'

'If you want to experience hell on earth, you go right ahead.'

'You don't want me to go to the swamp, fine. Point taken. My choice, girl. I don't give a frog's fart about curses and Aboriginal elders. Once Mackenzie's remains are found there'll be a formal investigation.'

'Kerry, let it go. Don't go near the swamp. It's evil.'

'People are evil. A swamp is a swamp.'

'You're too open, too sensitive. Please, don't go.'

'I'm willing to risk it.'

'I won't say I told you so.' Lacey rose and limped off around the dam to where she'd left her boots and socks. Then she went back to her work.

Kerry repacked the basket, and carried it back to his vehicle. Till Sean Merrin arrived, Kerry helped Lacey drag out fence posts and more tangled wire. She was, he supposed, a little like him—once he'd begun a job, any job, he had to see it through until the end. Lacey barely said a word although she did glance at him now and then. She had her beliefs, he had his. All he need do was overlook this little hiccup.

'You're really going to do it.'

'Yep.'

'Don't take your car. Let him take you.'

'Why?'

'Would you at least do something for me? Don't take your car. Leave it here, please. Keys in it.'

Kerry held his hands up. 'Okay, if that's what you want.'

She took no notice of his partial surrender. Kerry did not like the way she was looking at him—through him, around him, beside him. Her gaze was enough to freeze boiling oil. 'What?' he asked.

'Fire,' was all she said.

'What about it?'

'Your worst fear is fire.'

How the hell did she know that?

'That place feeds off fear.'

Kerry didn't say a word till Sean arrived in his wife's new hatch. Once, it had been white, now it was streaked with bright ochre colored bull dust. He sat in the passenger side and said, 'Get me outa here, will you?'

Lacey ignored Sean's attempt at a friendly hello—it wasn't the first, wouldn't be the last. She watched until the car turned left at the mailbox before she went back to work and whispered one word: Fools.

Kerry looked over at the swamp as they approached. It stood as a dead oasis across the heat-ravaged and semi-desert ground. Crown land. No one wanted it, not even the Aboriginals. It occupied about two, maybe three acres. To the north lay four square kilometers of salt wasteland. The prison site.

'No wonder the tribes don't want it. Don't fancy this myself, mate.' That was about all Sean had to say as the car continued on the wide, rough sweep around the swamp. The road wasn't used very often. On the left, Kilder's property boundary, on the right, grey reeds, ghost gums, wilga, river trees, paper barks, all dead from feet soaked in foul black water which never evaporated.

Lacey's underground river must surface here, Kerry thought. The place smelled like a sewer pit and was as welcoming to strangers as a white face in the Metro on a Saturday night. But both men had scoured through worse, looking for worse. If Elspeth Mackenzie's body was in this swamp, it'd only be a few bones. It wouldn't be as bad as searching for a decaying, sunken corpse.

'What was that you said?' Sean asked.

'What? I didn't say anything.'

'No, you said something. I heard something.'

Sean was about to stop his wife's car on the side of the corrugated road when all power, including electrics, drained, and the hatch, seemingly unpowered, drifted backwards, ignoring handbrake, drifting backwards evermore along a gentle incline until it finally stopped. What was this? Some kind of geomagnetic phenomenon?

Kerry felt someone in the back seat—a presence—and for a moment, he thought he heard someone breathing, too. Slowly, he turned. Nothing was there.

Sean had obviously felt something, too, but it was overridden by a tinge of fear mixed with confusion. He'd never had a car do this and was searching his mind for a cause. A reason.

Kerry looked at the swamp and knew the reason. Someone, something, whispered into his ear: *Get out of the car.*

Had he been watching a movie, he would have laughed.

Get out of the car, now!

Kerry obeyed. Sean pulled the bonnet latch and emerged.

Walk away, now. Quick!

'Sean? Sean, I think we better—'

Before he could finish, the car's battery exploded. For a moment they both thought someone had taken a potshot at them. Kerry was sure it hadn't been he who'd pushed Merrin away from the bonnet. But he was blamed for it. 'What the? How?'

Run!

Kerry pulled Sean to his feet and started running. A few seconds later the electrics caught. Kerry was gaining on a new sprint record when the fuel tank ignited and spewed out bright orange flames and thick, choking black smoke. And in the distance he heard the sound of a familiar car approaching. When the dust settled, he recognized his Rav, stopping a hundred yards away. But Lacey would drive no further. They had to walk to it.

Merrin, white-faced, could repeat only a few words: 'She's gonna kill me. She's gonna kill me,' as he looked back at what remained of his wife's new car.

For a moment, Kerry wondered which 'she' he was referring to. 'You okay?' he asked.

No reply except, 'She's gonna kill me.'

'I'll drive you home, mate. I think we'll give this a miss for today.'

Sean was too agitated to disagree.

Lacey didn't have to say I told you so. Kerry already knew.

CHAPTER 8

Kerry had almost forgotten what it was like to sit in a family home, at a dinner table, and soak in the distinct pleasures of being around youngsters.

Sean's wife had taken the news of what had become of her car as well as could be expected. Kerry sensed that the true verbal confrontation would begin the moment he left to return to Mallen. Which was why Sean was taking every conceivable opportunity to entice Kerry to stay, just a little longer.

Barbara Merrin seemed to be the type who would empty the contents of the crockery shelf at whoever was an unwilling target. She was a mousey, thin lady with pretty eyes—her only redeeming feature. Kerry studied the three kids and wondered where the two girls and one boy got their looks. The division of chromosomes had been favorable for all three.

Barbara was as tough as any police wife had ever been. She was used to strangers at the table, immune to the talk. So were the kids. The smallest, a girl whom Kerry guessed was about three, kept staring at him. The other two fought, grizzled about having to eat at the table, not in front of the TV. If Barbara knew of Kerry's arrest, she said nothing. Her attention was focused on one bright star hovering on the horizon of the near future—returning to civilization. She hated the bush as much as Annie would have.

'Kerry used to work with Demetri and Allan,' Sean said.

'What do you want? A medal or sympathy?' Barbara asked in reply, directing her question to Kerry.

'Some more of your lasagna would do,' Kerry said with a smile. Then she talked about lasagna and the origins of the recipe—some knife-wielding Italian woman. Eventually Sean said, 'They'll probably find it when the construction begins and they drain the swamp.'

'Find what?' Barbara asked.

'A body in the swamp. Just out of Mallen.'

'Is that where you went? Is that where you took my car?'

'Ah, yes.'

Kerry hardly listened to the accusations of broken promises. Well, Sean had promised not to take it over 120 and wash it when he got it home. There was nothing in the conditions that specified he couldn't accidentally incinerate it. And it being insured was not the point of the confrontation yet to come, either. It was the first decent car she'd had in ten years and it had taken ten years of part-time work...

Kerry pulled faces at the little girl, tried not to hear the rest of the argument. And he definitely refused to take sides.

After Kerry had eaten and declined yet another offer of a beer, hell, he could stay the night if he wanted, Sean reluctantly walked Kerry out to his car. The sun was setting and that was the reason for lingering an extra hour: Heading south-west into the blinding summer set of the sun, with too many large red kangaroos and road trains on the narrow, one-lane bitumen. Plus his hangover still lingered on the edges.

Merrin found yet another excuse not to go in and face his wife, who'd learnt more than recipes from her knife-wielding Italian friend.

'There's a few things I think you should know,' Sean said quietly.

Kerry knew the tone too well. He leaned against his car and folded his arms, waiting.

'Not all forensics are back yet, but time of death was between 4.00 and 6.00 a.m. Frank left a calling card and so had one other that night. We've got an 0 positive and an A negative. Purvis was A negative.'

Kerry was 0 negative.

'One partial print on the headboard of the bed indicates that whoever was there that night had traces of an olive oil-based cream on their skin. Perfumes also indicate it was most likely a cosmetic used by women.'

'What are you getting at?'

'Initially I thought it was a rape and murder. Now I'm not so sure. Personally, I think Ross was done by a woman. Maybe a gay woman. We found strands of blonde hair on the other pillow. Ross, as you know, wasn't blonde.'

'What are you saying here?' Kerry asked.

'How well do you know Lacey Kilder?'

'Oh, for Christ's sake.' Kerry got into his car and slammed the door. He turned the key in the ignition. Sean tapped on the window and indicated for him to roll it down. Against his better judgment, Kerry did. The car idled.

'Lacey's grandmother lived in Mallen. Elspeth Mackenzie was her cousin,' Sean added.

No deceit was present in Sean's eyes, just discomfort at relating news he knew wouldn't be digested easily.

'Her grandmother's name was Florence Lebsanft. She died in 1988. The property was called Rosehaven in those days. Now it's Rainbow Farm. Kilder bought it from her grandmother's estate. Look, I'm only telling you this because I took some hair from a hairbrush in Lacey's house yesterday when I was there. I have to close this fucking thing, Kerry. It's driving me insane.'

'You're barking up the wrong tree, Merrin.'

'People in Mallen I talked to told me the girls were an item.'

'That's bullshit.'

'Lacey's gay, mate. Twenty-eight people cannot be wrong.'

If Lacey was gay, Kerry was the Fairy Queen. 'First me, now her? You're gonna go through the entire town like a dose of salts, aren't you? Have you eliminated the cosmetics in Eadie's house? Have you eliminated her prints yet?'

Sean nodded. 'And there's something else. Lacey was visiting her grandmother at the time of Mackenzie's disappearance. Ask her. Ask her about the four years she spent in funny farms. You want proof? I have it. She's a diagnosed paranoid schizophrenic, Kerry. On medication, sure. But,' and he emphasized the word, 'she was charged with manslaughter a few years ago. It was thrown out of court at the committal. She had a QC on her case. A QC she later married.'

'Manslaughter? Who?'

'A male nurse when she was seventeen. Then she did an about face and accused one staff member of rape and two others of indecent assault while she was in.'

Kerry didn't want to know.

Sean stood on the footpath and watched the Rav disappear into the setting sun.

Kerry made the two hour journey home in one and a quarter. For a while he blocked all thought and emotion. It had been years since he felt this empty. Then faces continually replayed scenes in his mind's eye. Going down that narrow hallway, seeing the light from under the bathroom door. Calling out, keeping the old lady from next door away. Three kicks later the privacy lock shattered. Frightened eyes of a teenage girl, then the movement, so quick that he too had been cut. But he didn't realize it until later. Fright became terror, then it faded to despair as he saved the life she tried so hard to end; as he told her that nothing was worth dying for.

But she came very close.

Four years in a psyche ward for a botched suicide? Charged with manslaughter at seventeen? But why would she tell him? Why would she tell anyone? Her words echoing once again, *Kerry, there's something you should know about me.*

I know enough.

'Paranoid schizophrenic, my arse,' he whispered. Seeing things and hearing voices? Did that mean he was in line for a rubber room as well? No. He couldn't swallow that comfortably. She'd helped solve too many impossible cases as a psychic consultant. Merrin knew that but chose to overlook it. What had she said that day? Basing probable future on past experience? Merrin was grasping, that's all it was. Grasping. Blonde hairs on a pillow in Eadie Ross's bedroom. Lotion from one partial print. Purvis was a plumber. He'd most likely use some kind of lotion after he'd been crawling around in pipes, outlets. Merrin was desperate for a closure before his transfer. But too many traces of the past played like some heartless montage through Kerry's mind, any conceivable thing that one human being could do to another came as a reminder that anything, anything at all, was possible. People never ceased to surprise him. Some even shocked him. But Lacey? No, not her.

He didn't know what time it was, nor did he know how long he left the Rav idling at the five-ways on Weir Road. To the left was Starks Road and the swamp. Ahead, infinity. Right was home. If it could be called home after such a short time that felt like years. It was ten minutes to Lacey's. Two home.

An eighteen-wheeler stopped behind him, hit the air horn. Kerry raised a solitary finger and turned right. The semi pulled out towards infinity, crossed the river. Kerry couldn't go anywhere. He had a business to run, a few hours of sleep to catch before the alarm woke him and routine began again.

If anything could ever be the same again. But what was living if it was not full of change? If it hadn't been for Lacey's assistance he'd still be staring at the unpainted ceiling of Wilton watch-house, not pulling into his drive, parking beside his house, being greeted by a leaping Siamese cat that thought it was a dog.

Yang won the race to the front door. The verandah was littered with feathers. He'd been out hunting again, grew tired of waiting for the can of Whiskas. He looked terribly pleased with himself, though. The cat went in first, jumped on to the recliner and settled for the night. Or at least, he'd stay there until Kerry went to bed.

Kerry opened the fridge. There wasn't a lot to see except for half of

Ella's casserole with the Welcome Home note taped to the plastic film. Half a chocolate block. Seven beers. Kerry broke off a wedge of chocolate and headed for the bathroom. The mirror over the new basin reflected a face that looked as old and tired as Kerry felt. Yang jumped onto the basin and sat there awhile, yowling. He stretched out and a cold nose touched Kerry's chin. 'Yeah, you love me. I know. Fool.'

Kerry slipped the plug into the tub, switched on the taps and emptied half a packet of bath salts in until the water bubbled and churned a deep sea-green and hid that awful stain from view.

The cat watched him strip. 'What the hell are you staring at?' he asked as he kicked his jocks into the corner and waited for the bath to fill. But the cat kept staring. Not at him, rather, through him. Kerry had never known this to happen before. What'd it mean? Was he going to die? Meet with an accident? The stare was anchoring his guilt in paranoia.

'I know I owe her. I know I should at least tell her that she's a suspect. It's bullshit, pal. She's not gay, is she?' The cat just watched. He normally replied to any question. 'It's just talk. She wouldn't come across for any of the local dipsticks so she's got to be gay. It's just talk.'

Silence.

'Right?'

The cat finally yowled an affirmative. Kerry stepped into the tub. It was six feet long, narrow and deep. Kerry was six two. His feet were always upended on the opposite end of any tub he'd had. Till now. He lay back, sighed, felt his body relax. Blue walls, white ceiling. Should be reversed, he thought.

Yang jumped to the edge of the tub and braked when he saw the water so dangerously close. He was way too vocal tonight.

'What the hell's the matter with you, fool?'

The cat sat there, his thin, long body balanced precariously on a tub ledge four centimeters wide.

'What?' Kerry asked, again. He felt like some nut case actor asking a famous collie questions. Unfortunately this wasn't scripted, therefore Kerry had no idea what the cat was yowling about. So expressively, which made it worse. He'd heard that Siamese were loud and enjoyed conversations but this fool was worse than a nagging woman tonight.

'Piss off out of it.' Kerry sent a double handful of water at the animal and the cat leapt to the vanity basin, licked his coat and sent a death stare in return.

Kerry closed his eyes and couldn't recall the last time he'd had a bath he almost fitted in, let alone time enough to enjoy a soak without the phone ringing. No one called these days. The phone was as silent as a grave. Mallen as a place was even quieter, so quiet it was near comatose...

Fog rolled in across the lake. He looked over the side, the water was murky. Annie was in the boat, a little grey rowboat. She was rowing. He lay back, watching. He always liked watching Annie. The faces she pulled, the things she could do with her foot under a dinner table if the conversation got too boring, the laughter in her eyes promised quietly, later... later...

Catch me if you can. Her favorite game. The foot was touching him again. Toes gently pinching the inner thighs. Toes exploring.

The boat rocked a little, side to side, when she moved. The water was cool on his fingertips as he lay back again, open to the world, open to Annie. Laughing, boisterous Annie. His gypsy Madonna. Soft touches and small wet kisses from practiced hands and mouth and tongue, knowing what he liked, when, how, maybe even why. Who could tell with Annie? He reached down and touched her head. She didn't break rhythm. He curled his fingers in her hair and quietly begged her not to stop, never stop, don't... don't stop. The peak came too quick, too soon, too painful. And she wouldn't stop. Annie, no, no that's enough. But the hand reached out blindly for his face. Fingernails caught his lip, his chin. Burned a stinging trail down his chest. Annie! He pulled the head back.

It wasn't Annie.

He felt the rising scream but he wouldn't wake. The boat turned. Capsized. He couldn't find a way out. Something, someone, was holding him down, pushing him down. And laughter filtered in from the edges of an abyss. Laughter, like small kids playing.

Then, a miracle. The phone rang.

The weight lifted and Kerry struggled up from the bottom of the tub with a spluttering gasp. Able to breathe now, terror dissipating, he jumped out of the tub, grabbed a towel and opened the bathroom door. But no cat was there to shoot across his bare feet. There was no cat anywhere.

Still biting back a fit of coughing, Kerry wrapped the towel around his waist and answered the phone, pleased for the first time in his life that it had rung. He never thought anyone could be killed by a dream. A wet dream at that. Kids drowned in bathtubs, not thirty-eight-year-olds.

'Staines,' he managed to gasp.

'Kerr-ie?'

'Yo.'

'Lacey would be with you, non?' Emile sounded agitated. Very agitated.

'No, sorry, Emile. She's not here.'

'It is just that, well, how do I say? She did not appear for work tonight and I had thought she may have been with you for she is not answering her phone. It is unlike her not to call. I am, well, I am very concerned.'

'Can't help you, mate. Sorry.' Kerry put the phone down and noticed the cat asleep in his normal curl on the recliner. He wouldn't have dried that quick. And he couldn't slip through walls or closed doors, either.

Kerry whistled. Yang usually acknowledged a whistle with his presence, hungry or not. The tail flipped four times. Odd, very odd. Minutes ago he was trying to crawl up Kerry's nose.

Kerry touched his face. His chest. He looked. Three scratches, not of cat claws. Fingernails.

'Was it any good?'

He spun. The voice came from behind but nothing was there. He felt suddenly cold. The temperature in the room seemed to have dropped twenty degrees. A clammy hand touched his neck. Kerry tried to slap it away, unfortunately he was slapping at cold air.

'I said, was it any good?'

'Elspeth?'

Laughter echoed. Giggling. Kerry couldn't trace its origins.

'Elspeth, why can't you leave me alone?'

'I don't usually do this, Kerry, and I'm only doing it because I like you. If I was you I'd go and see Mags. Right now.'

'Who?' he asked aloud, but still he couldn't see anything.

'Mags.'

'Who's Mags?'

'Marguerite. I think she needs you.'

Then there was nothing. The wave of static dispersed and with it, Elspeth.

Kerry dressed, wondering when she'd come back. If she was watching. What she wanted.

Mainly, he wondered what she wanted. He searched his wallet for that card Lacey had given him weeks ago.

He dialed her number, but it rang out. He dialed again. It rang out six times. A phone ringing constantly for twelve minutes would be enough to make anyone answer.

If they're alive to hear it.

The laughter again.

Kerry grabbed his car keys. The feeling that had struck him the moment he touched Eadie Ross's back door had returned. Stronger than ever. He knew what it meant. He'd lived with it long enough to know.

He hesitated at the gate to Rainbow Farm—Rosehaven, as it was once known. The house was not visible from the road. Kerry rolled over the first grid, the second. Lights illuminated the patch and he glimpsed just how much work Lacey had accomplished in his absence that day. The fence was removed, the entire plot ploughed under. No trace of Frank's escape attempt remained. The homestead was in total darkness. Lacey's bike was in its place by the side gate.

Kerry stopped his car and expected to see a light illuminate one room. He looked at the time. Nine fifty. The dog didn't bark as he opened the gate and walked down the path. The cockatoo was also silent.

'Lacey?' he called.

Nothing.

The back door was open, the screen door locked. 'Lacey?' his voice echoed. He seemed to have experienced this before. Days ago. Kerry punched through the nylon fly mesh, unlocked the door. He fell over a mountain of sheets by the door, kicked a new packet of laundry detergent across the floor. Kerry found the light switch and wished he hadn't.

A twister had been though. Plates and glasses shattered not to pieces but powder. And the front door was off its hinges. Kerry stepped over the mess and found the floodlight on the front verandah. Lacey was lying, unconscious, at the bottom of the stairs, amid the roses. Roses that yesterday had been blooming. Now they were withered and brown. Dead.

Wasn't it Elspeth who hated flowers?

'Lacey?' He took a step down. The railing was loose, barely hanging. What the hell had happened here? The old dog sat nearby, teeth bared.

'Like her, don't you.'

Kerry froze. He didn't turn around. He knew who it was. He also knew now that the best tactic in this situation was to ignore it. It wasn't real. It wasn't happening. Elspeth Mackenzie was dead, and dead was dead.

'I said you like her, don't you.'

Kerry didn't react. But he couldn't move, either.

'I know you can hear me. I know you can see me. Come on, turn around and look. I know you want to see. Seen my tattoo up close? I've got two more, you know. But it'll cost you to see those two.'

Anger rose. Anger at himself for not being able to ignore the voice. He knew who it was standing in the open doorway directly behind him. No, not who. What. This time though, he knew she had a form. Not just a disembodied voice. 'You are not here. You are not real.'

The old dog was snarling now, but, Kerry noted, she wasn't snarling at him. The old dog saw the thing behind him, too.

'Christ, you make me laugh. You try so hard to be the good guy. You got no chance. I know what you are. What you've done. What you want and what you're doing here. He was right, Kerry. That cop was right. She *is* a dyke. She likes the girls. She loved Eadie. At least twice a week they got it on.'

'Go back where you belong. You're not supposed to be here.' He searched his memory, vainly, for all that crap Annie used to go on with. Light. Yes, that was it. Light.

'What would I want with light? It never done me any good. Forget the light, honey. I'm here now.'

Kerry could hear the footsteps. Real feet on wood. Coming closer. The old dog was frantic now but stood her ground, close to Lacey, protecting her. Kerry was determined not to look, not to show any fear. That, apparently, was the worst thing to do, because things like this fed on fear. Grew stronger from it.

'You couldn't do it, could you? You couldn't stop them dying. All you had to say was, don't go. But you didn't. Too proud to beg and they all died, didn't they? All of them. Even the baby. Yes, I know all about that. I know all about you. If you weren't pissed, you were stoned and if you weren't stoned you were… you had a problem, honey-bunny. A major, A1 problem. No wonder they were happy to see the last of you. But you still have a few uses, don't you?'

'You are not real.'

But the hand on the back of his neck certainly was. The hand caressing his neck, the hand slipping into his shirt sure was. It was warm. Soft. 'All you had to say was don't go. That's all she wanted to hear. But no, you watched them get on that bus.'

Even the breath was sweet. Too sweet.

'You're not real. You're not scaring me.' He resisted the attempt to turn his face to enable gazes to meet. He took one step down, towards Lacey. Elspeth Mackenzie appeared on the ground below. Just as he'd seen her yesterday. Young, beautiful. Dangerous. The old dog was attacking, but grasping at nothing.

'I told her not to. Warned her she'd only get herself hurt again, but she didn't listen.'

'You're not real.'

'I told her not to but she did.'

'You're not real.'

'I told you not to go near the swamp but you did.'

'You're not real!'

'I saved your life today,' she sang. 'I saved your life today and all you can do is say I'm not real? Do you know what real is? This is real. Me. See? See me?' She walked up the stairs towards him. One slow step at a time. 'Want to see what they did to me?'

'You're not real!'

'Look at me, Kerry! See what the bastards did to me!'

And with each step, her appearance altered.

'No!' Kerry, attempting to get away, fell backwards and had to fight to stop himself tumbling down the stairs and into the thing that approached. 'You're not real, you're not real!'

'Look what they did to me! I want someone to know what they did to me!'

She was one step below now, the stench was overpowering. 'You're not real, this is not happening!'

The hand of a once-beautiful young woman caressed his face.

'It only hurt for a little while. But they sat around, drinking. Left me there. Tied to a fucking tree. But now it don't hurt at all. I got them. Well, I got most of them. I ain't never letting them go, either. *She* thinks I should. Not me, though. I like having fun. And I like you.'

'What'd you do to her?' He looked at Elspeth again. The face was pretty now.

'Me? I didn't do anything.'

'Elspeth, why are you doing this to us? What have we done to you?'

No reply. The shape changed into a grey, swirling vortex and it flew at him so quickly he could not move aside. It caught his face and pushed him backwards up the stairs, so fast that he hit the door frame and bounced off it. Then it was gone.

Kerry felt nothing except the still, the incredible quiet, the empty silence. Dazed, he wondered where he was, why he was there. Then memory returned. Beside him, the door was off its hinges. The twister of Elspeth's anger. And Lacey amid her grandmother's dead roses. The dog had stopped its snarling. Soft, confused eyes stared at him. And the tail wagged.

Stumbling to his feet, Kerry took the stairs down, two at a time. The old dog licked her face, his hand. Kerry pushed it away. 'Lacey?' No reaction. He touched. Her face was lacerated, bruised. Blue eyes opened, tried to focus for a lost moment. She tried to talk, but nothing emerged.

Nothing that made sense, but not a lot made sense anyway. He didn't move her until he was confident there was no spinal damage and when he gently eased her over, she screamed at the movement because her left arm was broken.

He carried her upstairs. Her left eye was black, and breathing was not easy. He saw a multitude of scratches and bleeding lacerations, raw, swollen. 'It's okay. She's gone.'

'Be back—'

'Why? What the hell does she want?'

'You. Go home. Please? Go now?'

'No. No, I'm not going to let her win.'

'Go home! Forget you ever met me!' Crying now.

'Lacey? Lacey!'

She quieted for a moment and looked into his eyes. He had no intention of leaving, now or ever. It should have been comforting, but it wasn't.

'Listen to me. I have never voluntarily turned away from anything in my life and I refuse to be dictated to by some dead nympho with an ego problem. I have a right to live the way I want and no one, dead or alive, is going to interfere with that. She knows it. So don't you make this any harder than it already is by telling me to go when you know damned well that's the last thing either of us needs right now Whether you like it or not, I'm taking you in to Martinelli.'

'No.'

He ignored her and headed for her bathroom. And he took a moment to inspect the array of female necessities spread across the shelf under the bathroom mirror. A hand lotion. Olive oil based. He opened the bottle. The scent was light and lingering. He looked at it.

And Lacey watched from the door.

'What are you looking for?' she asked. Kerry turned. She was holding the regulation ice pack of frozen peas to her face.

'First aid kit?' he lied.

'In the cupboard.'

Kerry found the box, opened it and inspected the contents. 'Go sit down and don't argue with me.'

He tended her face first. Lacey said nothing, she simply stared into his dark eyes, reacting only when the antiseptic stung. The left forearm could have been fractured, sprained at the very least. She had partial movement of her fingers.

'You fuss too much.'

'I wasn't thrown down eighteen stairs into roses, was I? Move your fingers for me.' She tried. 'You'd better see Martinelli.'

'No.'

Kerry looked into her eyes.

'No,' she repeated.

'Don't like doctors?'

'Kerry, isn't there somewhere else you could be? There're forty-five other women in town who could really use this attention.'

'You need me more. I need to be needed,' he joked.

She said nothing else until he finished cleaning the cuts and wrapped her arm tight, perfect herringbones, three bandages thick. Then he made a sling. Once her left arm was bandaged and suspended, the pain lessened.

'You used to be a paramedic who flew in choppers.'

'Yep.'

'Air-sea rescue?'

Kerry pushed a glass of brandy towards her. 'Medicinal purposes only. Get it into you.'

Lacey sipped it, felt the immediate rush of warmth.

'I'll come back tomorrow and put the door back up. Needs new hinges.'

'Needs a new door. It's been warped for as long as I can remember. Grandma used to keep it jammed. If you wanted to go out to the verandah you'd have to go through her bedroom. The room was a child's nightmare, so it was easier to go downstairs, walk right around. I never liked this place very much when I was a kid. But once it was empty and repainted... I knocked a few walls out and I'm still working on the skylight. The rate I'm going, I'll be fifty before I get it right.'

Talking. Chatting. But the eyes were devoid of anything except pain. She couldn't hide it that well.

'Who beat you?' Kerry asked, as if by a touch he knew.

'It was ... it was Elspeth,' she lied. And he knew it was a lie.

'How about I drive you in to Dr Martinelli?'

'No.'

'Lacey, please.'

'No!'

He poured her another brandy and this time poured one for himself. Lacey rubbed her hair and stared at the table top, aware of Kerry's gaze, of all his unvoiced questions. Her answers could help him to understand her better—what she was. What she'd once been. What she still was. Frightened, untrusting.

'What's been said about me now?' she asked.

'To me? Nothing.'

'But you hear things.'

'I hear.' But he didn't want to say.

'I want you to go now.'

'I don't want to.'

'I don't want you here.'

'In case whoever did this comes back?'

'Something like that.'

'That arm needs attention, girl.'

'If I promise to see Martinelli in the morning, will you go? Please? You have to start work soon.'

'Have you got anything to help you sleep?'

'In the bathroom cabinet.'

He went back in and opened the sliding mirror doors on the small wall cupboard. The Pill, paracetamol, cream for dermatitis, a bottle of Serepax almost out of date and a bottle of chlorpromazine. Chlorpromazine for schizophrenia. Kerry opened the Serepax, shook two out. And he wouldn't leave until she'd taken them, until she'd allowed him to put her to bed.

He sat there a little too long, a thousand questions left unvoiced. She faded off into sleep, and only then did he comply with her wishes.

But outside at his car, Kerry stood motionless, unable to think properly. He looked up into the bright, star-lit sky and wondered. Perhaps he wondered too much, for in the end, he went home to shower, change and face the mixers and ovens once more. Not one moment passed when he didn't think of that girl.

But it wasn't Lacey on his mind.

CHAPTER 9

He knew she was in the bathroom with him, watching. And he knew she was two steps behind him during the walk to work. The presence was so close he imagined she was touching him—a hand on his shoulder as he opened the back door of the old bakery.

Once inside he felt alone. Alone and safe. He hit the light. Nothing happened. Fumbling in the darkness, he parted the venetian blinds. Moonlight filtered in. The street lights were on in High Street. There was no power failure. Fuses? Kerry cursed to himself, groped blindly towards the cupboard where the emergency light waited—an old kero lantern. A couple of candles. Fuse wire. He didn't particularly want to venture out into the dark again towards the tiny outhouse where the antiquated diesel generator resided. Making sure it wasn't just a blown bulb, he tried the lights in the shop front. Nothing. The radio with the inactive cassette player was also dead. But it had backup batteries. He flicked it to DC mode. Nothing.

Kerry spat a series of curses in triplicate. He was running late. He looked at his watch. Even it had stopped. Only one thing could have been responsible for this. Bloody Elspeth again. He knew that no amount of fuse wire would assist him now. 'Look, Elspeth, I know you're here. Give me a break. I need some power.'

'Come with me, Kerry. You'll have all the power you want.'

He turned to the voice behind him. Sitting beside the mixer, Elspeth. Aged eighteen again. Short blonde hair, long legs, and bright blue eyes. He wasn't shocked to see her, either. Just annoyed. At first.

She had a ladle in hand and was rubbing it against her thigh, down her leg. She cast him a look he wished he'd never seen. His mouth went dry.

'I know what you're thinking.' She threw the ladle to him. He caught it. 'You think I did that to Mags. But it wasn't me. Cross my heart, it wasn't me.'

'Fine. It wasn't you. Turn the power back on, please.'

She got off the bench and walked towards him. The kerosene lantern threw her shadow up the wall. And the closer she got, the more intense the static charge became. It was so strong that every cell on his skin, every hair on his body, was prickling. 'I know who it was, though,' she said and reached out to touch the old tee shirt Kerry wore. It depicted a marijuana leaf. He stepped back, he didn't like her getting too close. She stopped. 'You're scared of me,' she said, confusion in her bright eyes. 'Why?'

'Jesus, Elspeth—'

'You're scared of me because you think I'm dead.'

Kerry said nothing. Why argue with the truth?

'Dead, alive, there's no difference. I can do things you can't and vice versa.'

'What are you gonna do now?' he asked, trying hard to maintain a semblance of composure. It used to come naturally under the most extraordinary circumstances. But the trait had departed, quickly, forever. Elspeth touched her face, ran long nails through her hair. Very long fingernails He looked at her bare feet. The nails there, too, were long. Claw-like.

She turned away. 'Just thought I'd tell you what happened out there because she won't. She won't 'cos she's scared of him, see. But I chased him away before he beat her too bad. Threw some knives, plates, stuff like that. Made a good show to get rid of him. He left. Pretty quick, too. But the bastard doesn't hear me like you do. Makes it hard sometimes when people don't hear me. Can't see me. So when someone does, I make the most of it.'

'Who are you talking about?'

'Lenny.'

'Sergeant Gilmeister?'

'Yeah. He beat the shit out of Mags. I could have got him good but your mates would have locked her up for it, like they did to you. So I didn't.'

'You're going to get Lenny because he's the only one left?'

'Yes and no. There's another. And when you find out who it is you'll know who really did Eadie.'

'Is Eadie with you, too?'

'No, she's gone somewhere else.' Confusion crossed the girl's eyes.

'Who killed her?'

'You'll find out.'

'Jesus, Elspeth!'

'Oh, come on. I know what you're really here for. What you going to say? A spook told me?'

Kerry sighed.

She smiled.

'You're not making any sense.'

'Sense? Me?'

Why, now, was she being half decent? Did mental health issues run unchecked in her family line and carry the debilitation long after death?

She looked at him as if catching his thoughts and she grinned. 'I like the way your mind works, so how come you still can't figure me out?'

'I'd like to be friends with you, Elspeth, but you'll have to—'

'Have to? Have to is bullshit!'

'No! You hear me? No! This has got to stop! You have to stop this crap. You're dead. You shouldn't even be here.'

'You think I don't know that?'

Kerry wanted to run, but she'd only follow, as close as a thought, as quick as a heartbeat. From her there was no escape. 'What do you want from me?' he asked.

'No one's ever said no to me before.'

'Which is probably why you died the way you did. Shit, girl, don't you know what a pack of dogs is like? One mind, Elspeth. One mind. Those boys who took you to the swamp that night were of one mind, too, but you realized that too late. There was no way out, was there? You were nothing from the moment you agreed to go. You weren't Elspeth Mackenzie any more. Just a lump of meat. With no name, no identity. You were nothing.'

She didn't reply, nor did she look at him.

'I know where you were coming from. Hear me? I said were, not are. I've known people just like you.'

She looked up, half ashamed, half interested.

'You spent your life looking for love the wrong bloody way, girl. But it's over, and it's time you went on.'

'I like it here.'

'No. You stay around here because you want revenge. Revenge never ends. This will never end until you want something better.'

'I want you.'

'You can't have me. Not the way you want.'

There was a long silence during which Kerry was under scrutiny.

'You cannot stop what's meant to be. I like Lacey a lot and you'd better get used to that idea. Your time's gone. Gone. And even if I'd known you years ago I wouldn't have touched you. I would have been your friend, Elspeth. Only your friend. Now, I've got work to do, and I'd like you to turn the power back on because I've got a town to feed and frankly, you're giving me the shits right now.'

Elspeth seemed uncomfortable, disturbed. 'You would have been my friend?' There was nothing but child-like wonder in her voice.

'If you'd let me, and if you'd stop this behavior, I *will* be your friend. But you can't keep this up. You can't invade my privacy. Or scare the shit out of people any more. Especially me. Is that understood?'

She considered his offer but God only knew what she decided.

'I'll talk to Gilmeister. Rattle him a little.'

Her eyes smiled before it touched her mouth. A lovely mouth, Kerry noticed, then he realized that it used to be a lovely mouth.

'You think you'll find him?'

'I know I will.'

She laughed at that. 'Alive?'

'What do you mean?'

'You'll find out, Sherlock.'

'Look, you can stay and watch as long as you like, providing you sit there and be quiet. But you'll have to give me back my electricity. Please.'

Elspeth resumed her place beside the mixer and Kerry was relieved to find the electricity restored. A wave of bright surging light hurt his eyes, then resumed normal intensity.

In full artificial light, he could only see her in vague peripherals. His heart was ninety to the minute as he turned the radio on and sang very, very loud for the next forty-five minutes. As he expected, she soon became bored, and her presence faded. Only then he breathed normally again and stopped fighting the shakes. Was she really gone? Would she reappear at any moment? It seemed not.

He needed to talk to someone, anyone. But who? The only person who came to mind was Lacey, who talked to Elspeth, too, and had to take chlorpromazine because of it.

Maybe, he thought, I could go to Martinelli, say I'm hearing voices, seeing things, and chlorpromazine might block reception. And maybe, he thought, I'm open to her for another reason. But who would believe this anyway except someone else who'd experienced the same thing?

It was 3.00 a.m. Another two hours till daylight.

As the minutes passed, and his fear dissipated, the entire experience seemed an hallucination. An episodic aberration that began on his first night in Mallen. And now he was offering to make peace with a ghost?

Kerry fired the ovens, made a very strong coffee and took out his order sheets. Once filled, he'd fax them through to his supplier.

By the time the fax was engaged, he'd all but forgotten Elspeth's visit. One thought nagged. What if she was right? What if Gilmeister had visited Rainbow Farm?

He rang Lacey at 7.45 a.m. Twice. There was no answer. The shop was busy for the next hour and a half and during a lull at 9.15, she answered, cautiously.

'It's Kerry. I need to talk to you.'

There was silence for a little while. 'We can meet in the park by the river at about 2.00 p.m. if you want.'

The park by the river? What'd she think that was? Safe, neutral territory? Hadn't she listened to him last night? 'Lacey, are you okay?'

'I'll live.'

'Seen the doctor yet?'

'Kerry—'

'Look, it's past nine, I'm allowed to nag.'

'Park at two. Don't be late because if you're not there, I won't wait.' She hung up.

Kerry stared at the ancient wall phone momentarily before he mumbled, 'Shit.' The sensor at the door screamed. He parted the plastic ribbon curtain dividing the shop front from the bakery. Dora was waiting, without her normal bubbly smile. He felt more than saw the pain in her eyes but he said nothing while the routine transaction occurred. She was offering him nothing today which was unusual, so he asked, 'Bad news?'

Dora looked up into his eyes. 'I had a phone call last night. From a woman. She said she knew where my boy was. My Jack. Said she knew why he disappeared. Who would do that?' she asked, voice trembling.

One name came to Kerry immediately. 'What was said exactly?'

The handkerchief in the ex-teacher's hand was clenched tight. 'She said she knew where his body was. In the swamp with that Mackenzie girl.'

Kerry was on the other side of the counter before he realized he'd moved. 'Has anything like this ever happened before?'

'I'm not sure.'

'You're not sure?'

'After Jackie went missing a lot of strange things happened but it's been such a long time, Kerry. Why now? Why is it all starting again?'

What to say except, 'If she calls again, hang up immediately. Don't talk to her.'

'There's something else. But it's so, it's so—'

'What, Dora?'

'She asked if this was 127.'

'127?'

'It was my old number before 1985 when the automatic exchange was put in.'

'But if she'd rung 127 there'd be no connection.'

'My phone rang, Kerry. It rang. And it was Elspeth Mackenzie talking to me. I know it was. It's happening again.'

Kerry put his arms around her, half inclined to ask more, but knowing he shouldn't. He needed to tell her that he too was haunted by Elspeth but sharing a burden didn't necessarily alleviate suffering. After a little while, he drew Mrs Mallaby away. 'Dora, now mightn't be the time, but would you consider working here for me?'

A sparkle lit the woman's eyes.

'Award wages, say from twelve till five week-days? Would that interfere with your bowls?'

'Oh, no. No.'

'You will or you won't?'

'Oh, I will. I will.' She squeezed his hand, tight. 'But isn't there someone younger you'd prefer to have working here?'

'No. And I've been meaning to ask you this for a week now.'

'Would you like me to start today?'

Kerry arrived home at ten past midday to find a large envelope on his verandah. It was weighted with a rock to defy the non-existent breeze. He picked it up, felt the weight, shook the contents. Papers. Audio tapes. It hadn't been posted, either. Before he opened it, he knew who it was from. Merrin.

He threw the envelope on the table, put his frozen lunch into the microwave and all the while the envelope stared at him. Kerry drank a beer first, then sat at the table and studied the scrawled but legible block letters in black felt pen. He opened the envelope, slid the contents on to the table top. One cassette tape, photocopies of statements and a Record of Interview. No use playing the tape on the system. Kerry found his Walkman instead. And he ignored the microwave's bell.

He was listening to Lacey—a much younger Lacey during a recorded interview, a long time ago. He skipped the formalities and heard:

'Who came in?'

'Karl. The bald one. The ugly one. Said if I behaved he'd let me up.'

'You were restrained at the time of the assault?'

'No. No, he let me up. But I wouldn't talk to him. I wouldn't talk to anyone except Danny. I wouldn't eat, either. He got too close so I kicked him in the knee and that's how this happened.'

'You kicked him because he got too close?'

'It was the way he got close when no one else was around. I knew

126

what he wanted. What he always tried.'

'What do you mean?'

'I didn't want him touching me—I got him first. He tried to make me take the pills, but I wouldn't. I wouldn't because I didn't like what they did to me.'

'What was that?'

'I felt dopey all the time. Never knew what was going on, what was happening. Danny was the only one I trusted but they wouldn't let him near me till I behaved. He had a fight with Karl once. Karl used to wait till it was late and the sister had finished work before he'd take me to the showers and there was never anyone else around. Danny came in one night. I don't remember much about the fight, but I know it never happened again. Danny'd take me to the bathroom after that. Always with one of the lady nurses with us. Karl got in trouble and nearly lost his job. I never told anyone what he really did to me because no one would believe me. Except Danny. I told him. But all he could do was make sure Karl never got the chance again. I thought you wanted to know what happened last night?'

The tape paused as if no time had elapsed. But Kerry guessed a long time had elapsed. She was close to crying, so the interview was paused.

'Last night, Danny was taking me up to my room and he slipped. He slipped on something greasy on the stairs and he hit his head on the way down and—'

'Did you push him?'

'No! No! He slipped!'

Kerry ejected the tape, turned it over.

'After he slipped and lay unconscious at the bottom of the stairwell, what did you do?'

'I hid. I could hear Karl calling him. I had to hide.'

'Where'd you hide?'

'Under the stairs.'

'For how long?'

'I don't know. But I heard Jane crying that he was dead, that he broke his neck. I don't remember anything after that.'

Kerry read the other statement. Karl had supposedly witnessed the patient pushing the attendant down the stairs. And that is what the charge was based on. Her word against his. He found the photograph which accompanied the file. A teenage girl, face bruised, body bruised. Consistent with a beating.

Kerry stopped the tape and looked quickly at the committal transcript.

Not much of a case there. Two days of legal argument later, the magistrate threw it out of court. Kerry wondered how a teenager in a mental hospital managed to get a QC on her case.

A QC she later married.

Why had Merrin bothered with this? He must have thought her past relevant. Kerry didn't. If Lacey wanted him to know, like everything else, she'd tell him in her own time, in her own way. If he prompted enough. If he ever got to see her again aside from a safe rendezvous in public parks. He looked at the time. An hour and a quarter to fill in. Now or never, he thought.

Kerry walked into Denise's House of Beauty on High Street and asked for a haircut. The redhead whose name was emblazoned across her white shirt, ran her fingers through his hair and told him to wait. Kerry sat, picked up an ancient Cleo magazine and flicked through it. Out of the corner of his eye, he saw the display of cosmetics, shampoos, conditioners, waxes, make-up and body lotions. All with the same Greek label he'd found in Lacey's bathroom. Hope rose a little. He looked closer. Hand lotion. Body lotion for cellulite. Breast firmers. Foot conditioners.

Denise thrust her only other customer, an old lady, under a dryer, pushed a cup of coffee closer and turned to Kerry with: 'Righto. Basin.'

'I only want a haircut.'

'Basin.'

Being the only qualified hairdresser for fifty miles, she could treat customers as she wished. But once the warm water hit and the gentle scalp massage began, Kerry didn't want to leave. Then the hair was conditioned, rinsed and a towel wrapped around his head. A gas lift chair lowered to accommodate his tall frame and he was ordered to sit. He faced the mirror.

'All of it,' he said.

'All of it? No. No.'

'All of it.'

'Trust me,' the redhead said.

Two fatal words. 'To the shoulders then,' Kerry compromised, suddenly losing his nerve. He'd forgotten how he looked with short hair.

The visionary with the scissors and comb in hand studied his face and began cutting and talking. The woman knew more about Kerry than he did. He soon learnt why. Denise's sister-in-law was second cousin to Johnny Logan's wife.

When there was a break in the constant yapping, Kerry asked, 'Do you sell a lot of that Greek stuff?'

'Enough,' Denise replied. 'Now, if you'd come in for a perm, summer highlights, bikini wax or a facial I'd give you a complimentary bottle of breast firming lotion.' A wicked gleam lit the woman's green eyes. He took no notice—he'd learnt it was safer that way.

'You'd say that every lady in town's used this Greek stuff at some time, then?'

She thought for a moment, pausing reflectively. 'The majority, yes. It's very good and very hard to get. Can't import it any more...' She continued extolling its miraculous virtues.

When he sensed a break in the traffic of words, Kerry asked, 'Was Eadie Ross a regular here?'

'Poor Eadie. I've heard it was Frank Purvis. I'm not surprised. Nothing surprises me what that man could do.'

'You know he's dead, don't you?'

'An eye for an eye. Eadie was harmless.'

'Yes, I know.'

'When's the funeral? Does anyone know?'

'I don't. Sorry.'

Denise sighed and decided to answer Kerry's initial question. Was she a regular? 'She was here every three weeks without fail. She took good care of herself. Except for Decembers.' She continued on with what happened to Eadie in December. How she went into hiding for a week at a time.

'And what do you think about that?' he asked. Was it real?

Yes, it was real. Elspeth's revenge.

'Did you know her?'

'Elspeth? Yes and no.' Even Denise wouldn't elaborate on Elspeth Mackenzie.

'Does Lacey Kilder come in much?'

'Ah, Lacey.' The green eyes flashed. 'I've heard you two are an item. Didn't take you long.'

Kerry said nothing incriminating. It would have only been wishful thinking anyway. 'Is she a regular too? Does she buy that Greek stuff?'

'Eadie would drag her in for highlights and a cut. Do you know what she'd say? Cut it, Dennie, before she starts peeing on car wheels.'

Once the larynx was primed there was no stopping this woman. Kerry half listened, half wondered what was happening to his hair. Denise jumped from one topic to another as quickly as a bee in a carnival garden. She continued talking whilst his hearing was obliterated by the noise of the blow dryer.

She did a good job. His hair now hung to his collar, layered and shaped. Made him look a little younger. Twenty-three dollars later, Kerry walked out immeasurably lighter, the wavy, blown-dry hair tossed by the blistering southerly roaring down High Street. Next stop, The Arms for a liquid refreshment before the rendezvous.

Half a dozen snotty-nosed kids played with empty Coke cans in the gutter outside The Metro. 'How you going, matey?' came the call from inside the public bar. Kerry acknowledged the greeting with a gesture of hand, stepped around the kids and came to a sudden halt. He turned. He was being watched.

An old, white-haired Aboriginal man was studying him. Kerry immediately thought of the swamp. The sacred, no, the cursed ground.

The Aboriginals. Murrumbingal. He'll tell you...

The old man spoke more with his eyes than his mouth. And for a moment it felt as if they knew each other.

Kerry paused, wondering if he should offer to buy the old guy a drink. Talk awhile. Gently peel at the layers for information about the swamp. He looked back again, but the old man wasn't there.

'Where'd he go?' he asked the kids sitting in the gutter.

'Who?' a boy of about eight asked. Pale coffee colored skin, dark, dark eyes. A hint of mistrust there. Already.

'That old man. Is he your grandfather?'

'No old man here today. Pop's at home today.'

I'm seeing things again, Kerry thought as he turned away and crossed the road, heading for The Arms. Kerry took out his wallet, checked how much cash he had left and considered hitting the automatic teller when he heard one word:

'Djawa?'

He looked up quickly. Standing beside the public bar entrance of The Australian Arms, the old white-haired man who a moment ago had been in The Metro. For a moment Kerry didn't believe he was real. He couldn't have crossed the street so fast.

'Djawa?' he asked again.

'You talking to me?'

The old man nodded.

'My name's not Djawa. It's Kerry Staines.'

The old man smiled broadly. 'No,' he said, although the lips did not move. 'You are Djawa. Returning to undo what was done in the Dreaming.'

'Oh, for Christ's sake, you silly old—'

The old man disappeared in another blink of the eye.

Kerry, almost accustomed now to seeing things that weren't really there, simply shook his head and went inside. And hoped to God that no one had heard him talking to himself. He sat in the public bar, acknowledged a few regulars in his normal, quiet way. Chantelle was working, her mousy hair held high and tight in a Fifties style ponytail. She wore her jeans well. Poured a beer whilst lifting her right foot. He hadn't noticed that before.

'Hi, Kerry,' she said as she put his beer down. He hadn't asked for a beer, either. What he really wanted was a bourbon. Straight.

'Chantelle. How are you today?' He fumbled in his pocket for a small mountain of change, which he put on the bar so she could help herself. The beer would have to do.

'I'm good. You?'

'Fine. Fine. Is your—'

'I like your hair that way.'

'Thanks, love. Is your dad about?' Kerry asked.

'Out back,' she said. She had no trace of any accent, was as broadly Australian as anyone else in Mallen. She also had two more looks as Kerry picked up his beer and made his way past the lounge, the private bar and toilets, to the defunct beer garden area where Emile, on his own, was stacking empty kegs.

'Emile.'

'Ah, Kerr-ie. Denise has finally caught you, yes?'

'Yep.'

'Less of the hip-pee look *pour* Mallen, *alors, oui*?'

'Too bloody hot, mate.'

The Frenchman's eyes smiled, and as quickly as it appeared, the joy faded. 'You do know that Lacey phoned me this morning? She has broken her arm but she wants to work. I say to her there is no need, for Chantelle and I will manage.'

'How'd she sound?'

'Tired.'

'Want me to talk some sense into her?'

'If you can, *oui*.'

'Can I ask you something?' Kerry tried.

'*Oui*.'

'Did you know Lacey when she was a teenager?'

Emile considered the question. 'Yes and non. She stayed with her grandmother for short times only. Why is it you ask?'

'Was she in town when Elspeth Mackenzie disappeared?'

'Many were in town. Can it be she is a suspect now?'

Kerry didn't reply.

'Why is it you ask me this?'

'Talk is she's gay. That she and Eadie used to, you know.'

'Talk, talk. She and Eadie were friends. Why is it you ask?'

'No reason.'

Ah, but there was a reason. Emile hadn't worked a bar for twenty-five years and learnt nothing in the interim. 'You would listen to the talk of little minds? Here, what is not ordinary is despised. It is not my business what she does when she is not here. Nor is it my business whose arms she lies in at night.' Emile continued stacking kegs. 'But lucky arms they would be, *non*?' The glance in Kerry's direction was amused and, Kerry surmised, a little envious.

If only it could be that simple, he thought. 'How well did you know Eadie Ross?'

'Eadie? Why is it all these questions? Already I have told the police what it is I know. You cannot leave it rest. The police. It remains still. I say now that what is, will be. You have not lived here long enough to understand how it is. I would say leave alone, yet I know you would not listen so I would say be careful.'

'Some weird things are happening, Emile.'

'Accept them.'

'I have to know what happened.'

'You wish for a long, prosperous life? Accept and be silent. I am not the first to say this, I hope to be the last.'

Gazes met and Kerry eventually walked out, taking the long way to the park. His diver's watch, which had taken five minutes to reset after stopping last night, read 1.50. He crossed the road and sat for a while on the park bench. In the concrete at his feet was inscribed a name: Elspeth, 1977. A smiley face. He couldn't escape her anywhere.

The river was calming and he watched the steady stream of water trickle over the low dam wall. Behind him the deserted police station, the courthouse next door. Reaching to the five-ways, the row of upper class Mallen houses, mostly weatherboard, long, spreading, most with landscaped gardens, solar hot water systems on the roofs. Intermittent traffic crossed the weir bridge.

There was more rumor now. Rumor about the petition to the Police Minister. Mallen was about to be graced again by a uniform or two. Not before time. Kerry sat there and dreamed a little. He imagined slipping into uniform again, having an office like that one to himself. Testing for drivers' licences. Working the radar again. Performing peacekeeping duty between warring domestic factions. Reuniting the occasional family with its runaway. Only being called when someone wanted help and being largely ignored most of the time when there was nothing to do. And around here there wouldn't be that much to do. But it was only a dream. What had been would never be again, not now. Except perhaps the occasional phone call when someone needed a wall of a few years' experience to bounce an idea or two off.

A laden prime mover ground to a halt at the five-ways and Kerry turned his attentions to it. On the long, low trailer, a D9. Maybe a sub-contractor for stage one of Mallen Correctional Facility? The lone semi took Starks Road and disappeared in a cloud of bright red dust.

Kerry looked at the time again. Three minutes had passed.

A movement caught his eye. And another, from behind the bottle brushes further down the riverbank. He could see nothing directly, only in peripheral, but he could hear faint echoes of clapping sticks. Of voices. Kerry stood, his hip aching, and he limped on to the grass, towards the bottlebrush screen, past the vandalized barbeque on the riverside park. He parted a couple of flower and bee-infested branches. Mirage-like shapes. Some kind of Aboriginal dance? What was in the center of the circle? Some kind of bonfire? He took a step closer, magnetized by the half sight, the full feeling, the faint smells of roasting meat, the sounds of voices, long, low, wailing, off key. But he knew the song. Something, somewhere deep inside had recognized it and was reacting to it. He looked down. His arms were long, thin. Dark. Very dark. His legs, long and thin. Dark, very dark. His chest was bare, glistening with sweat where there was no white body paint. Scars there. Scars on his chest, his arms, his shoulders. The air was different. The air was almost warm. People there were beckoning him to come. Come and join them. Kerry took a step forward and all disintegrated with:

'James! James, you little shit, don't go near the water!'

Kerry jerked, his heart on fire. There was nothing now. Nothing except grass that needed a council mower. An overflowing rubbish can. And AUTHORITY SUX spray-painted on the side of the public toilets where that group of people had been dancing and singing only a second ago.

He wasn't black. He never had been, he never would be. Or so he told himself, but his heart refused to believe his lies. Kerry turned away, expecting to see that old man again, smiling at him, calling him Djawa.

'Jamie! If you go near that water, I'll bloody kill you!'

Kerry took a few steps back and turned. He saw a young woman pushing a stroller, calling a two-year-old back from the water's edge. A two-year-old who was deaf. Limping down to the water's edge, Kerry picked up the boy and put him down again at his mother's feet.

The woman didn't thank him. She swung out and smacked the boy on the side of the head, hard enough to rupture his ear drum. Then she forced him to the other park table, where she unloaded lunch.

Kerry dug in his pocket for his cigarettes and was about to light up when he saw Lacey coming out of one of the weatherboard houses—the doctor's house and surgery. Her left arm was in plaster from wrist to bicep. For a long while they simply exchanged long gazes. Kerry waited for a car to pass before he crossed the street. She looked no different to last night, except perhaps for the sun-bleached hair glistening in the sunshine. She didn't walk away. Rather, as he advanced, her study of her sandals became more intense.

The awkward moment lasted indefinitely. 'Hey.'

'Hey,' she said.

The plaster on her left arm was still wet, dark circles under her eyes, lips tinged grey.

'Decent shiner you've got there.'

She couldn't look at him. 'It was a clean break. You were right.'

Still having trouble breathing, too, he noticed. 'Coughing blood yet?'

'No.'

'How many ribs?'

'Two.'

'I thought so. Where's your wheels?' Kerry asked.

'At home.' She started walking, slowly, with a limp that almost matched his.

'How'd you get into town?'

'Dr Martinelli came out.'

'You could have called me.'

'You were at work.'

And the only happy martyr is a dead one, Kerry thought. 'How are you getting home?'

'Emile will drive me after work.'

'Think that's wise?'

'Bugger off and leave me alone.'

'Look at me and say that.'

She tried to, but nothing emerged.

'Lacey, I meant what I said last night. She's not going to come between us.'

'Stop her, Kerry. If you can.'

'Maybe I already have. I had a long talk with her very early this morning.'

Lacey watched him, cautiously. 'Don't believe her, Kerry. Never believe her. Promise me.'

Kerry touched her hand. 'Let me take you home.'

'You should be in your shop.'

'Dora's minding the bakery. Come on, it's not far to my place.'

'But I told Emile I'd be at work'

'And Emile doesn't want you at work yet. Give yourself a couple of days at least. How long will you be in plaster? Six weeks?'

'Henry said four.'

'Four. I'd like you to stay with me until you're fit for ... sorry, until you're well again.'

'You're delusional, Kerry Staines.'

'No. Just being practical. You can't ride a bike one-armed. There's not much you can do in the market garden one-armed either. Unless you want to suffer a punctured lung.'

'I can't live at your house.'

'Why not? I could sure use the company.' She was silent, trying to find excuses.

'We can go out to your place right now, collect the dog and that psycho parrot.'

'Kerry—'

I'm offering you a little security here.'

'I know.'

'I won't stop you from doing that book. Hell, I'm the world's best one finger typer.'

'Give me some time to think about it.'

Kerry counted back from sixty, confidence was rising with each heartbeat. 'Time's up.'

'I pay my own way. I won't be nagged about the ridiculous hours I keep. I sleep in a separate room.'

'Fair enough,' he said, a little disappointed.

'Only for a month, no longer. Just till my arm heals.'

'Four weeks,' Kerry said, trying not to sound elated.

They passed the tire service, petrol station, drapery and travel agent without another word spoken. Kerry backtracked at the florist's and he ducked inside, reappearing a minute or two later with a bunch of carnations which she took without a word. The look was enough.

'Damn it. I had it all rehearsed,' she said quietly as they limped on towards Margaret Street, and Kerry's arm slipped around her waist.

'So did I,' he said.

'People will talk.'

'They're talking now. Can't you feel it?'

Lacey looked up at his face, that incredible smile, so contagious. 'Shit,' she whispered.

'What?'

'It still feels like I won you in a lottery.'

CHAPTER 10

As he helped her into his vehicle, she was still laying down the laws, by-laws, rules and regulations of her temporary change of abode, so Kerry simply turned the volume up on his stereo to drown out the noise.

Lacey turned it down just as quickly. 'What'd you do that for?'

He said nothing. She didn't give him the opportunity.

'What'd she say to you?'

'Who?'

'Elspeth.'

'Oh, her. Not a lot. I did most of the talking.'

She didn't believe a word of it. Best to keep it that way for a little while, Kerry thought. 'I won't be home on Friday night. Logan wants me to play with the band at the B & S ball in Wilton. You can come if you want to.'

'Are you asking me on a date?'

He choked. 'Date? While I'm playing? No. It's not that I wouldn't, but musos and dating aren't necessarily compatible commodities. I just thought if you wanted to tag along ... if you don't want to be alone.'

'I'm used to being on my own.'

He said nothing further, but at any moment, expected, or hoped, that she'd break the silence on what happened the night before. Nothing came.

Eventually, he offered, 'Word is Mallen's getting a uniform soon. He'd have to be a sergeant at least if it's a one man station. Maybe Gilmeister will be posted back here.'

There was no reaction to the name except: 'He's been suspended.'

'That's right. I forgot. He's enduring an internal. What we call the barbed wire enema.'

'What you used to call, Kerry. You don't do that any more.'

He said nothing.

'You miss it, don't you.'

'What gives you that idea?'

Lacey studied the view. 'Kerry?'

'Hey.'

'What's Merrin said to you?'

'About?'

'Me. I know why you're doing this.'

'Doing what?' His feigned innocence was exasperating. 'Look, you don't have to stay with me if you don't want to. I simply don't like the idea of you being all the way out here without transport, that's all.'

'He's told you about me.'

Kerry slowed and eventually stopped, barely a mile short of Rainbow Farm's brightly colored mailbox. 'He thinks you could have killed Eadie.'

Lacey closed her eyes. 'How'd I manage that? I beat her up, raped her, shot her and framed you for it? Is that what he thinks?'

'Crime scene found a few strands of blonde hair in the bedding as well as fingerprints that have traces of a cosmetic cream sold by the local beauty parlor. He'll probably question you, take your prints for elimination. Now we know, sorry, they know, that she was visited by Purvis and another person, possibly Gilmeister, the night she died, but a woman was there as well.'

Lacey said nothing.

'Was it you?'

She turned her gaze to the window.

'Is that why Gilmeister visited you last night? To warn you to keep quiet about what you'd seen at Eadie's the night she died? You said no, he got rough?'

Lacey sat in the car, nausea rising, fighting for an exit. There was no movement except for tears welling in her eyes, tears she couldn't contain. 'Who told you about Lenny?'

'Elspeth. I called, you weren't answering. Emile had called you, too. He was concerned. Very concerned.'

Silence.

'It's not looking good, girl. You should have said something long before this.'

'How long till he comes to question me?' she asked, voice shaking.

'I don't know. A day or two. Depends on whether or not he gets a match from the hair he took out of your hairbrush.'

Lacey turned to Kerry, questioning silently.

'The day Frank Purvis died.'

Lacey turned back to the window. 'It's circumstantial.'

'It's probably enough.'

'What should I do? Get legal advice now? I don't want to get trapped again.'

'Again?'

'You already know! Don't sit there looking at me like that and pretending otherwise!'

'Okay. You want honesty? I know what happened when you were seventeen. I know about the charges. Merrin told me.'

'What'll I do?'

'Tell Merrin the truth. Tell me the truth.'

'I feel...I feel—'

She was out of the car just in time, throwing up into the bright red dirt on the side of the rough gravel road. And he was there, holding her upright, ignoring her futile attempts to push him away, finally offering her a handkerchief. She was white by the time he poured her back into the car. 'You think it was me. You think I killed Eadie,' she whispered.

'No. No, it wasn't you. Merrin will discover that for himself soon enough.'

Kerry stopped at the mailbox, got out and collected her mail. Lacey took it. She knew the handwriting on the only letter today, a letter as opposed to the normal run of uninviting windows. Craig. He must have scribbled some words of a personal nature, not dictated to his secretary. She opened it, one handed. Just an address, neatly processed in the middle of his fancy personal watermarked letterhead. The address of the only solicitor he knew in the south-west. The one who was still overseas.

'His timing was always impeccable,' she said quietly and looked at Kerry as he parked beside the house gate. 'He's given me a name of a colleague. But I asked for this for you, not me.'

'Trust me,' was all Kerry said.

Rainbow Farm was being abandoned until further notice. An hour later, the old black dog filled the back of the Rav, and the cockatoo, unable to fly or unwilling to taste freedom, calmly perched on Lacey's shoulder and talked excitedly during the entire drive back to Mallen. One suitcase of clothing, the computer, a cardboard box of food from her refrigerator and the box of research notes was all she needed.

'I feel I'm taking advantage of you,' she admitted.

'I told you, I can use the company.'

'I'm no company when I'm writing. That's one reason I live alone.'

Echoes of his own lifestyle were very loud. 'Why don't you do it any more?' Kerry asked.

'Excuse me?'

'The psychic detective thing. You were very good. I never believed in it personally, but I heard the reports one way or another, how good you were.'

'Do you still disbelieve?'

'Elspeth's made me see the light. Excuse the pun. Why'd you stop?'

'I got tired of proving myself. Tired of the ridicule, of the trouble it caused. If I wasn't a suspect, Sean Merrin would be very interested in what I'd have to say.'

'How'd you do it?'

'Psychometry. I'd hold an article of clothing if any was available. Sometimes I'd work from a photograph. But I never remembered what eventuated during a session. It was always taped. I was videotaped a few times. Worked in TV, radio, but—'

'But?'

'Not any more, Kerry. Never again. So don't ask me to.'

They arrived back at 11 Margaret Street and Kerry unpacked the car alone. He settled the cockatoo on an old hat stand that had lain under the house for twenty years, bedded the old dog under the house and talked to her in a quiet, soothing voice. Blue hazed eyes lit with a smile. Kerry thought that perhaps a bullet would be kinder as she wasn't eating much, arthritis was making it impossible to move. She struggled to her feet and tried to follow Kerry up the stairs till she realized upstairs was forbidden territory here, too. Give the smelly old mutt a week tops, Kerry thought, and I'll be digging a hole in the backyard.

Inside, Lacey waited in the kitchen. She was leaning against the table, and on the table the opened envelope. Kerry had forgotten to put it away. Another awkward moment ensued which lasted indefinitely. No use lying. She was as expert at sensing lies as he was.

'Oh, shit,' he whispered.

'This should have been destroyed.'

Kerry picked the envelope up, rammed the contents back into it, including the tape from his walkman, and he stuffed the package into the firebox of the wood stove. He took a lighter from his pocket and within moments the past was little but ash and smoke and melted plastic.

'I don't have much faith in yesterdays,' Kerry said. 'Need a hand unpacking?' he finally asked to fill the gap.

'No, thanks.'

'Make yourself at home. I'm going to crash for a couple of hours. Wake me at seven.' Kerry walked up the hall, into the main bedroom and he closed the door. He opened the French doors to the verandah. No breeze again. He stripped to his jocks and flicked the ceiling fan on. It whirred, grated and wobbled above as he lay on his back on the cotton bedspread. The breeze from the circulating air cooled the sweat and with the cool came sleep, a welcome stranger in daylight darkness.

Lacey stood at the French doors, sipped her cup of tea and watched him sleep. The cat arched around her ankle, greeted her quietly and walked past. He took his place on the end of Kerry's bed. His nose was bleeding already from one short confrontation with the bird. The phone rang but by the time Lacey had made it down the hall, the answering machine had engaged. She expected something witty on the tape certainly not: *Staines. Leave a message.*

Whoever it was did not like answering machines.

Lacey finished her tea, rinsed the cup and left it to drain. She walked into the living room and studied the photograph on the shelf above the fireplace—a woman with two children. She picked it up, took it from its frame and held it. A series of images flicked by her mind's eye quickly, so quickly it was a blur. She tried again, this time sitting in a huge recliner chair. She touched the woman's face first, left her finger there.

Only one image appeared, but it was all-encompassing. A young man with dark, possibly Grecian features, in a wide bed. And beneath him, choking back an orgasmic scream, the woman in the photograph. Nothing else came. This pretty woman was Kerry's wife, but her lover was not her husband.

Slipping the photograph back into its frame, Lacey put it back in place. She looked at the time. In her box of groceries, a frozen chicken which would cook while she performed other, more productive duties. She set her computer up on the kitchen table.

Two hours later, Kerry woke to the smells of roasting chicken and the sounds of the occasional bleep and girlish mumble punctuated with a sporadic obscenity. Which only served to remind him he couldn't walk around naked. He pulled on his jeans and appeared in the kitchen, scratching his head vaguely. Lacey turned quickly, looked at the wall clock in alarm.

'Smells good,' he said as he wandered past to the bathroom.

Lacey couldn't quite believe she'd been working constantly, without interruption or hardware failure for two hours. What was happening? Was Elspeth allowing her to do this now? The computer was gone and the table was set by the time Kerry returned from a much needed shower. He walked past again, a towel around his waist this time.

'We share the cooking, too,' he mumbled.

Half an hour later, he regretted the statement. Unlike Annie, this woman was magic in a kitchen.

'Did you sleep well?' she asked as she chased her meal around her plate. Kerry took pity and cut it up for her.

'Not enough. Who taught you to cook?'

'No one.'

'Yeah, well, no one taught me either but you'll make that discovery tomorrow night.' He left the table, threw a Bob Seger CD on to the audio in the next room, and returned singing a few bars of 'Old Time Rock and Roll'.

'I can't stand silence.'

'It makes you think.'

'Exactly. This isn't going to work. You know that.'

'What?' Lacey asked.

'You and me in separate rooms.'

'Is that why you asked me to stay here?'

No use pretending otherwise. He gave her a sheepish grin, his eyes teasing.

There was a knock at the front door. Which woke the old dog and alarmed the cockatoo as well.

'I forgot to tell you, someone called but didn't leave a message.'

'It was probably Dora. I showed her everything except the banking. It's probably her with the day's takings right now.' Kerry limped up the hall and opened the door.

But Lacey knew that it wasn't Dora calling. 'Jesus Christ, what the hell are you doing here!' She heard an unfamiliar male voice, but could tell from the tone and expression that he was more than an acquaintance. A long-lost friend by the sound of it.

'Was out this way, thought I'd call in. See how you were. Where's my beer?' the voice said.

Two sets of footsteps advanced along the creaking floorboards. Lacey watched the door and she was surprised to see the tall stranger walk into the kitchen. Her stomach turned in circles. She'd seen him before.

'Lacey, this is an old mate of mine from Brisbane. Demetri Aspromorgous.'

She smiled a hello, and saw the surprised glance that was aimed for Kerry. He ignored it, took a beer from the fridge and threw it to his friend. 'What the hell you doing out here?' Kerry asked and beckoned him to sit.

'Well, I got a new posting. New posting, promotion. At least it was supposed to be a promotion.'

'To what?'

'OIC, Mallen.'

'You? Officer-in-Charge? Jesus, was it a clerical error?'

'Kerry, can we talk?'

'Anything you have to say to me can be said here and now.'

Aspro glanced at Lacey. He was very uncomfortable.

'It's all right, Kerry. I have to unpack anyway,' Lacey offered. She rose from the table, put her plate in the sink and went into her room. She sat on the bed and stared at the wall, unable to hear what was being said in the distance, not wanting to, either. Her arm was aching, she'd eaten too much. But what made her nauseated was knowing that soon she'd be deemed responsible for driving a stake into the heart of another relationship, a friendship which had been strong for years. Or so Kerry had thought. Lacey closed her eyes. How in God's name could she be expected to be friendly to this man who had just walked in out of Kerry's past, knowing as she did that he'd slept with his best friend's wife?

'What the fuck's she doing here?'

'What I want to know is why you're here?'

'Did you get that stuff we sent you this morning?'

'We?'

'Sean and me. We both thought you needed to know.'

'And I thought you said you started tomorrow.'

'I am trying to help you here, Kerry.'

'Like you tried to help when I was under investigation and needed that fucking list? A list which would have had all charges dropped immediately but no one could find it? Like the night I needed your help and you hung up on me?'

'The inspector was sitting on my desk, for Christ's sake!'

Silence. 'Grady? That bastard's still Inspector?'

'He'll be Deputy Commissioner soon.'

'So you were shunted as far west as they could send you.' Kerry's anger was slightly fading.

'You know why I'm here.'

'And when you leave here tonight, you go straight to Merrin and you tell him that girl in there didn't do the Ross woman.'

'But she knows who did.'

Kerry lit a smoke.

'Merrin's questioning her tomorrow. I wanted to see you first.'

'Why?'

'To warn you to dump her, because when the shit falls, mate, I don't want you sprayed again.'

'You've already formed conclusions.'

'Kerry—'

'Lacey!'

'What the hell are you doing?'

'Lacey!'

Soft footfalls down the hall replied to the call. Kerry looked at his old friend. 'You hear what she has to say first.'

'But why wasn't this information offered sooner?'

'No one asked me.'

'What do you mean, no one asked you?' Demetri was astounded.

'I was never asked to give a statement or answer any questions.'

'You could have volunteered.'

'And get charged again? Like Kerry was charged because he found the body? Thank you, but no. Eadie asked me to come in. She needed me.'

'Why?'

'Because she called me at three in the morning and told me Lenny Gilmeister had raped her.'

'She never reported it?'

'Who was there to report it to? Local whores don't get raped. They lie there and take it. That's all she was—the local whore.'

'You were friends then?'

'No, we were lovers.'

Kerry choked on the beer he was sipping. 'You're bisexual?' Demetri asked.

'I am me. My sexual preferences have nothing to do with who or what I am. And I'm staying here, in a separate room, until my arm heals. But you'll make of that what you want, too. Eadie was alive when I saw her last. I had no reason to want her dead. I loved her.'

'Do you wear rubber gloves?'

The question took her by surprise. Kerry, too. 'No. I use cloth gardening gloves when I work in the market garden. I can't wear rubber. I have an allergic reaction to it. My skin blisters.'

'What brand of cosmetics do you use?'

'Nutrimetics. I get dermatitis if I use anything else.'

'What happened to your arm?'

She glanced at Kerry and he nodded. 'Len Gilmeister came to see me last night. He wanted me to say that he wasn't at Eadie's the night she died. I wouldn't. It isn't the first time he's threatened me. But it's the first time he's hurt me.'

'But there are no witnesses.'

'Just like last time. I was eighteen and a half and temporarily living in Mallen with my grandmother and my cousin, Elspeth Mackenzie. I'd gone into town with Eadie and Ells that night. The army was in town, on war games. Elspeth dragged me along, said it was time I lived a little. I'd just been released from… from an institution, all those charges had been dropped. I was confused, angry at the world. Eadie had gone off with some soldiers, so I decided to walk home, back to Rosehaven, a good four miles out of town. It was about eleven, midnight, I'm not sure exactly, when a ute stopped beside me. Frank Purvis was driving, Lenny was in the passenger seat. Mitch, Brady, Jack Mallaby and Eric Bateman were in the back of the ute. Elspeth was with them. They were all drunk. Elspeth wanted me to come with them for a party by the Bora ring, out near the swamp. It was her favorite place to *party*, as she called it. But I knew what her parties were like and I said no. I started screaming when Frank got out of the ute and put me in the back. It was Jack Mallaby who convinced them to let me go. They drove off. Elspeth never came back. No one ever saw her again but Lenny Gilmeister was the senior constable in town in those days and he filed a missing persons report. Frank said he saw her with some soldiers and no one did anything more. Lenny visited me the next day. He threatened to have me back in the 'funny farm' if I said one word to anyone about what I'd seen. It was either that or he'd make sure that if my body was ever found, it wouldn't be identifiable.'

Aspro said nothing, but the glance to Kerry needed no words.

'It's your word against his. There are no witnesses.'

'It doesn't matter, does it. My word's worth nothing. Not with my history of mental instability'.

'I wouldn't say that exactly. You don't deny being in the Ross house the night she died?'

'No. I was there, holding her while she cried herself to sleep. I didn't kill her. I had no reason to.'

'Thanks, love. Thanks. You can go back to what you were doing.'

Kerry walked Aspro to the door.

'I'll see what I can do.'

'Talk to Gilmeister before I find the bastard.'

'I would if we could find him. He's disappeared, mate. Disappeared.'

'Whose prints were on the headboard?' Kerry asked.

'The victim's.'

'Are you going to charge her?'

'Not if I can help it,' was all Aspro said. He took the stairs down, and turned back. 'It's good to see you again. Keep in touch, mate.'

Kerry stood in the night cool, watching his friend drive away. He leapt into the air when Lacey touched his shoulder.

'I didn't want you to know all that,' she said quietly.

'Let's just forget it.'

'Here. You look as if you need one.' She handed him his cigarettes and sat down on the top stair beside him. The cockatoo with its head under its wing mumbled, and down the end of the verandah, Yang waited his next chance.

'You okay?' he asked.

'I think so.'

'Do something for me? Don't sign anything, statements or otherwise, until I've read it first?'

'He's your friend and you don't trust him?'

'Well, put it this way, a well-turned phrase can turn innocence into provable guilt. I've done it myself—questioned some poor bastard for ten, eleven hours, put in a few additions in the Record of Interview, it's signed and, bang, you get it in writing. The basis of one or two extra charges.'

'You did that?'

'Sure.' Kerry studied the glow of his cigarette in the dark. 'If I knew I was right.'

'But I thought you—'

'Best not to think sometimes, girl. That part of my life is over now. Long gone. I didn't realize it till now. Can I ask you something?'

'If you want.'

'You really swing both ways?'

'What I felt for Eadie is not what I feel for you.'

'It makes sense though,' Kerry said quietly, more to himself than her. 'Turning to a woman for what you couldn't trust a man to give. And considering the past, I wouldn't blame you if you have fantasies of castrating every male you've ever known.'

'With a blunt butter knife?' She put her hand on his knee. He barely flinched. 'What time do you start work?'

'Two. This old me needs some sleep because in a previous life he was a grizzly bear without a cave to hibernate in. I'll see you tomorrow.' He leaned close, kissed her cheek and walked off into his room.

Lacey heard the door close and she sighed. She looked out at the tiny township. The neon lights of the Mallen Cafe blinked sporadically. For five years now the sign spelled MAL--N - AFE. Cars dragged up and down High Street. Teenagers home from boarding school would probably be out necking in the park by the weir, catching up on lost semesters of absence from each other. Or they were getting drunk in The Arms. The hundred-year-old hotel was the heartbeat of the town and without it, Mallen would cease to exist.

Her thoughts, idle ones, scrambling with fleeting feelings and imagery turned vaguely to Demetri Aspromorgous. She knew this was far from over. How could anyone think she would harm Eadie? Lacey felt the hand on her shoulder and she turned quickly, expecting to see Kerry. But nothing was there except the touch so familiar, warm, reassuring. Eadie's touch. *It's all right, it's all right.*

Despair, too much, too soon, flooded in and the tears she'd held back for too long finally escaped. Eadie was there as she'd always been before, holding her, yet not, caressing her hand, yet not, touching her face, yet not.

'You didn't have to die like that.'

It's all right now.

'Not like that.'

Kerry listened in the dark, wondering who she was talking to. But he dared not venture out and attempt any form of comfort because he knew exactly how it would end. Touching Lacey would probably conjure Elspeth, who was jealous. He wanted to give them both some more time to get used to this idea. What he needed now was some peace. It finally came when he heard the soft footfalls along the hallway. The lights died in succession. He followed Lacey's steps in his mind's eye and was on course perfectly, even to the soft 'ouch', when she walked into the bedroom door. Finally, he fell asleep.

Lacey turned the bed light on, sat on the bed which had once belonged to a little boy. She saw in her mind's eye, a tall two-year-old playing with toy trucks in a bohenia-lined driveway. Dark curly hair, huge dark eyes, six colored trucks all in a row. Kerry's son.

He never spoke of his family. If he didn't volunteer information, Lacey felt it futile to ask. Perhaps it was habit that he kept himself so much to himself. Time, she thought, he needs time. She pulled the covers back, slipped her Indian cotton dress over her head and off her arm and lay on the cool sheets, attempting to find a comfortable place for her plastered arm. She waited patiently for sleep to come.

The house was too alive. Lacey turned off the light and eventually opened her eyes to the shadows, shapes, flashes and streaks of light swirling about the bed. She recognized most of them.

'What do you want?' she asked, eyes closing, drifting away. 'What do you want now?'

From high above she watched the swamp fall, white skeleton by white skeleton, all swallowed by the black, stinking water. Chains, links thicker than a man's arm, pulling down the bones, letting hell loose. And an old black man stood in the bora ring, watching. Trucks, earthmovers driving around him. The old man, unaware of the machinery, choking dust. He looked up at Lacey and he pointed. Lacey woke screaming so loud that Kerry, about to take a sip of his 1.00 a.m. heart starter, spilled the lot down his shirt.

Blinded by the sudden light, a hand on her arm. Kerry. He was leaning over the bed, talking. She couldn't hear the words.

'They're going to find, they're going to find—'

'What? What are you talking about?'

'Bodies. Lots of bodies.'

'Where?'

'The swamp. The site. The old man, the old man you know, yes, you know him, he pointed at me. He showed me. He wants me to stop them, Kerry. Stop them from draining the swamp because it'll only set the evil free. He keeps saying "Wanambi. Wanambi." What's *wanambi*?' Her eyes were cloudy from mists of bad dreams. She tried to get out of bed.

Kerry held her down. 'You were dreaming.'

'No, no, it's not a dream. It's going to happen.'

'What.'

'They're going to upset the balance. It has to be left alone. People are going to die. I have to stop it.' Again she tried to get out. 'Let me up! For God's sakes, let me up!'

Kerry let go. He had to—the squeal was piercing. 'You can't stop it.'

Lacey picked up her dress from the floor, struggled into it. 'I can. I will somehow. That old man, he'll help me.'

'You can't stop heavy machinery! You had a nightmare!'

'No. No.'

'A few days ago you told me the swamp was a breeding ground for evil. Now you're going out there to protect it?'

'No. Don't you see? I'm protecting the town! Those workmen at the site!'

'I don't want you out there.'

'You think I want to go?'

'Don't!'

'Don't tell me what I can or can't do!'

'How you gonna get there?'

'I'll walk! It won't be the first time!'

'Lacey—'

'Keep out of this, Kerry. For your own sake, keep out of it. Stand aside and let me go.'

Annie was there in her eyes. That fierce, unstoppable defiance. And like Annie, he watched her walk away.

'You know where I'll be!' he called to the darkness. Lacey, already crossing the street looked back. For a heartbeat, he prayed she'd change her mind. Most of his prayers were never answered, why would this be any different? Lacey disappeared into the darkness.

Kerry turned to the solid wooden wall and punched, once, twice. He halted at the third. That old Aboriginal was standing in the hallway, pointing. Kerry, partly frozen by the sudden soundless reappearance, followed the pointing hand. He was hit with images, sounds, feelings. But it went no further. 'No!' he screamed. 'I don't want to know!' Then it was just him again. Ready to punch the wall. 'I've had enough.' One word echoed into his brain. One word which haunted him for hours.

Wanambi.

CHAPTER 11

'Hello, what's this?' Luke put his pint mug down on the dusty ground, chased the persistent fly for the thirtieth time that morning, and nudged his fellow worker.

Jamie, who was preoccupied with better thoughts of where he would rather be—smoking dope up in the Daintree—woke from his fantasy and followed Luke's pointing finger.

'Didn't know there were any white girls this far out. What's she got?'

'Looks like an esky. Might have a beer in it, huh?'

The two earthmoving contractors watched numbly as the pretty girl with the broken arm stopped walking, perused the area as if choosing a suitable site for a picnic. She spread her travel rug and sat cross-legged, and one armed, adjusted her huge hat. It looked as if she were there to stay.

For a moment Luke and Jamie stared, transfixed by the sight, then each turned to the other and shrugged.

Luke called, 'Hey!'

The girl looked up.

'What d'you think this is? A picnic?' Jamie closed his eyes, wincing. Some joke. 'What you think you're up to?'

She pretended she didn't hear.

'Now what?' Jamie asked.

Luke picked up his mug of tea, finished it and rose from his folding chair. He looked at the time—smoko was over half an hour ago anyway. Didn't matter. They were on their own for at least another two days. With forty-eight hours allocated to clear and level the site, the job would take only six providing they had a fair run at it. Not a lot they were contracted to do, really. Just clear already dead timber and level the area. He and James weren't required to clear the swamp. By the look of that, it'd take three weeks, twenty-five more men and would delay construction another month.

Luke pulled up his football socks and walked to where the girl sat. Again she looked up and smiled politely. He had a daughter almost as old as this one. Her smile was nice. Actually, she was nice so he decided to approach the same way. Nice.

'Listen, love, you're a bit early. We're not expecting the protesters here till next week. So get on your bike and bugger off out of it.' It seemed as nice as Luke ever got.

'Sorry,' was all she said, casting her bright blue gaze towards the transportable quarters. 'Best both of you leave. Now. While you still can.'

Just what I need, Luke thought. A fruitcake.

'Look, honey, we've got a job to do and we can't bloody well do it while you're sitting on your arse fair in front of the D9. Now, piss off out of it before you get yourself hurt.'

'You don't realize what it is you're doing. You don't understand what is going to happen tonight if you persist.'

Saying things like that, so calm, too. 'You're trespassing on government land, love. Now be a good little girl and piss off or I'll have to call the boys in blue. And we don't want that, do we?'

'You're interfering with sacred ground.'

Here we go, he thought. Rape, pillage and plunder via heavy earthmoving machinery. 'Move. Come on, love.'

'No.'

'Jamie! Call the cops!' Luke yelled, hoping the threat would be enough to displace her.

She just smiled. Go ahead, the smile said.

Jamie obeyed the order. He walked to the white dual-cab pick up and opened the passenger door.

'Cell phones don't work out here,' the girl said. 'Nothing works out here. I'm surprised the machinery's done this much.'

Luke leaned on the blade of the Cat and fumbled in his pocket for his smokes. 'Yeah? And why's that?'

She was different to the normal rabid protester, this one was pretty and likeable. Very pretty.

'Why? This ground is haunted. There's four square kilometers of it. To the centimeter.'

'Haunted. Right.'

'Haunted and cursed. It goes back ten thousand years to the Dreamtime.'

'Yeah?'

'Yes. Once it was a fertile piece of land. The swamp was the only natural spring for a hundred miles. Warring tribes used to fight over it.'

Nothing's changed, Luke thought.

'The last battle was a terrible one, so legend goes. No one survived.

The battle goes on though, in the early mornings. Hear it, see it, feel it... Legend has it that anyone who walks in here is never the same afterwards. If they live, of course, to walk out again.'

Something about the serious gaze accented the words. For a minute, Luke nearly believed her. 'Early mornings, huh?'

The two had arrived, offloaded, driven back to the pub in town, where they'd stayed overnight and began work before dawn. They'd yet to spend a night on the site, let alone hear, see or feel anything in the early morning.

'Hey, Luke! Phone's not working!' came the call from across the dusty flat.

Luke looked at the girl, still cross-legged, her arm in plaster.

'You felt something the moment you arrived, didn't you, Luke? Your first impression was, "Jesus, it's not worth ten grand", because the hair on the back your neck prickled with static. You didn't like this place then, you don't like it now. Is it really worth ten thousand dollars to you?'

'How'd you know about that?'

'Leave before it's too late. The evil here knows neither day nor night.'

'What do you want me to do now?' James asked. Luke turned to his offsider. 'Go into town and call them.'

'You sure?'

'Just do it.' Luke killed his cigarette butt.

'You're being given a chance to leave while you still can. Ignore this and you'll die.' She opened her cooler and took from it a picnic lunch. Luke saw a thermos of tea. The girl offered him a sandwich from a Tupperware container. It was thick country bread, he hadn't had any of that since he was a kid. He took a sandwich. Soft. The crust was hard. In it, tomato, lettuce, cheese. Luke squatted against the D9 blade and shooed the flies. He could see Jamie driving off, tires spewing dust, towards town.

'Nice sanger,' Luke said after the dust cloud settled and silence ruled.

'I thought you'd like it. Would you care to see something?' she asked. He said neither yes nor no, he simply watched as she took something else from the esky—papers encased in a plastic sleeve. She handed it to him. An aerial photo of the Mallen township from 5000 meters and there it was the prison site. When she said four kilometers to the centimeter, she wasn't kidding. Even from 5000 meters it was an anomaly, like it shouldn't be there. A perfectly square dust bowl, except for the swamp on one corner.

'Legend goes that anything dead thrown into the swamp regains life, but not life as we know it. A girl was murdered around here many years ago. Her body was thrown in the swamp. I suppose the excavators will find it.'

Luke took another bite of the sandwich. 'What do you mean, dead things live? Get up and walk around again?'

'People have seen her. The Aboriginals call her the bagini. A pretty girl with sharp claws who forces any man she meets to make love. Usually a bagini lets them go afterwards. But not this one, she's different.'

Luke had never believed fairy tales, even fractured ones like this girl was spinning. 'Live around here, huh?'

She pointed to the farmhouse in the west. They'd driven by it on the way here—both had commented on the rainbow-colored mailbox. But it was Luke who'd said, 'Thought it'd be too far out for hippies here.'

Jamie, who considered himself a closet hippie, had simply grunted.

'Maybe you're telling people all this crap because you don't want a prison next door to you.'

'I don't want innocent people dying unnecessarily.'

'What's your name?'

'Lacey.'

'You make a real nice sandwich, Lacey love. But, by Jesus, you talk some crap. Be a good girl and bugger off now. You're too pretty to get arrested.' He threw the sleeve back and leant against the blade once more.

He was making no moves, why should she? Lacey picked up another sandwich and sipped her tea. The police could probably remove her, warn her, and she'd return next morning.

Emile sighed to the man and called for his daughter to tend the bar in his absence. 'Monsieur, police is not necessary. We have someone in town who will help her see reason.' Emile walked to the bakery. Dora was working the counter. 'Kerrie is in?'

The familiar face appeared around the corner. 'Yo. What's wrong now?'

'It is Lacey. She has seated herself in front of a Caterpillar and refuses to move.'

'So?' Kerry asked, trying hard not to smile at the mind picture Emile's words had created. Knowing Lacey it'd take more than a D9 to move her, too.

'You would talk sense to her?'

'She won't listen to me. Call the police.'

'But—'

'Emile, call the police.'

'*Non*. I cannot.'

'Yeah? I can.' Kerry lifted the phone, dialed Wilton Police and asked for the officer-in-charge. Emile couldn't quite believe what he was hearing or seeing. Perhaps what was said about the two being an item was only gossip after all. Kerry eventually hung up and Emile stared at him in total disbelief.

'Look, Emile, I've retired. I took your advice. And the new guy in Mallen won't be on duty till Wednesday.'

Emile glanced at Dora, who didn't know where to look, so for the second time she rearranged the cream buns in the display case. 'After all she has done for you, you would now stand aside and watch her be taken away?'

'She's a big girl. She's made her decision.'

'So have you, too, I see.'

'Ah-ha.'

'Then I have misjudged you.'

It wasn't exactly what the Frenchman had said, but the tone that said the most. Emile left, upset, and Kerry noticed Dora's questioning look.

'What?'

'Nothing. Really, nothing.'

'Dora—'

'It's not my business to take sides, Kerry, but in a town like this we have to stick together. Lacey isn't always right and not many people understand her, but she's not often wrong, either. And if she's sitting in front of an earthmoving machine, there's a good reason for it. Now, I can mind the shop while you're gone.' That school-teacher look was back in her eyes. It was impossible to argue with it. 'She needs you even if she doesn't know it.'

After a few seconds of confused indecision, Kerry said, 'Watch that bloody slicer while I'm gone,' and he took his work coat off. 'No. Just don't use it at all.'

Dora Mallaby smiled.

Barely ten minutes later, Kerry's Rav drove by, and continued up High Street.

Kerry took the track in. On approaching the swamp today there were no caterpillar races up and down his spine, no voices in his ear warning him to get out. Just a rough makeshift track leading off Starks Road and into the government ground. As bare as the Simpson Desert in summer and just as hot. Kerry saw the transportable quarters, one Hilux dual cab, an eighteen-wheeler and the earth- movers. The rest of the workers would come in time, the concreters, brickies, electricians...

And there she was, having a bite to eat with the two earthmovers. Kerry sighed as the three turned to the approaching vehicle. What's she telling them? he wondered. Is she filling them with horror stories about ancient curses and the walking dead? Good one, Elspeth, he thought. Here's some more victims for you. Kerry was straight to the point, as always. 'What the hell are you doing?' he yelled as he stepped out of the car, feigning anger, one of his best acts.

Lacey offered him her thermos, a peace offering of sorts.

'No. Lacey, we have to talk.'

'So talk.'

Not in front of these two strangers, Kerry thought. But she had no intention of moving. 'Cops'll be here in twenty minutes.'

'Good.'

'I called them.'

She looked up at him, disbelief clouding her eyes.

'Didn't think I would? Look, you can't stop construction. At most, all you're doing is wasting time.'

'Delaying,' she corrected.

'You want to get busted for trespass and Christ only knows what else?'

Kerry looked away from her grin.

'Okay, fine. You're on your own.'

'Kerry?' she called as he turned back for his car. 'What?'

'Don't you want a cup of tea while we're waiting?'

'No. I have a business to run.' He climbed into his car, hesitating momentarily and again his better judgment reappeared. He called out, 'Come back to town with me.'

Lacey shook her head.

'Do you know what you're doing?'

'Yes.'

'One person cannot make a difference, girl!'

'That's your opinion.'

'No, it's my experience! Think I never tried?'

'Kerry!'

Too late, he was gone, churning dust clouds with spinning tires. But he didn't go back to town. He waited for an hour and a half till the cops came. Luckily, it was Peter Jameson.

'What is wrong with you!'

'Don't talk to me like that.'

It was an hour past sundown and she was in his kitchen cooking dinner for two, one-armed. Rejecting any offer of assistance. A walking martyr. The only happy martyr was a dead one, but Kerry declined the temptation to voice this—she'd heard it a thousand times already.

'I've nothing against protesters providing—'

'It's a cause you believe in? Kerry, for the last time, if construction continues people will die.'

'Did you tell the earthmovers that?'

'Yes.'

'And what'd they say?'

'It's a joke to them. But you should know better.'

'Should I?'

She put his plate down. Mainly salad, camouflaging a solitary crumbed chop.

'It was quiet there today. Nothing happened.'

'Exactly. The place is waiting.'

'You were lucky. Lucky it was Jameson, and not the new OIC.'

'I'm not doing this for notoriety. I'm doing it to—'

'Save lives? Crap. Sometimes I wonder about you.' Kerry's anger had lost its effervescence. This girl was no different to Annie in some ways. 'You gave them your word you wouldn't go back tomorrow.'

'No. You gave your word for me. Remember? As if I don't have a brain of my own. Am unable to make my own decisions.'

'I'd like you to help me in the shop.'

'You have Dora. She needs the job more than me.'

'Lacey—'

'If I get busted, it's my problem!'

She was reading his mind again.

'Why can't you just let things happen?'

'Why can't you take your own advice?'

'Okay, that's it. I'm outa here.' He pushed his plate away, grabbed his keys from the end of the table.

'Where are you going?'

'Fucking mad! Care to join me?'

The back door slammed.

'Child,' Lacey whispered to herself.

Luke and Jamie had finished their meal of bacon and beans and had locked themselves in the temporary quarters—home for the next couple of days. The Honda generator powered the one light and fridge, and a small desk fan was set on high to chase the mozzies away. The quarters were screened but didn't refuse entry to tiny, green biting bugs.

Jamie was spooked, a remnant of a childhood spent mostly locked in a dark closet. Once the earth revolved to darkness, the six-foot-two weightlifter's fears overrode sanity. It was too quiet, too still, not even a whistle of a breeze outside. The sky was as black as ink with not a star in sight yet. Cloud cover was thick and blanketed any reflection.

'Think what she said was true?'

'Hey?'

'That girl today. Think what she said—'

'Oh, for Christ's sake, Jamie.'

Silence, except for the rumble of the generator. 'What was that?'

'What.'

'Sounded like footsteps.'

Jamie, on his bed, had his back to the thin wall. From the window he could see no sign of civilization for miles—not even a light from the farmhouse in the distance. But he knew footsteps when he heard them and he thought he heard breathing, too, till he realized it was his own. 'There's some bastard outside, Luke.'

The cellular phone buzzed, short and sharp. It hadn't worked since they arrived, now it was making noises.

'Sunspots,' Luke said and flicked the page of People magazine, sipping at his beer, reaching for his smokes. He fumbled blindly. None left.

The new pack was on the dash of the ute. Outside.

'Go get me smokes, mate.'

'Piss off.'

'Take a leak for me while you're out there.'

The lights died after the generator's final cough. Now it was incredibly quiet. A loud silence. 'Fill the Honda while you're out there, too,' Luke said.

'You come with me.'

'Jesus Christ, no wonder you're still living with your mother!'

'Got no choice about that! Divorce wiped me out. Where are the candles?'

Luke stood, reached for the box of candles and threw them to Jamie in the darkness. 'Friggin great sook,' he mumbled as he walked to the door. The thin flooring reverberated with each of Luke's footsteps. The door opened, and hot night air blasted inside, along with fifteen mosquitoes the size of ten cent pieces. Luke left the door open.

'Close the fucking door!' Jamie yelled after him.

No reply.

Jamie moved off his bed, and, lit candle in hand, went to the door. 'Luke! Bring us the Minties on the... Luke?'

Not a sound. A faint moon was rising and with it came a little light now and then, but not enough to see with any clarity.

Heart loud in ears, Jamie called out again. 'Come on, you bastard, no more of your jokes!'

He knew Luke too well already. It was only their first job together, but he'd heard a lot about him, too. Once he found a weakness he hammered away till either the fault strengthened or it snapped altogether.

Not a sound now. Anywhere. Then came the soft crunch, not a man's footsteps at all. Unless the bastard was tip-toeing in bare feet. No, he'd definitely gone out in his thongs.

There was no sign of life at the ute, parked about twenty meters away.

'Shit, mate, where are you?' The voice echoed for a good square mile, returned it seemed, in a bounce off each corner of that square. But if Jamie didn't venture into that dead zone outside, Luke's joke would have no target. So Jamie shut the door, locked it from the inside. On the card table, Luke's smokes. He touched the packet. Empty. No joke here. He really did need his new pack, but he couldn't hear him at the ute getting the drum of diesel for the generator, either. Just footsteps outside, walking around the hut. Sounded like something being dragged, too. What'd he found now? Another log for tomorrow night's fire?

Jamie waited for the inevitable banging on the wall, guaranteed to scare him whether he expected it or not. Expecting it was worse though and Luke knew it. So Jamie reclined on his bed again, and turned on the crackling transistor radio. Batteries sounded a little flat. Funny, they were new yesterday. 'Sunny Afternoon' was playing. He sang along to as many words as he knew. Then someone banged on the door. Three times. 'Let me in!'

'Up yours,' Jamie replied quietly, and picked up Luke's magazine. What was the mad bastard up to now? he wondered and turned the page. He was out there, running around the hut. Tripping over things in the dark. Banging on the walls. Scratching, screaming, yelling. Then a solitary, 'Oh, Jesus, no!' echoed for miles, again in a square. And then there was nothing. Except the radio, the candlelight.

His fooling around. Damn him. Jamie turned another page, looked at it, saw nothing. Guilt was rising. That's enough, Jamie thought and turned the radio off. He unlocked the door. No one was there. 'Oh, for

Christ's sakes, I've had enough of you!'

Then he saw something on the ground, a few meters away. It looked like his mate. Jamie took the one stair down, nudged him. No movement. He crouched, half expecting Luke to grab at his ankle or something stupid.

Nothing.

'Luke? Mate? You okay?' He turned him over.

Terrified wide eyes met his gaze. Luke looked white, drained of all blood, or so it seemed in the rising moon darkness. Jamie stepped back, any sound choking in his throat. Footsteps again. Jamie was frozen, except for the movement of his eyes. He saw a girl's smooth legs, shining in the reflection of the moonlight. All he remembered was her smile, her face, the outstretched hands, and his own scream. Then there was nothing.

CHAPTER 12

Kerry had no intention of going home that night. He considered visiting The Arms as he drove down High Street, but drinking to camouflage a problem was expected behavior and he'd come to Mallen to change old, established ways. So he looked the other way and turned left. Realizing there was nowhere to go, even less to do, he parked for a while by the weir, watching a couple of night fishermen sinking more beers than bait. For a moment he was tempted to go down and talk to them but he stayed in his car, unwilling to invade others' privacy without good reason.

Down the street, lights were on at the police residence. Demetri was moving in. It seemed he already had a visitor, too. A Mercedes was parked in the drive, behind the police car. It was either Emile Rollet's or George Cooper's. Probably Cooper's, Kerry thought. The short bald man was sole owner, editor and operator of the fortnightly Mallen Beacon—all gossip and no news in its four pages. George had approached Kerry for his life story before his first week in Mallen was done. So Kerry bought a year's advertising for $200, talked a lot but said nothing, and had posed for a photo—one of the worst Kerry had ever seen of himself.

Unwilling to converse with George again, Kerry patiently waited for forty-five minutes until the Mercedes left, and then parked his car on the overgrown footpath.

The front door was wide open, the narrow hall littered with empty boxes. The Beatles at brain mush volume screamed 'Strawberry Fields Forever' from deep within the old weatherboard house. Kerry knocked futilely, he knew. Still no reply. He walked in, stepping through the obstacle course. 'Migraine?' he called.

No reply.

He turned right into the kitchen. Nothing except traces of chaotic habitation. Kerry took the three stairs that led down into the backyard. A laundry, a toilet by the back door. The light was on. Exactly what George's interview had given me, Kerry thought amusedly. The shits. He went back inside where he inspected the contents of the fridge. It was half full of beer and little food, a good indication that no female lived here. He'd heard rumor that Aspro had married again—a girl from the tax office this time.

Kerry was halfway through a beer when Aspro walked in, and saw Kerry perched on the edge of the kitchen table.

'Jesus Christ!' Aspro squeaked, hand to chest.

Kerry looked behind. 'Where?'

'Bastard!'

'What'd I do?'

'You could have told me you were coming,' Aspro said as he washed his hands at the kitchen sink and dried them on his pants.

'Like you do?' Kerry asked.

'Yeah, well, it wasn't exactly a social call.'

'Need a hand?'

Aspro lifted a large, heavy box of crockery on to the table and pointed to the overhead cabinet. Kerry unwrapped and stacked, and nothing was said for a little while.

'Sorry about last night,' Demetri said.

'Forget it. I won't. How big's your area?'

'Sixty square miles.'

'Alone?'

'Alone.'

'This is married quarters.'

'Shit, you're observant.'

Where's the other half?'

'In Brisbane. She wouldn't come.'

'Oh. Sorry.'

'Don't be. I'm not. Heard from Sean yet?'

'No. Should I've?'

'He's not proceeding with your woman. The case is closed.'

'Gilmeister resurfaces.'

'No. It's closed.' Aspro threw an empty box down the back stairs. 'Fini, pal.' He wasn't happy at all.

'So it's all been laid on Purvis. Very tidy.'

'Yeah. And I have been officially told to mind my own fucking business.'

'Who by?'

'Alf Graham.'

'Think you'll like it here?' Kerry asked, eventually.

Aspro studied his surroundings for a moment before asking, 'Do you?'

'I don't know yet. The people are... well, you'll find out. What'd George want?'

'You bastard. You sat in your car and waited till he'd gone?'

'Yeah. Do I look stupid? What'd he want?'

'My life story. Angled for some dirt.'

'Did you tell him you were eligible?'

'For what?'

'Jesus, you did. The ladies'll keep you busy.'

'Yeah? Might make it worthwhile after all. What are you doing here, Kerry? Shouldn't you be at home with the little lady?'

'Is it that obvious?'

Aspro studied him for a little while. 'She kicked you out, huh? You had a fight and she kicked you out of your own place?'

'She's trying to delay construction of the prison. Won't listen to reason.'

'Yeah, I heard. She's another Annie You know that, don't you? Soon as I saw her, I knew.'

'She's nothing like Annie.'

'If she's nothing like Annie, what the hell are you doing here? Why aren't you at home? Your home, I might add.'

'Filling in some time.'

Aspro consulted his wall clock, stuck firmly in the side of a box. 'You love this girl?'

'I don't know. Probably.'

'Go home and find out. Before you get that unwanted look, take a squizz. See all this crap? I've got one day and half a night to find a home for it all. It's great to see you again but can we take a raincheck? Go home, for Christ's sake.'

Kerry finished the beer. 'That's one thing I miss. A dependable friend.'

'Bloody go home. I was watching last night, mate. Saw the way you looked at her. So go on and piss off out of it. I'll get nothing done if you hang around too long.'

Kerry parked under the house and woke the old dog. She barked four times before she recognized the voice. Kerry took the back steps two at a time only to find the back door locked and he had to find the key that fitted.

It was nearing 10.00 p.m., the kitchen was spotless and no trace remained of the meal he'd pushed aside. Which disappointed him somewhat, because he could have eaten anything not nailed down. He made a coffee in the microwave and took it into the living room, expecting to see Lacey watching TV or one of his movies. No sign of life but the light was on in her bedroom. He knocked on the door. No reply.

'Lacey?'

He knocked louder and opened the door. She was sitting on the floor, her back to the door, a Walkman on her head. And she was singing. An angel's honey voice.

Kerry leant against the door for a few moments, watching, listening. Even he didn't sound so good laying down a voice track unaccompanied. And he'd never heard this before, it sounded ancient. Haunting. Celtic. When silence fell, he applauded and Lacey turned quickly. Then she covered her face, ashamed. She slipped the Walkman off.

'How long have you been standing there?' she asked.

'Twenty minutes?' Kerry walked in, sat on the bed. He covered her shame by saying, 'That was lovely.' Kerry offered Lacey a sip of his coffee.

She took the cup. 'Is this a bad habit of yours, walking out to avoid an important issue?'

'Can I?' he asked, ignoring her question and indicating the Walkman. He took the tape out and walked away. A moment later another angelic voice was issuing from the four 100-watt speakers lining the living room walls. After an exasperated sigh, Lacey followed him out. Kerry was leaning back precariously in the recliner and for a moment she was tempted to help it over a little, to see him fall on his head. She hit the stop button on the tape deck instead. Silence fell.

'I was listening to that.'

'We have to talk.'

'Fine. Me first. Why'd you lock me out?'

'I wasn't locking you out. I was just—' Her voice faded.

'He won't come looking for you here.'

'You don't know him like I do.'

'Lacey, he has to get past me.'

'During the few times you're home, sure. Johnny Logan brought your guitar back. It's on the verandah.'

'Did he fix the valve amp?'

'He didn't say. He was more interested in knowing why I was staying here.'

'What'd you say?'

'The truth. That it wasn't permanent. That I was only here using your body for sex.'

'To hell with my mind, huh?'

'Something like that.'

Kerry studied her for a moment before he rose and walked by. And near the front door lay the Strat in its original case, the Fender valve amp.

He plugged both in, and tested the amplifier. *Toccata* at varying levels of volume and expertise issued forth.

'He wanted to know if you were still playing at the B & S!' Lacey yelled.

'What'd you say?'

'I said yes! Probably! Are you still upset with me!'

'What?'

'I said are you still upset with me?'

'What?'

'Kerry!'

He stopped playing. She'd turned the power off and stood with arms folded, defensive in front of the switch. 'I don't understand you. Where'd you go? And why did you go?'

'I went out because I felt like going out. Turn the power back on or I will.'

She stood there defiantly, without any intention of complying, but she baulked a little as he took the old guitar off and laid it against the wall gently. A prized possession. Fragile. He took three steps towards her.

'On,' he commanded quietly.

'No.'

'On,' he said again, more emphasis this time.

'No.'

'Why not.'

'It's past ten. You're violating a by-law. Noise pollution.'

'I don't have neighbors to complain.'

A tiny smile crossed her eyes, her stance remained unaltered. 'Oh, I see. I know what you're doing.'

'Now you know how it feels. Don't stop me, I won't stop you. It's called compromise. You want to get busted for trespass?'

'No, but something has to be done.'

'You'll come to me to bail you out. Every time.'

Lacey pulled a face. 'It's not a capital offence. It's only trespass. A minor annoyance.'

'A minor annoyance that costs money every day construction's delayed.'

Lacey smiled. Half victorious, half cautious.

'Okay, you win. You want to be a martyr, go ahead. I don't give a shit. Power. Now.'

Lacey didn't move. 'I want your word.'

'I will not interfere.'

'On any grounds whatsoever.'

'I will not interfere.'

'One more thing.'

Kerry rolled his eyes.

'Can I use your car? Please? It's a long walk out there and I can't hitch with any other protesters because they haven't arrived yet and—'

'Oh, man, I don't believe you.'

'Please? I won't beg. I absolutely refuse to beg.'

'But you'll take the car anyway. Probably hotwire it if I keep the keys. Yes?'

She considered it. 'Yes.'

Kerry walked to her, looked down into her face. She was so damned pretty tonight, unbelievable lights in her eyes. 'All you had to do was ask.' With a smile and a flick, power was restored. Lacey sidestepped. But Kerry's interest in the old Fender had swiftly departed. There was one thing she could not do successfully and that was tease.

'What'd you really say to Logan?'

'I was upset that you'd run off.'

Kerry backed her into a corner. 'What'd you say?'

'Must I reiterate?' she asked, touching his hand, holding it. 'Because I meant what I said.' Promises lingered in her eyes again. Lacey stood on tiptoe and planted a small wet kiss on his cheek.

He was more than a little confused. 'Is this a yes or are you just teasing me?'

'It's yes on one condition.'

He did not like that word—condition.

'It's my way, tonight. It's *all* my way.'

A smile crossed his eyes as Lacey led Kerry down the hall and into his bedroom. And again, he knew there was a God somewhere.

Kerry kissed her hair—his silent thank you. Even if he still hurt, especially that bite on the inside of his thigh. But she'd kissed it better six times so far. Now she was semi-exhausted, sleepy, using his arm as a pillow. It was hot, the ceiling fan working overtime to cool sweaty bodies. This time she wasn't ashamed of letting him see her naked, to the contrary, she was stretched out and limp beside him, beads of sweat rolling from her face, along her neck, on to the sheets. Kerry wet his finger, dissected her body with slow, deliberate, gentle lines.

'Can I ask something?' His voice was soft, almost non-existent as he circled the darkened nipple, wet it with his tongue. Big blue eyes simply watched. 'What was it like with Eadie?'

'There's no comparison.'

'Please?'

All was quiet for a short while. 'We turned to each other in desperation, I suppose. For closeness. Another's touch. An understanding touch.'

'No, I mean... you know.'

'Kerry, I can't talk about things like that.'

'Of course you can. I'm only curious.'

'No, you're not. The thought of it turns you on.'

'That's all it ever takes with you. A thought.' He kissed her, light but lingering and returned to his slow, deliberate dissection, watching what his touch did to her skin.

'We never planned it,' she whispered. 'The first time was one Christmas Day a few years ago. We were at my place, watching the sunset, sipping wine, talking. She told me she thought she loved me, that she'd understand if I ran away. But I didn't. I felt the same way about her. It was a gradual thing, though.'

'What happened? What was it like?'

'She wanted to see me naked and I was drunk enough to comply. It was so hot anyway. So I showed her. She touched me. It felt different. Different to any man's touch, except maybe yours. She was soft and gentle and as vulnerable as I was. What about you?'

'What do you mean?'

'Have you ever—no, I suppose not. I'd be insulting your manhood by even suggesting it.'

'Me? Shit, no. If anything I'm a closet homophobic. I had a mate who was gay, though. Poor bastard worked Vice. I've been approached two, three times. I thought I could play any role allocated. I was wrong. I reacted badly.'

'Why did you ask about Eadie and me?'

'It's been a fantasy of mine to watch. Nothing else. Just watch.'

'Some fantasies are worth more left unrealized. Only some.' She rolled close, put her leg over his and touched him in much the same way as he'd touched her—with curiosity, wonder. How long would the feeling last? 'I wondered about you the first day I saw you here. I was in town. Eadie was helping you unpack your car. I thought—' She sighed. 'No, I hoped, and I wished and I almost prayed. Then you spoke to me at The Arms that same afternoon and my first instinct was to run. It's something about you, Kerry. I still can't believe I'm here, now, with you. Doing this.'

'You're inflating my ego, girl.'

'I've got a big pin that'll bust your balloon.'

Kerry watched the ceiling fan and for a lost moment wondered how this was going to sound. Wondering would not get him very far. 'If I told you I loved you? Would that make you run?'

'No, I'm not like you.'

He put his arms around her, held tight. 'I have to go.' He kissed her mouth and rolled from the bed. Lacey took his pillow and watched as he lazily put pants on.

'Do you like what you do now?'

'Baking? It's okay. But I'd rather be here with you. Just don't get busted today.'

She smiled.

'Go to sleep.' What he needed was a cool drink and a shower, certainly not the prospect of leaving for work. Kerry kissed her forehead, covered her with the sheet and ventured out into the still darkness alone. Every floorboard creaked with each step. Kerry closed the kitchen door, turned the light on and took a Coke from the fridge. It was half gone by the time he reached the bathroom. And here lay evidence of a female's presence. He'd believed it would never happen again, but there it was—a red mate for his blue toothbrush. A small array of cosmetics, not that she needed any, in a little plastic basket. Kerry had barely wet his skin when the phone rang. Who the hell would be calling at this hour? He answered, dripping, naked.

'Kerry?'

'Aspro?'

'Did I get you out of the cot, mate?'

'No, I'm on my way to work.'

He heard the creaking of the door and turned. Lacey was leaning against the doorway, her curiosity aroused. It was ten to one, who'd be calling at this hour?

'Something here you better see.'

'What is it?'

'Can't say on the phone. Give me a couple of minutes, will you? It won't take long.'

Stunned urgency in the quiet voice. Kerry had heard it before. 'Okay, I'll be there in ten.' Kerry hung up. 'Demetri's found something he wants me to see.'

'That Greek guy who'd already put the rope around my neck before he'd even met me?'

'He's okay when you get to know him.' But she wasn't convinced. He saw that in her eyes. 'I've got to go.'

'Put some clothes on first,' was all she said before she turned and headed back to bed. His bed. So much for the list of rules and regulations.

Aspro was waiting on the front stairs of his new abode. He hadn't changed since Kerry's visit a few hours before; if anything he looked plain tired. He threw his cigarette into the overgrown garden by the stairs, and this time he shut the door once Kerry had walked in. The place was still an obstacle course, slightly less dangerous to the unsuspecting. Aspro led his old friend into the main bedroom. 'I was about to crash when I saw this sticking from the ceiling.' He pointed.

Kerry looked up at the high tongue and groove ceiling and saw nothing except a few dusty cobwebs. Aspro put an envelope into Kerry's hand. An aged document envelope with the State Government emblem. In it, photographs. Old faded Polaroid photographs. Of a half-naked young woman, her hands tied with nylon rope.

'Know her?' Aspro asked and lit another smoke.

'It's Elspeth Mackenzie. I'd know that tattoo anywhere.'

'Keep looking.'

Kerry slipped the first Polaroid to the back of the bunch.

'Know them?' Aspro asked.

Kerry studied the photograph. Elspeth, beaten and lacerated, held to the ground while another was being caught in the act. Literally.

'Purvis. Younger, but it's Frank Purvis. I can't see the other's face clearly. Looks a little like Gilmeister—what I've seen of him anyway. I'd know an arsehole anywhere.'

'Gilmeister,' Aspro said, 'was the last inhabitant of this place. I'd say he stashed these seventeen years ago and forgot where he put them.'

Kerry flicked through the Polaroids and with each a more bitter taste rose in his mouth. 'You know what you've found here, Migraine.'

'Yeah, I know,' was all Aspro said.

Kerry was studying the final photograph—Elspeth Mackenzie dead, or so it seemed. 'Is there a photocopier in the office?'

'Yeah. Yeah, this way.'

Kerry followed. 'Something else I'd do if I were you, mate.'

Aspro, looking pale as he always did when confronted with such niceties of life, turned as he unlocked the office door. 'What?'

'I'd send copies through to Belinda. No one else need see them yet. Just Belinda. Chances are, the originals will get lost very quickly. And if you're told to lose them, give them to me.'

'You take copies.'
'Oh, I intend to.'
'But you were never here.'
'I was never here.'

CHAPTER 13

It was three in the morning by the time Kerry finally sat with a strong coffee and the static of the insomniac's show for company. He took the sheets of copy paper from his pocket, sipped his coffee and unfolded the papers. Seven photographs, three on one page, four on the other. How easily it could have been Lacey there that night.

He didn't have to see much of the darkness-bound background to know the location. If indeed there was a bora ring at the prison site, it shouldn't be too hard to find before the scrub was pushed. Not that there'd be much evidence remaining after seventeen years.

Kerry stared at the pin board on the wall opposite his tiny desk. A few notes were stuck there for his own memory's sake—like Dora's time sheet. She always started ten minutes early and left fifteen minutes late. And lately they met in passing only. So Kerry paid her an hour's overtime a day. Her loyalty was worth every cent. He looked back at the copied photographs, knowing that soon it would all be over. If it wasn't already. Intuition alone told him that Gilmeister hadn't disappeared voluntarily. That Lacey's fear of him coming back for another chat was unwarranted.

'What'd you do with him, Elspeth?' Kerry asked the still darkness. Nothing. Not even a hint of her presence to raise his hackles, touch him with fear. 'Are you off giving someone else a hard time tonight, honey?' Honey. Why am I calling her honey? Why am I talking to a dead person?

He rested his head in his hand, looked down at that final photograph once more and his whisper this time was, 'What'd they do to you, girl? What did they do?'

He closed his eyes. From the edges of a wide, deep cavern overhead he heard laughter. Female laughter. And he was there. An unseen observer, seeing, hearing, feeling...

'Stop, Frankie! Stop!'

The ute skidded to a stop on the potholed, corrugated gravel. A girl was walking in the dark, alone. A pretty girl with long fair hair and a heart-shaped face.

'Come on, Mags! It's a party!'

'No. No, I don't want to. Just leave me alone!'

Lenny got out of the ute, picked her up under one arm and deposited her in the back with the others, others Kerry had never seen before. But there was one, a nice-looking youth, no more than nineteen who kicked and punched away the grasping hands of the cowboys with him. There was one who set her free.

Dora's boy, Jack.

'Your loss, you stupid bitch!' Elspeth called and the ute burnt rubber, taking off sideways in the rough gravel. And the girl, head down and crying, continued on her long walk home.

The ute eventually stopped at the fence line fifty yards from the edge of the swamp and the six, laden with ready-mixed rum and Coke bottles, fumbled their rowdy way in the dark across the rocky ground. The swamp rose high in the near distance, a grasping skeleton in the moonlight.

'What's over there?' someone asked. Half a mile to the south, a tent city—the army's enemy forces.

'Keep the noise down, for Christ's sake.'

A party ensued—these people gathered in a circle. Elspeth with them, taking turns at each other's ready-mixed bottle of rum and Coke, mostly tucked under Gilmeister's huge arm as she sat beside him on an old log.

'Who's going first?' she eventually offered.

'Me. I don't want seconds again.'

'Shit, Lenny, you got yours before. No, I choose for a change.' She stood, swaying, stepped precariously on to the log and looked down at the expectant faces below. And she was cheered on as she started to strip—first the white lace top which she flung over her shoulder, then the black bra. She strutted a little, offering a chance to touch, withdrawing. Then she fell backwards and lay there giggling. That was when Frank brought out the rope. She didn't like the look of that. 'No way. No bloody way! If this is what you bastards got planned, you can stick it. You hear me?'

'Mitch! Brady!'

'Come on, guys, this isn't funny. No. No!' Hands caught behind her back. 'I don't like this. I get claustrophobic!'

'Bullshit. You're gonna love it.'

'No. No, I want to go home. Now! I'll scream!'

Frank wrapped the rope around her neck and pulled tight. 'Scream? No, you won't.' She tried to kick, push him away. Futile. 'Eric, get that tape. It's in the back of the ute. Now!'

Eric bounded over to the ute, searched blindly and reappeared with a roll of wide adhesive plumber's tape. 'I don't think this is a good idea. You said it was just a party, man.'

'You don't want a bit? Fine. Shut the fuck up and watch, you wanker.'

Elspeth kicked Frank in the knee and took off, hands tied behind and tripping on the trailing rope. She made it to the fence and was halfway through when Frank caught her and pulled her out. She screamed, her legs and hair tangled and tearing in the barbed wire.

'Frankie, don't! Don't! Let me go! Please, let me go.'

Frank bound the wide silver tape around her mouth till nothing but muffled pleadings could be heard. He carried her over his shoulder, set her down at the base of half dead gum tree, and tied her to it. Nothing happened for a little while.

'Where's Jack?' someone asked.

No one knew.

'The gutless bastard's done a runner. Fucking typical.'

'Forget him, Frank,' Lenny said. 'He's probably still running. I'll have a chat with him tomorrow.'

The five remaining—Purvis, Eric Bateman, Gilmeister and the two cowboys, Mitch and Brady, all merrily drank on. No one listened to the muffled pleas coming from the base of the tree. After a while, Gilmeister rose and walked to her, took a huge swig of his ready-mix. He untied the rope from the tree, not from her hands. Elspeth tried to run again, but a handful of hair cut that escape short. She fought as best she could till Gilmeister kicked her to the ground.

'Someone give us a hand here. Hold her still,' he commanded.

A steel-capped work boot came down on her chest. Each time she moved, the heel dug in. Frank, towering above, lit a smoke and smiled down at her. Mitch took the photograph while Gilmeister stripped her shorts off, spread those long legs wide.

Muffled pleas of no, no, no, whilst the cowboys watched and shouted, yes, yes, yes!

The horror continued, seemingly without end, each taking turns, except Frank. He simply watched, held, held and watched. And Elspeth, torn and bleeding, tried to crawl away. A hand clamped on her foot and dragged her back to the tree. This time more rope was used, so tightly bound it bit into her throat.

'Think that's too tight?' someone asked.

Frank looked back. Blood trickled from her neck, down her body. 'Nah.'

'Jesus, I don't know about this,' Eric said.

'Fuckin' walk if you wanna go.'

Thunder roared in the distance. The sky lit with a lightning strike. A few spots of rain began to fall. Someone cursed. Eric decided he'd had enough. He took one last look at Elspeth. A look she saw and pleaded with. 'Help me', her eyes implored. *Help me.*

But he walked off into the darkness, alone.

'Everyone finished?' Frank asked, looking up at the encroaching storm.

Confirmed by grunts.

'My turn, then.' He had a smoke first, watched her as the others took their half-empty bottles and made their way back to the ute. All except Gilmeister. He had the polaroid camera in his hand. 'You want to do her?' Frank asked.

'What?'

'Top her.'

'Why?'

'Jesus Christ, did you cheat on your exams?'

'Shit, Frank, she won't say anything.'

'Can't take the risk. Think about it.'

'Hell, I don't know…'

'All we have to do is get our stories together and watertight. No worries.'

Elspeth was partly conscious, face turning blue. They looked at each other.

'It's got to be done.'

Gilmeister shook his head.

'You can go sit in the ute if you don't want to watch. I'll tell you when.' Frank flicked his cigarette butt away and unzipped his pants, stepped out of them. And he took her as she was tied. With hate. She was choking, crying, trying to scream. He didn't care. H, enjoyed it. Especially the flashing of the camera in the darkness. He was almost done when he said, 'Say goodbye to Ells, Lenny.'

Gilmeister didn't move as Frank reached for the knife in his boot and showed it to her just to see the terror light her eyes a little more. He turned to Gilmeister. 'Change your mind, huh?'

'Just walk away, Frank. Please. Just walk away.'

'Yeah. In a minute.'

Frank looked into Elspeth Mackenzie's eyes, and cut the tape, tore it from her face, her hair. There was hate in her eyes now. Hate that amused Frank. She was still choking on her curses, struggling for freedom. Then she screamed. It was loud, piercing. Heard probably two miles away. But it was also very short. Frank drove the knife in under her left breast and twisted it. Blood poured from her mouth, her eyes rolled and she hung limp, held only by the nylon rope.

'Jesus, why'd you go do that!'

Frank stepped away, pulling up his pants. 'Gimme the camera. Gimme the fucking camera!'

Gilmeister passed it over, robot like. 'There was no need for that.'

'What you going to do? Arrest me?'

Frank took the final photo, another flash in the darkness, as Elspeth lay dying. He handed the camera back.

'That's enough, Frank. Enough!'

Frank tilted her head back. Satisfied now, he pulled out the knife, cut the rope and watched her topple. She lay on her side, unmoving. Frank wiped the knife on her hair and walked off towards his ute.

Gilmeister was frozen.

'You coming or not?'

The rain began in earnest. And the party was finally over.

Daylight. A scene change in a movie. And darkness. And daylight once more. A patrol car stopped by the fence and a uniformed senior constable emerged. He climbed through the fence, walked to the gum tree. But nothing was there. He panicked. He ran in circles, ever-widening circles, calling. Then he saw the tracks of something being dragged. The tracks led to the foul brackish water of the swamp. He followed, and there she was, lying in the shallow black putrid mess. Only minutes from death. Gilmeister looked in the direction she was heading—Rosehaven. Her grandmother's farm. He sighed, bright eyes clouding with indecision.

He walked into the stinking shallows and took the service revolver from his belt. He stood over Elspeth Mackenzie, looked down into her fading eyes.

She said something almost incoherent, but he heard traces of a threat. *Kill you. Kill you all...*

He shot her twice and dragged her body into the deeper water. But she didn't sink. So he dragged a log into the swamp, to weigh the body down.

And there was no more.

Kerry opened his eyes. The coffee in his hand was cold. His hip had locked from remaining stationary too long. And something was burning, too. 'Oh, shit!'

He looked at the time. It was five to four and thirty-eight loaves of bread were burning. Opening the ovens, he waved away the thick smoke and cursed. Then the tears came. He couldn't stop them: perhaps it was the culmination of a lifetime of dealing with humanity's darkness. Breaking point finally reached. He ran for some fresh air. He was shaking, ill, till he felt a hand on his shoulder and he knew that touch. It was Elspeth.

'Well, you asked what they did to me, so I showed you,' she said. 'It doesn't hurt any more. Honest, it doesn't.'

'Get away from me!' he yelled into the hot night air. So loud that lights came on in the post office next door. Within moments, Ella's head, curlers intact, poked out of her open bedroom window barely thirty feet away. 'Kerry, are you all right?'

He tried to pretend otherwise: But another wave of nausea overtook him.

A few seconds later, the middle-aged post mistress was beside him, patting his back. 'Goodness me, you're a mess. I can call the doctor for you.'

'No. No, I'll be all right. It's a virus.'

'Eddie used to help Eric sometimes. I can call him for you.'

'Eddie?'

'Eddie!' came the screech, guaranteed to decalcify anyone's spine. A man Kerry had never seen before poked his head from the window.

'What?'

'We need some help here!'

Alert the entire frigging town, Kerry thought as he tried to stand upright, and ended up leaning against the back door of the bakery, knees jelly.

'You don't look at all well.'

'Just need some Maxolon—' But some sanity would be better.

Half an hour later, Ella, dressed only in a summer nightie, was mopping the bakery floor, Eddie was mixing another vat of dough, and Kerry was sitting at his desk, head back against the wall, watching Martinelli's face as the old man prepared a syringe. Kerry offered his arm.

As he gave the injection, the old doctor noticed the sheets of paper at Kerry's elbow. But he said nothing except, 'What you need is a little fresh air, son.'

Kerry rolled his sleeve down, picked up the papers and followed the doctor out, still shaky. 'How much do I owe you for that?'

'Later. Pop in whenever you need a chat. For now, I suggest you go on home, sleep for an hour or two. Have some toast and tea—sweet tea. Get that blood sugar back up.'

Kerry watched the old man get into his car and drive away. Blood sugar? He looked up at the night sky, tried to ignore the cramping in his gut.

Annie. She'd go off and meditate, end up in a trance and later, she'd eat a full packet of chocolate biscuits. You'll get fat. Fat and crazy, he'd say. To which she'd always reply, a true spiritual encounter always lowers the blood sugar.

But that hadn't been a spiritual encounter. Surely to God it was just a nightmare. Kerry went back inside and took a handful of chocolate bars from the counter display. After two he felt considerably better. Almost alive.

Ella had gone home but Eddie remained.

'Kerry Staines,' he said quietly, offering his hand.

'Yeah, I know.'

The hand was ignored. Friendly type, Kerry thought. 'Ella said you used to work with Eric Bateman.'

'Sold to him.'

'You're the original owner?'

'Nope.'

Fountain of information, here.

'You bake too much. End up broke. Too much waste.'

'No, I don't have much wastage.'

''Cos you give your day old to the Abos. Far as I'm concerned, that's waste.'

Yes, Kerry gave his day old to Sheryl, a woman barely thirty years old who had twelve kids to feed. Only nine of them were hers.

'Big mistake. Be better off selling it to Mick Logan.'

'Johnny's father? Why?'

'For his pigs. Shouldn't feed the coons. Only breed up more.'

Kerry wasn't certain if this man was joking. Somehow, he didn't think so. 'Thanks for the hand, Eddie. I can take it now.'

'You're making a mistake,' Eddie grunted and left without another word.

And Kerry was pleased. Thirty-eight loaves down. He sighed, poured the dough into the tins and started over, two hours behind.

It was a busy morning. A succession of people in and out, all lingering for a chat. Asking how he was feeling now And was it true he'd be marrying Lacey Kilder soon? Was it true that the new policeman in town was an old friend of his? The only person he was pleased to see was Lacey. And the shop was full at the time, so he served her last.

'Multigrain's a little late. Be ready by lunchtime.'

'Are you ok?' she asked, frowning.

'Fine. I can bring it home, you know. There's no need to buy it. Unless you're planning another picnic down by the swamp.'

'Give the man a medal.'

'Lacey, please. Not today. I need to talk to you when I finish up.'

'If there's no multigrain, I suppose two of the high tops will have to do.'

'Please, this is important.'

'So is what I have to do. Where did you hide the car keys?'

Kerry fished them from his back pocket. *Love you*, she mouthed just as Chantelle walked in, expecting the day's order of dinner rolls to be ready as normally they were.

Oh, shit, Kerry thought. This day will never end.

Barely an hour had passed before Lacey returned, parked the car nose in, not tail in. She came into the shop, shaky and agitated. Sheryl was collecting the day old bread. Lacey had never seen her smile very often, but lately she kept all her smiles for Kerry. Lacey waited, impatience rising steadily because now they were talking. He was doing this on purpose, making her wait.

'Gidday,' Sheryl said on her way out.

'Sheryl.'

When they were finally alone, he said, 'Back so soon? Another warning this time?'

'There's no one there.'

'Ah, so your stories scared them away. You should be happy.'

'Kerry, I said there's no one there. Just a Hilux, a semi, and the D9. The quarters were wide open but I didn't go in. Something's happened to those two men. I know it has.'

'They might be in town.'

'No, did you hear me? The ute is there. How did they get to town? Walk?'

Kerry sighed. 'It's nothing to do with me. Go tell Aspro.'

'He's not there either. There's a note on the door that says he's in Wilton till two o'clock.'

'What do you expect me to do?'

'Kerry, I didn't like the feeling I got out there.'

'Well, you shouldn't have been there in the first place.'

'Kerry Staines, you're being a pain in the arse!'

Kerry studied her thoughtfully. Then he turned away. Lacey ducked under the counter and followed him. 'I think those men are dead.'

'Look, they could be anywhere.'

'Kerry, please? Go out there with me?'

Kerry took a dozen trays of dinner rolls from the ovens, emptied them into a rack. 'I can't go any bloody where for at least another hour. So don't stand there nagging me, do something constructive and bag these. In half dozens.'

Lacey leaned against the wall and folded her arms defiantly.

'Please,' he said quietly. "When Dora comes in, we can go.'

Kerry was relatively quiet during the drive. He let an eighteen-wheeler through at the fiveways and glanced at Lacey beside him. She was upset. Pale. Fidgeting. 'You think Elspeth's got them.'

'I don't know what's got them. All I know, what I knew would happen has happened.'

'Why would she bother with strangers? Wasn't she only interested in the ones who killed her? Or contributed to her death at least?'

'I have already told you what Elspeth was like. Any man would do, Kerry. Anyone at all.'

'How'd she die?'

'What?'

'Elspeth. How'd she die? She talks to you, right?'

'Yes, she talks to me.'

'How'd she die?'

'She was knifed. It took her three days to die.'

'Where was she stabbed?'

'Why don't *you* ask her?'

'Me? Come on.'

'You can pretend you have no contact with her, but that's what I first recognized in you. You're more than just intuitive. You're a pure channel. A medium.'

'Where was she stabbed?' he asked again. Lacey thrust her finger into his ribs as he drove.

'Someone came back a day or two later. That's what she says. He came back and finished it. Are you satisfied now?'

'Who came back?'

'What's my life worth if I say who came back?'

'I doubt very much that Lenny Gilmeister is a threat to anyone any more.' Kerry took the papers from his pocket and handed them across. 'Aspro found these photographs when he was moving in. And I was coming out here, later today anyway, to take a look around.'

One look was enough for Lacey. 'They took photographs?'

'Yeah. I once worked on a case that involved snuff videos.'

'What's that?'

'Actual videotape footage of people being tortured and killed. Nothing surprises me when it comes to the workings of the human mind.'

'Why are you asking about Elspeth now?'

'She showed me what happened. Mainly because I asked. Like the eternal fool, I wanted to know. Need anything from home while we're out this way?'

'No, thanks.'

'Do you know where the bora ring is?'

Lacey nodded. 'Why?'

'That's where the assaults took place. I want you to show me, because once I find that bora ring I'll know exactly where to look.'

He was quiet for a little while. They passed the mailbox to Rainbow Farm, and the road deteriorated further. Churning clouds of bright red dust billowed behind. 'Did I tell you that you look very appetizing today?' Kerry asked.

'No.'

'Well, I just did. Don't you ever listen?' He glanced at Lacey and smiled. It soon faded. He could almost read her mind. 'And those men aren't dead. Twenty bucks says they're pulling scrub right now.'

'I hope you're right.'

'Darling, I'm never wrong.'

'Do you admit it when you are?'

Kerry remained non-committal. He took the rough track in for the second time in two days. The hair on the back of his neck immediately saluted. gooseflesh whizzed up and down his left side.

'Do you feel that?' Lacey asked.

'Feel what?' Kerry parked a distance from the Hilux, which was still where it was parked originally. The driver's door was open He looked at Lacey and said, 'Stay here. Do not get out unless I ask you to. I mean it. Bloody stay put.'

'You feel it too!'

Kerry got out, slammed the car door. He looked in at the Hi Lux. A packet of molten Minties on the dash. Keys in the ignition. Ho didn't touch. He squatted at the campfire and touched the ashes. Cold. Scum and flying ants floated in the open billy. A few cigarette butts, footprints. The diesel generator was on, out of fuel. The lead intact. The door to the trans portable quarters was ajar. Below the donga steps, in the dirt, a dark congealed fluid in a sunken pool. Saltbush, its leaves sprayed with old blood. Kerry squatted, put his finger into the stain on the ground. He felt it, smelled it. Blood.

Walking up the stairs, he opened the door with his elbow. No one inside. A People magazine, the centrefold's erogenous zones decorated with candle wax. A beer can upended, spilled on the floor. Overflowing ashtrays. Dirty socks on the floor. A pair of workboots. No struggle.

Kerry walked out, back to the car. He leant on the passenger window. 'Go back to town and if Aspro's still not in, call Wilton. But talk only to him. No one else. Tell him I want him out here, a.s.a.p. You go home. I'm not sure when I'll be back.'

'You can't stay here on your own. You're too vulnerable. You have no protection.'

'Vulnerable, my arse. I'll be fine. Just go, please.'

'But you wanted to know where the bora ring was.'

'Lacey, I don't want you here.'

'Unless I show you, you'll never find it.'

He looked at the time. 'OK. Then you leave. You do exactly as I've asked. Understood?' There was no argument. He opened the passenger door and helped her out of the car. Lacey put her huge hat on and took his hand, tight. They walked off together.

'They're dead, aren't they,' she asked.

'I can't say.'

'You don't have to.'

Lacey led him past the D9 and across the bare, dusty flat. She stopped to get her bearings and turned left, towards the north-west. Ten minutes later, Kerry saw it before she did. He put a hand out to stop her moving one more step.

'I know now,' was all he said.

'What do you mean, you know now?'

He could see the swamp, but more than that, it was all so familiar. Too familiar.

'Go. This is no place for you.' Kerry walked ahead, alone. Lacey had no intention of going back, not yet. Not until she'd seen what he had seen. But for a moment, something held her back. Common sense perhaps. She wanted to tell him, 'No, don't go in there'. But nothing would come. She watched him walking, without his limp now. It seemed as if someone else was pushing his remote control. He came to a stop in the middle of the ceremonial bora ring—a wide circle of stones, laid countless years ago. What was he doing? Standing there eyes closed, hands raised? Fear hit immediately in a nauseating wave. 'Kerry! Don't!'

The man in the circle, a stranger now, turned to her. His eyes were black with rage. He pointed a solitary finger at her, said something incoherent. It was another language. Lacey recoiled. He turned again, this time to raise his face to the sky. He was shouting. Wailing. She'd heard this before, or something similar, at tribal displays down by the weir on Australia Day.

'No!' Her scream and its force was enough to wake the dead. Invisible strings snapped. Kerry dropped to his knees, then to his face. Lacey ran without knowing she was running, pushed by an invisible hand. A helping hand. Lacey touched his shoulder. He raised his head, turned to her. But he wasn't Kerry. 'It's the circle. Get out of the circle!' she yelled, pulling him and half dragging him along the bare ground.

The silence was incredibly loud for a long moment. He got up slowly, wiped his hands on his shirt.

'Man, that was weird.'

'What did you see? Who were you?'

'I was, I was… shit, I don't know.'

He had lost all threads of reality, she saw it in his eyes as he searched his mind for an end to the confusion. Then he reached for a cigarette, lit it with shaking fingers and drew in deeply. 'What are you doing here? You shouldn't be here. I told you to…' His voice faded.

'What? Talk to me!'

'You're a woman. You shouldn't be here. Anywhere near here. It's…it's…'

'Sacred?'

He whispered an obscenity and looked at his hands. 'I'm not black. No, no, I'm not black. I'm white.'

'How many times has this happened to you?'

He looked into her eyes. 'Twice,' he said, voice barely audible. 'It's this place. Something about this place.' He drew in on the cigarette again, but he held it like he'd hold a joint. And she knew as she watched him that he wished it was something stronger than plain tobacco. 'You better get into town.'

'I'm not leaving you here on your own.'

'Do as I say,' he said calmly and looked at her coldly.

There was a threat there and she felt it. 'No. If we go, we go together.'

Kerry glimpsed something in the distance, something curled around the base of a gum tree. Elspeth's tree. His blood iced. He didn't have to see the face to know who it was. 'Stay here, Lacey. I mean it.'

She obeyed, but couldn't contain her curiosity. 'Kerry, what is it?'

He looked back.

'What is it!'

'Go, now! I don't give a shit who you call, just get someone out here!'

'What is it!' she screamed, running his way. Angry now, Kerry was fast losing patience. He blocked her from getting any closer.

'No! No, you don't want to see this.'

Lacey used her plastered arm to push him away. 'What? What is?' She stared for a second before realizing exactly what it was he didn't want her to see. And she stepped backwards, hand to mouth, gagging from the sight.

It was Lenny Gilmeister. What was left of him, anyway. And lying near his knee, a Beretta handgun.

Kerry waited until he heard the Rav's engine start and soon saw clouds of dust rise in the distance.

But how long would he have to wait here until someone came? He lit a smoke with shaking fingers and inhaled deeply. Damned if he wasn't chain smoking again.

Looking back to the body half-hidden by the tree, he realized exactly where he was sitting—on the outside of the bora ring, on a log. Where the *party* had been. Elspeth had been standing on this very log when she'd strip teased the boys, unaware of the terrors yet to come her way. So long ago.

Kerry rose, kicked through the saltbush behind the log. Buried in the dirt, an old Bundaberg rum bottle. He kept kicking at the dry dirt, most of it impacted. From under the log he'd been sitting on he glimpsed something black. Using a stick, Kerry raked it out on the third attempt. Female underwear—a black lace bra. Rotten. He flicked it from the end of the stick, pushed it back where he'd found it. Two paces on, he dug around a little more. And there it was. Not white any more. Rotting, too. The lace top Elspeth had been wearing that December night in 1985.

Kerry carefully extinguished his cigarette butt and slipped it back into his packet. It was too late now to ignore the feelings, the images in his mind. Elspeth's revenge. That's what the hairdresser had said. First, the cowboys—Mitch and Brady. Eadie had informed him of that ten seconds after he'd arrived in town. *Bullshit they hit a roo.* Then came Eric Bateman's suicide on the kitchen floor of his house. *Do it, you gutless bastard, do it!* And Frank Purvis, suicide by police.

Now Lenny Gilmeister. All gone. Or were they?

Jack Mallaby had disappeared barely three months after Elspeth. Did she really need any help righting the wrongs?

'Show me where you are, Elspeth,' he whispered as he moved towards the swamp, that magnet to his curiosity. He was in his work clothes, loose shirt, old jeans, sneakers. It'd mean burning the lot.

Kerry knew he shouldn't be doing this. If he had any sense, he'd be with Lacey right now, finding help. Getting the authorities in. If he had any sense at all, he wouldn't be doing this. He'd be back at the shop, being apathetic about Elspeth, and the two missing workmen, like everyone else in Mallen—apathetic. If it doesn't involve me, I do not want to know. Insanity always overruled logic, maybe even self-preservation. He was drawn into the nightmare again, willing or not. Someone else's nightmare, always, until now.

What had once been here? he wondered, looking down at the stretch of stagnant, stinking mire, where that underground river touched the surface, which probably meant there was more than one bottomless hole hidden amid the shallows. And one wrong step would mean a plunge into infinity.

In his mind he saw Gilmeister's legs sinking to the ankles in the shallow murk. He scanned the area, looked back to the direction of the bora ring. The gum tree. From that tree, Kerry calculated the shortest route to the swamp, took fifteen paces to his left and two paces ahead. He sank to his shins in the crap. This was probably where the dying girl lay, looking up into a service revolver, resigned to the fact she'd soon be dead.

Gilmeister, a brick of a man before middle-age spread won the race, had also been a front row forward with the local football team. Six two, 100 kilograms of muscle.

Kerry took three steps further into the swamp, sinking in thick mud to his knees. Four meters out was a split log rising at a forty-five degree angle, a meter above the waterline. He walked in further, until the slime and stagnant murk reached his chest. Under his feet, mud, sticks, rocks, slime. He reached down, fumbling blindly, hands as eyes. He pushed the log away. It belched, an awful sound. Sickening. He reached down again, this time almost submerging totally, desperately trying not to allow the putrid mess to touch his face. Kerry touched vertebra. There was no mistaking that sensation. A human vertebra. He gripped it and pulled. It was stuck. Kerry moved forwards slightly, touching what felt like the curve of a pelvis. He went the other way, following the vertebra with his hand till he touched rope. And the bones of a hand. Maybe two hands. He pulled and the bones disengaged from what seemed to be the wrist. He brought it up as gently as possible. Part of a human hand—a thumb.

He felt stripped of all emotion. There was just a haunting emptiness inside him, no more, no less. Kerry waded out, stripped off his shirt and tied it to the closest marker he could find. Then he sat on the edges of the swamp and looked at the time. His watch was covered in mud. Between his feet, the bone.

He sat there immobile for almost two hours till he heard the sirens approaching.

The voice of the gods, screaming with hunger. And there was something else, too. Something he hadn't heard for a long time. It was the sound of a chopper closing in. He looked up and it eventually appeared from the east. A Jet Ranger. The Channel Ten News.

CHAPTER 14

Lacey was sitting on the front stairs, praying that the next vehicle sighted would be Mallen's new police car, driven by Kerry's friend, the one she didn't like or trust. It was 4.00 p.m. now, what was taking so long? The phone rang and the machine took the call half a second before Lacey could reach it. She picked up, interrupted Kerry's brief, cold, recorded message with, 'Yes, hello?', hoping in vain it would be Kerry. But it wasn't.

'Is Kerry available?' The hesitant voice was surprised. It was also female, but deep, gravelly, and what some people would call provocative.

Lacey wished she hadn't answered. 'No, sorry, he isn't here right now.' She couldn't place the voice, didn't like the feelings associated with it, either. Who was this? An old girlfriend re-establishing contact?

'I need to speak to him. What's his work number?'

'He's not at work.'

Lacey heard several stifled curses. 'Would you give him a message?' It was a polite, if not cool, question, one that needed no reply. Lacey remained quiet, waiting. 'Tell him Belinda called. I'll be contacting him within, say, the next six hours, and I'd appreciate it if he could be sober.'

Oh, would you now? Lacey thought. 'I'll tell him you called.'

The woman with the gravelly voice hung up. Lacey stared at the phone before she put it down, too, and she whispered, 'Bitch.' Then she heard the words which she'd feared for so long. A news flash on TV.

'A report just to hand. A grisly discovery this afternoon at Mallen, far south-west...'

Demetri slowed at the fiveways and indicated a turn.

'Just take me home,' Kerry whined.

Aspro turned anyway, took the street by the river. 'Just checking on messages. I'm expecting one from Belinda. Be half a fart.'

'I'll try not to breathe,' Kerry mumbled. Dirty, stinking, hungry, thirsty and tired. He sat in the passenger seat of the patrol car, half naked, itching all over. The only life in the swamp had been leeches and mosquitoes. Hordes of them.

When the cops had eventually arrived, Kerry ventured back into the swamp with Aspro, Jameson and Leon Prior, all of whom, of course, took overalls from the boots of their respective vehicles.

The news chopper was banned from photographing from the ground but it was not restricted from the air. Kerry knew that the shots of the remains coming out of the swamp piece by piece would make it to the next news broadcast heavily edited. It'd have to be. Shots of Gilmeister's body were allowed only after the immediate scene was covered by tarpaulin. Kerry had wished a little more than ill to befall the journalist taping the grim scene.

It was Pete Jameson who had literally stumbled across the second set of skeletal remains—probably Jack Mallaby's—one bullet hole in the side of the head, plus the back of the skull was fractured. Most likely by a rock, dropped from a great height. Kerry kept his opinions to himself. One look was enough for him. Dental records would be used for formal identification and both sets of remains were being sent to Brisbane. Last he heard, anyway.

A fight had erupted between the male journalist and Leon Prior over the cameraman catching Peter Jameson hysterically throwing up. That footage was definitely banned, human interest or not. Worse, Peter had to stay on regardless, searching for the two missing workmen until the backups arrived or darkness fell, whichever came first.

Aspro had taken Kerry home—the 'civilian' with no further part to play. Not a lot had been said for the past four hours. The handgun beside Gilmeister's body was formally identified as Kerry's, the one stolen weeks ago. Ballistics would test it but Kerry already knew that it was the weapon used to kill Eadie Ross, and Len Gilmeister by his own hand. Or so it looked. While the questions began—who, how, why—Kerry remained silent. They'd piece it together eventually. He knew who, how and why already. How he knew was best kept to himself because nothing could be proved.

Still the emptiness remained. He was dead inside. As dead as he'd felt when he'd watched his baby daughter die. When he held her tiny body to his face and screamed. At least back then he'd been able to scream.

The office door slammed. Demetri came out, still in his filthy overalls, a curling piece of fax paper in his hand He got into the driver's side. 'Major crimes is involved now.'

Kerry said nothing. He looked the other way. Major crimes should have been involved in 1985, he thought, and it would have saved us all some unwarranted suffering, and maybe, Kerry counted, it would have saved six deaths. Not Elspeth though. Nothing would have saved her.

It could have been Lacey there too if Jack Mallaby hadn't fought to let her go.

When Demetri dropped him home, Kerry got out without a word and didn't look back. Demetri eventually drove off. Lacey was waiting for him. She'd bathed, and looked pretty and fresh. But she always did. Except when she was working in her market garden. Kerry came to a standstill at the bottom of his stairs, leaned against the railing and tried to conjure the energy necessary to put one foot on the stair. Then the other. Eighteen times.

'I'll run you a hot bath,' Lacey said quietly. He nodded and looked up at her again. For a moment that stranger returned to his eyes. And for a heartbeat, Elspeth was there, too. Unsure of what to say, Lacey added as she turned and walked away, 'I put a six pack in the freezer for you. And I asked Eddie if he'd bake the quota for you tonight. I hope you don't mind me doing that.'

The last thing he needed was the prospect of facing the mixers and ovens and being polite to people, if polite even existed in his vocabulary any more. Kerry took a deep breath and climbed the remaining stairs slowly. Each one felt like Everest. He still hadn't said a word. He simply leaned against the bathroom wall and watched the hot water filling the tub.

Outside, Lacey kicked his filthy clothing down the back stairs. All of it would have to be burnt jeans, socks, underwear, sneakers...

Kerry lay back in his tub, soaking off the stink, his fingers curled around a beer. He sighed at the sound of the gentle tap on the bathroom door.

'Can I come in?'

No reply. The doorknob turned. Lacey entered, a jug tucked under her plastered arm. In the jug, another frosting stubby of beer. She wore a black cheesecloth dress. It was touching the floor and almost transparent. Almost, but not enough. A low neck, caught with a drawstring, and a tiny gold cross was embedded between those freckled, full breasts. Annie used to wear those dresses, too, but not as well. Maybe Aspro was right. Maybe I do think this lovely creature is another Annie.

Lacey closed the bathroom door and replaced the flat, warm beer with the fresh one.

'Thanks.'

She sat on the edge of the tub and the cat watched from the vanity basin. Without a word, Lacey reached for the jug and shampoo. She sat on the edge, closer, and washed his hair, her touch more relaxing than Denise the hairdresser's had been. Far more erotic, too. Then she squeezed some of her liquid soap on to a sponge and washed his back in strong circular strokes. The dress was wet on one side, clinging to a hugely erect nipple. Why isn't she wearing underwear? his mind asked, vaguely.

'It hurts to see you like this.'

'I'll be okay,' Kerry said, tipping his head back for a better look. I should come home like this more often, he thought. I like this treatment very much.

'Lie back.'

He obeyed, sipped his beer.

Lacey, one-handed, washed his arms, his chest, with the same strong circular strokes. 'Don't stop there,' he said softly, the hint of a tease in his eyes.

Lacey tried to ignore it and handed him the sponge. 'Are you hungry?'

'Yeah.' He couldn't remember the last time he'd eaten.

She closed the door as he was about to say thanks. So he sculled the beer and scrubbed his body until his skin was clean again, and finally rinsed off under the shower. The water slurping down the thirsty drain was black. But nothing could take the smell away. Maybe it was simply adhered to his nostrils, stuck there for ever.

He shaved his face, half wondering why his razor was dull. It begins again, he thought, searching for a disposable, finishing the job quickly. He found the aftershave that set his skin on fire. It worked a little like violets, anaesthetizing the olfactory nerves.

He couldn't smell a thing now. Pausing by the mirror above the vanity basin, he scrutinized the face staring back at him. The dark hair, so dark that sometimes it shone blue. Dark olive skin. Eyes so brown that when angry it was difficult to distinguish between iris and pupil.

Adopted at age three? For a brief, confusing moment, he wondered if his mother was Aboriginal. Or half caste at least. He'd been told that she was barely fifteen years old. He'd never wanted to know any more about her except for an occasional passing thought. His memory of early childhood was negligible. Such thoughts strayed while the eyes remained locked on the reflection's vacant gaze.

Why was it always Kerry stepping forward, without fear, towards a group of colored youths? He was so unlike his colleagues, who usually tossed for the chore and the most fearful always lost. Colleagues who, when trouble was averted by a few words, always said, without fail,

'How come they always listen to you? What is it about you that attracts them, Staines?'

'Flies to shit?' Kerry would reply.

With a sigh, he wrapped a white towel around his waist. He couldn't remember having white towels. Well, maybe there was one, Lacey saw it, freaked and did the laundry? The cat followed him into the kitchen and wound around his ankles while he leaned against the fridge and watched Lacey at work. Cooking something exotic, or so it appeared. He still couldn't believe the miracles this girl could perform in a kitchen. To think these flavors were lying, hidden, undetected, undiscovered in his cupboards...

He watched her for a long time. Her hair was down today. Falling in waves across her shoulders, tickling her back. She was barefoot, too. The line of the legs through the black, vaguely transparent cheesecloth stopped suddenly at the black bikini pants. Nothing else though could he define. She turned, reached for a bottle of herbs. 'Are you brand new yet?' she asked, smiling slightly.

'Almost. Smells great,' he lied. He couldn't smell a thing.

'So do you.'

'Used my razor, huh?'

'I left mine at home.'

'Come here.'

'I'm cooking.'

Kerry walked to her, looked down over her shoulder. The food being pushed around the fry- pan was far less interesting than the rise and fall of those glorious breasts. One look, such as it was, and his entire body was on alert. 'Any appetizers on the menu?' he whispered, slipping his hands around her waist, and pulling her into him. So she could feel it, too.

'Kerry, it'll spoil,' she whined.

Ah, that whine. He'd heard that before. 'I make great Vegemite sandwiches. Or honey. Yeah, honey. I'll coat you in honey and—' He nuzzled her hair away, chewed gently on her neck. She tried to object but couldn't. Kerry reached over and turned the hotplates off, moved the frypan.

Clean, sweet-smelling fingers cupped her breasts, tight. She put her head back against his shoulder and exuded tiny sighs. The lights finally turned green after an eternity on amber. Kerry fumbled with the drawstring on the dress and virtually tore it aside, spun her to face him. With one sweep of hand, the bench was vacated. Glass shattered, plastic containers bounced, spewed floury contents across the floor. He lifted her to the bench and hungrily began his assault.

Lacey, almost shocked by his sudden urgent need, fumbled to find something to hold on to as he took her quickly while he was standing. She didn't close her eyes and nor did he, for his were lit with a strange glow. Intense. Frightening. This wasn't the considerate, responsive man she thought she knew. He just wouldn't stop. He was hurting, rough. Not gentle. Not caring. She felt the rage inside him and couldn't understand where it came from or why he was transferring it to her. Into her. He had to let it out. Any way. Give it to anyone.

The touch was nearly hate-filled now. He was grasping, squeezing, biting, pumping so hard. Her fear exploded to the surface. 'Kerry, no. Slow down, you're scaring me. You're hurting me!'

He didn't hear a word.

She tried to push him away, one armed. He was far too strong. 'No, Kerry, no!'

He reached for the knives screwed to the wall near her ear. One was in his hand now, and it was huge. But it wasn't Kerry holding that carving knife. It was Frank Purvis. Frank Purvis mumbling obscenities. She screamed in terror. A scream which cut more than the hot night air. It woke the old dog who reacted violently. 'Frank's in you! Get him out, Kerry! Get him out!'

Kerry, wherever he was, heard that scream. And as quickly as it began it was over. All movement ceased. Breathless, confused, disorientated. He looked into her eyes. Tears there. Of pain. Physical pain. And fear bordering on pure terror.

Whatever, no, whoever had overtaken him slowly slithered back into its dark hole. He saw the carving knife in his hand. The blade was up. Inches from her body.

'Oh, fuck.' He dropped the knife, withdrew. There was nothing left now. Nothing except confusion. 'I'm sorry. I'm so sorry...' He tried to cover her breasts but the dress kept falling off her shoulders. His fingers were shaking, he couldn't find the drawstring. Bruises were appearing now Big ones. Bite marks, half a breath from bleeding. 'Oh, Jesus Christ, I'm sorry,' he whispered again, stepping back, turning away. 'It wasn't me.'

Lacey, almost impaled against the wall, remained as she was. Stunned now that the terror had passed. But her heart still beat with a quick ferocity, so quick and forceful she thought it would explode. Kerry wrapped the towel around his waist again, picked up her pants from the floor. Lacey slid off the bench, her knees almost refusing to lock when bare feet touched floor. She was shaking, hurt, and, one-handed, she tried to cover her nakedness. She clenched her dress together, a death-grip. No words would come, from her, or him.

He was looking at her with quick, guilty glances from terrified dark eyes. In his outstretched hand, her pants. 'I don't know what happened. I —' He took one step towards her. Lacey snatched the pants. Her feet found wings and she bounded up the hallway, into her room.

Kerry heard the door close, and within seconds he could hear the crying. He closed his eyes. Anger, uncontrollable and violent, burst inside him. He sank his fist into the wall, once, twice, splitting knuckles, feeling nothing, least of all pain. He went into his room first, found a pair of jeans on the floor and he put them on. But he hesitated at her closed door. 'Lacey?'

The crying was more of a whimper now. She tried to say, 'What?' three times before it was successful.

'I didn't— Jesus, girl, it wasn't me.'

For five long seconds, a thick silence hung in the air.

'You hurt me. You hurt me...'

Crying again. He opened the door. She was on the floor in the corner, curled in a fetal knot. The horrors he'd witnessed in the swamp that day were nothing compared to this sight. He stepped in. She flinched. His knees objected when he squatted. His hip, too. But he ignored it. Six times he reached out tentatively before he found the courage to touch her hair. And again she flinched. Curled tighter. How many apologies could he offer?

'I need—I need—'

'What?'

'Some ice. I think.'

When she turned her head and looked at him, the eyes of that teenage girl burned once more into his memory. What have I just done? was his only recurring thought. She'd worked so hard to overcome past terrors, to get on with life. With living. What have I done?

'Ice?'

She uncurled from her knot, unclenched her fist, let him see what he'd done.

'It wasn't me. It wasn't me.'

She looked into his misting eyes. And she nodded. 'I know.'

But he knew she'd never trust him again.

Kerry put the hematoma ointment back in the first aid case in his bedroom. She hadn't said a word to him this past half hour. She was out there now, cleaning up the mess he'd supposedly made. Her silence was annihilating.

All he could remember was touching, nuzzling, expectant of another unplanned lovemaking session. Spontaneous. Next he knew she was screaming and he had a knife in his hand. But he hated knives, hated them with a vengeance. She'd never let him touch her again. Never.

Kerry, in the solitude of his room, sat on his bed and stared at his hands so long without blinking that his eyes dried. And because of it, tears stung. Tears to wash it all away. And she was out there cooking. He could smell it in the air. Permeating everything. He'd never trust himself again. Never let go like that again. Ever. Maybe she was safest away. Right away. Maybe he'd just take her home because at any moment, she'd come in and she'd say, 'Kerry, I want you to drive me home. I want to go home, now.'

The bed beside him indented. Kerry waited, expecting to hear the words he'd already rehearsed. But a hand touched his hair.

'I know it wasn't you.'

'No excuses,' he said, twice, because his voice wouldn't work the first time. He looked at his hand, the split knuckles. 'I'd willingly cut off this hand rather than ever hurt you. You know that. But I did, I did.'

The fingers were in his hair now. 'Talk to me. You *have* to talk to me.'

'I'm not sure what it is I feel right now.' He turned to her. The quick glance into her bright eyes was just too much to take. 'I don't recognize it, Lacey. How can I describe it or explain it? Or make excuses for it.'

'Try.'

'No. If I look at you again it wouldn't be you. It'd be—it'd be—*her.*'

'Elspeth?'

He lay back, put his arm across his face and tried hard to fight the despair welling. He came very close, but he couldn't cry. It was what he needed to do, he knew that, but he couldn't. The topography of his life had split down the center, the edges were breaking away, leaving rugged cliff faces, deep narrow caverns. He'd slipped. Fallen. And this woman he loved but barely knew was trying desperately to throw him down a line.

'I love you,' she said softly, daring to touch him. His arm was sweaty, hot, tense.

'No, girl. You don't know me.'

'Yes, I do.'

'No. No one knows me. Not even me'

An asexual touch now, on his shoulder. A touch like a mother's. A mother he'd tried to escape from, some woman's prison of comfort before it annihilated the freedom of his manhood, such as it was.

'Talk to me, please. Tell me what it was.'

'I can't.'

'Try.'

'No, you're making this worse.'

The touch lifted, Kerry rolled the other way. His back to her. He was angry now, angry she could even be half understanding. He kept it contained. His entire body was tense, agitated. He was full of anger, more productively expressed today out there at the prison site, that murky graveyard, but not expressed at all, only contained in silence, till loosed on someone familiar. Someone he loved. Probably the only person he loved. It was the way of most men. And most women knew to leave them alone for they felt the signs and retreated quietly. But not her.

'It's nothing personal, girl. I can't talk. That's all.'

'You've never tried hard enough.' The hand on his back now.

Kerry buried his face into the cotton bedspread for a moment. But it smelled of her. Everything smelled of her. So he rolled to his back, put his arm across his eyes again. No good. 'Oh, Christ, what's happening to me!'

She held him as best she could, tight. He drowned in the maternal softness, was calmed eventually by the deliberate beating of her heart. She held him so long that he never wanted to be set free. She rocked him, soothed him with a forgiveness he didn't deserve.

'Tell me what happened to you today,' she softly demanded and drew him away, purposely ignoring the tear-stained face. And his words, when they came, were hesitant, unsure. Two false starts, then the wave descended.

'I had to find her, Lacey. Me. I had to be the one to find her. Can you understand that?'

Lacey didn't reply. It wasn't really a question at all.

'I had to know, I had to prove to myself that I wasn't insane. That I wasn't just seeing images or hearing voices in my head. That there was a *reason* for it. I had to prove I wasn't delusional. That yes, I could make it all go away. Disappear. Solve it. Put it to rest for ever.'

'I know,' she said, prompting softly, lying beside him on the bed now. Eye to eye.

'I knew exactly where she'd be because she showed me. She showed me. You know what I felt out there today?'

'No.'

'I had my hand on a human vertebra and you know what I felt? Nothing. Not a fucking thing. There should have been something, girl. Despair, anger, rage, shock. Satisfaction that finally, finally, I'd found her body. That what I'd seen happening to her was real. But I didn't react. I thought, if I found her she'd let me go, she'd let us all go. She'd go on, fuck, this is ridiculous.' He sat up, rubbed at his face. 'I found the skeletal remains of a young female. I'm acting like I know her.'

Lacey remained quiet, watching.

'She wanted me to know, to do something, and there's fuck all I can do.' He was quiet for a moment. 'The gun near the body? It's mine. They think, because they want to think, that Gilmeister did Eadie, then himself. That's the scenario now. But it doesn't make sense. None of it makes sense. I saw that body, Lacey. Like you did. But I saw in a different way to you. I did not see a suicide when I looked at Len Gilmeister.'

'Kerry, let it go. You have to let it go.'

'I can't do that. I can't.' Kerry rubbed his hands through his hair before he stood to full height and turned in an agitated circle. 'It's too neat. I don't like neat.'

'Kerry.'

'No. I know, girl. I know.'

'What? For God's sake, what?'

'Demetri finds incriminating photographs. A few hours later we find Gilmeister dead. He was dead before the photos surfaced. He was dead before his body was put near that tree.'

'What are you saying?'

'Someone else was there at the swamp, Lacey. The night Elspeth died, someone else was there.'

'Kerry, let it go. It's going to destroy you if you don't let it go.'

Kerry turned to her, studied her for too long a time. 'You know who it was out there the night she died.'

'No. No.'

'Gilmeister wasn't the only person you're threatened by. There's another one.'

'There was no one else! Let it go! It's over!' Tears, big ones, filling her eyes now.

Kerry was immune. 'No. No! Don't you understand? She wouldn't still be here if it was over! She never showed me all of it. Why, Lacey? Why?'

'Kerry—'

'Why didn't she show me all of it? Why did I do to you what was done to her? Huh? I could have killed you. I was half a fucking heartbeat away from sinking that knife into your heart. Whatever was in me wanted you dead, like Elspeth. Something was in me, Lacey. In me. No, it's not over.'

'Come and eat now?' she tried, knowing it was futile.

'I can't eat.'

'For me? Please?'

Silence.

'Please? Shit, Kerry! Look at me!'

He did, a side-on glance.

'Look at me. I could have gone. I could have run away screaming. I damn near did. I could have said no more. No, it's over. What we might have had has gone. Did I? No. No, I am still here because I *know* it wasn't you. I know who it was in you. It was Frank. Frank Purvis. I saw him transposed on your face. I saw him and I screamed. But he can only hurt me if you let him. Do you hear me? You can't let this happen again.'

'You think I willingly allowed that happen?'

'Bury it, Kerry. Bury it now and close your door because if you don't, you'll die, too. It will be me, then you.'

Kerry walked out to his verandah, breathed in the hot night air. It was clean, almost pure. After a long while, Kerry said, 'I need some space right now, Lacey. I don't know when I'll be home. Don't wait up.' Kerry touched her arm, an absent but gentle squeeze of goodbye.

'The keys are in the car,' she said quietly.

'There's one more thing I never want you to forget,' he said at the bottom of the stairs.

Lacey waited expectantly.

'I have never cared about anyone the way I care about you.' Then he was gone. It wasn't quite what she needed to hear, though.

'What's happening to you?' she whispered as she watched him drive away.

Chapter 15

Choices arose again. He had two. He could keep driving, or he could not. There was no other option. Except perhaps that other magnet, a magnet to his need, The Australian Arms. And, as if destined, he saw the parking space right outside the entrance to the public bar.

'Frank Purvis, my arse,' Kerry said softly, thrust the Rav into Park, turned the lights off and killed the engine. Elspeth's prompting voice was loud, loud and internal. The hair on the back of his neck prickled, but Kerry mumbled an obscenity, took the keys from the ignition and got out of the car with one thought foremost—ignore her. Ignore her or go stark raving mad.

He locked the car from habit alone—most people in Mallen left windows down, keys in the ignition, for that way, car keys could never be lost. Theft in this godforsaken hole of a place was still largely unknown. He should have been thankful but at that moment, all he wanted was the safety—if it could be called that—of some place familiar, like a city where one million other people did not know him and had no time to judge. Kerry walked into the bar. It was 7.00 p.m. and not many people were about this midweek day.

'Ah, Kerr-ie. We have not seen you for ... oh, such a long time.'

'Emile,' he said and sat down. There was no chance of offending a drunk tonight by taking his barstool—no one was here. 'Bourbon, pal. Straight. And keep it coming until I lose consciousness. And when I do, don't even throw a blanket over me.'

'Ah,' Emile sighed, curiosity rising. 'I should then mark an X for the spot where you were last seen alive?'

'Sounds even better.'

Emile poured the bourbon and watched. It was gone within two seconds. The dark eyes watered, Kerry took a deep breath and nodded. Another was poured. 'I have seen this in old western movies,' Emile said, a little concerned. 'Perhaps I can join you?'

The tense anxiety was fast flooding away.

Emile poured himself a drink, sipped it, and tended the slow bar, all the while watching Kerry closely.

Kerry, mind now thankfully inactive, turned on the barstool and watched the only other occupants of the bar playing eight ball. One was complaining about the bend in his cue, goosing the other player each time he lined up a difficult shot. The cue touching backside didn't delay the inevitable. It was a clean cut into the side pocket. Kerry expected a fight to erupt at any moment, but it didn't.

He stayed there for half an hour, calmly numb, the best way to be. To hell with broken promises. To hell with each new day. To hell with everything. He fumbled in his pocket for his smokes, lit one and inhaled deeply. He studied the glowing end, carefully, at first half wishing it was a joint. Then the wish became a need. Intense. Maybe Aspro had a stash? He looked again at the two pool players and decided it was futile. Those two wouldn't know marijuana from kikuyu.

Dammit.

Emile was back, half leaning on the bar. 'How is our Lacey now?'

'Okay, I think.'

'I feel her loss here. Deeply. A month without her will be difficult.'

Kerry looked into Emile's eyes. He couldn't read what lay there. 'She'll be back.'

Emile scratched his head. 'It is true that she was ... how do I say... beaten by Gilmeister?'

Kerry nodded, wondering how the Frenchman knew.

'All comes back. This is the way of life. It all came back to Gilmeister, *non*? This, too, I hear. This is perhaps why you are here, *non*? Washing away what it was you saw, today at the swamp?'

'I can't comment, Emile. I'm in enough shit already, mate.'

'Usually, I would say, "Emile, keep what is on your mind in your mind", alas—'

"I can't comment.' Kerry still couldn't decide if Emile's interest was curiosity or need. A mixture of both, maybe. He didn't pursue the matter and, for half a moment, Kerry hoped he'd be left in peace.

'How is the business?'

So much for hope. 'Fair to middling.'

'I have heard that you are employing Edward.'

Edward... 'Eddie? Yeah, sort of.'

'The fingers on that one are light. This I know myself.'

'Point taken. Anything else you want to unburden while you try to pry me open?'

Emile grinned. 'I am but being neighborly. You are a businessman, I am a businessman. This we have in common. Perhaps you would consider joining our Progress Association?'

Kerry nearly choked. 'And get involved in cat-fights over what color to paint the public toilets? Piss off.'

Disappointment rose in Emile's eyes. 'Council then? An ally I would need.'

'Emile—'

'The town will grow, Kerr-ie, with the prison so close. It will grow. I have many ideas. Many for the future of this town. My town.'

Kerry had forgotten that Emile Rollet was the town mayor. 'One reason I moved here was to escape politics. I served my time, Emile. I did not rise because I did not kiss arse on cue. And nor would I lie to satisfaction.'

'Consider ?'

Chantelle came down the stairs, ready to work again after a short tea break. She was pleased to see the hotel virtually empty. More pleased to see Kerry again. Emile walked away, busied himself at the dishwasher. Kerry watched the antics of the two—father and daughter deliberately avoiding each other.

'Hi. Haven't seen you around for a while,' Chantelle said.

'You're looking prettier each time I come in.'

'You're just saying that.' Her face flushed.

'I never say things I don't mean.'

She noticed that the bottle of bourbon was half empty now Two hours ago, it was three nips from new. 'Has he asked you yet?' Chantelle said.

'Who, about what?'

'Dad. Has he asked you about standing for election?'

Kerry pulled a face.

'We need a little fresh blood on the council. Or so he says.'

'One or two recent vacancies, right?'

'Just one.'

'Let me guess. The friendly neighborhood plumber.'

'If you don't like the idea, just say no. But not directly. Dad gets his own way far too often around here and doesn't really understand the word no. I told him to leave you alone. Now he's shitty. And he'll stay shitty for three weeks,' she said, her final words loud enough for her father to hear, and as soon as Emile closed in, Chantelle moved off in the other direction. Kerry sensed the antagonism between them ran deep indeed. In fact, he could have sliced the air with a hatchet whenever they came within three feet of each other. But it had nothing to do with him. Nothing.

Again the Frenchman leaned on the bar. 'Before I forget. There is a woman here today. Asking where it is you live. Can I think of her name?'

'Belinda,' Chantelle called from the other end of the bar.

'*Oui*. Belinda.'

'He wouldn't tell her where you lived,' Chantelle said, raising her voice again and not needing to because the bar was echoingly empty.

'I did not say because I do not like being the sandwich filling!' Emile turned back to Kerry.

'She's in Room 4,' Chantelle announced. 'Or she was. I thought I saw her go out half an hour ago. She was talking to Have-a-Chat Logan. I think he told her where you lived. No one else would. But Johnny was pretty pissed, too, so God knows where she ended up.'

'Is she a tall, skinny woman with red hair and lots of freckles?'

'Oui. Very alluring.'

'Jesus, Dad, you're old enough to be her father.' Kerry bit back a smile. 'It's fine. No domestics tonight, not over me.'

Emile was very interested in this woman asking for Kerry. 'She seems mysterious. Always a mystery is good.'

'Well, I wouldn't describe her like that. I used to work with her.'

At that moment Chantelle swept past. 'She said that, but Dad didn't believe her. He said she was far too beautiful to waste her life asking questions about strangers. Something like that.' She lowered her voice and said, 'Time you learnt a new pick-up line, Pop, and stopped being jealous of younger men.'

Jesus, Kerry thought. Here we go.

'Again, I say I am not in the habit of—'

'Look, Emile, it's okay. She wants me, she'll find me.'

'She had the hungry look.'

'The hungry look?'

'*Oui*. It was not food she wanted.'

Kerry had to look away. This was becoming a circus. Chantelle delivered the line which was scratching the surface in Kerry's mind: 'Dad, how many bourbons have you had?'

'At times,' Emile sighed, 'I think, what did I do to deserve the daughter I was sent? For here it is, my one chance in far too long of perhaps, well, need I say?'

Lacey heard the authoritative tap. She eased the axe-head aside, opened the front door. A woman, thirty at the most, wearing tight jeans, a white shirt and a checked jacket stood waiting patiently on the verandah. She had short, spiked red hair that accentuated the eyes further. Intelligent eyes. But she was reaching for the cockatoo and was in danger of losing a finger. He never took to strangers easily. Much to Lacey's disgust, the crest lifted. He turned his head to one side and whispered, 'Give us a kiss.' The bird liked her, not so Lacey.

'Beautiful bird. Is he yours?'

'Look, I don't want to seem rude but I have my own beliefs and I don't want to buy anything.'

'That's a first,' Belinda said, amused. 'Is Kerry in?'

'Linda? Was it you who rang earlier?'

'Belinda. Belinda Barlow. Major Crimes, Special Division. May I?'

'May you what?'

'Come in?'

'Kerry's not here. I'm working.'

Belinda's all-encompassing gaze immediately picked up what Kerry obviously could not. How many times had he described his ideal woman to her as they drove around the city, together, alone? Was that all men wanted? Blonde hair, huge mammaries and little brain? 'Fine,' Belinda said. 'I'm in Mallen making enquiries into the 1985 disappearance of Elizabeth Mackenzie. Will you tell him I was here? I need to speak to him, urgently. I can't find him.'

'Her name was Elspeth. Not Elizabeth.'

'You knew her?'

'She was my cousin.'

'Cousin. Right. So you must be Lacey Kilder?'

'If I had identification on me, I'd show you to prove it. But obviously you don't know the correct procedure, do you, Belinda?'

Belinda bit back a smile, stopped scratching the cocky's head, and took her identification from her pocket. She was a Detective Sergeant. 'Kerry's an old mate, okay? Now, I have walked half the bloody town because some brainless cowboy artist with a mouth like the floodgates of the Warragamba Dam gave me the wrong directions.'

Johnny Logan, Lacey thought, reminding herself to give him a hug when next they met.

'I'm tired, I'm pissed off and I don't want to sound rude but I have no other reason for seeing Kerry again apart from catching up on old times.'

Lacey said nothing for a moment. 'Kerry's changed.'

Belinda turned and scanned the night-time darkness that was Mallen. 'Obviously.'

'And he doesn't drink much any more either. Nor does he do drugs.'

Belinda seemed relieved to hear it. Relieved or surprised, hard to tell which. Lacey was unsure whether to approach openly or turn and run.

'Do you know how long he'll be?'

'No. I learnt early not to let him sense any restriction. That way he always comes back.'

'To you.'

'Yes, to me.'

'I get the message. Which is the shortest way back to the hotel on High Street?'

'If you want to come in and wait, come in.' Lacey stepped aside as the tall woman accepted the biting invitation. The perfume she wore was faint, a dusky exotic one. Italian boots clapped a light applause on the floor. Lacey wondered how many males in town were now suffering from kinked necks. Of all places to stay she chose The Arms. Emile would be in fantasyland right now. 'What time did you get into town?' Lacey asked, trying to be pleasant. It wasn't easy.

'Around five. It was the longest, most boring drive of my bloody life. God Almighty, how can anyone live here voluntarily?'

Lacey showed Belinda into the kitchen. Unlike most faces that paled under fluorescent light, Belinda's glowed. And she was also photographing every detail of the house with her eyes, a habit she shared with Kerry. Or perhaps one he taught her. 'Tea? Coffee? Something cold?' And fattening? Lacey thought, but didn't add.

'Cold, thanks.' Belinda stripped off her jacket, folded it on the end of the table. 'Been here long?' she asked and opened the Coke bottle Lacey offered.

'Be specific.' Lacey poured the soft drink into a long glass.

'Here. Mallen,' Belinda elaborated. Lacey handed her the glass. 'Thanks, this is great.'

'Sit down,' Lacey said as she shut down the computer. 'How long have I been here? Well, one half of my family came from Mallen originally.'

'How long have you known Kerry?' Belinda asked, casually.

'It seems all my life.'

'Oh,' Belinda said, 'Like that? Well, I hate to admit it, but I envy you.'

'Why envy? You don't know me, apart from others' opinions neatly typed and shoved in manila folders. Opinions which I am sure you've already read.'

Belinda had misjudged—blonde plus jumbo didn't necessarily equal brain-dead, not with this one, anyway. 'Well, let's not call it envy. Let's call it wanting something you could never have. I could only work with him. And we sang together. But anything else bar a working friendship was next to incestuous behavior. Or so he used to say. Don't think I never tried. Trust me, Lacey, you're safe.'

'He might feel differently towards you now that his circumstances are altered.'

'I doubt it. He knows me too well. He also knows I'm in town but he keeps avoiding me. What's that tell you?'

Lacey said nothing.

'No, you're more his style. He likes his ladies soft, feminine. It takes a lot of work to keep him in one place, though. My perspective, you see. The outsider looking in. Hell, after sex with a guy like him, what else is left?'

What's she saying? Lacey wondered as she watched her, half curious, half cautious. What's she playing at?

'Relax, I'm not here to steal him away from you.' There was silence for what seemed like a very long, uncomfortable time. 'The house has got a nice feel to it. You live here? Permanently?'

'You already know where I live. You know who I am. Tell me, what am I supposed to call you? Miss? Mrs? Miz? Or Sergeant?'

'Belinda's fine.'

She stretched her long legs out, crossed her feet and jiggled. She was a little uncomfortable and pretending otherwise. 'You don't trust me, do you?'

'After what I've endured this past week? No, I don't trust you.'

'I'm not working right now.'

'Which is the same as saying Kerry's retired. But he hasn't—it's still in his blood.'

'Lacey, I need to know what the hell is going on in this town.'

'Wait till Kerry comes back, then we can all talk.'

'Look, I can understand your distrust—'

'No, Sergeant. You can't. You are not me.'

Belinda reached for her icy Coke and sipped it. 'Is it true you were with Kerry today when he found that suicide? That sergeant from Wilton?'

Lacey nodded.

'You knew the deceased?'

She nodded again.

'How are you handling it?'

'I'm relieved.'

'Excuse me?'

'I'm pleased the bastard's dead.'

'Can I ask why?'

Lacey rose, loosened the drawstring. 'He did this to me on Sunday night. He also broke my arm. You see these bruises?'

Belinda looked at the dozen or so deep, fresh bruises spread liberally across the shoulders, throat, breasts. She winced, an automatic reflex. 'You reported that?' she asked, rising, inspecting the back, where no bruises were visible.

'It did no good. It was a case of closing ranks even tighter. Just like before. Will you tie this for me?'

Belinda obliged the request and retied the draw-string into a perfect bow. 'Were you raped?'

'He wasn't that stupid.'

'That's why Kerry brought you here.'

'One reason. Yes.'

'Some people I've spoken to are saying you'll be marrying soon.'

'Were you surprised? Because I am. No doubt it'll be news to Kerry, too. Tell me, do you always acquire background information from gossip?'

'We speak to people.'

'And what are people saying in Mallen?'

'Not a great deal so far.'

'Do you honestly think it'll get better? That suddenly a few select individuals will be willing to sell the town's dark secrets for the sum of a good night's sleep? My best friend already tried that. They haven't released her body yet.'

'You've been through a hell of a lot.'

'That's a serious understatement.'

Belinda studied the depths of the long glass. 'One thing aggravates me, Lacey. Mind if I call you Lacey?' She didn't wait for a reply. 'You know how it is when there's a tiny stone in your shoe and you'll be damned if you can't get rid of it? How it's just an annoyance at first but the more you're aware of it—'

'Shoot.'

'If you're the only surviving witness to this crime, if there was a crime at all—'

'Oh, there was.'

'When the forensics report is in my hand, then I will believe it. This is off the record, okay?'

Off the record, my arse, Lacey thought. 'Okay.'

'I don't understand for one, why you decided to live here permanently. Given that, according to Sergeant Aspromorgous, you were a witness and threatened on more than one occasion.'

'I had the opportunity of buying my grandmother's property. It had sentimental value, as well as having the only permanent water in the area. I've since turned it into a market garden. Parts of it, at least, and I'm getting tired of explaining my existence to people like you.'

'But you were one witness preceding the alleged events that took place in December, 1985. You left town soon after your cousin disappeared, and twelve years later you return.'

'Economics. The geography was coincidental.'

'But you say you knew all along why your cousin disappeared, and because of that your own personal safety was threatened. Why come back?'

'Why be forced to live your life running away? My time had come to turn around and face it, defy it. And I did.'

'And you're still alive. You see, Lacey, if there was a crime it was covered up by an expert. An expert too good to allow one loose end to unravel. So you tell me, if everyone involved in this alleged murder is dead now, why are you still alive?'

'Knowing what happened and being involved is not necessarily the same thing. And what's to say that if Kerry hadn't arrived in town perhaps I wouldn't be alive right now?'

'No. I put it to you, Miss Kilder, that if Kerry Staines hadn't arrived in town, none of this would have happened at all. Edith Ann Ross would not have been silenced for what she, too, supposedly knew. Frank Purvis would still be alive. And so would Leonard Gilmeister.'

'You don't know that for sure. No one does. What's my crime here? I'm still alive and you think I shouldn't be? Because that's all you've got and that's all you'll ever have.'

Belinda sighed. 'Are you sure you don't know how long Kerry is going to be?'

'I told you, I'm not his keeper. He may even be at work right now. Who knows? I don't put a tracker on him.'

'Where's the bakery?'

'Main street, next to the post office.'

'Thanks for the drink.' Belinda rose, put on her jacket. 'What are you writing now, if I can ask?'

'A book about my cousin.'

'Is it fiction?'

'It may as well be. Seems no one wants to recognize that she even existed.'

'I am expecting a positive identification within twelve hours. And I'll need to talk to you in depth, tomorrow, or the next day.'

'Isn't once enough for you people? I've told Sean Merrin. I've told Demetri.'

'I'd like to hear it for myself. Form my own opinions.'

Lacey walked her to the front door. 'Who else are you speaking to?'

'Everyone who knew Elspeth Mackenzie, Edith Ross, Frank Purvis, Len Gilmeister.'

Lacey watched Belinda walk down the stairs. 'Hope springs eternal.'

Belinda turned. 'Excuse me?'

'People will tell you nothing.'

'I have my ways,' Belinda replied with a smile.

'Mallen has its ways, too. The cemetery's proof of that. Be careful who you talk to.'

'Who I talk to or what I ask?'

'Both.'

'I see. Is this a psychic warning?'

Lacey smiled. 'Oh, you have done your homework. Do you want a psychic warning?'

'Oh, please. Please.'

'Get into your car and get the hell away from here as quickly as you can.'

The phone rang. Emile took it and Chantelle returned to view, this time wiping the bar down, slowing greatly when she approached Kerry. He lifted his glass. 'I know why you're drinking yourself into oblivion,' she said, glancing back to make sure her father was still on the phone. 'I heard a whisper about what you found at the swamp today. Is it true?'

'Honey, I can't comment.'

'Why not?'

'There's been no formal identification.'

Was it really Len?'

'Who?'

'Oh, you mightn't know him—it was before your time. Len Gilmeister. He used to be the copper here before the station closed and he was transferred to Wilton. I heard it was him, that he'd shot himself, that you found the body and it had been there a couple of days.'

Where'd you hear this?'

'Peter Jameson's fiancée, Karen, told me. We're best friends. Peter wants to resign now. I didn't think he was tough enough to be a copper anyway. Tough inside, I mean.'

'Is that what you think's the main selection criteria?' Kerry asked, watching the way she kept polishing the one spot.

'Kerry, this Belinda you used to work with—is she a detective like you were?'

'Yep. And your old man's the wrong gender for her tastes.'

'Really?'

'Really.'

'That's why you were so amused.'

Kerry took a cigarette from his packet, looked up at Chantelle and asked, 'Know anywhere I can get something with a little more life to it?'

Her face went red again. 'Oh, I don't know…'

'I'll pay.'

'I don't know…'

'Don't know or can't decide? I swear, my use only. No one will get busted. Please?'

She saw the imploring, desperate expression in his eyes, recognized it for what it was and looked for her father once more. Still safe. He was on the phone, watching her. 'Meet me in the car park after closing.' She continued her polishing.

Kerry glanced at the time. Half an hour to fill. 'What else did they find at the swamp today?' she asked, shyly. Softly.

'I can't say.'

'Is that why she's here?'

'Who?'

'Belinda.'

'Buggered if I know.'

'If she's here because of Len and Eadie Ross and Elspeth Mackenzie, and I know she is because I heard her asking Dad things, and if she talks to you, will you tell her to go? Please? To get right away?' Chantelle kept looking back at her father, still on the phone.

'Why?'

Gazes met. Something, Kerry wasn't sure what, passed between them. But his gut turned circles. She moved on quickly, fear lighting her eyes when her father returned to the bar—his very presence pushing her away. Kerry was adept at seeing a lot and indicating otherwise. Maybe she knew that. 'Grief?' he asked.

'*Oui*,' Emile replied. 'A council matter. One which will never end.'

'I've been thinking,' Kerry said. 'I won't give you a no just yet about the election.'

'You would consider standing?'

'*Oui*,' Kerry said.

'You would allow me to nominate you?'

'Give us a few days to get used to the idea. It could be the bourbon talking, or I've been listening to your daughter too long. She's very convincing. Very convincing.'

Kerry literally saw the wave of relief flood the Frenchman's eyes. 'I will see you again, then?' Emile asked.

'It's more than a definite possibility.' Trouble is, you're not going to like it much. Kerry watched as Emile talked quietly to his daughter before taking his car keys from the top of the cash register and departing.

'Chantelle?'

She came towards him.

'Do you know who Murrumbingal might be?'

She thought for a moment. Had she heard that name before or not? 'Murrumbingal... it's familiar. Isn't he a tribal elder?'

Kerry shrugged.

'Oh, I see. The swamp spooked you, too. Across the road might be the best place to go. If you're game enough to walk in that is, and silly enough to believe in wanambis and baginis.'

Wanambis? For a second his heart leapt. 'Baginis and wan-whats?' he asked.

'The mythical creatures that live in the swamp.'

'Tell me about them.'

'It's all bullshit. As if anything like that could exist. I mean, hell, a giant snake that lives in the rockwells and eats anyone who touches the water?'

'Is that the wanambi?'

'You believe this?' she asked, incredulous. 'You actually believe in some woman with claws that preys on unsuspecting men for you-know-what? Jesus, you do.' She pulled a face, tried to contain her amusement, without success. 'Across the road. They'll tell you all about it. They like scaring the shit out of us white people with their gruesome stories.'

Across the road, The Metro hotel. Kerry turned, only now realizing how much effect the half bottle of bourbon was having. Through the blinds on the public bar window, he had a clear view across the street, clearer if he'd been sober. Seven or eight Aboriginals on the footpath. He'd never been afraid of them. Till now. Because his reason for approach was fantasy. Baginis. Wanambis. Having delusions that he was a black man.

Chantelle was sitting down now, filing her fingernails, watching the clock.

'Why do we have to meet in the car park?'

'Because my stash is in my car and I'll get shot if I leave the bar unattended.'

'Oh, fair enough. You hate this town, don't you.' She raised her head, laughed his comment off and continued filing.

'Got a boyfriend?'

'No.'

'How come?'

'I'm always working. No one around here takes my fancy anyway. Bloody cowboys with one-track minds. No thanks.' Standard answer to a standard question. Or it would have been if she hadn't sent a silent message to Kerry as he sat alone, drowning his sorrows.

Something in the eyes sparked more than a little interest. He wondered how old she was. 'Ever thought of leaving Mallen?'

'All the time.'

'Why don't you?'

'I can't leave Dad alone.'

'Just you and your dad, huh?'

'Has been for seventeen years.'

That magic number, seventeen. It lit Kerry's interest like a flashing neon sign. 'What happened to your mother?'

'She died. Drowned in the weir when I was a baby.'

'I'm sorry, love. I shouldn't have asked.'

'Ah, what's it matter? I never knew her. Never seen a picture of her, either.'

'Why's that?' Kerry asked, interest rising, brain clicking into gear.

'Dad might tell you. He sure as hell won't tell me. Maybe I look like her, I don't know. Sometimes I don't care much, either.' Chantelle looked up at the wall clock. Only a few minutes to go. 'Drive around to the car park. I'll close early.'

An invitation such as this Kerry could not refuse.

There were two cars in the car park. Chantelle's Hyundai, and a yellow Ford. But his attention was soon diverted.

A full bag of glorious head cost him thirty-five dollars. Which meant that there had to be a local with his own plantation. Kerry already had a fair idea of who that local would be. He rolled his first in the car as he was parked under the house, and he smoked it whilst sitting on his back stairs. A gift from the gods. Lacey's old dog sat by his knee, nudging his hand every few seconds for another pat. So Kerry talked to the smelly old mutt for a long time. And tried to remember where his pipe was. Had he even brought his utensils with him?

He eventually floated up the stairs, fumbled at the locked door far too long. He couldn't find the keyhole, and he was starving to death. He had the munchies bad.

Lacey unlocked the back door and Kerry literally fell inside, tried his best to avoid her. 'Gidday,' he chirped, half hanging off her. Lacey closed and locked the back door.

'What on earth have you been drinking? Smoking? You reek.'

'Nah. Perfume of the gods, darlin'. Perfume of the gods.' He stumbled to the fridge, opened it, looked for food, any food, cooked, uncooked... He grabbed a huge carrot. It was gone in seconds. Celery. It too, lasted a short time. The bread in the freezer was frozen. He threw it over his shoulder.

Lacey just watched, sighing. Amused one moment, despairing the next. Then amusement hit in full. 'Where'd you get it?'

'What?'

'Where'd you get it? Do you think I'm stupid?'

'You? Nah. You wouldn't like to knock me up some—'

'No, I wouldn't.'

'Oh, come on. I'm hungry.'

She tried to step past. 'I'll see you tomorrow at midday. Eddie rang. He can't make it. You've got to work. Wonderful news, isn't it. Good night.'

The information floated over his head. Kerry took out a container of chocolate-chip ice-cream, a large spoon and sat at the table. 'I thought you were going to bed?' he asked.

'Kerry, you have to go to work.'

'Nag, nag ...'

'I'm not nagging.'

Kerry turned, a little too quickly, saw her standing in the doorway and looking disgusted. He thought the ice-cream a safer sight. 'I tried to warn you.'

'About what?'

'Tried to tell you what an animal I am. Deep down inside. Where I live. Sometimes. I think.'

Lacey sat at the table and watched him eat too much ice-cream too fast. Any moment now, he'd be complaining of a headache. 'You have to go to work.'

'Yeah, yeah.'

For now, he was slightly amusing. How would this same scenario be, though, in months, if not years' time, whenever he felt the need to escape and promptly drowned his consciousness in mind-altering substances?

'Anyone call?' he asked.

Lacey shrugged.

'Shit, that's strange.' He was peering into the depths of the ice-cream container, a frown trying to form on his face. 'An old mate's in town. She was trying to contact me.'

'An old friend or an old flame?'

'Belinda? Jesus.' He recoiled at the thought. Whatever the thought was. 'I told you about her. We used to catch bad guys together. We used to sing.' He paused. Something lit his eyes. A thought strayed and remained there too long, biting at common sense. 'Yeah. Sing. Jesus, I feel like playing.'

'Kerry, don't.'

He looked at her, surprised.

'Don't drag the amplifier out now. Get some sleep. You have to go to work. Please, go to bed and get some sleep?'

'Come with me. I've never done it in a bakery before. Have you?'

'Kerry, is that all you think of?'

'I know what I'll do. I'll coat you in strawberry jam. No, I don't like strawberry jam. I'll coat you in something else and lick it all off and—'

'You are disgusting.'

'You are beautiful.'

'Go to bed. I've already set your alarm.' Lacey took the ice-cream away. He lunged for it. 'No! Go to bed.'

'You come too.' He tripped on something invisible as he reached for her.

'For God's sake, brush your teeth. I mean it!'

He saluted, stumbled into the bathroom. There were two of him in the mirror and he didn't like the look of either.

Lacey lay in Kerry's bed for twenty minutes before visualizing the reason for the delay. She padded out, down the hall, through the kitchen and finally into the bathroom. He was asleep on his feet, toothbrush in mouth, head resting on the vanity basin. She put her hand on his shoulder and he woke, fighting for a moment before nearly choking on the toothbrush. 'Come to bed.'

He rinsed his mouth and she led him to his bedroom. He didn't know where he was. He kept asking 'whose house is this?'

She undressed him as best she could, put him to bed.

'You are, you know,' he mumbled.

'I'm what?'

'The most beautiful woman I have ever known. Most tolerant, too.'

'You missed your true vocation,' Lacey said.

'Yeah? What was that?'

'You should have been an actor. You'd be living in Beverly Hills.'

'Without you? Couldn't even consider it.' He brushed stray wisps of hair from her forehead, lowered to kiss her. But she turned her cheek ever so slightly.

'Don't ever do that to me again.'

Kerry pulled back, stared up at the ceiling fan. 'Do what?' he asked, folding his hands under his head.

'Hurt me.'

'I didn't do that to you. It wasn't me. You saw who it was.'

'I meant, don't hurt me by playing childish games, making me feel a fool for believing your lies.'

Kerry swallowed a fast rising lump and reached out, snaked his arm under her head.

'It's not funny. It hurts. It really hurts.' She rolled in, as close as the plastered arm would allow. Hot breath on his shoulder. He was stirring again. Quickly. She worked a magic on him that was volatile. One look into her eyes was usually enough, but her presence so close was overpowering. He tried to ignore the rising need. Two, three, four times a day would never be enough for him. In the dim past of clouded yesterdays, once had usually been enough. So it was true—he did love her. 'I'm sorry,' he said softly.

'Sometimes I don't know who you are,' she said quietly, easing her body deeper against his and closing her eyes. 'Night,' she whispered.

'Night.' Kerry reached over and turned the bed- light off.

What seemed like moments later, the alarm screamed. Loud.

And he had the mother of all hangovers for his 1.30 a.m. breakfast.

Kerry heard the knock on the back door of the bakery at 6.15 a.m. He emptied his trays, opened the door. Demetri was there, more out of uniform than in it. He looked as Kerry felt, like he'd been hit by a runaway bus. Kerry didn't like the look in those eyes. Then Leon Prior stepped in. 'He knows,' Demitri said.

'Motor mouth,' Kerry said. 'You'll never bloody change.'

CHAPTER 16

Kerry had just finished the day's baking. He called Dora in, but she couldn't come. She was being interviewed by police again, this time about the disappearance of her son. 'Kerry, they told me they were almost sure they'd found Jack,' she had said. 'It was just as she told me on the phone. Just as she told me.'

'Well, that's...' no, it wasn't good. 'I suppose it's a relief for you, love. I don't know what else to say.' After a few consoling words—from whence they came he had no idea—he eventually hung up. He felt sick. His hands were shaking again. He called Lacey. She answered, a little sleepy. 'Babe, I need you to help me out for an hour or two. Maybe longer, I don't know.'

'What's wrong?'

'I can't say on the phone. Can you get down here, quick?'

'Kerry, you sound terrible.'

'Please, babe. Come down?'

She was at the bakery within eight minutes of his hanging up the phone and she did not like what she saw when Kerry opened the back door to let her in. He was ill and it had nothing to do with last night's binge. He closed the door, and was walking in circles, dragging fingers through his hair. 'That friend I was asking about. Belinda. The one trying to contact me.'

'What about her?'

'Demetri pulled her out of the weir this morning.'

Lacey didn't know what to say for, perhaps, too long. 'Anything I can do?'

'I have to see her. You understand that? We go back too far to—Jesus.' Tears in his eyes. 'I haven't finished here. There's buns to ice and fill and—'

'Go. I'll see to everything here. Go!'

He didn't hesitate.

Lacey waited until the car reversed out of the alley beside the bakery before she lifted the phone.

There were two police cars parked outside the doctor's residence and surgery—Aspro's patrol car and an unmarked. Kerry knocked on the surgery door. Leon Prior opened it and stepped aside. 'Down the hall, second on the left.'

'Anyone see this?' Kerry asked as he turned back.

'Half a dozen people.'

'Good.' Kerry walked in to Martinelli's surgery.

Aspro was standing by the window. On hearing the footsteps he turned and nodded, looked away again. On the surgery table, Belinda, very much alive.

Martinelli, with a very odd expression in his eyes, touched Kerry's arm as he slipped past. 'A word with you, son.'

'It can wait.' He looked at Belinda. 'You're too ugly to be a corpse, anyway.'

'She didn't give you the message, did she?' Belinda said as she sat on the exam table, huddled in a blanket.

'What message?'

Belinda didn't say. Aspro was too quick. 'Emile Rollet called five minutes ago. Said he was driving across the weir bridge at 9.35 last night. On his way to a councillor's house for some meeting or other. Said he saw a woman standing on the bridge, looking down into the water. He stopped, asked if she was all right. He drove on.'

'That was incredibly well-timed, but then again, news travels fast around here,' Kerry said without expression, his gaze resting on Leon Prior, who couldn't look at him for any length of time. What is it now? Kerry wondered. Shame? No, just discomfort because I outrank him. 'Time the body was transported. Lie down, Sarge. You're supposed to be dead.'

He stood alone watching the coroner's van depart.

Down the street, four people were watching, which was good, and in the distance, barely fifty meters away stood the weir bridge. He was so deep in thought that Kerry jumped when Martinelli put a hand on his shoulder.

'Strange business this, son.'

Kerry looked into the ageing eyes. 'Tell me how the Emile Rollet's wife died, Henry.'

'Oh, that was a long time ago.'

'I need to know.'

'What was her name now? Yes, Jasmine. Lovely girl.'

'What do you remember?' Kerry asked, still staring at the bridge.

'The six-month-old baby she left behind. Sad that. Very sad indeed.'

'Was it suicide?' he asked, already too aware of who would have been the initial investigating officer at the time. Gilmeister.

'Life, son, is suicide. From the moment we're born we begin to die. And things like this only accelerate the process.' Martinelli tapped the packet of cigarettes in Kerry's breast pocket, turned and walked away. 'Follow me.'

Dr Martinelli searched the depths of his ancient filing cabinet and eventually withdrew the Rollet file, opened it. 'She was a pretty girl, nineteen at the time she died. Eighteen when she gave birth. It was a bad delivery, a fortnight early and almost spontaneous. I delivered that baby on the floor of the hotel. Almost lost them both.'

'In your opinion, was she suicidal?'

'My opinion? No, I shouldn't think so. Problems, yes, but suicide? She loved that baby too much. Clung to it like a lifeline. But she'd said a few things to me in confidence over the years.' Now the old man was gazing at the weir bridge, too, but from his window. 'I remember one day in particular. She was sitting opposite me, right in this room, baby in arms. She said, "Henry, I can't face it".'

'Face what?'

'Sexual relations with her husband, Emile. He's got another woman, she said. Well, I didn't tell her that he had three I knew about. Two of them are dead now,' Dr Martinelli said and turned his tired gaze to Kerry. He didn't have to say any more, but Kerry tried anyway.

'Was Elspeth Mackenzie one of them?'

The old man said nothing, but his eyes replied. Kerry exhaled slowly. 'Eadie Ross?'

Martinelli gestured.

'You can't tell me because the third is still alive. Still living in town. A patient of yours.'

'Son, I see a lot. I hear a lot. I know the people in this town. I've birthed them and I've buried them, too. You can take what I'm about to say or you can leave it. It's up to you.'

'Fair enough.'

'I was out for my walk last night at eight-thirty. I walk from half past eight to half past nine every night. My walk takes me past your place up there in Margaret Street. This friend of yours, Belinda, we met in George Street and talked for quite some time. Lovely girl. It seems she was trying to find your house. I showed her. And I waited for a little while, hoping, I suppose, that she'd allow me to walk her back to the hotel. I didn't think it would take long as you weren't home. I'd seen your car at The Arms. But when Lacey let her in, I knew it was futile waiting for her to come out. I'm telling you this because I know who you are, son. I know why you're here and I have known ever since you arrived in town. I'm not a fool, nor are the inhabitants of Mallen. For the most part, anyway. Strange business this. Very strange. I want no further part in it. Do you understand?'

Kerry studied the old man's eyes for a moment before he nodded and said, 'It's almost over anyway. Thanks for your cooperation today, Dr Martinelli.'

The shop was open, two of the early morning regulars were coming out. They each greeted him and Kerry reciprocated from the car window as he parked in the alley. He unlocked the back door with his key. Lacey was reading a magazine and looked up when he walked in. He seemed like a stranger.

'You okay?' she asked.

'Yeah, fine.'

She'd bagged the rolls, filled the buns. Kerry was caught between anger and confusion. He didn't dare look into her eyes, fearing his reaction would be very unfavorable.

'It's been quiet,' Lacey said.

He looked at the time. Ten to eight. He knew it was going to be one hell of a long day.

'The gossip's already started,' she offered, sensing something was not right.

'This fucking town runs on it.'

Lacey closed the magazine, rose and stepped towards him. He turned away. He had to, anything not to look into her eyes, anything not to touch Emile Rollet's third woman.

'What happened?'

'No one knows. It seems she jumped off the weir bridge. Or fell. Or was pushed. Demetri was taking his morning run when he saw her in the river.'

'Anything I can do?'

'Yeah. Yeah, but I think you've already done enough.' Kerry jumped the counter, locked the door, turned the sign to closed and drew the blinds as well. When he turned to face her, he was someone she'd never met before. There was no sign of a limp when he vaulted over the counter again. She stepped back, instinctively.

'When did you talk to Emile last?' he asked.

'Last night. I wanted to know how he was managing without me.'

'And?'

'He wants me to come back as soon as I think I can manage. Kerry, what is it?'

'How well did you know Jasmine?'

'Who?' she asked, eyes filling with fear.

'Jasmine. Don't you remember her? She'd be a year older than you. If she was still alive.'

'Emile's wife? Kerry, that was so long ago.'

'Did you know her!'

'Not really.'

'Not really?'

'Who were your friends in 1985?'

'What?'

'Who were your friends in 1985!'

'Elspeth and Eadie. What's wrong?'

'Elspeth and Eadie were busy fucking Emile Rollet, but you never knew his wife? Your two best friends at the time were involved with a married man but you didn't know what they were doing?'

She was shrinking. Literally. Backing away, trying to get to the door. Try all she liked, Kerry would not let that happen. Not yet anyway. As she backed off, he approached.

'Eadie was definitely alive the last time you saw her?'

'Kerry—'

'Answer me!'

'Yes, of course she was!'

'She told you Gilmeister had raped her.'

'Yes!'

'Then Frank Purvis visited, threatened you with what, exactly, if you talked?'

'What's happening? Why are you asking me all this?'

'He threatened you with what!'

'He said he'd kill me.'

'He *said*? Why didn't he? Six foot two, ex-SAS? He could have broken you with one hand but you scared him away, is this right?'

'Yes!'

'And what kind of firearm was it, Lacey?'

'I don't know... a shotgun? I was scared, I don't remember.'

'Well, that's convenient.'

'What's happening? Why are you asking me this? You're scaring me.'

'It was also convenient how Sean Merrin saved you the trouble of blowing Frank Purvis's head off. What was it? Coincidence?'

'I don't know what you mean.'

'Oh, yes, you fucking do.'

Lacey made the dash for the back door. Kerry caught a handful of hair and restrained her against the wall. 'How'd you do it, Lacey? How'd you manage to drag Len Gilmeister's body to the swamp? Did you drag it by the tractor? Is that how you did it?'

'You're crazy! He was going to kill me! He'd hurt me!'

'But Elspeth frightened him off? No. You shot him. Someone else came. You called someone else. That someone else took him away for you. Took him to the swamp. Then called me so any involvement would be minimal.'

'You're crazy.'

'Yeah? Maybe I am. You were the last person to see Eadie alive. She was the one who stole my handgun. She saw it in my house, and she was scared. What was she scared of? What she knew was coming?'

'I don't know. Maybe.'

'She showed it to you, didn't she? What'd she say to you? How do you work this thing? Is that what she said? You killed Eadie, too?'

'No!' Lacey screamed. 'I loved her as much as—' Her voice faded.

'What? As much as you love me? As much as you love Emile Rollet and Christ only knows who else in this fucking hole?'

Lacey looked up into his eyes and she whispered two words. 'Prove it.'

Which proved one thing only. She didn't know him. At all. His hand fisted in her hair. But she was immune to his anger. A small smile played on her lips.

'Prove it', she said again.

'You set me up. You set me up, you pulled me out. You weaved me into your intricate little web of lies so tight… I'll tell you one thing, Lacey. You are very good, but not that good.'

'Prove it,' she whispered, confidence rising.

'You never loved Eadie. You never loved Elspeth. You hated them both. They were stealing your man. A married man at that. Then his wife takes a convenient nosedive from the weir bridge. Why? Did she find out about you?'

'You're not even close.'

'Tell me!' A demand.

'So far away.'

'Am I next? Am I? Is the swamp gonna get me too? Or do I just meet with an accident.'

Silence. He stared down into her eyes. Eyes that lacked fear, that lacked emotion of any kind. She was better at this than he was and he'd had twenty years of practice.

'Belinda talked to you last night. She talked to you, you didn't like what she had to say so you called Emile. Who left barely two minutes after he hung up. I was in the pub at the time. Did you know Emile saw Belinda on the bridge at 9.35 last night? Is it coincidence that my friend died like his wife died? Why, Lacey? Was she too close, too? Asking the right people wrong questions?'

'Prove it.'

'I can.'

'You'll fail.'

'Your barrister husband taught you nothing.'

'Let go of me.'

'Gonna cry rape?'

'Why not? I'm a better actor than you.'

A smile touched his eyes but not his mouth. 'You really think so?'

'I know so.'

Kerry let go of her hair and stepped back. 'Perhaps it's time I introduced myself. Detective Senior Sergeant Staines, Major Crimes. Special Division.'

'You're bluffing.'

'Do you think anyone with half a brain would actually buy into this pissy little town, huh? Without a good reason? You made the job worth while, though. Oh yes, very worthwhile.' The gaze began at her feet, ended at her eyes. 'But that's just a fringe benefit.'

She didn't move. He expected she would. He expected she'd attack. Scream, hit, punch, kick, scratch. Anything. She did nothing except stand there staring at him, frozen. And believing.

'You gained my trust? Maybe you did. I needed you to think that, anyway. But I sure as hell got yours. You fell right in, Lacey. Right in.'

She still said nothing. Tears were welling in her eyes. He wouldn't be moved, emotionally or physically. But he wanted to. How he wanted to.

'Sergeant Barlow called you yesterday afternoon. You want to know how I know? There's a tap on my phone. Everything incoming, outgoing, is recorded. Would you like me to prove it? I can. Because last night when she walked into that house I've been living in, she was wired.'

Lacey still could not move. She couldn't read his eyes. Fear rose, fear of the creature he had transformed into. Fear of her own foolishness in believing he was The One. 'You're bluffing,' she tried, voice shaking.

'Elspeth, Eadie, Purvis, Gilmeister, now Belinda. My friend, Belinda. Do you really think I'm bluffing? Are you willing to take that risk? Or is that brilliant mind of yours already searching for a way out of this?'

The tears forming erupted, sailed down her face. She made no sound at all.

'Emile Rollet is going down, and he's going to take you with him. Five people are dead, Lacey. Possibly six and you're implicated. If you're lucky you might get to see Rainbow Farm from your cell window, but you'll never see daylight again. That's where you'll be, sweetheart, on the inside looking out until the day you die. You know that, anyway,' he said and put his hand in her hair once again. The touch was gentle, though, kind, like he used to be, yesterday. When she thought she knew who he was.

'I can help you. You know I can.'

Her heart was wild, her knees turning to jelly. And he knew it. He felt it. He fed from it. Her fear, her confusion. Her pain.

'Tell me the truth,' he whispered and used his thumb to wipe away the tears. So kind. So nice.

'I didn't kill Eadie. I loved her. I loved her so much.'

Silence.

'I didn't kill that bastard Gilmeister either, but I wished to God I had. Emile loves me. We're business partners, but nothing else. It didn't work any other way. That woman last night, Belinda, yes, she came here. She wanted you. I knew she did. But I wanted you, too. To myself. All to myself. I thought you were the one. The one for me. As soon as I saw you. Something inside...'

He just watched. Felt. Heard. But he couldn't sense any lies.

'You say your phone's tapped? Then you've heard what Emile said to me.'

'Tell me again.'

'He said she was asking questions. Wanted me to keep you two apart. I had to call him if she showed. I didn't think she'd... I tried not to like her but I did. I told her to get away, but she probably thought I was jealous. I was, Kerry, I was. If she was wired you'd have heard what I said to her and what she said to me. She was like everyone else. She looked at me, made her decision and tried to crucify me.'

Kerry had never seen an expression like it before. Pain that deep could not be faked.

'I never loved Emile, but I own half of the hotel. I didn't tell you because I would never have known if it was me you loved. Me or my money. You want the truth? I just told you the truth.'

A trace of the man she once believed she knew rose in his eyes.

'I didn't kill anyone. But it doesn't matter. You've convinced yourself I have. You used me and I trusted you. I told you things I have never told anyone in my life. It proves one thing, though. The talk is true. I am mad. I am crazy but only because I believed in you. I don't care what you do. I don't care any more.'

Kerry let go. She put her hand on the door. 'Before I walk out of here I want you to know something.' She turned, looked into his eyes. 'I have never forgotten your voice. All these years I have never forgotten. I didn't give my name, did I, Kerry? But I'm sure the conversation was noted somewhere. Or recorded. It was ten minutes past ten on the night of 15 October this year. I called from Henry Martinelli's office and he was right beside me the entire time. Because he wanted this over with, too. Or don't you believe a word he has to say, either?' She looked at him as if for the last time, and she whispered, 'I loved you.' Then she turned, opened the door and walked out.

CHAPTER 17

Kerry was sipping on a mug of coffee and leafing through a mountain of papers and photographs when Demetri tapped on the door, and said, 'Ready yet?'

Kerry looked up. 'Send her in.'

Chantelle was ushered into the interview room. Her face registered a little more than surprise the moment she saw Kerry behind the desk, his feet up.

'Chantelle,' he greeted. 'Sit down, sweetheart. This won't take long.' He ground out his cigarette in the ashtray and watched her eyes. 'Kerry Staines, Detective Senior Sergeant. But I think you know that by now.'

Chantelle sat. She was uneasy and incredibly nervous, especially after last night in the car park. That meeting was foremost on her mind. Maybe she'd stood too close or something. He'd kissed her last night. It was long and wet and she'd almost melted. And he'd held her tight and she'd felt him, too, so hard against her. She'd felt a real fire inside for the first time, and he'd told her how pretty she was. How one day she'd make someone extremely happy. Why couldn't it be him? But it was no good thinking that way. He was nearly twice her age. She'd said it didn't matter. Kiss me again? Touch me. Like this? he'd whispered, eyes almost laughing. I like it when you touch me like that. Where is it, darlin'? I need some, bad. Later, after consideration, she should have held back on the weed until she'd got him in the back seat. But he looked too desperate for some grass. And maybe he never wanted her anyway, maybe he just did that to make her feel desirable. All it did, though, was make her feel pretty bad all night long.

She should have known better but common sense always got in the way. She'd sold him a bag of head for thirty-five dollars even though it had cost her sixty. She'd thought that if she sold it to him cheap, maybe he'd come back once a week or something. Maybe he'd even get sick of Lacey Kilder, want someone younger. But that was last night. It sure wasn't today. He was a fucking undercover cop. All along.

Fuck.

'Tea? Coffee?' he offered.

She shook her head. She couldn't look at him.

'I want to ask you a couple of questions about last night.'

She dared not look at him except in quick glances. He was leaning back in his chair, clicking on a biro. In, out. In, out. 'I got it from Johnny,' she said quickly. 'Logan.'

'What?' Kerry asked.

'The stuff. You know.'

'Stuff? What stuff?' he asked, a smile in his eyes.

'You mean this isn't about—'

Kerry shook his head. 'I don't know what you're talking about.'

Relief flooded in so fast it almost swept her away.

'You remember when I was in the bar last night?'

'Yeah.' She was so happy and relieved, she'd answer anything.

'When the phone rang at about twenty past nine, you answered, right?'

'Yeah.'

'Who was calling?'

'Lacey.'

'Are you sure it was Lacey?'

'Yep.'

'Your father never told you where he was going?' Hesitancy flickered across her eyes. 'It's okay, Chantelle. Really it is.'

Eventually, she said, 'He never said where he was going, but he didn't have to. As soon as he said council business I knew it was Lacey. She was always phoning him when she got lonely or something went wrong. That was before you came here.'

'Were they close before I came here?'

'I don't know. Probably, it's hard to tell.' Chantelle wouldn't look at him.

'Do you know if they were ever intimate?'

She looked around the room, trying hard to find something interesting.

'Honey, you can't tell me anything I don't already know.'

She nodded, then shrugged, unsure. 'Jeez, Kerry, I don't know. Probably. I know Dad wanted her, like he wanted that friend of yours. But whether Lacey did, you know, with Dad, I can't say. He never said, she never said. She's a real private person. Real private. I know Dad didn't like it much when she took a shine to you.'

'Okay. Your mother died when you were a baby, right?'

'Yep. I told you that last night. How pissed were you?'

'I just go over it in my mind aloud sometimes. And, yes, I was pretty pissed as well, but not that pissed. Do you know how your father met Lacey?'

'Before my time, I know that much. Through Elspeth and Eadie, I think? I'm not sure. Sometimes it was hard to believe things Eadie would say. You know how she was a bit twisted. Really twisted if she'd been drinking. And when she was drinking she always tried to tell me things. I was always stuck with her. Lucky me.'

'What would she say?'

'Things like, how hard it used to be telling Elspeth and Lacey apart. How for cousins they looked more like twin sisters except for one thing. Well, two things really. You know, Lacey's got big, yeah, well, you should know about that from what I've heard. Is she really living with you?'

He didn't answer, because at that time he didn't know. He doubted she'd still be in his house, though. Not that he'd have blamed her if she left, especially after that morning. 'Basically, all you knew about Elspeth Mackenzie was what Eadie Ross used to say when she was drunk.'

'I guess so. Yeah, if you put it like that.'

Kerry offered Chantelle a cigarette. She took one from his packet and he lit it for her. His eyes were soft and kind when he flashed the Zippo. God, she thought, I came so close last night, too. Bees swarmed in her belly again, her face roared with fire. Why was he looking at her like that? She looked down at the table and whispered, 'Ta.'

Kerry sat back and lit his own cigarette. 'What time did your father come home last night?'

'I don't know. I watched movies in my room till two or so.' She looked into Kerry's eyes. 'I couldn't sleep.' She looked away again and Kerry was thankful she did.

'So you don't know.'

'Nope. I really don't give a shit what he does or where he goes.'

'Chantelle, did you speak to the woman who occupied Room 4?'

'A bit. She was asking about you. About Lacey, Elspeth, Eadie... Remember I told you you'd better convince her to get out of town?'

'Yes, I remember. But you never said why.'

Sudden fear lit her eyes. A lot of fear.

'Chantelle, I need you to answer the question. It's fine. No one will harm you in any way.'

'I thought she was here because of the photos I found.'

Silence ruled. The poor girl wasn't sure what to say or do and for a moment nor was Kerry. He thought he was beyond surprises. 'What photos?' he asked.

'Jesus,' she said quietly. 'Do I have to?'

The look he sent cut off any escape bid, physical or verbal.

'They were photos of Elspeth Mackenzie with some guys. The first couple looked pretty awful, and the others? Shit, they were... oh, God.'

Kerry gave her a moment to continue.

'They were old Polaroids. Really old. The color had faded, they were ... what's it called when it's gone brown?'

'Sepia?'

'Yeah, all my baby photos are just like them, the same color. I thought they were taken with Dad's old camera, the one he still uses sometimes.'

Leon and Demetri, who were watching from the tiny two way mirror, were suddenly listening hard.

'He takes a lot of photos, doesn't he?'

Her gaze dropped again. 'Says he likes looking at... you know.'

'Naked women?'

'Yeah, but the pictures I found, they were different. They were not, you know, normal.'

'He doesn't know that you found them, does he?'

'No. Shit, no.'

'Talk to me, Chantelle. What did you do when you found them?'

'I put them in the new copper's house before he moved in. I opened a back window, put them in the ceiling of the biggest bedroom, so he'd see them. Did he find them, do you know?'

'Why did you do that anonymously?'

'So people would know it was Frank Purvis who killed Elspeth. Not Lenny. He wasn't like people are saying. He wasn't. Not that it matters any more, because he's dead, too. How long's this going to take? If I don't open on time and Dad drives by and sees the pub closed—'

'We're nearly done, love. Where were the photos when you found them? How'd you find them?'

'I was putting the laundry away up in his room. They were in an envelope taped to the top of his underwear drawer. The tape had come off, it was hanging down a little and I touched it. I thought, this is where he's hidden them. He never kept photos of my mother, you know. I don't even know what she looked like. So I opened the envelope because I knew he wouldn't be back for a few hours. They sure weren't photos of my mother.'

'Where was he that night?'

'He went to see Lacey. He had that look in his eye. It was the Sunday night before she moved in with you. Next I hear she's broken her arm and can't come in to work. It was all I needed.'

'You do the laundry all the time?'

'Yeah, and everything else.'

'Think back to the next day after your father visited Lacey. What state were his clothes in?'

'Real dirty. Yeah, mud, black mud. And stink!' she whined, rolling her eyes. 'I remember asking him what he'd been doing. He said he'd been helping Lacey out in the paddock.'

'Why would he do that?'

'Buggered if I know. He doesn't like getting his hands dirty. Maybe it's because she owns half of the hotel, helps us out a lot. He wants to buy into her property. I don't know, Kerry. I don't understand their business arrangements. I don't care. I just want to leave Mallen. I can't stay here any longer. Boring bloody hole of a place.'

Kerry took several photos from the top file. 'Tell me if these are the photographs you found in your father's underwear drawer.'

He handed them over.

Chantelle looked at the first one. She nodded and handed them back.

'All of them, Chantelle. I know it's not nice but please.'

She looked through all the photographs quickly and handed them back, crossed her arms and hugged herself tight.

'Detective Constable Prior will take a statement from you now. He will then accompany you to the hotel where I suggest you pack a few clothes and personal items. It'd be advisable if you went with him, Chantelle, and not inform anyone at all of your whereabouts until you are informed to the contrary. Do you understand?'

'What, shut up about where I go?'

'Yep.'

'It was Dad, wasn't it,' she said softly, tears forming but not emerging.

'Thanks for your help. You can go.'

She rose unsteadily and didn't look at him. 'I thought you were too good to be true.'

The door closed and Kerry sighed, picked up the biro again. He clicked it a couple of times, then he snapped it in half. Did he need anyone else telling him what a prick he was?

Demetri came in, saw the look in Kerry's eyes and wished he was elsewhere.

'Has Martinelli given his statement yet?' Kerry asked.

'Uh-huh.'

'He'll testify?'

'Yep. Will the daughter?'

'Oh, yes.'

'Did you ask?'

'A bag of head says she will, pal. What can I do you for?'

'You want Emile yet?'

'No. No, I don't.'

'You sure?'

'Uh-huh. Trust me on this one.'

Kerry went home and parked under the house. There was no barking from the old dog today. Lacey had gone, although some of her clothing remained pegged to the line in the backyard. He'd known it would eventually come to this, anyway. Hope, however vain, always failed when battling reality.

The old house was empty. There was no toothbrush next to his. No cosmetics in their neat basket. Kerry walked into the room she'd lived in for a few days that felt like a soft forever. The room was devoid of all trace of her. Very empty. Except for Elspeth standing in the corner. Smiling.

'You haven't won, yet,' Kerry said, more to himself than to her. His phone rang. He answered before the machine took it.

'Prior. I want to hold him here. I don't want to question your judgment but I think you're making a mistake, sir.'

'We will do this my way. It has been my way from the beginning. It is also my responsibility and I have sweet nothing to lose. I want an admission of guilt and we will not get an admission any other way. I know exactly where he is going to go and I am going to be there waiting. I also want the swamp dragged. I have a feeling those missing workmen are there.'

'Why's that?'

'I want it dragged. ASAP.'

'Sir.'

'I also want someone to give me a lift out to Rainbow Farm and I want to wear the wire Sergeant Barlow left in the office for me. Send a car, Leon. And get the Rollet girl out of town now.' Kerry hung up, chose what he needed from his collection, loaded it and went outside to wait.

There was one vehicle parked by the house gate—Johnny Logan's ute. The patrol car pulled up behind it.

'Stash this heap somewhere it won't be seen,' Kerry ordered.

'I think this is a mistake.'

'I don't give a shit what you think. Move your arse.' Kerry got out of the patrol car and Demetri scanned the area for a place to park. Wide open space was all he could see.

Kara met Kerry with much joy, as if she hadn't seen him in weeks. Kerry rubbed the old dog's ears and vaulted over the gate. 'Watch the dog,' Kerry said. 'She'll tear your leg off.'

Demetri looked down into the smiling eyes of the cross-bred Labrador guarding the gate and waiting for him to emerge.

Kerry walked towards the back door of Lacey's high-set house, and the cocky in the cage by the laundry asked what the fuck he wanted this time. Kerry didn't hear the words he'd been repeating to the bird constantly over the last few weeks—his attention was focused on Johnny Logan, who was standing at the top of the stairs. The screen door was half open. 'She doesn't want to see you, man.'

Kerry kept walking regardless, took the stairs two at a time. He put his foot in the door before Johnny could close it. 'You can leave. Now.'

'I can't do that,' Johnny replied.

'If you don't leave now, John, I'll have a swarm of narks on your doorstep before you can scratch your arse. What's it to be?'

Kerry knew Logan's loyalty wouldn't be very strong. He could hear Lacey calling him back and there was no reply to her incessant, 'You can't leave me here on my own!'

'Lacey?'

Kerry stepped inside and heard furniture moving from the living room. By the time he peered around the corner, he was met with a frightening sight—a scared female holding a 12-gauge sawn-off shotgun. She was trying to load it. Impossible with the plastered arm. Under the coffee table was a great cavern in the floorboards. He didn't have to look to know what lay inside.

'For Christ's sakes, put it down before you hurt yourself.'

She was still trying to load it.

'Lacey!' He took three steps towards her, defying common sense, and he knocked the shotgun from her grip. She tried to hit him. Kerry pushed her on to the sofa. She scrambled off it. He pushed her back again and held the shotgun out of her reach over his shoulder before some serious and unnecessary damage was done.

'I have nothing to say to you!'

Kerry ignored that and threw the shotgun to Demetri, who had walked into the living room. 'Put it away, Demetri. You haven't seen it.' Kerry indicated the cache in the floorboards and he looked back at Lacey.

'You're going to listen to me. I did not lie to you, Lacey. Not all of this has been a fabrication. With regard to our recent conversation, all I can say of that is … Demetri, make yourself scarce.'

'Jesus, make up your mind,' Aspro mumbled as he left the room.

'I had to know, girl, okay? I had to say those terrible things so I would know.'

'Terrible? Is that all you can say? Terrible?'

'Have you spoken to Emile Rollet today?'

'I have nothing to say to you!'

'Have you spoken to him!'

She turned her face away. She didn't want to look at him.

'You have. Good.'

She looked back, surprised, confused.

'I want Emile to believe he is suspected of pushing Belinda Barlow from the weir bridge.'

'What are you saying?'

'She's fine, Lacey. I wanted the town to think she drowned. That another body had been added to the growing list. Which is why I'm here because Rollet is coming. I don't know when, but I know he will.'

'I don't understand.'

From under the denim coat he wore, Kerry withdrew a huge semi-automatic handgun, checked its load and slipped it back into place. 'Maybe Frank Purvis did top Eadie and maybe we will never know for certain but I want Rollet for Gilmeister's murder. He wasn't shot at the swamp, Lacey. He was shot in this house whilst you lay semiconscious down there in the roses. As soon as you heard Gilmeister coming, you called Emile. Well, you should have called me, saved us all some grief. For not informing the relevant authorities, you could be charged with being an accessory to murder.'

'It wasn't like that!'

'What was it like, Lacey!'

'I was too frightened to say anything!'

'Is that why you staged that ridiculous protest? You knew where Gilmeister's body would be and you wanted someone to find it?'

She nodded.

'Do you still hate me?'

She wouldn't look at him.

'I tell you what, how about I make us a cup of coffee?' Kerry reached for her hand. It was a touch she recognized. He led her out into the kitchen. Lacey sat at the table, held her head in her hand. He was filling the jug.

'I'm not an accessory to anything and you know it.'

'You've assisted me greatly in this, cooperated as much as you were safely able and I'm going to make sure that's taken into account.' Kerry plugged the jug in, turned it on and looked back at her. 'Makes it impossible when one breaks one's own rules, though.'

She looked up. The once-bright eyes seemed dull, lacking animation. 'Meaning?' she asked, expressionlessly.

'I have tried to convince myself I feel nothing for you but the result's absurd. Where's the sugar?' he asked.

'There's a jar on the shelf which spells S.U.G.A.R.'

There was silence for a little while, except for the cockatoo's screechings. Kerry stood by the window, peering out and seeing nothing but the beginnings of Mallen Correctional Centre in the distance while he waited for the jug to boil. It had to be the slowest in history. 'It doesn't matter now whether you believe what I'm going to say or not. I'm going to say it anyway. What I feel for you I cannot explain in words. Nor can I compare it to anything I have ever known before. Whatever it is, girl, it doesn't fade and it doesn't bore me and believe me, that's a first. You might think I'm some kind of low-life gutter rat right now and you'd be within your rights thinking that, but I never intended to use you or hurt you.'

'Look at me and say that.'

Kerry turned. She was watching. 'You're up to your ears in shit, girl, but it doesn't change how I feel. I love you,' he said, gaze intent and unwavering. 'And I know you needed to hear this sooner, but I took it for granted you already knew. None of what I felt then, or now, was, or is, a lie.'

'But your coming to Mallen certainly was. And if that was a deception, Kerry, then everything that's happened since has been, too.'

Kerry walked to the back door and looked out. Demetri was by the cage, talking to the screeching cockatoo while he rubbed the old dog's belly.

'I never wanted to lie to you.'

'No? Coming out here, supposedly retired, buying the old house, the bakery, settling into the town?' She was drawing invisible circles on the table top. She'd do that on his chest sometimes when they were sharing a bed.

'That was real.'

Her circles enlarged.

'Around the same time I bought the bakery, we became involved in an initial investigation based on your information. I was three months from retiring, so I approached the boss about letting me be relieved of other duties to take this one. My last job. Alone and undercover. It's true that I haven't retired yet, that I am still active, but in three weeks time I am free. And I mean that literally.'

'Did Sean Merrin know about you?'

'Not until six hours after I was charged with Eadie's murder.'

'Leon Prior?'

'This morning.'

The jug finally boiled. Kerry made three coffees.

Lacey watched. Some of the ice inside had melted. The feelings she tried so very hard to bury were once again resurfacing. 'Are you going to stay in Mallen?' she asked.

'I might. Providing I'm accepted back into the town. Providing I can still see you. And providing I can find an apprentice, because once the prison's established I expect to be extremely busy. And so will you with your market garden. Which is why you never sold this property, isn't it? What with its permanent water, good soil that'd grow any damned thing and 400 extra people needing food. Purely business, babe. Just like me.'

A smile touched her eyes, but she turned away so he wouldn't see it touch her lips. Kerry put her mug on the table and he perched on the edge, very close to her. 'Any questions?' he asked, sipping the coffee he'd been craving the past hour.

'Was Annie real?' she asked, drawing circles again.

'Yes, she was. Michael and Julia, too.'

'Your mother?'

'Lacey, my only lie was saying that I had retired when I was still active.' He wanted to touch her hair. 'I don't ask forgiveness for this mess but I do ask for some time to make amends. If you'd let me. If you'd ever trust me again.'

The circles became triangles. 'While you're here waiting for Emile to show, have you considered he might be on his way to France by now?' The geometric designs were closing in on his thigh. At any moment Kerry expected to be touched.

'He's not going anywhere.'

'You're so sure.'

'I'm not often wrong, but when I am, I admit it. No, he'll be here. There's one loose end remaining, girl. You. I believe the only reason you're alive right now is because he loves you a little too much and I can surely understand how he feels.' Kerry got off the table and called, 'Demetri! Coffee's up!'

No reply. He walked to the door and for a moment couldn't find Aspro. Then Kerry saw him in the patrol car which he'd parked behind the bougainvillea. It seemed he was talking on the radio. Kerry whistled. Demetri looked up at the house, and realized he hadn't hidden the patrol car successfully.

A moment later the car's engine started. This time he parked it behind the machinery shed where it was definitely out of sight. Kerry came back inside, muttering to himself.

'What do you look like in a uniform?' Lacey asked.

The question was unexpected. 'Why?'

'I'm curious.'

'I have a couple of photos at home.'

'Which home?'

'Here. Can I show them to you tonight?' A lot, perhaps too much, lay in her reply. 'It's time I cooked for you. I might even let you hear the song I wrote for you. We might do it right for a change, Lacey. Might even stretch the credible elastic by pretending that none of this ever happened. Are you good at pretending?'

'I hope so.'

Aspro's boots thumped on the back stairs, but Kerry didn't move from his place on the table's edge. Lacey picked up her coffee mug. He'd never made coffee for her before but he must have been watching how she took it because it was white and sweet. He must have seen more than she realized.

'Two things,' Demetri said as he picked up his coffee mug. 'Those missing workmen have been located in Charleville. Shit scared. They're on about some kind of spook or something that came out of the swamp. Some girl with... I'll have to tell you later, mate. It gets better apparently. A lot better.'

'Spooks in the swamp, huh?' Kerry quipped offhandedly, noticing the smile appear on Lacey's face and hoping his own remained well hidden. 'Eighteen, nineteen? Blonde hair? Nails like claws? Insatiable?'

'You know about that?' Demetri asked, incredulous.

'You said two things, Sergeant.'

'Oh, yeah. Rollet just turned into Starks Road. Looks like you're right. He's coming this way.'

Kerry mumbled to himself again, finished his coffee and snatched the mug from Demetri's hand. He tipped the dregs down the sink, rinsed the mugs, dried them, put them away. 'Make yourself scarce and don't surface unless I specifically call for you. And don't hide yourself like you hid the frigging car.'

Demetri took the back stairs.

'How'd he get to be a sergeant?'

'Clerical error,' Kerry said lightly. 'No matter what happens, I am in the next room. Here's your chance to prove if you're as good an actor as you say you are. A lot's riding on this. A lot. Understand?'

Lacey nodded and listened to what Kerry had to say.

Emile didn't knock before he came into the house. 'The police are here?' he asked.

'No.'

'They have been?'

'No.'

'There are many tire tracks.'

'I asked Johnny Logan to bring me home. We made a couple of trips. What do you want? Can't you see I'm busy here?'

'Leave this,' he said, and hit the power button on the computer.

'Emile!'

'We have to go while there is still time.'

'What?'

'We have to go. Now. You and me.'

'I can't go anywhere.'

'Oh, yes, you can. We will go now.'

'No, Emile. I can't.'

'Who is here?'

'No one. No one's here.'

'Then come!' he insisted.

'No. Emile, sit down. Please.'

He sat, although he didn't want to. Lacey took two glasses, opened the fridge and poured juice. 'There's something I have to say to you and I want you to be quiet and let me talk. Please.'

Emile watched carefully.

'Kerry's asked me to marry him. I said I would.'

A knife in the heart would have been less painful and less of a shock or so it seemed. Lacey's mouth went very dry. Her hand shook as she lifted the glass of juice.

'I'll sign the hotel back to you if that's what you want. I don't care if I lose money, I love him. I'm not letting this chance slip past me.'

Emile was very quiet. Lacey didn't like the expression in his eyes, only because she didn't know what it was. She knew soon enough when he stood, angry. 'Non. You will come with me. Allez!'

'I don't want to. Don't you see? Kerry and I were meant to be. Not you. It was never you.'

'For all that I do, this is what I have now? Nothing? Chantelle has gone. You would leave me too?'

Can I do this? Lacey wondered. 'You shouldn't have pushed that woman off the bridge! She didn't have to die! Eadie didn't and Lenny didn't, either. It's too much, Emile. Too much. I should never have come back here. I should never have let you talk me into it!'

'There is nothing the police can prove and I did not, how you say, push anyone off a bridge!'

'If there's nothing, why are you running away?'

'I am not running away!'

'No? Chantelle found the photographs you took of Elspeth and the boys!'

'It was not me! They were not mine!'

'How can you prove they weren't? "I was minding them for a friend"? How is that going to sound? Chantelle found them and virtually gave them to the police! She's talked, that's why she's gone! The cops are looking for you right now. They know about Lenny. They know you shot him here and dumped his body in the swamp. Jesus, Emile, what happens to *me* if they find you here?'

'This cannot be true.'

'It is! And it's only a matter of time before they find you. You can't run.'

'Us, *cherie*. Us.'

'Us? This has nothing to do with me. It never did!'

'It was all for you! Always it was for you!' He was touching her now. Her skin was crawling from the arm sliding around her shoulders, how he hugged her tight.

Kerry, where are you, why aren't you here stopping this! her mind silently screamed.

'You will not be with him. I will not allow it. Non. Non.'

'Well, I am, Emile. I'm already with him. I love him.'

'Non. It was *I* who saved you. *I* who gave you back your faith. Who taught you how it is to live again.'

'You helped murder my cousin.'

'It was not I.'

'They'll say you were there, watching. Taking photos. Photos the police have. Photos they can prove were taken with your old camera because they have that, too. They'll say you shot Eadie.'

'Frank shot Eadie.'

'Like Lenny shot himself?'

'He had hurt you!'

'You didn't have to kill him!'

Yes, yes, Kerry silently prompted. Admit it, you bastard, admit.

But he said nothing. It was too quiet out there. Kerry almost peered around the corner, then he heard: 'Come now. Leave all of this. Come with me. Come to Bordeaux. Already I have the tickets.'

'No!' The crying was real, genuine and futile.

'Come!'

'I can't. I can't.'

'Without me, there is nothing.'

'No. No, you're wrong.'

'You will not come?'

'No!'

'Then, *cherie*, to hell will you go.'

Kerry heard the piercing scream and stepped into view, the Browning aimed at Emile's forehead. He saw many things at once, but most of all he focused on Lacey's bright terrified eyes and the switchblade at her throat. Here we go, he thought, mouth drying, and palms sweating.

'Put it down, Emile. Put the knife down.'

'Let me go, let me go—' Lacey whimpered as her head was pulled back hard by a handful of hair.

'I will kill her.'

'No, you won't.' Kerry was focused on the Frenchman's eyes. For a long time there was no movement and no sound. Lacey was rigid.

'I did not push that woman from the bridge!'

'I know you didn't. Put the knife down, slowly, very slowly.'

'I am not a bad man, this you know!'

'Put the knife down! I don't want to do this, but I will. God help me I will.'

'She comes with me now or she dies.'

'I'm not going to let you do that.'

Demetri appeared, silently, on the back landing. He had the back view only of Emile but doubted he could disarm him without injuring the girl in the process.

'Sergeant Aspromorgous, who's standing right behind you, will not hesitate, Emile. I know him. You don't.'

Demetri followed the lead but the service revolver in his hand was visibly shaking.

Emile turned, taking Lacey with him. The knife bit into her throat, a thin line of blood trickled down her neck. Her eyes were wide, her face white.

'Decide, Emile. Decide if it's worth it because this is suicide!'

Emile was backing his way to the door and Kerry nodded. Demetri misunderstood the meaning. He retreated slowly, went down the stairs backwards. Balancing on the top, Emile, still with Lacey in a death grip.

Then the old dog shot out from the laundry, took the stairs at lightning speed and sank her teeth into Emile's calf, attacking, shaking her head, tearing his leg. Emile let go of Lacey's hair, a reflex action. She put the plaster to good use and lifted her arm high, cracking him under the chin. But he took her with him when he fell.

Demetri kicked the knife away and pulled Emile off the woman. The dog was still attacking and Demetri made no attempt to call it off. He kept his service revolver aimed, ordered he get on his stomach and put his hands behind his back.

'She okay?'

Lacey was on her face on the concrete, crying, unable to move.

Kerry called the dog off, but it snapped at him when he got too close to Lacey. He ordered it to sit. Eventually, the old dog obeyed. She was as agitated as everyone else, riding high on her adrenalin rush, too. Kerry turned Lacey over. 'You hurt?'

'No. I don't think so.'

Kerry pulled her to her feet but her knees were jelly so he held her upright and had a quick look at the puncture in her throat. He put his hanky over it. 'Hold it, tight.' To Demetri he yelled, 'Get that bastard out of my sight!'

As Demetri led the handcuffed town mayor away, he had to raise his voice to be heard over the din. 'I'll send a car for you!' he yelled because Emile was crying and cursing in his native tongue and Kara was still nipping at the man's ankles all the way up the path.

'It's over, babe. It's over,' Kerry whispered soothingly.

Lacey passed out and Kerry's legs almost caved in when he tried to catch her. The cocky was screaming obscenities and Kerry realized it had been screaming the entire time. He just hadn't heard it.

As he carried Lacey upstairs, he was shaking, badly.

He laid her on her bed and noticed a movement in the corner. Elspeth was sitting cross-legged on the dressing table.

'I told you. I told you.'

Kerry walked out and returned with Lacey's first aid kit. The puncture wasn't too deep. He found a butterfly closure.

'Where were you when I needed you?' Elspeth asked.

'Go annoy someone else.'

'You're no fun.'

'I could have told you that.' What am I doing? he asked himself silently. I'm talking to a dead person again. Hell, why not? 'What'd you do to those two guys?'

'Which two guys?'

'You know who I'm referring to. The guys at the prison site?'

'Oh, those two. What'd you think I did to them?'

'Elspeth?' He looked at her. She had a very satisfied look on her face. 'Forget it. I really don't want to know.'

'What would you like me to do to you? I can, you know. Anything you want. And I know exactly what you like.'

'You're not going to go away, are you?'

There was no reply so he looked towards the dressing table again. She wasn't there. He turned the other way. She was leaning provocatively against the doorway.

No doubt in the near future there'll be 400 maximum security prisoners with huge smiles on their faces, Kerry thought.

To which Elspeth said, 'How many?'

'Four hundred.'

'Four hundred guys? Wow.'

'I've got an idea, Ells. You interested?'

For the next few days, Demetri Aspromorgous carried a perpetually surprised look on his face, probably from a succession of wet dreams about a beautiful young blonde. She was insatiable.

236

CHAPTER 18

'Amen.'

Hallelujah, brother, Kerry thought. He watched Lacey touch the minister's hand, watched the straggle of black-clothed people walking back to their cars.

It was almost over.

Kerry was Brisbane-bound until the fifteenth. The bakery had temporarily closed until that date, and not many people were talking to him, although it seemed that most believed the rumor that he'd been pulled out of retirement for one final job. Kerry let them keep the fantasy as it suited his needs for present and future. Mallen had started to feel like home and he hoped it would be so once again.

Lacey was talking to Chantelle Rollet now, hugging her. And Chantelle had hold of Leon Prior's hand, too. Silly girl, he thought and walked back to his car. He leaned on it, waiting. He should have been long gone but there was another flight he could catch from Charleville tomorrow. It'd mean another lie about his delayed reappearance at Headquarters, but better a lie than letting a good friend down.

Jack Mallaby's remains had been interred yesterday and, throughout, he'd held Dora's hand. Today, it was Elspeth Mackenzie and Eadie Ross lowered into adjoining plots. Hardly anyone came to this ceremony, though. Lacey bore the financial responsibility for Elspeth and Eadie, being the only friend of one and only surviving relative of the other. She hadn't shed a tear yet, not that Kerry expected she would. And nor had she spoken to him much; the relationship was strained, to say the least, hardly existent at the most. But surprise lit her eyes each time she looked at him, as if shocked that he was still there. He was still there because he wanted to be. There was no other reason.

She eventually said her solitary goodbyes to each open grave and turned away. Kerry was waiting, sunglasses on. They were reflector ones she wanted to crush. He opened the car door for her and she said nothing as she sank down into the stifling interior. Kerry closed the door and got in. He turned the ignition on, set the air-conditioning to high. It took a few moments before the temperature was bearable.

'When's your plane leave?' she asked.

'Later,' he replied. 'I've got time.'

'Kerry, I said there was no need for you to come.'

'I knew them both, too. It went okay for a funeral.'

There was silence for a while. Maybe that had been the wrong thing to say. Again. 'Where would you like to go now?' he asked.

'Tahiti,' she said softly.

Kerry drove off, muttering in a very English accent, 'James? Tahiti would be nice.' He glanced at her. She was staring from the car window. He wanted to tell her how good she looked in black, with her hair up like that but nothing came except, 'I have to go. I don't have any choice. I told you.'

'I know what you told me, Kerry.'

Quiet ensued, too much quiet. He needed some music, but didn't think rock 'n' roll suitable for a drive home from a double funeral.

'How long do you think he'll get?' Lacey asked, allowing him to know what her train of thought had been.

'Mandatory life. He confessed and is going to plead guilty so there won't be a trial.'

'Even though he was defending me.'

'He would have killed you, too.'

'No one knows that for sure.' But she touched the adhesive cover on her throat anyway. It had required a stitch and already it was itching, pulling each time she moved her head.

After a little while she asked, 'Would you have shot him, Kerry?'

'Yep.'

'If it had been me?'

'Jesus, Lacey—'

'Just curious.'

'Well, you shouldn't be. Where do you want to go?'

'Want or need?' she asked, looking at her time. 'Better drop me off at the hotel. I have to open.'

Nothing else was said until Kerry came to a stop at the public bar entrance to the Arms. 'When will you change the licensee sign?' he asked.

'When you're the manager,' she replied.

'News to me,' he said.

'Why waste a business brain like yours, Kerry Staines? I'm buying Emile out and giving Chantelle the option of staying if she wants. She said she'd stay until you came back. But she has stars in her eyes now. I think she's taken to Leon with a vengeance.'

238

'Yes, I noticed. It's a hell of a job alone, Lacey, running a pub.'

'I know. I'm counting on you coming back.'

'I will,' he said. 'Who's helping out till then?'

'Ray Macquarie and Johnny, Chantelle and me.'

'What about the farm?'

'Didn't I tell you? The government's offered me twice its value. I'm taking it. I've been assured it will be kept as a market garden worked by the inmates.'

'And what about us?' he asked, his most important question left until last.

Lacey patted his knee and got out of the car. 'You know where I'll be,' she said before she closed the door. 'Go, before you miss your plane.'

She watched as he drove down High Street and turned left towards the five-ways. Sighing, she looked at the old Labrador lying across the entrance to the public bar. There was a Siamese cat trying to swat at the wagging tail.

Kerry didn't take the road to Wilton, he turned left instead and continued on till he approached the caravan park and there, he crossed the one-lane bridge and drove on, into the black side of town. The neglected side. Gravel roads, no garbage collection and a leaking water main producing a bog that four kids were playing in. He drove on, past rows of identical fibro houses with decrepit fences, roofs, broken windows. None bore house numbers, but then again there were no street signs either.

Abandoned, rusting hulks of cars rested permanently in overgrown front yards. Kids playing street cricket gestured obscenely as he interrupted their game by stopping, calling out. A boy of around thirteen walked towards him, paling bat over shoulder.

'You lost?' he asked.

'Probably,' Kerry said. 'I'm looking for Murrumbingal.'

'Who?'

'Murrumbingal. I think he's a tribal elder.'

The kids crowding by the car window took a while to work out who this Murrumbingal was. One of them decided it must have been old Ted. 'You go down there, go right, and right, and right and it's a white place with a Valiant in the yard.'

Right, right and right, is that right? Kerry looked into the rear-vision mirror, said thanks to the boys and he U-turned, stopped the Rav opposite the house with a Valiant in the yard. The car had been stripped of anything valuable a long time ago. On the front porch of the shanty house sat a very old man, a mane of white hair framing his ancient face.

Kerry turned the engine off and wondered if he should go ahead with this. It made no sense. He should have been on his way to Charleville by now.

The old man just watched.

Nothing to lose, Kerry thought and emerged from his car. He locked it and pocketed his keys. Four kids of various ages and degrees of color hid under the porch and watched him approach. He pretended not to see them.

The old man didn't acknowledge his presence. Kerry stood in calf-high grass and looked at the ancient man sitting on an even older recliner. Ripped, torn, squeaking as he rocked.

'Excuse me?'

The old man barely flinched. Kerry spoke louder. 'Excuse me? I'm looking for someone called Murrumbingal. Can you help me?'

'Sheryl, he's here.'

The woman who came into his shop every day appeared with a naked two-year-old on her hip. 'Gidday,' she said, all teeth and joy.

'Sheryl.'

'Don't mind the cranky old bugger. He's been expecting you for a long time. He's blind and he don't hear too good either. You gotta yell at the silly old bugger.'

Something touched his shoe. Kerry looked down. Little arms and hands were poking at his legs. He stamped his foot and the kids retreated, squealing. The old man grinned. All Kerry saw was a shock of white teeth equal in color to the hair. The old guy was so black, his skin seemed polished. 'Come on in, Djawa. Come on in.'

Inside, the house was cluttered with clothes and toys, but there was a minimum of furniture. The old man knew exactly where he was going.

Kerry was handed a warm beer in a dirty glass and he doubted the wisdom of this visit as each second passed. Kids shot through the house screaming.

'You's a white fella?' Murrumbingal asked. 'Yes, I am.'

'You coming back here or you going back to the city where you don't belong no more?'

'Ah, I'll be coming back.'

The kids were using the house as a race circuit till the old man bellowed, 'You bloody kids git outside!'

Peace reigned. Kerry sipped the beer and was motioned to sit down. He did, after he moved a toy truck from an old lounge before he impaled himself on it. The two-year-old without pants sat at Kerry's feet and played with the toy. A wheel came off, he handed it to Kerry, who without a word, put it back on and shot it across the bare floorboards. The child brought it back for him to do it again. Which he did, over and over.

'You want to know, don't you, white fella?'

White fella. Jesus, Kerry thought. 'I need to know a few things, yes. That's why I'm here.'

'Soon as I saw you I knew who you was once.'

Kerry looked into the sightless eyes. I'm in the wrong house, he thought. I'm surrounded by maniacs.

'Might be blind, white fella, but I can see. You don't remember, do you?'

Kerry looked at the house again, thought of his mother, his father—the ones he'd known—and the urge to run was strong, almost undeniable.

'They filled you with bullshit, boy.'

'Excuse me?'

'Bullshit stories. You wasn't born in no city. You was born here. They come take you away. Them white fellas got you 'cause your daddy was white. Raised you white. Taught you white ways. But I seen you and I knew you'd be comin' back here one day. I seen him again in your eyes back then, back in '54. Was 29 May, 1954.'

Kerry's birthday.

'She was still a kid, your mother. Didn't know what was happening. Screamed so bad. She nearly died on us. Then they come take you away, away from here. Don't like it much, do you, white fella.'

Kerry's only thought was of Elspeth, perched on the car window, displaying her wares and asking him who jumped the fence, mum or dad?

'Finish that beer. We'll go for a walk. Just you and me, away from these bloody kids.'

Kerry looked at his watch. It was too late to catch that flight now. He sculled the warm beer, thanked Sheryl for it, ruffled the two-year-old's hair, and followed the old man out. He almost offered to assist him down the two stairs, but thought twice.

'Feel it, don't you.'

'Feel what exactly?'

The old man turned to him, put his hand on Kerry's forehead, then his chest. 'Here. You know why you're here, so don't bullshit me. Just tell me what you seen.'

Kerry told him, hesitant at first, about the experience by the river barely a week before. He was also about to tell Murrumbingal about the bora ring, too, but the old man was talking again.

'You know, before my time, before my grandfather's time, it was ceremonial ground there. A meeting place. Long gone now. Long gone.'

'Do you know what happened to me? I can't explain it. I thought you might be able to.'

'Yeah, spirits working, helpin' you remember things. Where's your car, white fella?'

'Across the street.'

'I tell you what. You take me to the swamp and I'll tell you a story when we git there.'

'Used to come here sometimes,' Murrumbingal said as Kerry walked him across the ground towards the bora ring. The prison site was deserted today, and the swamp's pungent aroma intensified by the stifling heat and non-existent breeze. It seemed that every time he came here, the stink got worse. 'Elders used to come here. Spirits show us why. This place used to be a good place, you know. Used to be a magic place long before white fella come. Tribes all over come to shelter and water here, this spot, this place. Was a good place then. Good water, lots of lilies. Ever tried lily roots?'

'No, can't say I have.'

'Dunno what you been missing, white fella. Was way back when,' the old man said with a sigh. 'You want to know what happened way back when?'

Kerry was standing in the middle of the bora ring, nothing was happening today. The old man was sitting on that log, shooing flies.

'You want to know, white fella? You want to know who you was, what you did?'

What Kerry wanted was an escape. Instead he heard himself say, 'I guess so.'

'Way back when there was a small tribe used to live here. Way back when. They was happy, way back then. But one day this outcast comes. His name was Djawa. Outcast. Lived on his own. Stole some women. Stole em at night, right out of their family's house he would. Right away from the husbands he stole em. Smart bugger, Djawa. Got the women magic'd. Got em to slip him food. Lie with him. Gave him sons they did. Men tried to kill him, but they couldn't. Too sneaky for that, see. Then one day he goes away. He steals his sons. The women cry.' The old man sighed and Kerry was half listening to the Dreamtime bullshit story, wondering the sense in this anyway.

'He weren't no outcast. He was from the tribe on the other side of the river. Bad ones, them, real bad ones. And fight! Jeez, they could fight. So he goes back to them, this Djawa, takes his sons, teaches em to fight and kill and they all come back before dawn one day and they kill everyone. Even the women who cried. But the last one to die, he was the spirit man. He called up Wanambi and he cursed this place, made it dead, no good for nothing. He cursed and the place died right away. Stunk of the dead. Wanambi rises cos he's called up. Wanambi swallows Djawa and his sons and all his people who come to steal this place. This good place. Place stays dead till Djawa sees his wrong.'

Kerry waited for more. But there was no more. 'Wanambi. What exactly is that?'

'The snake.'

'And you're telling me I'm this Djawa? This outcast?'

'Spirits show me this long ago when I looked into the baby's eyes.'

Which spirits? Kerry wondered. The ones from a bottle?

'Sit down now,' Murrumbingal said. He took from his baggy pants a jar of white clay paint. 'Sit!'

'Look, this is a crock.'

'End this now!'

The old man moved quickly with incredible strength, too, and before Kerry knew it he was on his behind in the middle of the bora ring, with the old man streaking white clay across his eyes and cheeks. He didn't like the feeling of the sticky stuff on his skin. Nausea rose.

'Spirits bring you here to show you. So see. See white fella, see!'

The air hit Kerry in a heavy wave. What was bright summer daylight became dim. The colors were different, the air was sharp, biting. In the east, the rising glow of dawn broke across the horizon. Around him, lean-tos and inside, semi-naked black bodies, deeply asleep. With him, others, although he couldn't see them. They crept in, through the fertile oasis surrounds, spears raised. He could see them now, twenty, thirty of them and he was there leading them, some ancient black warrior with painted skin and long bare feet, feeling nothing except excited anticipation. But there was barely a sound except for breathing. Axes of stone tied to wooden handles were raised high, ready to strike. One blood-curdling yell followed by screaming, crunching as axes struck skulls, as spears pierced backs and breasts and bellies of the young and old alike, of men and women and children, even babies.

One remained prone at his feet. Hatred in the eyes. Incomprehensible words spat with hate as the left hand raised up, pointing a bony finger to the east, the north, the west, the south. Then at him. The voice calling up the protective spirits to avenge the massacre, but the spear came down into the throat, impaled the chief to the ground.

A victory dance lasted for ever. Bodies dragged away and burnt. He claimed the oasis as his own. But the spring water turned sour. The trees died. The water lilies shrunk, turned brown and the roots poisoned his woman first, then all who ate. He watched his people die. Till only one remained without the strength to walk. He was watched by a huge black crow as he slowly died of thirst. It was over. Done.

Kerry touched his face. White clay, hardened, tightened his skin. Numbly, he looked around. Murrumbingal was sitting on the log, watching with his blind eyes. And nothing Kerry had ever experienced was as real as that which had just occurred. A moment lasting indefinitely. But what did it mean? Was it some spirit magic that had turned this oasis into a quagmire of decay? He tried to tell himself it was pure fantasy. A fairytale better kept for stories around a campfire at night. Stories to scare gullible children.

Murrumbingal sighed, chased some flies and asked, 'What you see, white fella?'

'Wanambi didn't swallow anyone. They died of some kind of sickness. Fever. One by one.'

The old man grunted. 'Undo,' he said.

'What?'

'Undo. Or those white fellas living here soon'll die, too. Same way.'

'I can't undo it.'

Murrumbingal laughed.

'I can't, man! Jesus Christ, if it happened and I stress if, it was centuries ago. What the fuck can I do about it?'

The old man sighed, waited for him to stop reasoning it away. 'White fella talk. All white fella talk.'

'I am a white fella!'

'White fella talk. Ashamed of being black. Ashamed someone might find out.'

Kerry put his head on his knees. That topography was splitting again, taking his sanity—what was left of it—down the ragged hole, too. 'What do you want to hear!'

'You are Djawa now. What are you going to do?'

'If I'd known what was going to happen I wouldn't have—'

'What, white fella? What?'

'I would have done something. Anything but that.'

'Who you sorry for? Them or you?'

'All of them! Everyone!'

'Feel it strong, don't ya, white fella.'

'Don't call me that!'

'Feel the fear, don't you, white fella. Was the fear swallowed up this place, and it ain't gone nowhere since. It stayed. Undo it.'

'But I can't be him!'

'Undo it!'

Kerry turned to the old man and for half a heartbeat, he wasn't Murrumbingal at all. He was the man who lay prone at his feet, the finger raised, till impaled by a spear in the throat. Kerry, his right arm over his eyes, and it seemed, on remote control, guided by remorse, by a memory of a past which would not let him be, pointed with his left hand to the east, the north, the west and finally, the south. Nothing happened for a little while.

Murrumbingal said one word. 'Watch,' and he turned to the swamp.

Whatever it was rose up out of the black water and into the air, formed in a congealing mass of putrid murky cloud and kept rising until it dispersed into the clear blue sky above. An incredible stillness settled over the entire site. The deep stench of decay eased. The only sound and sight breaking the still was a huge black crow, aarrking as it landed on the fence, fifty meters away.

Kerry turned to the old man, half expecting he wouldn't be there. But he was. He was rising, moving his tired bones with difficulty. Kerry tried to move, too, but his hip had locked.

'Take me home, white fella,' Murrumbingal said.

Kerry, still with the clay on his face, stopped the car outside the elder's house. He didn't go in and nor did the old man move for a little while even after Kerry had said, 'You're here. Home.'

'Gone now, white fella.'

'What? What's gone?'

The old man laughed. 'Long ago. It's gone.'

I wish to God I was, Kerry thought. What foolishness had even brought him here in the first place? Dreamtime bullshit stories. He knew that if he drove by the swamp again, it'd be the same. Nothing would have changed. Nothing.

'You gonna help us, white fella?'

It was a question which needed no reply. All Kerry wanted was to get back to 11 Margaret, scrub the clay from his face, change, throw his bag into the Rav and drive.

'See this here? See where we live? Been a long time since council's done much. What you reckon, white fella? Once you mayor, you gonna do something for us? Or you gonna pretend we don't live here, like all them others?'

Kerry stifled an exasperated laugh and banged his head on his steering wheel.

'What you reckon, white fella?'

Kerry glanced at the old man. He was staring straight ahead, at something only he could see.

Kerry thought, I have the bakery. I have a manager's job at the pub, too. Mayor? Me, for God's sake? Mayor? 'Murrumbingal, one person cannot make much of a difference.'

'Not if he don't try he can't. See you, white fella. You'll be back.'

'You reckon, black fella?' Kerry called from his car window.

'Yep. Spirits told me.'

'Spirits, my arse,' Kerry mumbled, trying hard not to laugh.

Murrumbingal shuffled his way across the corrugated road, shooing the swarm of kids who ran to meet him.

'What you bring us, Pop? What you bring us?'

Kerry drove off. He needed a bourbon, bad. But that could wait, it would have to.

Julie Harris is the Australian author of *The Longest Winter, No Exit, Anna's Gold, The Diamond Factory, Beyond Laughter: The Marie Corelli Story, Kizzy, A Tear of Blood, The Edge of Nowhere, An Absence of Angels*, and more. She has been published in Australia, USA, UK, Germany and France.

Her writing, which crosses most genres, has been compared to Harper Lee and Jack London.

Julie lives with her husband in a small country town on the Darling Downs in Queensland, Australia.

www.ingramcontent.com/pod-product-compliance
Lightning Source LLC
Chambersburg PA
CBHW031946240626
47153CB00003B/884